To Sarah

RP

CW01271525

The White And Silver Shore

by

Rosalin Peaceweaver

Prayer on p.7 © Caitlin Matthews, from *The Celtic Devotional* (Godsfield Press,1996)

ISBN-10: 1542594839
ISBN-13: 978-1542594837

To Molly and Seb

Although the storyline and the characters in this book are entirely fictional, the event on which the story is based is true.

There are a number of Gaelic names and phrases used in the text of the story. The names of the places referred to on the Isle of Skye have been anglicised; this is the way that visitors to the island would be most likely to encounter them. The mountains, however, are an entirely different species. They are older than the language itself, and I have retained their Gaelic designations.

At the back of the book, you will find a list of all the Gaelic terms used, with their pronunciations and translations.

PRAYER FOR COURAGE

TO RE-ENCOUNTER SITUATIONS, PLACES OR PEOPLE WHICH HAVE SHAKEN CONFIDENCE

I will rise, I will go back
To the white and silver shore.
I will have courage,
As the sun does rising and setting.
At birth and death, the gift of life is precious,
Soul-life streaming down the strand.
I will go as the sea in its turning,
I will rise, I will go back,
I will rise.

Caitlin Matthews

1

Helen had sneaked out of work early, asking her friends to cover for her if anyone checked up on her whereabouts. She had replaced her uniform with a rather spectacular red plastic coat, which she belatedly realised wasn't exactly going to help her appear inconspicuous, but which she had originally chosen precisely for its overt showiness.

'It's so important to show these people you mean business,' she'd told her best friend Bev, when they had cooked up the plot together.

'How is a red coat going to do that?' Bev had asked.

'Don't you know anything about colour language?' she'd responded. 'Red is a power colour. It says you're ambitious and determined and ...'

'And potentially very angry and a trouble-maker,' Bev had finished for her.

'Oh no, do you think so?'

Bev had giggled. 'No, not really. Just winding you up.'

Now that Helen was sitting in the back of the taxi wearing it, she wondered if Bev had been right. It was such a vivid red – no subtlety in it at all. And it wasn't just the colour that was so intrusive; it was the sound. She now realised every time she moved even the slightest amount, the coat announced her to the world.

During the first few minutes of the taxi ride, the driver

had repeatedly turned round to try to work out exactly what the strange noise was. Helen had just about managed to hold her nerve enough to smile sweetly each time it happened, and was very relieved when he stopped shifting in his seat and concentrated on driving, albeit still glancing in his rear-view mirror from time to time, as if perplexed as to why anyone would want to dress in such a strange manner.

She had to admit she was beginning to wonder, too.

But no, she reassured herself, privately. *It's the whole point. I'm not just anybody. It's really important I make my presence felt.*

Emily Hough wasn't just anybody, either. It was crucial that Helen made a big impression today, because this meeting could literally change the rest of her life. The thought instantly made her feel sick, and she had to swallow hard to keep her nerves level. *Breathe, Helen girl, breathe,* she reminded herself. *If you don't remember to breathe properly, nothing's going to impress.*

The journey across Battersea was not a long one, which was just as well. She had had to sneak into the back yard at work to do her voice warm-up exercises, and didn't want the effect to wear off. She trusted that Miss Hough would give her some proper warm-up time when she arrived. Surely someone as big as she was in the music world would understand the importance of that.

She began to feel sick again as she reflected on the enormity of the audition she was about to perform. She had always wanted to be a singer, from as far back as she could remember. As a young child, she had loved singing to her dolls and teddies, and had subjected her family to weekly concerts in the living room, singing anything new she had discovered since the week before. Pop, folk, opera – all was fair game to her young mind.

When her parents had suddenly disappeared out of her life – both killed in a car-crash – her song selection had changed to exploring laments and sad ballads, until her aunt couldn't bear it anymore and forbade her to sing in the house.

She had been twelve, and had started at that point on her secret career, becoming adept at finding hidden and secluded places to practise.

Her school friends and their families had been much more supportive. Many of them had known her since she was little and enjoyed hearing her sing. Particularly Bev and her parents. It was largely their encouragement that had kept her dreams alive.

'You really do have a lovely voice,' Bev's mum would say, on a regular basis. 'I hope you get the chance to do something special with it one day.'

Well, now that chance was here. If she could show her true potential today, there was every possibility she could win a scholarship to music college, and study singing properly. How amazing it would be to spend her days trilling out scales and studying notation, instead of serving repeated portions of burger and chips.

The taxi pulled up outside a large Victorian terrace with a brass plaque on the wall, just above the doorbell, announcing it to be the home of Miss Emily Hough, ARCM, FRAM.

Helen paid the driver and got out of the car. She smoothed her red plastic coat for the last time, now regretting she'd chosen something so loud – literally. It wasn't helping to boost her confidence at all, now that she was actually here. She heard the taxi drive away. *Come on, girl,* she encouraged herself. *It's now or never.*

She braced herself, taking another strong breath, checked her watch to make sure she was on time, and stepped onto the stone staircase with its fancy black ironwork. *There's posh,* she joked quietly, trying to steady her nerves.

She reached up for the large brass knocker adorning a huge wooden door, then decided the doorbell might be a better option. The house was large enough that a knock might not be heard. She pressed the button and waited.

Nothing happened.

Oh, God, how long is it polite to wait before trying again? she agonised. She left what she guessed was sufficient time for someone to come up or down from another floor, then pressed the bell again, praying that it didn't sound impatient.

There was still no response.

She began to panic. Suppose she'd got the wrong time. Or the wrong day. Or even the wrong address. *Don't be daft, girl. It could just be that the bell doesn't work. Try the knocker.*

For the second time, she reached up to take hold of the ornate brass lion's head, but as she lifted it, the door began to open. She breathed a sigh of relief and lowered her hand again, in expectation of the familiar face she had recently been studying on the internet.

But the door stopped moving. It had opened a few inches as she touched the knocker but had now come to a halt.

That's not right, she thought. She'd come across unlocked front doors on holiday in the Highlands but no-one in London did that. She wondered if this was the protocol for a pre-arranged audition.

She decided to try giving the door knocker one last attempt. After all, if the doorbell wasn't working, Miss Hough still wouldn't know she had arrived, and it seemed only proper to announce herself.

She took hold of the brass head again and gave it three sharp taps – and watched in horror as the door swung completely open, revealing the body in the hallway.

She knew the body was dead the moment she saw it. It wasn't just the lack of movement that gave it away; there was something missing in the energy of the body. She'd seen dead bodies before.

Oh God.

Just for a brief instant she contemplated turning her back and running, a thought gone almost as quickly as it arrived. She knew she had to check, to take action. She forced herself to move and entered the hallway, crossing to the body. As she got closer, she realised her first impression was correct. A nasty pool of blood was congealing under the head, and the limbs were all at odd angles, as if they didn't really belong to the rest of the body.

Nevertheless, she quickly ran through a vital signs check, just as she'd been taught on the first aid course at work, though it took every bit of her courage to touch the cooling flesh. Yes, Miss Emily Hough FRAM was definitely dead, but hadn't been so for long.

She began to shake, not sure who she felt more sorry for – herself and her shattered dreams, or the poor lady lying at her feet. *She must have fallen coming downstairs,* Helen surmised. Though that didn't quite account for the blood flowing from her head. The wound was clearly visible, not underneath the head, next to the floor. Perhaps she had hit it on the banister as she fell.

Helen reached into her pocket to pull out her phone to call emergency services and realised she'd left it in her work uniform when she'd changed into her new red coat. *Damn.*

Uncertain for a moment how to proceed, she sat down on the bottom step of a grand flight of stairs leading to an upstairs floor. Presumably the ones Miss Hough had fallen down. She realised she would have to leave the body to go for help.

Then she heard a voice. A man's voice talking to someone else. She got up, expecting someone to come through the front door, but instead there was the sound of another door being kicked open.

The noise came from a floor below where she was standing. *Someone already in the house?* She just had time to think how odd that was before she heard the voice again, accompanied by the sound of footsteps coming up a creaky staircase.

'No, there's nothing down here. Searched everywhere.'

A second voice said something she couldn't make out.

'Oh, I've dealt with her. She won't give us any trouble.'

Helen flew into action. She spotted a nearby door, slightly ajar, which she prayed led into a room she could hide in, and dashed through it, silently cursing the noise her damn coat made as she moved. She discovered she was in a cloakroom. Once inside, she pushed the door back to its original position, so she could just see through the slit, and stood as still as she had ever stood in her life.

'What was that?' The second voice was audible now.

'Dunno.'

Helen didn't even dare breathe as two men briefly came into view. One was clothed in a smart, but traditional, suit. The other was wearing a black leather jacket – and carrying a gun.

She stifled a gasp, feeling herself go hot and cold all over. She willed herself not to shake.

'Looks like the front door's blown open.'

'Christ, man. Do you want everyone to see? Get it closed.'

The black leather jacket moved out of view, revealing the face of the man in the suit. He was an older man, perhaps in his mid-fifties. Clean-shaven, with short grey hair, carefully combed to conceal what Helen guessed was a bald patch. He had steely blue eyes, and carried an air of authority about him. Someone used to getting his own way.

The men were discussing what to do.

'We can leave her here. No evidence pointing to us. Didn't even have to shoot her. Stupid biddy fell straight down the stairs when I hit her.'

'You're positive she's dead?'

'Yeah, absolutely.'

'And you've searched this floor?'

'Yep. Nothing here. Just like downstairs.'

'Then let's go through upstairs.'

The men began to ascend the staircase, and Helen soon heard them ransacking the floor above. They weren't looking carefully. They were chucking things everywhere.

Now would be her chance to escape. While they were

making so much racket. Could she risk coming out of the cloakroom? What if the front door didn't open? She'd be a sitting duck if they glanced down into the hallway. But if she stayed put, she risked being found when they came back downstairs after their search.

She began to ease open the cloakroom door, and for the umpteenth time that day, regretted her ridiculous coat, as it creaked loudly with every movement she made. Inwardly, she swore. If she ever got out of this alive, she was *never, ever,* going to wear anything like this bloody coat again!

She decided she would have to ditch it. It might make a noise as she took it off but she could muffle some of the sound by pushing the cloakroom door closed. That would at least make a quiet get-away possible. And she guessed she only had a very short time to do this.

She made a decision, and unbuckling the belt, let the coat slide to the floor. Fortunately, the cloakroom had ample space to do so easily, and she was able to step over it and open the door again without creating any more noise.

The men were still busy searching, judging by the sounds she could hear. Very tentatively, she began to pass through the doorway, into the hall, and to cross towards the front door.

Thank God she was wearing sensible shoes – suitable for standing in to sing, not clattery high heels. She ignored a temptation to turn and look up the stairs. She focused on quietly placing one foot after the other on a steady journey across the tiled floor.

'Stop.'

She froze in her tracks. Not daring to turn around, she waited for the gunshot, the sound of feet pounding down the stairs, voices shouting – something!

'I think I might have found it.'

Oh my God. They hadn't seen her.

She ran to the door, covering the remaining distance in seconds. She grabbed hold of the door handle and pulled with all her might. The door flew open, and she charged through it and out onto the street, running with every bit of energy she had, down the road and out of sight.

Helen ran as far as she could before she was forced to stop by the pains both in her legs and her chest. She'd never been more grateful for all those years of lung-expanding exercises. She'd run to the end of the street, and then turned alternately right and left at each corner she came to. This had helped her to run a good distance without having to stop and think about direction. She figured if the men had seen her leave, it wouldn't matter what direction she took; they'd be faster than her. But if they hadn't discovered there'd been someone else in the house straight away, the more she could complicate her route, the better.

She finally came to a halt and leaned up against a wall in an alleyway, breathing hard. She bent over to ease the effort of getting sufficient air back into her lungs. They felt as if they'd been squeezed dry. Her pulse was sounding in her ears, and her head felt like it would explode.

As her breathing became easier, she tentatively took a glance at her surroundings. No-one appeared to be following her. The alleyway was completely empty. That was when the tears began to fill her eyes, quickly brimming over as she gave in to huge, gulping sobs. Now she began to shake. *Oh my God, oh my God, oh my God.* The full impact of the last fifteen minutes of her life hit her.

Questions flooded into her head. *How? What? Why?* She felt completely overwhelmed, and sank to the ground to cry some more.

Suddenly, she heard someone singing.

She looked up and saw an old lady entering the alleyway, dressed in a tatty overcoat, and carrying an array of colourful bags. Helen started as the woman moved towards her, then realised she was harmless. Nothing to do with the incident she'd just witnessed at all.

'Are you okay, dearie?'

Helen nodded, finding herself unable to speak just yet.

'Boyfriend, is it?'

She nodded again.

'Don't you worry. They're not worth it. Here, have this to cheer you up.'

The woman reached into one of her bags and pulled out a squashed, cold, sausage roll.

'Better for you than any man.' She handed it to Helen, and continued on her journey through the alleyway, still singing quietly to herself.

Helen let the disgusting piece of food drop to the ground. She needed to decide what to do. She needed to go to the police and report what she'd seen.

She got up and walked to the end of the alleyway where the old lady had headed and discovered it opened onto a busy, main road. She didn't recognise where she was, but that might not matter. Battersea must have its own police station, and that couldn't be difficult to find.

She stopped the next person she saw before she ran out of courage.

'Excuse me. Can you tell me where the police station is?'

The man, who looked about her age, eyed her suspiciously. She realised she must look a sight. She was out without a coat on a chilly afternoon, but obviously sweating profusely, and probably with tear stains on her face. Not surprising if he backed off.

He muttered something that sounded like 'No, sorry,' and pushed past her. She got a tissue out of her handbag and wiped over her face. Then tried again.

The next people to pass her were an elderly couple who turned out to be quite chatty.

'Oh, you're going in completely the wrong direction. You need to head back to Hastings Road, then turn right and follow that road right to the end, and …'

Between the two of them, they delivered a complicated and confusing set of instructions, which Helen had no doubt would get her to the police station if she could memorise them, but at the moment, her brain didn't seem to be capable of that. She waited for a pause in the dialogue, and smiled sweetly.

'Thank you so much.'

She turned in the first direction they'd indicated and set off, crossing the street to put some distance between herself and more unhelpful chatter.

At the corner, she turned onto another busy road and kept walking. Her mind was doing cartwheels. She kept replaying what she had just gone through, over and over, trying to convince herself she really had witnessed it. That it wasn't some horrible dream from which she would wake up suddenly.

She realised she'd been walking a while, so approached the next person coming towards her to get further directions, hoping these would be easier to remember since she was now closer to her destination. This time the information was much clearer.

'The station's just round the next corner, but I'm afraid it's not open any more.'

Helen looked at the woman she'd stopped, not comprehending.

'I'm sorry … ?'

'They closed it down last month. The building's up for sale.'

The woman, who was wearing a large, furry hat and mittens, was friendly enough, but this wasn't helping Helen any.

'You're obviously not from around here.' The woman could see her bewilderment.

'No.'

'Well, they've moved all their business to Rosemary Lane and Wandsworth Stations. Not especially helpful, really, but Rosemary Lane's not far from here.'

Helen felt that her day was getting more and more difficult to manage. She suddenly felt very weary.

'Are you alright, dear?'

'Yes, yes. I'm fine.' She didn't feel as if she wanted

anyone fussing over her at the moment. She just needed to get this whole foul mess handed over to someone in authority. Why was that so hard to accomplish?

She responded to the woman's questioning face.

'No, really. I'm fine. If you could just give me directions … ?'

Once more, she listened to a set of instructions, and made her brain pay attention. This time she repeated what she'd heard to make sure she'd remember. It sounded near enough to walk, despite the fatigue setting in. 'Thank you.'

She set off again.

Ten minutes later, she saw the police station come into view.

Thank God. The adrenaline in her body had subsided a little now. The walking had helped to settle her. She was beginning to feel the cold in the air, and she was very tired, but at least she was thinking more clearly.

She walked into the yard, just as a squad car pulled in on the other side. Two officers got out, followed by a man in a suit.

Helen gasped. She recognised him instantly. *They can't have caught him already? Surely?*

Something was wrong. She stopped in her tracks, realising the man she'd seen in Emily Hough's house was not being manhandled, or even directed, into the police station. He was not handcuffed, nor being restrained in any way at all, as far as she could see.

She watched in stunned disbelief as one of the officers turned to him and spoke, addressing him as 'Sir.'

2

Katriona lifted her head from the myriad of papers on her desk to look through the window of her study at the magnificent views. She was still learning to become accustomed to this. How was it possible for one person to be so fortunate? It seemed almost unfair. She watched as her partner, Elayne, and their dogs, Molly and Alice, herded a small jumbled group of sheep down the hillside and into the paddock behind their house.

She sighed contentedly and went back to studying her paperwork. The crime rate on the island was ridiculously low, and mostly to do with Friday night excesses and petty theft of – and by – tourists, rather than serious detective work, so she was doubly fortunate to be able to live here and continue with her profession, currently as a consultant detective for the Specialist Crime Division within the newly-organised Police Scotland.

The phone rang and she picked it up, tucking it under her chin so she could continue sorting papers as she spoke.

'Hello?'

'Hi, it's Gavin.'

'Gavin. How lovely to hear from you.' She left her papers to themselves, and enthusiastically took the phone over to her comfy chair, where she could curl up for a good conversation. 'How's the big city?'

'Much the same, really. Busy as ever.'

Katriona realised how much she'd missed the sound of Gavin's cheery voice. He had been a good friend and colleague when she worked in London.

'More to the point,' he said, 'how's the quiet life suiting you?'

The decision to leave her high-flying and fast-paced life in the metropolis had not been an easy one. She had worked hard to gain a position of authority and respect within the police force. Even in this supposedly open-minded era of equal opportunities, there were still characters who believed women could not grow brain cells, and even if there were such an anomaly, parading it in the midst of a man's world was just bad taste, so Gavin's friendship and support had been particularly valued.

'Loving it.'

'Really?'

'Yes, really. It's very different but it is *so* beautiful here.'

Gavin made a sound that could have been a snort. 'So you're not tempted to come back to us?'

'Not in the slightest.' They both laughed, a moment reminiscent of their time together.

'So what are you up to at the moment?' Gavin asked.

'Just watching Elayne bringing in the sheep.'

'No, workwise, you idiot. Got any interesting cases on the go?'

'Nothing as ground-breaking as you, I'm sure. I was just finishing off some paperwork, actually. A serious case of contraband.' She tried to sound sincere but Gavin knew her too well.

'You're joking?'

'Well, only a bit,' she acknowledged. 'One of the small distilleries over towards Loch Ness reported missing cases of their vintage single malt. The stuff kept disappearing somewhere between their warehouse and the buyers.'

'Doesn't exactly sound like mega-crime.' Gavin's comment reflected the comparison she was sure he was making with whatever he was working on at the moment.

'Oh, you'd be surprised. Whisky of that age carries a considerable value, and this was repeated theft over several months.' Katriona was aware she might be trying to justify her work a little too enthusiastically.

'How come you got involved?' Gavin asked.

She wondered if he was just being polite, and explained about the checked stock that was regularly dispatched from the distillery, yet arriving with the buyers as empty bottles.

'Since they're in Germany, no-one could work out exactly where along the route the bottles were being stolen. There was such a huge potential area to be covered, they felt they needed to get a detective involved at each end to co-ordinate the investigation, liaise with Customs, and so on. You know the drill. So they rang me.'

'And you, of course, solved the case?'

'Of course,' Katriona retorted. 'Have to prove my worth as a 'part-time' detective'.

That had been the jibe from many of her colleagues at her leaving party. Mostly good-humouredly, but she knew some really believed it.

'Actually, it was quite amusing,' she continued. 'I suggested they might start with trying some old-fashioned police work.'

'Yeah?'

'Well, they'd been tracking the transit of the whisky by CCTV up to then. Checking each key point along the route - you know, loading, unloading, at the dockside, and so on.'

'So what did you suggest?'

Katriona grinned to herself at the recollection. 'They'd established that the disappearance of the full bottles was definitely happening in this country, so I suggested they physically tail the lorry.'

'Heaven forbid!'

'Yeah, they were all so glued to their technology, it hadn't occurred to them to go back to old-fashioned 'leg-work' – well, 'car-work' really. Something about it not being cost-effective.'

'What?'

'To be fair, tailing someone through the Highlands is a whole different ball-game from tailing someone through Haringey.' Katriona pictured the two very different scenes in her mind and wondered how to convey some of the difference to Gavin.

'I mean, there's only one road for a start-off. So you have to get several cars from different jurisdictions involved along the route. It's a bit obvious if the same car follows you for a hundred miles or so, without attempting to overtake.'

'I guess so. Presumably you caught the culprits?'

'Yep. Turned out to be quite easy.' She was getting warmed up with her story now. 'The truck only went about twenty miles or so down the road. The drivers stopped off at a breakfast café, just outside Fort William – and there's only a handful of those, I can assure you. They went inside to eat, and whilst they were in there, a white van turned up – with their own set of keys – and unloaded some of the full bottles and replaced them with empties. Quite clever, really. Keep it small-scale and local. And the drivers could legitimately claim they had nothing to do with it. Well, nearly.'

'So you're telling me no-one had spotted this?' Gavin's voice on the other end of the phone sounded incredulous. 'What about the CCTV at the café?'

'Oh, Gavin. You have no idea. This is a different world up here. They don't install CCTV at every shop and café like London. Driving up here, you can travel fifty miles or more without seeing anything but trees and mountains.'

Gavin was clearly having problems envisaging this. 'How on earth are you managing?'

'Mostly, I'm managing really well.'

'Only mostly?'

'I would say that's one step up from working at the Met.'

'Point taken.'

There had been years of hard work, dedication and increasingly thick skin involved for Katriona to gain a position as DI, overseeing her own team of investigative officers. And even then, she had continually met with opposition, both from men in the lower ranks, who simply could not stomach being told what to do by a woman, and from men in the senior ranks who felt constantly challenged by her sharp intelligence and accompanying success rate.

'So tell me how things have changed there,' she probed.

'Here? Well, we're now squeaky clean and ultra-respective – particularly of our female officers, of course.' Gavin spoke with his usual sarcasm about his place of work and his colleagues.

Sometimes, Katriona wondered why he continued to work there, but she knew the answer. His love of the job, and the few genuine friendships he had, were enough for him. He didn't expect total job satisfaction and was never surprised when he got screwed over by someone he worked with.

'No, I would say we're pretty much as we were when you were here.'

'So the internal investigation hasn't made a difference?'

'Not really.'

The last case Katriona had worked on before she left had involved assisting IPCC with exposing a group of 'bent coppers'. She had played a significant role in the investigation, working surreptitiously to collect evidence, and while that had ultimately felt like a powerful contribution to make, it had cost her. The stress of the situation, added to the daily stress of the job, had taken its toll on her health.

That was when Elayne had insisted it was time to do things differently. An architect by profession, Elayne had always wanted to design and build her own house. Her beautiful creations had been one of the reasons Katriona had been drawn to her originally, and when Elayne had shared her dreams of the perfect home, built into the landscape of a small-holding, the magic had utterly captivated her.

It had taken a few years of patient waiting to find exactly the right piece of land and, she had to admit, more than a few years of patient waiting on her partner's part, before Katriona had felt ready to embrace the dream. But both of them had happy childhood memories of growing up in the Highlands, and both of them knew and loved Skye almost as much as they knew and loved each other. When this particular plot of land had come on the market, it had felt exactly right, and they had gone ahead with the purchase and then the initial building, about two years ago. So when the investigation came to a close, it had been easy to put the finishing touches to the beautiful house and Katriona had finally surrendered to the inevitable.

Gavin spoke again. 'Jack the Lad's been rather quiet since then, though.'

Jack Foster – known to many on the force as Jack the Lad, though never to his face – was a senior officer based in the station, who often seemed to have a hand in suspicious goings-on, but who, somehow, always evaded any proof of his involvement. Katriona had been convinced he was co-ordinating the activities of the circle she was investigating but he was particularly good at covering his tracks and, ultimately, when the axe fell, he had remained out of its reach.

'Perhaps he's finally realised we're on to him.'

'Maybe. Not your problem any more.'

'No.' There was just a hint of wistfulness in Katriona's voice. 'So what *has* been happening? What's the gossip?'

'Well, actually, I do have news. That's the reason I rang.'

'Oh?' Katriona's ears pricked up.

'Tricia's expecting a baby, so we've decided to go the whole hog and get married.'

'Oh Gavin. That's wonderful. Congratulations. I'm so pleased.'

'Yeah. Thanks. I am, too.'

Gavin liked to present a front to his colleagues of being robust and fairly macho – one of the lads. It was the culture of the force, and Katriona knew it suited him just fine to fit in that way at work, but she'd got to know him outside of work, too, and had seen the gentler, kinder side of his character.

It had been something of a struggle for him to reconcile the two aspects, but falling in love with Tricia had given him the motivation to explore his 'feminine side', as he liked to call it. She knew he was really happy with her, and the stable home-life they'd created together had given him the anchor he needed to embrace the rougher hardness associated with the job.

'So when's the day?'

'In a couple of months. December 15th. We've found this fantastic place out in the country for the ceremony and so on. It's like a stately manor. They do everything. You know, big posh room for the legal bit, ballroom for the party. They even have rooms for the guests to stay overnight. We've taken over the place for the whole weekend, so anyone who wants to book a room can do that.'

'Sounds fantastic.'

'And we'd love for you and Elayne to come.'

Katriona opened her mouth to thank him for the invitation, thinking at the same time how difficult it would be to arrange such a trip from so far away. But before she could say anything, Gavin continued.

'I know it's a heck of a long way for you to come, so Tricia and I want to pay for your accommodation for the weekend. They even take dogs in part of the hotel, so you can bring Molly and Alice with you. I know you never go anywhere without them.' He did, indeed, know her well, and the generosity of his offer was too much to turn down.

'Gavin, we'd love to. That's so kind of you. It'd be great to see you again. Oh, what a lovely surprise.'

Their conversation drifted on for a while longer – mostly with reminiscences of Katriona's time in London – before Gavin had to hang up and get back to work.

Katriona reluctantly replaced the phone on her desk. She *was* lucky to be able to live here but there was a part of her that definitely missed the cut and thrust of what she'd had before, and she felt a little envious of Gavin still being in the midst of it all. But one had to make choices, and Elayne was right – taking care of her health *had* to be a priority.

However, she had to admit, an unexpected bonus of working up here, was that she had finally gained an easy respect from her colleagues. They actually valued the time and effort she put into the work, and her willingness to go the extra mile – literally! There weren't too many detectives who would take on responsibility for such a huge geographic region, and her dedication met with approval. Despite the odd twinge of nostalgia, she really wouldn't have it any other way.

She allowed her gaze to shift once again to the views visible from her study window. This was an exceptionally beautiful plot of land. Tucked away in the tiny village of Torrin, it was remote even for Skye.

Yet interestingly, it was also on the tourist route to some of the most spectacular views in the universe – at least as far as Katriona was concerned.

The twisting road between Broadford and Elgol, although nearly fifteen miles in distance, was single-track the entire way. There were numerous passing places along the route to enable two-way traffic and – supposedly – overtaking, though this possibility often didn't occur to the visitors who traversed its length every day.

There had been many occasions when Katriona had been stuck behind a sight-seeing tourist for five or six miles before the thought had penetrated that they could let the faster car past. But, actually, for Katriona, this just added to the charm of the place. It served, constantly, to remind her of the importance of slowing down to a healthy pace of life, instead of living as she had always done before – driving herself into the ground.

Her thoughts were disturbed by the sound of the backdoor opening.

'Hi.' Elayne's voice accompanied the sound of wellingtons dropping on the kitchen floor. 'Fancy a cuppa?'

'Yeah, that would be lovely. Shall I make it?' She called through from her study.

'Nope. That's okay. You finish off what you're doing. I'll serve it in the conservatory.'

This had become a regular bit of humour between them. Since finally moving into their delightful new home, they often enjoyed afternoon tea in the conservatory, complete with china teapot, cupcakes on a stand, even lace doilies when the fancy took them. Just because they could. It was sheer delight after years of grabbing mugs of muddy water on the go.

Fortunately - as they were both still too busy to contemplate baking - they lived only a few hundred yards from the Blue Shed Café. The only eating place within six miles in either direction, it had been a stroke of genius to convert the old community shop into a cheery stopping point for the passing tourist trade, specialising in home-baked cakes as well as locally-crafted goods for sale. The current proprietors, Linda and Dave, continued the success of the original enterprise by adding their own delicious soups and hot toasties to the outstanding menu.

Katriona had picked up two pieces of chocolate Tiffin this morning when she'd walked the dogs down to the lochside – her regular routine on a 'working-from-home' day. At this time of year, the sun had not yet managed to climb over the cliffs at the sea-end of the loch on its daily journey over the water, where it would highlight the peaks on *Rhum* before sinking out of sight behind *an Cuiltheann* or the *Cuillin*, as most people knew them. The air had been sharp and fresh, the light subdued, creating an air of expectancy in the valley.

With no clouds in the sky, the top of *Blà Bheinn*, three and a half thousand feet above her, had been visible and she'd relished his towering presence overseeing the early morning goings-on. Later on, if the sky remained clear, the blue waters in the loch would sparkle and dance in the sunlight, and *Blà Bheinn* would gaze down on his own reflection.

'Work going well?' Elayne touched her gently on the shoulder to bring her out of her reverie.

'Yeah. Just tidying up the paper work from that incident at Inverlochy.'

'Oh, the one at the distillery.'

'That's the one. Hey, let's not talk shop. I've had enough for now. Where's that tea?'

They wandered into the conservatory where, sure enough, a delicately arranged tray of teacups, plates and traybakes stood waiting. The three-sided glass room allowed the surrounding landscape to be almost part of their own décor. The Red Hills, directly behind their little house, glowed in the late afternoon sunshine, living up to their local name with breath-taking accuracy.

Each of the rounded peaks had gathered a wispy piece of white cloud which sat like a decorative collar around its top. To the west, *Blà Bheinn* and *Clach Glas* had also gathered some evening cloud, which was playing with the sunshine to produce spectacular effects in the fading daylight.

After Katriona had shared the news about Gavin's wedding, they sat in silence for a while, drinking in the beauty of the scenery.

'I'm thinking about taking that job on,' Elayne mused, as she poured a second round of teas.

'What – the one for Island Homes?' This was a Glasgow-based firm, with a local office on Skye, who specialised in building modern houses which blended unobtrusively with the Hebridean countryside. They often contracted out the design element of construction to various Highland-based architects, particularly if the client had requested it. In this case, the clients were a Skye couple who'd left a few years ago to 'make good' in the music industry. Having succeeded in grand fashion, they were now returning to the island to set up home, and had specifically asked for Elayne as their architect.

'Yeah, Donald and Fi. You remember them. They've

bought that piece of land over by Dunvegan that I was telling you about. I really like what they want to do with it.'

Katriona smiled. It was lovely to see Elayne's enthusiasm shine through her eyes. The start of a new project was always exciting, and she knew it wouldn't be long before initial sketches were being plastered on the walls of Elayne's workroom with requests for comments.

'I'll get the crayons out, shall I?'

'Better order some more, I think.' Elayne laughed, and reached for another piece of Tiffin. 'Mm, this is delicious – even by Linda's standards.'

'I thought it looked pretty good when I called in this morning. She said they were expecting a large group of hill walkers today.'

'Yeah, Bill told me they'd got a party booked when I saw him yesterday.'

Bill ran a very successful hostel for walkers and climbers, just off the main road through Torrin, tucked into the countryside on the edge of the loch. Even in the shorter days now on offer – the autumn equinox being a few weeks ago – there were still people whose passion for the *Cuillin* Mountains drew them back here year after year, making use of every bit of daylight they could to explore the glorious landscape and experience the grandeur only possible from three thousand feet above sea level.

It wouldn't be long now before the first snows arrived, dusting the tops enticingly and adding a fairy-tale element to scenery that was already unbelievably stunning. And with the snow would come a fresh batch of climbers, intent on tackling the most difficult and dangerous routes through the snow and ice to scale *Sgùrr Alasdair*, or maybe the Inaccessible Pinnacle, or to walk the ridge between *Gars-Bheinn* and *Sgùrr nan Gillean.*

Katriona and Elayne sat a while longer, chatting about their day and catching up on news from neighbours, until the sunlight outside began to fade and Elayne suggested they take a twilight stroll out to the shore down the little lane behind No. 9. The village was small enough that each house was known either by its name or its original croft number, rendering the need for road names redundant.

Katriona happily agreed. 'But I must finish my paperwork when we get back – I'm away to Inverness tomorrow.'

She normally undertook the two-hundred-mile round trip once a week, enjoying the opportunity to meet her colleagues in person and to catch up on what the current crime scene was doing, as well as revelling in the amazing scenery en route.

'Okay,' Elayne responded, as she collected the teacups and piled them onto the tray. 'I'll make tea so you can get an early night.'

'Thanks.' Katriona smiled and reached out a hand to show her appreciation of her partner's gesture, touching Elayne's shoulder as she leaned over the table.

Elayne turned and kissed her gently. 'It's a pleasure, my love. A real pleasure.' She turned and picked up the tray, making her way to the kitchen.

Yes, thought Katriona, *it is, isn't it?*

3

Helen was sitting in a grubby little café, just off the high street, trying to make sense of everything. Her hands trembled as she lifted the coffee cup to her lips. She didn't drink coffee much – it wasn't good for her voice – but she felt she needed it after this latest shock.

She had backed out of the station yard so abruptly that she had crashed into a uniformed officer walking in behind her. Her attempts to remain low-key and insignificant had not been very successful.

'Can I help you?' the woman had asked – inevitably. She'd had a mixture of concern and suspicion on her face.

Helen remembered muttering something that resembled an apology, and had pushed past to get away as quickly as possible, hoping she hadn't been noticed by anyone else. Not that anyone would recognise her, she now realised. No-one knew she'd been at Emily's house – yet.

She stared out of the window at people passing by – a standard tea-time rush hour. Schoolkids were chatting in groups, winding each other up with silly teasing. A couple of them were tentatively holding hands without looking at each other, seemingly both embarrassed and excited by their mutual attraction. Cars moved slowly along the street, queueing at the traffic lights – end of the work day, going home. Shoppers carried plastic bags filled with supermarket goods, and vegetables from the grocers on the corner. It started to rain.

Everything seemed so normal. Helen's world had been rocked to its core, yet everyone around her was continuing their daily business as if nothing had changed. She found it difficult to comprehend. She tried not to cry – again.

A noisy group of workmen entered the café and slid into the benches on the table next to hers, disturbing her thoughts. The waitress from behind the counter brought over a tray with four mugs of hot tea.

'Hi, Cynthia. And how are you today, darlin'?' one of the men asked, loudly.

'All the better for seeing you, of course,' the girl joked.

'Better not tell Harry, then,' another of the gang chipped in. There was laughter, as he thumped his workmate in the arm.

'No chance.'

The banter continued for a few minutes before the girl returned to the counter to take someone else's order. Clearly a regular routine. Everything around her, thought Helen, was regular … normal. She longed to be able to slip back into that world. To let go of the last few awful hours. To pretend she'd never made the discoveries she had. It was all too much.

Then suddenly, through the shock and self-pity, she made an important realisation. If she hadn't seen the man in the suit when she had, if she'd got as far as reporting the murder before she'd encountered him, things would be way, way worse. If that had happened, he would know who she was and what she had seen. A dawning reality hit her – if things had unfolded that way, her life would be in danger!

A man willing to arrange Emily Hough's demise for the sake of whatever he had been hunting for, certainly wouldn't hesitate to dispose of her. No, she'd actually had a lucky escape. And – she now thought – it had given *her* the advantage. As soon as 'Detective Grey-Suit' (it somehow helped to give him a nickname) identified who she was - and that seemed inevitable - he would be tracking her down. No doubt about it. She needed to get away somewhere safe. Out of London. Put some distance between her and – and him!

At least she had a headstart. He'd be unlikely to work out who she was quickly. Even if the two men realised someone had been at the house, there was no way they could know it was her. She began to breathe a little easier and sipped some more coffee. No, she had some time to decide what to do, where to go.

Then she remembered the red plastic coat! Now sitting innocently on Emily Hough's cloakroom floor. As soon as anyone conducted a serious search of the house, the coat would be found – and it would be pretty obvious it didn't belong to Emily. Was there any way it could be traced back to her?

An image of the taxi driver appeared in her mind. He would certainly remember it. If there was a public appeal for information ….. *Oh God.*

No, be logical. She probably had some time to execute an escape plan, depending on how soon someone found the body. Well, that could be hours – days, even.

No, wait. Emily had said she would fit in Helen's audition before she left for Manchester. She was due to give a performance at The Bridgewater Hall tomorrow so presumably was booking into a hotel this evening. That meant the alarm would likely be raised in the next three to four hours. Once that had happened, she guessed the police would visit the house and discover the body – possibly quite quickly since she was an international celebrity.

Helen decided the first thing she needed was money. She had some savings in her account. She began working out the best way to get hold of them. How much could one take out at a cashpoint? She couldn't remember. She only dealt with small withdrawals ordinarily. She paid for bigger items by card. Clearly, she couldn't rely on that method now. She'd seen enough thrillers and TV crime series to know how traceable that information was.

She finished her coffee and crossed the room to where the waitress was chatting to a friend who had come into the café. The girl looked up as she approached.

'Excuse me,' Helen asked. 'I wondered – is there a cashpoint near here?'

'Yeah, there's one just down the street.' The girl pointed in the direction she'd come from, then resumed her conversation with her friend.

'Thanks.' Helen turned to leave. 'Oh sorry. Could I get a sandwich to go?'

'Sure.' The girl pointed again, this time to the stack of pre-wrapped sandwiches sitting in a plastic cabinet next to the till. 'What flavour?'

'Oh, cheese and tomato'll be fine.' Now that she'd thought about food, Helen's stomach rumbled. It had been hours since she'd eaten.

The girl removed a sandwich from the shelf and handed it to Helen in exchange for a five pound note, then scrabbled in the till, searching for change. The normality of the transaction rubbed against Helen's impending sense of panic. From now on, every time she stopped to buy something – even something as simple as a sandwich – she was increasing the chances of her being found. The thought was chilling. She was going to have to plan her escape very carefully.

Helen retraced her steps down the street in the direction the waitress had indicated. She found it terrifying to be walking back towards the police station but, in the first instance, it seemed sensible. She was pretty sure all that stuff about there being cameras in cashpoint machines was true, but information placing her in this vicinity at this time was not going to create a problem. By the time the police accessed it – if they did – she'd be long gone. And she needed to get hold of cash as quickly as possible.

Although the rain had eased a little, she became aware she was now getting both cold and wet. She looked around and saw there was a bargain clothes shop on the other side of the street, squeezed in between a jeweller's and a newsagent's. She crossed over as the traffic came to another halt, waiting for a traffic light change. Yes, there were cheap waterproofs for sale. Cheap enough that she could pay for one with the money she'd brought with her for a taxi-ride home.

She chose a dark blue coat that had little substance but would keep her dry. She decided, with just a trace of irony, the colour was anonymous enough for her not to catch people's attention. She put it on and headed once more for the cashpoint. It then occurred to her that she could do the 'hoodie' thing. She could use the machine, keeping her head down and her hood pulled up. It wouldn't necessarily mask her identity completely but it might help to confuse the picture.

Oh God, now I'm starting to think like a criminal. The idea was very upsetting but Helen was beginning to understand that, at least for the time being, she was going to have to give something like a performance, and she knew how to do that. She began to take the requisite deep breaths that were customarily part of her preparation for presenting a role, and found she could access the quiet focus inside that she always used when she was on-stage. It was a trifle wobbly, but it was there. The panic in her head subsided somewhat and she began to 'be' that person on the run.

Now feeling much more confident about her ability to pull this off, she joined the cashpoint queue, behind a guy in jeans and fancy leather boots with studs and chains on them. She kept her head down and made a pretence of admiring the detail. As the woman at the front of the queue – a mother with three young children, one in a pushchair – finished her transaction and began to move away, one of the youngsters jolted her arm and she dropped her card. The guy in the boots reached down to pick it up for her and noticed Helen staring.

"Cool, huh?" He couldn't resist.

Helen smiled but said nothing. She didn't need to get

into a conversation with anyone at this point. The guy turned back to take his turn at the screen, and a few minutes later, Helen had collected two hundred and fifty pounds to stash in her bag – the maximum this particular machine would allow her.

Her first goal partially accomplished, Helen's confidence increased. She considered what else she would need to execute her plan. More clothes. More money. An escape route. She wondered whether going back to the flat to retrieve some of her own clothes was a sensible strategy. Since she had some time before anyone would consider looking for her, she decided it was more sensible than spending the little money she had on new clothes. Good, that was one decision made, but it now necessitated making another. Her flat was on the other side of London. To get home was going to involve time and expense. Could she afford to do it?

She felt herself going into a state of panic again. Every step she tried to take out of this horrible mess seemed to increase the complexities of it. Aware that her self-pity was about to surface once more, and knowing how that would go, she made herself resume her breathing techniques to clear her thinking.

She didn't know exactly where she was, or how to get back to where she'd come from. The whole point of taking a taxi to Emily's house had been to remove the worry about travelling from the experience. A helpful idea if one is attending an audition, but using a taxi now ran the risk of making her memorable, as well as being ludicrously expensive. She came up with a compromise. Get a taxi to take her to the nearest bus station, where she could maybe work out a route home using public transport.

With every little step she accomplished, and every small decision she made, Helen's confidence grew. A short taxi-ride and three bus journeys later, found her back at the end of her own street, where she felt a bit more comfortable about everything. In fact, as she opened her front door, it was almost possible to believe that none of the rest of the day had really happened. She was tempted to trust to luck and not do anything rash like running away. Perhaps she could get away with it. Perhaps her identity wouldn't be discovered. Perhaps no-one would ever find out that she'd been there.

She knew none of that was likely to be true, but she was tired and cold. Arriving home *was* comforting. Maybe she could just take a little nap, have a cup of tea, assess her situation …

She flicked on the radio as she filled the kettle to make a pot of tea. Then reached for a few slices of bread to pop in the toaster. There was post on the table. A credit card bill for her. A couple of leaflets from the local take-away, offering a deal on delivered pizzas. She noticed Bev had opened an envelope addressed to her and now propped up against the clock. There was a note written on the outside: 'Is this brilliant or what? See ya later. Bev.'

Whilst Helen had travelled across London, she'd reflected on how much she should share with Bev about what had happened. She knew Bev would want to help but she also knew that might put her life in danger, too. So she'd decided not to tell Bev anything, but to just disappear. It would worry her friend immensely that she wouldn't know what had happened to her but if she didn't know anything, she couldn't be forced to tell anything. That was, Helen thought, safer for both of them.

Bev was out this evening, at a gig with her boyfriend, so Helen had known she could come back to the flat, unobserved, to collect what she needed. Now, seeing the friendly note, she toyed with the idea of leaving one in return, but there was nothing she could say that would not arouse suspicion. She wouldn't suddenly just go off to visit someone without having told her friend about it, beforehand. It wasn't what they did. Even *Don't worry, I'm okay* would cause as much anxiety as saying nothing. This was such a horrible position to be in, but she really didn't want to implicate her friend in any investigation that followed.

As she stood in the kitchen, trying to decide what to do for the best, the local news came on the radio. Helen listened in horror as the newsreader announced that the body of Miss Emily Hough had been discovered in her home. 'Police are investigating a burglary at the scene. Witnesses are requested to come forward with information.'

How? How had they found her so quickly? Decisions made, Helen ran around the flat, collecting clothes, toothbrush, a packet of biscuits, a bottle of water and finally, her diary. This contained all sorts of useful information – useful both to her and to the police. Her mind in a frantic whirl, she glanced around quickly to see if there was anything else she should take with her. She saw her iPad sitting on the arm of the sofa. It would give her contact. She could get on-line and keep track of things. But it might be traceable. She just didn't know. She left it where it was and went through the front door into the night.

4

Gavin had arrived at the house at the same time as the Forensic Pathologist. That particular section of the street had been cordoned off and crowds were gathering behind the blue and white tape his officers had used to designate the 'no go' area. It was still raining, though not heavily, and now it was dark, so the scene was lit by the cold white rays from the energy-efficient street lamps and the flashing lights of two police cars and an ambulance.

Not for the first time, he experienced the disturbing mixture of deep regret and excited anticipation in attending the eerie scenery created in this way. There was always an air of unreality about the early stages of an investigation – like being in a fantasy world. He was aware some of his colleagues really got off on this. They felt it as a boost to their egos, or even like getting high. He knew it was important to his sanity to remind himself there was a dead person – not just a dead body – involved.

'So, what have we got?' he asked the officer at the door, who was overseeing proceedings, collecting the information to pass onto him.

'Sir. Emily Hough, aged sixty five, international classical singer. Head has sustained an injury, possibly from a blunt object, but the body appears to have also fallen, or been thrown, down the stairs. Looks like several broken bones.

Probably died on impact. The doctor is going over all that right now.'

They walked into the house together, where Emily's body was lying in the hallway, and the rest of the house was busy with various forensic personnel and police officers taking measurements, photographs, fingerprints and samples of all kinds.

'The burglary was systematic and destructive. Every room, bar the small bedroom, has been turned upside down, but nothing of obvious value has been taken. All the usual stuff like jewellery, laptop, cash deposit box – that's all still here. So it looks like someone was searching for something very specific. Our guess is the last room is untouched because they found it.'

Gavin raised his eyebrows. Now that was unexpected. What ever could the old dear have been into that would initiate a break-in like this? He made a relatively quick overview of the body – position, location, injuries, etc. – and began a tour of the house with Charlie.

Sergeant Charlie Parker – his dad had been a jazz aficionado – was a good copper. Gavin liked him. They'd worked a number of crime scenes together. Charlie was efficient, conscientious and, most important, accurate. He was a real stickler for not avoiding the clues that didn't fit. His meticulous work had led to several successful convictions over the last year since he'd joined the branch.

They moved together from room to room, Gavin taking in an overall impression of what had happened, Charlie feeding him essential relevant information. Gavin trusted his team to pick through all the evidence in its detail and come up with a very useable report. At this stage, he could afford to focus his attention on the bigger picture rather than having to worry over the niceties.

'What do we know about Emily? Was this her main home?'

'Yes, Sir. She always came back here between tours, and spent about half the year in full residence, when she was working on recordings and such like.'

'And how do we know this?'

'From the neighbour, Sir. Mrs. Annie Thomas. She's known Miss Hough for years, since the lady moved in. By all accounts, they were quite friendly – good neighbours, you know. It was Mrs. Thomas who found the body.'

'Oh?'

'She knew Miss Hough was due to go to Manchester tonight for a concert tomorrow, so when she got home from work and saw the front door open, she came in to check everything was okay. One of the officers is taking her statement next door.'

'The front door was open?' Gavin was surprised.

'Yes, Sir. I thought that was odd, too. Maybe whoever was searching had to leave in a hurry and didn't stop to make sure it was closed.'

'Is there any CCTV out front?'

'Just checking that now, Sir.'

Gavin thought it would be very strange for a burglar to leave by the front door. Even without security cameras, his or her chances of being seen were too high. It seemed very careless. There must be another explanation.

'Where's the back door, Charlie?'

'Downstairs, Sir.'

Sergeant Parker led the way down the twisting staircase to what would once have been a traditional cellar and coal bunker, now beautifully transformed into a small recording studio. The soundproof door at the far end was wedged open and one of the forensic team was dusting it for fingerprints. He stood up from his crouching position as Gavin and Charlie came into the room.

'Hello, Tom,' Gavin greeted him. 'Haven't seen you for a while.'

'Hi, Gavin. No, I've been away on a course. Training to be a super-forensic.'

Tom was one of the 'characters' of the forensic team. Unlikely ever to take up a leadership role, his brilliant and unpredictable brain made him invaluable. His ability to interpret clues and piece together seemingly unrelated and miniscule pieces of evidence, never failed to be astonishing.

Inevitably, his appearance reflected his unusual and chaotic – to Gavin, at least – thinking. His hair, naturally black, sported streaks of orange, matched by the ornate spectacles he currently had pushed up over his forehead, making his fringe stick out at odd angles. He always wore several interesting pieces of jewellery, both round his neck and on his fingers. He also liked to wear studs.

Gavin had often wondered whether there was any part of his body that wasn't pierced, but had never quite summoned the courage to ask him. Today, Tom was wearing the usual nose and ear pieces, and Gavin found his sight straying, as ever, to the large black-rimmed circle that lived permanently in Tom's left ear. The same thought ran through his head as it always did when he spoke with Tom – *that must hurt.*

'Found anything of interest so far?'

'Nothing.'

'That's disappointing.'

'No, that's just the point. There's nothing. No fingerprints, no footprints, no stray hairs or threads. This was a professional job, Gavin.'

Gavin felt the hairs on the back of his neck prickle. There was something very disturbing about this scenario – aside from the obvious fact that someone had died. He had the strangest feeling that they were on the edge of something much bigger and much more sinister. He looked around at the violently emptied drawers and cabinets, their contents scattered over the polished floor. What the hell was all this about?

'Charlie, is there anything broken or smashed up down here, or is the mess just from things being thrown around?'

'No, Sir. All the recording equipment is intact. The computer screen's not been damaged. All the electronic stuff is fine. It definitely has all the hallmarks of a thorough search rather than sheer vandalism.'

'And do you get any impression of what they may have been searching for?'

'Something small enough to fit into one of these.' Charlie pointed to the broken drawers of a neat little desk file. 'Every small box and container we've come across so far has been ransacked.' He moved towards the door Tom was working on. 'Back door's through here, Sir.'

Tom stood to one side as Gavin and Charlie carefully passed through the doorway into another cellar room. This one was lined with shelves which had housed hundreds of CD's, audio-cassettes and even vinyl records, many of which had been swept to the floor and consequently broken.

'Christ. Someone wanted something really badly. There's a fortune in here and it's just been ignored.' Gavin turned back to Tom who had resumed working on the door. 'Tom, where's your boss?'

'Angela? She's upstairs.'

'Right, well, when you get into this room, just go carefully.'

Tom looked at him quizzically.

'Sorry, that came out wrong. You lot are always careful, I know. What I meant was – aside from what you need to do to collect evidence, get some officers to retrieve what they can of the CD's and stuff. Call me a softie, but it looks like this is a lifetime's collection. Maybe we can retrieve a good part of it. It just feels criminal to chuck it away. You can liaise with Charlie, here. He'll organise you some people.'

Gavin turned away and walked towards the glass-panelled backdoor, set in the far wall. Behind him, Tom and Charlie exchanged looks. He knew they would, but something about this wanton destruction had got to him. He didn't normally care much about people's belongings – couldn't have said what happened to most of them – but this felt different. There was something down here that called for respect. Maybe there was someone to inherit all of this. If not, he was sure someone would cherish such a collection.

Am I getting sentimental in my old age? As Gavin was only in his early thirties, this explanation seemed unlikely.

Charlie joined him at the backdoor. It looked out onto a charming patio lit by solar lamps and lined with elegant containers holding various plants. A few small tasteful statues completed the picture. They weren't the usual garden ornaments – the hedgehog or the smiling Buddha. These looked more like commissioned pieces. Once more, he was struck by the burglar's single-mindedness in ignoring items of obvious value.

'Do we have a key?'

'Lock's been broken, Sir.'

Gavin reached out a gloved hand, and, sure enough, the door pulled open easily, revealing where the catch mechanism had been expertly broken.

'Is this where they came in?'

'We think so. Here, let me show you.' Charlie went through the doorway and turned abruptly to his left. 'There's a covered path here, Sir, which leads round to the street.'

Gavin followed him under a splendid archway of finished roses, neatly pruned back for the winter. The path traced the outlines of the house to a pretty garden gate, which opened to reveal a passageway running along the side wall. Gavin could see pedestrians passing by at the other end. He walked along, curious to see how obvious the opening was from the street.

As the alleyway ran along the full length of the house, it was quite long and dark. He looked up to see if there was a security light fitted – though, of course, during daylight, that would be irrelevant.

So, whoever had broken in had just walked down here in broad daylight? No, that didn't seem likely. He reached the street-end of the alleyway, and discovered it also had a gate, which had been left open. This was tall enough that, when closed, the street would not be visible from the garden gate.

'Was this open when the team arrived?'

'I don't know, Sir. I'll find out.' Charlie reached for his

radio.

'Later, Charlie. Just make sure you let me know.'

'Sir.'

Gavin stepped out on the street.

'I wonder how busy this is during the day. Charlie, get your statementing officers to ask the locals.'

Although there was a significant crowd gathered behind the tape, he guessed this was normally a quiet road. There were only residential buildings here and it wasn't on the route to anywhere significant. Which meant two scenarios were possible. Either it was so quiet that no-one had been around to witness the intruder, or it would have been obvious to anyone who happened to be looking that a stranger was entering the premises. He hoped for the latter.

A young officer, whose face was new to Gavin, approached them.

'Sir, no security cameras anywhere. Not even a personal porch device.'

Gavin sighed inwardly. He totally understood why people – older ones particularly – didn't want to live a life constantly observed, but it did make his job harder. Sometimes he wondered, facetiously, how coppers had caught anybody in 'the good old days'.

He thanked the officer and began to lead the way back along the passageway. Charlie stopped as if a thought had occurred to him. 'Maxwell, you were first on the scene, weren't you?'

'Yes, Sarge.'

'Do you remember whether the gate was open when you arrived?'

There was a pause while Maxwell tried to recall.

'Yes, Sarge. It was. I remember because it was quite breezy and the gate was banging against the door post.'

Gavin's ears pricked up. 'So it was unlocked but not actually open – like it is now?'

'Um. Yes, Sir.'

'What are you thinking, Sir?' Charlie asked.

'I'm thinking that someone may have left in a hurry. Front door open. Side gate left unlocked, perhaps not even closed. Maybe – just maybe – someone disturbed whoever was here and made a quick get-away essential.'

'But if that was the case, why didn't that someone report the burglary?'

'That, Charlie, is a very good question.'

Gavin spent the next twenty minutes or so completing his tour of the house. It was the same story in every room. No clues left behind, evidence of systematic searching, total disregard for anything personal or obviously valuable. It would take Forensics quite some time to go over everything so maybe something useful would turn up before they were through, but he wasn't holding his breath.

Having seen as much as he needed to on the upper floor, he found himself returning to the hallway where the doctor was finishing up his preliminary examination of the body and arranging its removal into the ambulance. He was about to ask Dr. Humphrey for his initial thoughts when three things happened all at once.

First, a police officer came out of what Gavin had assumed was a cupboard in the hallway, holding a very vivid red plastic coat. Second, Constable Maxwell re-appeared, carrying an appointments diary. And third, Inspector Jack Foster walked in through the front door.

5

Huddled in her warmest coat, and wishing she'd remembered her gloves, Helen sat on a park bench and tried to consider her options. She wasn't making a very good job of it. After leaving the flat, she'd wandered around the streets for a while, attempting to come up with ways of getting out of London unseen. The intrusion of modern technology was becoming very apparent to her.

She couldn't go anywhere where there might be crowds, like shopping malls or main roads because there would be CCTV. She couldn't get on a train because paying for her ticket with a credit card would be traceable, and therefore also her destination. She didn't have enough cash to allow her to buy a journey of any distance. That would've left her needing to get more cash at the other end, which would involve a cashpoint of some sort. Even taking money out at a post office ran the risk of her being caught on camera or remembered by the assistant.

She'd considered the cashback option offered at supermarket checkouts but that brought her back to the CCTV problem, and anyway, she thought you could only take out very small amounts of money that way. In any case, most of these options involved using a debit card – and that would definitely leave a trail.

For a brief while, she'd thought about trying to hitch a

lift out of the city but that had its own dangers – nothing to do with being identified. The best kind of lift would be a long-distance one, like a lorry or a truck, but that meant getting herself to a service station, or at least a transport café, and she was back to the problem of being caught on camera, as well as the fact that asking for any individual's help exposed her terribly. It would require a level of trust she no longer felt willing to test out.

One thing she could do, she thought, was get something to eat. She'd had nothing of real substance all day and was now feeling very hungry. She checked her watch. Tony's would still be open. She went in there about once a week to get fish and chips so he wouldn't think anything of her coming into the shop. Chances were, if he was asked later, he wouldn't even remember which particular night she was in. That seemed the safest option. Checking on her surroundings, she'd retraced her route back to his little café and bought fish and chips 'to go'. She'd taken them into the park and had sat in the cold, relishing both the taste and the warmth on her hands through the wrapping paper.

But now she had no idea what to do next. Although eating had made her feel better initially, she had since begun to feel despondent again. Was she going to be reduced to sleeping on a park bench? And even that wouldn't be safe because she knew one of the local community officers regularly came through here during the early hours of the morning. She was well and truly trapped. It seemed like the only thing she could do was keep walking the streets, and that wasn't any kind of long-term answer. Inevitably, the tears came once more.

The sound of loud, cheery voices startled her. A group of young men were making their way along the path, obviously happy on a drink or two, chatting and singing football chants. She pulled her hood further over her head, and tried to look inconspicuous.

'Helen?' a voice asked.

She didn't respond.

'Is that you? Helen, are you okay?'

She lifted her tear-stained face to look up into a familiar one.

'No, Petey, I'm not. I need help.'

Unbelievably, Petey was probably the only person in the world she could trust right now without running the risk of dragging him into a scenario he wouldn't want to be part of. Petey was one of life's free spirits. He lived on a canal boat and, although he regularly moored at various points in the city, he spent just as much time travelling the waterways through the surrounding countryside. Helen wasn't sure how he made a living but she knew he was not averse to being – at least marginally – on the wrong side of the law.

A philosopher at heart, Petey disliked authority, convention and containment. He and Helen had first met some years ago when Helen was walking the canal in Regent's Park. Too young and innocent to know any better – as her aunt would have put it – Helen had been entranced by the pretty boat, with its little shuttered windows and stacked firewood on the roof, and had got chatting with the fascinating man who'd been off-loading a bicycle to ride to the shops.

At the time, she'd felt envious of the freedom and flexibility of Petey's life-style, but as they'd got to know each other during his intermittent visits to her locality, he'd encouraged her to keep exploring her own freedom through her singing, telling her that one day – if she was true to her heart – it would lead her on many exciting adventures. Well, that was painfully true now, Helen realised, as she gave into the emotion of the last twelve hours and wept openly on his shoulder.

Petey had sat down on the bench next to her and waved his friends on. 'I'll see you soon, yeah?'

Then he'd stretched two musty-coated arms around her and pulled her into a very welcome hug. When she stopped crying, he offered her a purple rag to wipe her face and asked, 'Whatever's wrong?'

'Where do I begin?'

'Well, how about over a cuppa back on the boat? It's bloody cold out here, once you've stopped moving.'

'Tell me about it.' Helen managed a little smile and showed Petey her hands, now red with cold.

'God, honey, how long have you been out here?'

'I don't know. Several hours.'

'Come on. It's not far. Let's get you warm.' He reached into the deep pockets of his brown overcoat and retrieved two tatty knitted gloves. 'Here. They're not much, but they'll do for now.'

Helen pulled them on gratefully, and took the arm he offered her. He began to move in the direction of the main road. Helen hesitated.

'Petey, is there a back way?'

'What d'ya mean?'

'A route we can take that's more … private. Less chance of being seen? No security cameras, cops, that sort of thing.'

'Dear God, Helen. What've you got yourself into? Sure, there's a back route. No problem.' He turned them around and headed for the trees lining the far side of the park. 'Just stick with me.'

Petey led the way along a convoluted route between woodland, parkland and various backyards, until they reached a relatively secluded spot where his boat was tethered. Inevitably, within the city confines, the area was lit by streetlights, so Helen pulled up her hood again as they approached the boat and climbed on board. Once inside, she felt able to relax a bit.

As she settled herself next to the wood-burner, Petey got the kettle on and dug out some biscuits from one of the myriad of tiny cupboards lining his kitchen. Helen looked around at the neat arrangement of everything one needed to live comfortably, all squeezed into a miniscule space. She'd only been inside the boat a few times before and it always both fascinated and amazed her that so much could be fitted into such a tiny space without feeling crowded.

Petey handed her a very welcome mug of hot tea. 'So tell me about it.'

Helen sighed. 'It's a long story.'

'That's okay. I'm not going anywhere.'

Helen gasped as a crazy idea came into her head.

'Petey, are you planning to stay here for a while or were you on the move?'

'Oh, I was just about to leave London,' he replied, reaching for a biscuit. 'But it's no problem. You know me. I don't generally have plans. I'm happy to stick around for a bit, if it'll help.'

'No. I mean … Just the opposite. I don't suppose … Could I hitch a lift with you?'

'Of course. Where to?'

'You need to hear why before you agree.'

'Do I?'

'I think so. You might not want to get involved.'

A seriously worried look crossed Petey's face. 'I think you need to share, Helen – as they say.'

So she did. She took him step by step through everything that had happened that day – technically, yesterday now – from the taxi ride delivering her to the audition, to Petey finding her on the park bench. He was a good listener, and let her tell the story at her own pace, allowing her to fill in the details she felt were important. He didn't interrupt until she had finished, though when she described the scene at the police station, he had given a low whistle, and got up to refill their mugs from the teapot.

When she finished, his first response was to reassure her.

'Helen, honey, I get your predicament, but I really don't think you need to be quite so paranoid. Most CCTV is wiped clean at the end of the day. It's only kept if there's been an incident, like a robbery or something, so no-one's going to know about your movements today.'

It seemed a strange turn-around for Petey to be telling

her not to worry about surveillance.

'But once they know they're looking for me – well, once *he* knows, that police officer …'

'Well, yes, to a certain extent, but unless they think you're actually the murderer, they're not going to be putting out a BOLO, as they say in America. And I don't think your Detective Grey-suit can be raising a high-profile alarm without drawing suspicion to himself.'

'Really?' Helen began to feel a little calmer.

'Yeah. I mean, they don't even know you've been there, do they?'

'I guess not. Unless …' A thought occurred to Helen. 'Unless Miss Hough had me listed in her appointments diary.'

'True. But there must be loads of Helen Clarke's in London. It would take them a while to find the one daft enough to wear that red coat.'

Helen laughed, and felt the relief that brought. 'Yes. You're right. I got myself into a right state.'

'Nevertheless,' Petey offered her another biscuit. 'You are right to think about lying low for a while, I think. You can't be sure who you can trust within the local police now, so maybe getting out of London, and reporting what you've seen at another police station, is an option.' He caught her face. 'And, yes, I'd be very happy to help you with that.'

The two of them talked late into the night, going over what had happened to Helen once more, and then chatting about happier things, catching up on each other's lives since they last met. Around three in the morning, Helen felt herself starting to fall asleep, the exhaustion of her day hitting her.

'You take my bed, honey. I'll kip in here,' Petey said.

Helen tried mildly to protest but was actually too tired to try hard. Petey showed her the bedroom which had a wonderfully inviting three-quarter sized bed, nearly filling the little cabin. He handed her some pyjamas out of a wardrobe neatly hidden in the wall.

'Here. Too big, I know, but they'll do.'

She took them gratefully, as he gave her a gentle kiss on the cheek.

'Goodnight, honey. Sleep as long as you like. I'll pop out and get us some breakfast in the morning. You just stay low if I'm not here when you wake up, okay?'

She nodded.

'Thank you.'

She spoke quietly, all her energy now gone. As soon as he closed the door, she was undressed and in the bed within seconds. She didn't remember anything else.

6

The forensic team had worked through the night, so when Gavin arrived at his desk the next morning, there was an initial report waiting for him. As had been suggested yesterday, there was none of the usual evidence such as fingerprints, so the supposition that this was a professional job seemed more than likely. That, however, raised more questions than it answered.

Gavin was still puzzling over Jack Foster's interest with the case. It was most unusual for him to turn up at a crime-scene – even on a case assigned to him. He was notoriously lazy and generally relied heavily on the work of his subordinate officers. Inevitably, he was happy to take the credit when their work was successful but just as happy to blame them when a case crumbled.

Similarly, it was rare indeed for him to work 'after hours'. He did not subscribe to the concept that a senior officer should put in whatever time was needed to solve a case. So to see him at the crime scene last night was nothing short of extraordinary. Gavin found his comment that he'd 'just been passing' very unconvincing, but could not come up with any other explanation. He *felt* it was suspicious that Foster had put in an appearance but without more information, he couldn't follow up on his feelings.

He grabbed his Starbuck's coffee and decided to visit Dr.

Humphrey to see if he'd come up with anything more useable. As he left his office, he saw Tom approaching.

'Mornin', Gavin.'

'Morning. Disappointing report.'

'Well, yes. In the ordinary way of things, I suppose it is.'

'What's that supposed to mean?'

'The great thing about not finding the obvious is that it seriously challenges you to look deeper.'

Gavin gave him an exasperated look.

'We took more samples after you left, and the team have been working on them. You never know what might turn up.'

'But nothing yet?'

'Not as such, but …'

'But what, Tom?' Gavin was getting impatient. He didn't deal with the abstract as well as Tom did – particularly first thing in the morning.

'It's just that last night, when we went upstairs to join Angela, there was a laptop on the bed in the main bedroom.'

'So?'

'I didn't think anything of it at the time – and it's been collected for the team to work on, anyway. But now I'm wondering if it was significant – the fact that it was open, as if someone had been using it, and it had shut itself down after being left.'

'Could've been Emily Hough. She might have been using it upstairs when the burglar found her.'

'It's a possibility.'

Gavin could almost hear Tom's brain working.

'What if the object the murderer was after was a flashdrive?'

'A flashdrive? What makes you think that?'

'Well, we found a box in that room that had housed several, and they'd all been emptied on the floor.'

'But that was true of pretty much everything in the house.'

'Yeah, but if you were searching for a particular

flashdrive, and you saw a laptop, you'd start trying them out, wouldn't you? Booting them up to read the files list. Suppose someone was doing that on Emily's laptop when they got disturbed?'

Gavin nodded thoughtfully. 'Is there any way of telling what that particular computer was doing, prior to shutting down?'

'Absolutely. The digital guys will be able to read the computer's history. That'll tell you what its last action was. I'll get Bryan onto it.'

Bryan was the latest addition to the digital forensics team. He was only eighteen but was considered a genius in his field, having already completed a university degree. Not surprisingly, he had quickly earned Tom's respect.

'Thanks, Tom. Let me know if anything interesting turns up, but I won't hold my breath.'

'Well, it's a theory.'

Gavin agreed it was and actually felt it was quite plausible. All the indications last night had been that the search carried out by the burglar had been for a small item, and a flashdrive certainly fell into that category. He left Tom to his cerebral meanderings and continued on his visit to the morgue.

Dr. Humphrey was actually waiting for him when he got there. Gavin looked surprised.

'How did you know I was coming?'

'Tom's trying out some new device or other. It bleeps when someone enters the corridor, and translates the CCTV footage into a print-out of someone's name – if it recognises them. Doesn't always work, though. It told me yesterday the Chief Super was on his way, and it turned out to be Angela. Not quite sure how that happened.'

Dr. Humphrey laughed. He often trialled new bits and pieces for Tom. It appealed to his sense of the ridiculous.

'Have you managed to come up with any information from the body, Doctor?' Gavin asked.

'Yes. Time of death – I'd estimate sometime between two and four in the afternoon. Cause of death – blow to the head with a blunt object, causing an initial concussion, which was then exacerbated by the fall down the stairs. This broke her neck, as well as several bones in her arms and legs. It was a horrendous fall. Thankfully, I believe she was unconscious when she fell. The object used to hit her was oblong with rounded corners. I'm guessing the butt of a gun.'

'A gun?' Gavin was taken aback. This case was getting murkier by the hour.

'That's certainly what it looks like. I've taken swabs and photos and sent them off to Angela's team.'

'So we're definitely looking at murder, aren't we, rather than accidental death?'

'I think so, Inspector.'

Gavin paused. 'Just to be sure, I suppose you've examined the body for evidence of anything else?'

'You mean like sexual interference, or aggravated assault?'

'Yeah.'

'No, there's nothing to indicate anything else took place. All the bruising is perfectly consistent with the fall. There's no evidence of fingerprint bruising like you'd get with strangulation, or toecap bruising from being kicked, for example. And all the bruising was inflicted while she was still alive. So you're not looking at a hate crime, here.'

'Thanks.'

Gavin experienced a wave of pity for the old dear. How awful that she'd been at home. Clearly, the burglar had had no interest in her at all. She'd just happened to get in the way. Which begged the question once more of what on earth she had in her house that someone would want so badly.

He turned to go.

'There is one thing you might find helpful, though.'

'Yeah, what's that?'

'I removed this from around her neck.' The doctor held out a plastic bag containing a chain and locket. 'I wanted to show you before I sent it on to Angela's team.'

'Isn't it just a medical information locket?'

'Yes, but it doesn't contain any medical information. No blood group or named drugs, or anything of that sort.'

'Really?' Gavin took the bag and examined the contents carefully. The locket opened to reveal a tiny piece of paper with a number on it. 2450.

'Any idea what this means?' he asked.

'Not a clue,' said the doctor.

Gavin made his way back upstairs to his office. One of the frustrating things about working a case of this kind was that you never knew what pieces of evidence were significant. It was also one of the fascinating things, if he was honest. It was like trying to solve a puzzle or a crossword. The process of following what might be irrelevant lines of thought, of trying to make non-matching clues fit together – that was what kept him doing this job, despite the stress and aggravations it involved.

Talking of aggravations … When he got to his office door, he discovered Jack Foster sitting inside, leafing through the forensic report. He suppressed a surge of irritation. Although Jack was a Detective Inspector like himself, technically he outranked Gavin due to his longer career in the force, so it generally didn't pay to challenge him directly.

'Hi, Jack. Can I help you?'

'Just wondering if you've found anything of interest yet.'

Gavin hesitated. He was certainly not going to volunteer information when he had no idea what Foster's real intentions were.

'Nothing particularly significant.'

He took a seat behind his desk and looked expectantly at his visitor. One of the best ways to get the upper hand with Foster was to get him to reveal his thoughts first, and this was best done by playing it cool. Foster had little patience, especially when he felt people were keeping things from him.

'Nothing that might lead to the identity of the burglar, then?'

'Not yet.'

Gavin felt that prickling on the back of his neck again. Something was out of order here. He waited.

'Or any clue about what was taken?'

'No.'

'Right.' Foster got up to leave. 'Just wondered if I might be of assistance, that's all.'

His attempt at nonchalance was almost laughable, and to Gavin, highly suspicious.

'Really?' He couldn't help himself.

'Oh, didn't you know? The case should have been mine, only the switchboard couldn't reach me at the time, so I feel a trifle – shall we say – proprietorial about it. You'll keep me posted, right?'

There was a definite hint of threat beneath the words, which Gavin presumed was intended to intimidate him but which only served to confirm his notion that there was something more going on here than mere professional jealousy. He smiled, and looked Foster directly in the eye.

'Of course,' he lied.

Much of the morning was taken up with routine trawling through statements from neighbours, constructing a storyboard, re-reading the forensics report and similar basic but essential activities. For Gavin, it was all about getting a flavour of the case. At some weird, alchemical level, he knew that the evidence would start to make sense if he let the energy of it seep into him.

He would never have shared any of his thinking with his colleagues but he was all too aware that catching serious criminals had as much to do with intuitive leaps of the mind as with systematic piecing together of evidence. Those detectives who were only willing to utilise logic and 'hard facts', were rarely as successful as those who allowed a touch of creativity into their detecting, and this was now something he cultivated.

By lunchtime, he was feeling more strongly than ever that something very sinister had taken place at Emily Hough's house – something that was way bigger than a bog-standard, interrupted burglary that had inadvertently ended in murder. There was no doubt that Miss Hough had something very particular in her possession that someone else was intent on acquiring, and that someone was even prepared to kill for, but so many questions surfaced as a result of this idea.

Had Emily interrupted the burglar herself? Did she know she had something that someone might kill for? Or had it, perhaps, been planted on her, maybe during one of her international tours? In which case, she would be completely unaware of the danger she was in.

Or had she herself got involved in something sinister? She really didn't seem the type to practise smuggling but you never knew. Drugs, perhaps? Or diamonds? Both could be concealed in small packages, though probably not so small as the size of a flash-drive. And if it turned out that Tom's theory was right, and it was a flash-drive they were looking for, that meant she was probably smuggling information of some kind. Then one had to consider the murky world of spying or espionage.

Gavin decided he was getting carried away with himself. More groundwork was needed before he considered possibilities like that. He called Charlie into his office.

'I'm sure you're already onto it, but I want you to check what Emily Hough has been up to over the last month or so. You know, if she's been overseas, performed or visited somewhere significant … You know the drill.'

'Yes, Sir. I've got one of the officers doing that just now. I'll get him to report to you asap.'

'And relatives. Did she have any family?'

'No children, Sir. She was never married. Her career seems to have been her life. Her parents are both dead now. Died during the last ten years. Records show she had a sister.

We're trying to track her down.'

'Good. Keep me posted. Any further with finding that Helen person listed in her diary?'

'Not yet, Sir. There are hundreds of Helen Clarke's in London. It'll take some time, I'm afraid, unless we get a lucky break.'

'Seems odd she didn't have any contact details written in with the name. You're sure she's not listed in Emily's address book?' They had found a rather beautiful and exquisitely hand-written book next to the phone in Emily's front room. Along with stunning photographs, presumably of many of the places Emily had visited, there were addresses, phone numbers and e-mail details for all her personal friends and colleagues.

'Definitely not in there, Sir.'

'Which probably means,' Gavin mused, 'she wasn't someone Emily knew.'

'I agree, Sir. She seems to have kept her business and her personal life quite separate. She obviously did quite a bit of teaching – one to one stuff – but all her students' names are listed in her appointments diary. Some of them are regulars. Some just appear once with their contact details next to their names.'

Charlie paused. Gavin could see he'd just had an idea.

'Go on.'

'I wonder if she did some kind of assessment work, like auditioning. Perhaps she had connections with some of the big music colleges, and they sometimes asked her to listen to someone, give her opinion. Maybe Helen Clarke was just a last-minute arrangement, slotted in quickly before she left for Manchester. She certainly didn't have anyone else listed for that day. Or the day before, in fact.'

'That, Charlie, is a good idea. See if you can follow it up.'

'Yes, Sir.' Charlie turned to leave, but paused at the door.

'Something else?' Gavin asked.

'Just wanted to clarify, Sir. We are reporting directly to *you*, are we?'

Gavin looked up sharply. 'Yes, Charlie. All information comes to me first. Please make sure everyone understands that. 'Circumspect' is the order of the day.'

Charlie nodded. 'Yes, Sir. I'll make sure that the staff are all clear on that.'

So, Gavin thought to himself as the door closed, he wasn't the only one who thought Jack Foster might be up to something.

Charlie had been one of the few lower-ranked policemen who had assisted with the investigation into corruption last year. In fact, that was how he'd come to join the Met, being brought in from a smaller branch outside London specifically to investigate dealings 'on the ground'. He had quickly picked up on suspicious activity surrounding Jack Foster and was able to highlight officers who appeared to be passing him information surreptitiously, but like the rest of the team, had never been able to uncover any conclusive evidence that would implicate the inspector.

The experience, however, had left him wary of the senior man and, clearly, he had noticed Foster's interest in this case. Since the investigation, 'circumspect' had become something of a code word for those working in close proximity with Foster whenever there was information that needed handling with care.

Late in the afternoon, when Constable Maxwell had taken over his turn at the front desk, a young woman arrived.

'Can I help you?'

'Yes, well, I hope so. I need to report a missing person.'

'Oh dear,' Maxwell turned on his sympathetic look. 'Right. Best let me have the details.' He pulled out a large notepad and the requisite form from under the desk.

The young woman continued without prompting.

'It's my best friend – my flatmate. You see, I didn't go home last night. I was out with my boyfriend. We went to this gig, and it was really late when it finished, so we went back to his house, 'cos it was nearby and …'

Maxwell knew better than to interrupt an anxious person. Even within his short experience, he'd discovered allowing someone to tell their tale in their own way was much the best course. Let them spill out what seemed important to them, listen carefully for significant information and often the reported incident sorted itself, when the member of the public remembered where they'd left the 'stolen' object or recalled the message left to say the 'missing' person would be late home.

'… so when I got home after my shift and discovered she wasn't there either, and some of her things are gone, which is very odd – and, of course, her phone was still sitting in her pocket at work …'

The woman petered out and looked apologetically at Maxwell.

'Sorry, I'm rambling, aren't I? It's just not like Helen not to get in touch for twenty-four hours. Especially after such an important audition.'

Maxwell's ears had pricked up at the mention of a Helen, and when the woman also mentioned an audition, he realised this could be really important.

'Perhaps you could tell me her full name?'

'Helen Clarke. Helen Rosemary Clarke.'

Maxwell felt cold shivers running down his back. He began to fill in the form in front of him.

'And how old is she?'

'Nineteen.'

'And you last saw her … ?'

'Yesterday afternoon, when she left work early to go to an audition.'

Maxwell cleared his throat.

'And where exactly was the audition?' He held his breath.

'Somewhere in Battersea. A woman called Emily Hough. She's an – '

'International classical singer.' Maxwell finished for her.

'You know of her?' the woman asked in surprise.

'You haven't seen the news, then?' he asked, gently.

'No, what news?'

Maxwell debated internally whether he should tell her now, or get her upstairs first and let one of the senior officers do so. He decided it was probably kinder to share the information straightaway, rather than increase her anxiety with needless speculation.

'Miss Hough was found dead in her home last night.'

The woman gasped. 'Oh my God.'

She paused, letting the news sink in. 'But what about Helen? Is she okay? Where is she?'

Steadily, Maxwell responded. 'We don't know. Look, Miss … ?'

'Hutchinson. Beverley Hutchinson.'

'Miss Hutchinson. Can I ask you to come through and speak to one of our senior officers? Your information is going to be very helpful to our investigation, and will also mean we can now start looking for your friend properly. Up 'til now, we had no idea who Helen Clarke was.'

Maxwell moved across to the locked door leading to the inside of the station, intent on getting Bev onto the right side of it, in case she disappeared, too.

'Can I just ask what she was wearing yesterday?'

'Oh, that's easy. A ridiculous red plastic coat.'

7

Helen sat across from Petey at the table in his kitchen area, watching the late afternoon sun drift in through the porthole windows on the starboard side of the boat – or was it the port side? She could never remember. She felt quiet and calm, and much more able to face her difficult situation than she had twenty-four hours ago.

She'd woken to the enticing small of bacon frying. For a moment, she hadn't been able to place where she was; then, as she took in the neat little room encompassing her bed, she'd remembered the awfulness of the day before, and Petey's kindness the previous night. She'd climbed out of the deliciously warm covers, wrapped herself in the tartan dressing-gown Petey had left out for her, and made her way into the 'galley'.

'Mornin' – or should I say 'afternoon'?' Petey had smiled a cheerful greeting.

'Morning.'

She'd grabbed the warm cup of coffee he offered and plumped herself down at the tiny table, ready to share a hearty breakfast. She was starving.

'What time is it, then?'

'About three o'clock.'

Helen had initially been horrified – partly by her apparent rudeness to her host but mostly because she was so anxious to get her escape plan underway, and now she'd lost more than half a day. When she attempted to share her worries, Petey had simply suggested she pop out the 'front door' and take a look around. Surprised by this suggestion, she'd taken her coffee with her to stand out on deck and view the surrounding countryside.

'Where are we?' she'd asked in amazement.

'Somewhere between Walthamstow and Enfield.'

'Petey, you're amazing.' She'd given him a big kiss on the cheek in sheer relief before they'd both gone back inside to eat.

Now, after twelve hours of sleep, a fantastic fry-up and the knowledge that she was a considerable distance from the location of yesterday's events, she began to relax a little and to feel more capable of making plans.

'I thought we could follow the Lee Navigation north as far as Hoddesdon.' Petey suggested. 'From there we've got a couple of options.

'We could continue north up to Hertford, or we could go east towards Bishop's Stortford along the Stort Navigation. The police won't be monitoring public transport yet, and even if they were, they'd be looking inside the London borough first, I would think. So you've probably got a selection of choices: trains, coaches – even hitching a lift, if you feel like it.'

Petey got up to clear the table and start washing up the plates and cooking utensils. Under normal circumstances, Helen would be quick to offer to do the task herself, but she was busy running her checklist in her head again.

'Problem?' Petey asked, getting the hot water going.

'Yeah, I've very little cash. I've got plenty of savings – well, enough, anyway – but I can't get hold of them. I had thought, yesterday, I might risk going to the bank to take them out, but that would mean going back into London, now.'

She looked up at Petey. 'Please don't think I'm not grateful that you've got me out of London without being seen, Petey. I feel so much better than I did yesterday. It's just that every problem I solve seems to throw up another one.'

Petey smiled. 'I get that.'

He picked up the frying pan with two large yellow hands and plunged it into the soapy water. He looked most peculiar wearing rubber gloves with his usual attire. Helen giggled. She hadn't expected him to be house-proud, but looking around the boat she could see he kept the place immaculately and she guessed, for a long-term boater, this was probably essential.

'Don't knock it,' he grinned. 'Want another cuppa?'

'Yes, please.'

Leaving the pan to soak for a while, he put the kettle on again to make another brew and came over to join her at the table, while it boiled.

'I have an idea about the cash,' he said.

'Oh?'

'Easy, really. I can lend you some.'

'No, absolutely not.' Helen felt genuinely shocked by his suggestion. 'Petey, you can't. You hardly know me. Besides, I need quite a bit. I'm not ...'

She felt the tears threatening to come again. She swallowed.

'I'm not going to have access to my account for the foreseeable future. I need enough money to survive on and to get me somewhere a good distance from London – and I don't know how long I'll need to be away, or if I can get work, and ...'

Petey put out a hand, sensing her rising panic.

'Listen, Helen love. One of the beauties of a life like mine is that you don't need to rely on banks and such-like. In fact, they probably wouldn't give me an account – no stable address, you see. I'm not a bona fide person in their eyes. So if I can't participate in the system, I'll find ways to circumvent it.'

He got up to fill the teapot.

Helen forced her anxiety to subside. After all, she was not in any immediate danger. She'd got time to listen to any crazy plan he had, even if she later decided not to follow it through.

'We'll just leave that to brew.' Petey popped a bright red knitted teacosy over the pot. 'Another of my hidden talents.' He made a dramatic sweep of his arm to indicate his handiwork.

Helen giggled again. 'I'm impressed.'

'That's better,' he said. 'Now, follow me and I'll impress you some more.'

He led the way back into the bedroom, where he proceeded to tuck Helen's bedclothes into neat folds around the edges of the mattress.

'Oh sorry, Petey. I hadn't got around to making the bed yet.'

'No, don't be daft. That's not what I'm doing.'

Helen watched in amazement as he lifted the end of the bed and tilted it up against the wall where she now realised there were hooks that allowed him to attach the mattress by means of fabric loops on its sides, so that the entire bed was held in an upright fashion, flat against the bedroom's panelling.

Then he knelt down and scrabbled with his fingernails, loosening a floorboard in the space where the bed had been. Lifting this out, he revealed a small handle which he then pulled towards him. A trapdoor. Helen gasped as a large dark space became apparent, too small to count as a room but deep enough for Petey to drop into up to his knees and long enough that a person would be able to lie down in it.

Petey flicked on a light switch, illuminating the space. He grinned at Helen. 'You never know when you might need something like this.'

She nodded, wondering not for the first time what kind of life Petey led.

'And,' he continued, 'it makes a great place for the safe.'

At the far end of the hidey-hole, tucked out of sight

under the adjoining floorboards, Helen could now see a small grey door with a combination lock on its front.

'Wow. You think of everything,' she gasped.

'Sure do,' he agreed, and began to turn the 'tumbles' on the lock. The door opened smoothly, revealing two shelves. A number of wrapped packages sat on the top one, and the lower one held a cash box which Petey pulled out and handed up to her. 'Here, take this.'

Helen took the box which was surprisingly light while Petey locked up and closed everything behind him. When he was done, there was absolutely no indication that such a secret place existed. The floor looked just like the flooring in the rest of the boat.

They took the cashbox back into the kitchen and placed it on the table. Petey poured the tea, then reaching up to the top shelf positioned over the sink, he brought down a pretty red tin which jangled as he moved it. He took the lid off and tipped the contents onto the table. A jumble of keys, all different sizes and shapes, spilled out across the wooden surface. He shuffled them around until he found a small flat silver one, then piled all the others back into the tin.

'Do they all open stuff?' Helen asked.

'No.' Petey grinned. 'Mostly decoys.'

He now pushed the little silver key into the lock on the front of the cashbox and turned it, lifting the lid. Inside was a stash of used banknotes of all varieties – five pounds, ten pounds, even some twenties and fifties. Helen gasped again. She'd never seen so much money in one place.

'Petey, there must be hundreds in there.'

'More like thousands, I hope,' he responded. 'So how much do you need?'

His cheeky grin and his unbelievable generosity were too much for Helen. She burst into tears.

'Look, love. You'll pay me back. I know you will. And you can see you're not going to leave me short. Besides, I'm in the middle of another deal. That's why I chose this route out of London. I'm off to a meeting tomorrow in Bishop's

Stortford.' He got up to refill their mugs. 'Thought I'd kill two birds with one stone, so to speak.'

Helen was dumbfounded. She didn't know what to make of any of this. Had she really had a stroke of amazing good luck, or had she run away from one murky situation only to land herself in another?

Petey saw the consternation on her face. 'Don't worry. You don't need to know anything about it. The money's clean. The deals are – well, maybe not legal – but definitely not treacherous.' He paused. 'And the cops are not after me, if you're wondering about that.'

The thought had crossed her mind. It would be rather stupid to be running away from one lot of police only to plunge herself into the arresting arms of another lot.

'Seriously, you're safe. You're just temporarily – what shall we say? – underground.'

Helen looked across the table into Petey's cheerful face. He had deliciously deep, dark brown eyes which radiated a sense of security. She'd always guessed his lifestyle wasn't exactly above board, but actually this kind of help was just what she needed right now. Petey was happy to sit slightly on the 'wrong' side of the law, so wasn't at all concerned about helping her. Added to that, his undeniable knowledge and skills at maneuvering in this new underworld she'd fallen into, were truly a godsend. She decided to trust him.

'Thank you,' she said, quietly. 'I promise, as soon as I can, I'll get the money back to you.'

Having totally surrendered to this strange new life, Helen decided she might as well enjoy it. She spent the next couple of hours on deck, revelling in the warm autumn sunshine and the lovely scenery which Petey steered them through. She'd had no idea there was such gorgeous countryside so close to London, and the canal route kept them mostly well away from noisy traffic and train lines so that the experience – aside from being 'on the run' – was delightful.

Petey turned out to be something of a bird watcher, so

was able to point out lots of interesting sightings which she would have missed on her own. The trees lining the sides of the waterway were in the process of turning their leaves, so that in between the fresh light greens that yesterday's rain had polished up, there were fabulous yellows and golds, with occasional bursts of red berries.

The birds were busy flying in and out amongst the colours and chattering about it. Petey pointed out robins and chaffinches, easy to see with their red and rose pink breasts, and then small flocks of birds that landed for a while, making a bush seem alive with fluttering before rushing off to another haunt. Long-tailed tits, with their pretty pink and grey markings. Goldfinches with their red 'masks'. Helen was enchanted.

Then suddenly, Petey put his finger to his lips. She could hear a bright, insistent piping call, a few yards along the banking. Then a startling flash of electric blue skimmed the water's surface, racing past them so fast she almost didn't see it.

'A kingfisher!' she whispered, feeling the privilege of the moment.

They met very few other boaters along the route. Petey had said it would be quiet at this time of year. Each time another vessel came in sight, Helen decided it would be prudent to pop back inside the boat temporarily. At first, Petey thought she was being too dramatic, but they talked about it for a while and he began to see where she was coming from.

'I guess I've lived outside the system for so long, I forget how obsessed people can get with things like spotting criminals.'

He grinned at the chagrin on her face.

'Petey, I'm being serious here.'

'Sorry. I know. It's true though. When you live a life like this, the world that other people find so important does gradually become irrelevant.'

Helen could understand why he would think this, having

spent a few hours idling along the water, and she could see the attraction of living disconnected from the complexities of what she had always considered a 'normal life' and choosing to be more in touch with the natural world, but she didn't feel it was anything she would want to do herself on a more permanent basis.

'I do see your point, though.' Petey interrupted her thoughts. 'Perhaps it would be a good idea to disguise you a bit.'

'What?' That idea hadn't occurred to her.

'Well, even just cutting and dyeing your hair would make you less obvious. I mean, if people are looking for a long-haired redhead and they see a girl with short, dark hair, they're not going to notice her, are they?'

'I suppose not,' Helen answered slowly, caressing one of her auburn locks as it sat on her shoulder. The thought of losing her lovely hair was pretty shocking.

'It'll grow back,' Petey said, with a grin. 'I'll pop off the boat in the morning and go shopping for you. See what I can find. You'd better make me one of your lists.'

'You're really getting into this, aren't you?' Helen asked, responding with a cheeky grin of her own.

Petey just whistled a jaunty tune as he turned back to steering the boat.

They moored just around twilight, alongside some fields. A full moon was coming up over the scene, illuminating the stubble left from harvesting in a patch close by and the lovely green of a meadow next to it. Small movements in the grass every now and again indicated that the evening wildlife was coming out to play. As the last of the daylight disappeared, an owl hooted across the open countryside, followed by a sharp bark.

'What was that?' Helen asked, as they fixed the last of the ropes to hold the boat securely overnight.

'A fox.'

'Really? I've never heard one before.'

'Helen, you really haven't lived, have you?'

Helen wasn't sure she'd agree with that statement but was willing to accept that there was definitely more to experience about life than she'd anticipated.

They went inside to prepare supper, then spent a quiet evening chatting, going over possible plans for Helen's get-away and generally getting to know each other a little more.

Helen began to realise just how much Petey loved the way of life he'd chosen and that it wasn't something that had just happened to him. He had a profoundly gentle aspect to his character that genuinely relished living amongst the plants and animals he encountered on his travels. He also had a really strong aversion to being told what to do by anyone, and obviously truly valued the freedom this life allowed him. In fact, it was clear he would have been extremely uncomfortable living in a house, or even in one place, for any length of time.

She discovered she didn't envy him. In fact, as the evening wore on, she began to miss her little flat in North London and the friends she would normally spend the evening with. Grateful though she was for this escape route, this was not the life for her. She desperately hoped there would be a way through this mess so that she could return to the way of life she'd chosen.

Despite her long sleep into the day, she found she was still very tired, so around ten o'clock or so, she excused herself to climb back into Petey's very comfy bed. She had briefly offered to take up the couch bed in the 'living room', but Petey wouldn't hear of it. Besides, it made more sense for him to be able to move around the boat and for her to have the option of sleeping in.

'Just stay out of sight in the morning if I'm not around when you wake up,' he'd instructed. 'I'll probably get going early and I'll pop into town, like I suggested, to get your stuff.'

Helen had agreed, too sleepy to consider anything else, and wished him goodnight.

As Petey sat out on deck, looking at the stars and smoking his joint, he released a silent prayer of gratitude for his beautiful life, thanking the heavens he was not in Helen's position. He listened to the late news on his little portable radio, and decided he wouldn't share with her what he heard until he really needed to.

8

After a long but satisfying day of registering paperwork, catching up with colleagues and participating unexpectedly in an ongoing investigation, Katriona set out to drive home under the stars. Travelling in the dark through the Highlands was always a magical experience. Very different from travelling in the dark through London.

For a start off, it was truly dark. The sweeping roads which traversed the landscape here had no lighting of any kind, which meant that, on a clear night like tonight, it was perfectly possible to see the stars. In fact, with no street lighting to interfere with the view, she was always surprised by the overwhelming number of stars she could see. The sky was littered with them, almost as if someone had taken a spray gun to the black canvas and was determined to fill every available space with bright specks of varying sizes. She found it breathtaking.

Over the months she had been making this journey on a regular basis, Katriona had started to pick out various constellations in amongst the jumble. The Plough, with its seven large striking blobs of light had been the first one she recognised, as this had been visible in the skies around London from a suitable venue. But now she was able to make out subtler configurations as well, such as Cassiopeia with its pretty 'W' pattern and Cygnus, its five stars depicting the body of a flying swan.

As she got to know more, she had begun to feel as if she were among friends, so that driving home from her work day in Inverness was not at all the chore it had been when she'd worked in the 'big city', and equally was not the scary experience she'd expected when she'd first agreed to take on the consultancy job.

Making this long journey on a regular basis had been one of the aspects of the work that had made her hesitate. Driving in London was always a fraught experience, but at least if one broke down, there was easily accessible help to hand. Out here, she'd feared one could be stranded for hours (even days, she'd imagined,) without sight of another human being.

That was the other aspect that made this kind of journey so different. Instead of the scenery being populated by shops, houses and factories, it was startlingly only scenery. Mile after mile of stunning watery expanses, marching coniferous forests and, most impressively, towering mountains with their powerful craggy faces and thundering waterfalls.

When she and Elayne had first moved here, it had been high summer, with the typical Highland ranging sunshine illuminating the staggering views for roughly twenty two of the twenty four hours of every day, leaving a short space either side of midnight when the skies would allow a calm, but slightly eerie, gloom to coat the landscape. Katriona had then remembered her childhood, playing out 'til all hours, not believing her parents when they called bedtime and struggling to settle to sleep when, even with drawn curtains, the daylight stretched into the night.

This glorious feature of the summer had made her early journeys to and from Inverness a real delight. It hadn't mattered how late she'd wanted to work, she could always drive home in daylight! And during those first few months, she had come to know and love the mountains in a similar way to how she now knew and loved the stars, so that when the autumn had arrived, and she had found herself required to drive more and more in the dark, she also found she knew which of the mountains was watching over her at any given point along her route.

And the mountains weren't the only thing watching. One of the most unexpected and enthralling features of driving at night was the deer. These magnificent and gentle creatures lived high up on the moors and crags, but Katriona had discovered that when darkness came, they tentatively made their way to the lower slopes, even to the roadside in the more remote spots. Then she would sometimes catch sight of a moving wave of brown bodies, or a collection of staring circles of light as her headlights caught the startled raised heads of a grazing herd. She always felt when this happened, that it was she who had strayed into their territory, rather then the other way round. That the solitary winding road, making its way steadily along the various valleys of the route, was an impertinent intrusion into the wilderness these beasts had claimed as their own for centuries.

Yes, she reflected, it was worth the weekly trip to Inverness just to have the experience of driving home.

Tonight, as she drove, she was also thinking about her day. It had been exciting to sit in on a case again, even though she had not been taking a leadership role in the investigation. A particularly nasty murder had occurred a few weeks ago in Cullaird Wood. The Specialist Crime Division had set up shop in Inverness Station and quickly worked through the evidence, arresting the obvious suspect within the week. But since then, other incidents had come to light, making the original arrest suspect, so the team had been called back in to review the case.

Katriona hadn't been involved in the original investigation so the Super had considered it fortuitous that she was there today when the team had met, to give an opinion 'from outside the case'. She'd been glad of the opportunity to stretch her brain cells a bit, and had enjoyed talking through her thoughts and ideas with members of the team, some of whom she hadn't seen for a while. *Sometimes, I miss that companionship.*

She stopped the car and got out to stand in the solid darkness surrounding her. *Sgùrr na Càrnach* and *Sgùrr Fhuaran* stretched above her as high as she was able to see, even shutting out the stars. This was the gloomiest part of the journey – even in daylight. Travelling through the *Cinn Tàile* mountains, past the Five Sisters, could feel quite ominous as the peaks were very high and, at points, so close to the road that the valley felt extremely claustrophobic as well as remote.

Here, in this part of the journey, one did not revel in the expansiveness of the landscape. This was much more a place of introspection. Not for the first time, Katriona glimpsed the insight that if one was not able to live with oneself – if someone were too dependent on the company of others – then this secretive valley would quickly show that up, and the place could become terrifying. She had been terrified here herself in the past.

Pausing to stare into the darkness, she breathed with the strange, exotic landscape and listened to its message. Tonight, it reminded her of why she'd left the ominous and claustrophobic atmosphere of working in London. She reached out as if to touch the nearest rocks which, although they seemed so close, were actually quite a distance from where she stood.

'Thank you, my Sisters,' she whispered.

She would not have admitted to anyone in the world – except, of course, Elayne – that she talked to the landscape; but even as she spoke, she realised how much this place had changed her over the comparatively brief time they'd lived here. She felt as if she was retrieving long-forgotten parts of herself, parts which had seemed easy when she was a child, but which she had pushed away when she'd started out in the 'big world'.

Being 'fey' just didn't cut it in London – it made you vulnerable, scorned. But here it felt natural and real. She knew that despite the apparent lack of excitement within this new life she'd chosen, she experienced being alive far more deeply here than she ever had before. Whatever its disadvantages, she didn't really want to go back. She hoped she'd gradually find the courage to embrace the sparser parts of her existence, like Elayne did.

She was often in awe of how Elayne 'did' her life. From the outside, it appeared to other people that she had it all. Certainly the money she earned as an architect enabled plenty of choices that would be denied to many, but Elayne invariably made ones that removed her from the complexities of modern life and seemed to connect her to a deeper place.

She consistently chose simple solutions, both in her work and in her life – solutions that resonated with the truth of the landscape, her personality and her talents. Her designs were recognised for their elegant and stylish simplicity and had gained her the reputation she now held within the architectural world. She somehow had the ability, thought Katriona, to let go of everything extraneous and to reveal, beautifully, what actually mattered.

Nothing shook Elayne. She remained as solid as these mountains. But Katriona knew this surety about herself had been hard won. Elayne had shared with her, quite early in their relationship, some of the appalling history of abuse which she had suffered as a child. It had shocked Katriona sufficiently that Elayne had refused to tell her the whole story. She had found it hard to understand how someone so beautiful had stood before her, when she learned the truth. Why wasn't Elayne angry? afraid? crushed? All of which would have been Katriona's responses to such a terrible scenario.

It was the quality of Elayne's forgiveness that had inspired Katriona to stay in the relationship and try to learn how to love that deeply. The same quality she saw in every one of the houses Elayne designed – a simple, persistent searching for the truth at the core which, when revealed, she honoured with an almost sacred embrace. No wonder people lined up to live in her creations.

Taking in one last breath of the magical dark air that surrounded her, Katriona climbed back into her car to push on with the last part of her journey home.

Not far now. Coming out of the end of the valley, the road became a comparative highway, travelling alongside Loch Duich, with increasing glimpses of the water glinting under the stars and a newly risen moon, until she caught sight of the outlines of a solitary castle tower, perched on its own little island at the edge of the water as it joined the vast expanses of the sea.

Castle Eileen Donan. All lit up like a beacon signalling the gateway to another world. Katriona knew when she reached the driveway leading to the castle from the road, her island – Skye – would become visible, like an enormous ship sailing out into the water as she rounded the bend. She always relished this part of the journey. It was as if the island itself came out to greet her, revealing itself in all its grandeur, and suddenly becoming so present that she always wondered how it was possible for it to stay hidden up to this point.

From here, it was a short run of eight miles to reach the bridge. In principle, Katriona and Elayne hated the bridge. Opened in 1995, it had destroyed forever the precious disconnection of Skye from the mainland.

It was an elegant enough construction from a distance, resting delicately on an off-shore islet before arching its way across Loch Alsh; but driving across it, there was no longer a semblance of feeling that one was crossing from one reality to another – which was what Katriona considered a bridge should be. The smooth design allowed traffic to follow the road from the tip of the Kyle without any intimation of leaving land behind to soar over the water. There was no sensation even of landing on the other side. One simply suddenly found oneself in Kyleakin – as if nothing of importance had taken place at all.

Whenever they could, Katriona and Elayne used the

community-owned ferry between Glenelg on the mainland and Kylerhea on the island, but this only operated during daylight hours through the summer and not at all once the season was over, and the only other ferry now linking with the mainland meant travelling as far south as Fort William and picking up the traditional 'road-to-the-isles' out to Mallaig. So Katriona had resigned herself to using the bridge whenever it was essential and was grateful that it made coming home from Inverness possible late at night.

A few minutes later, turning left at the Broadford Hotel, she picked up the little lane that quickly became a single-track road, winding its way across open land under the benign presence of the Red Hills, until the majestic outlines of *Blà Bheinn* became visible against the starry sky and the last few miles brought her into Torrin.

Everything was quiet. Only a few lights showed behind closed curtains as she passed. Most of the community would be in bed by now, but she knew that Elayne would be waiting up for her, as she always did.

Crossing over the cattle grid as quietly as she could, she could see the welcoming porch light on their front door, providing just enough light to illuminate the short driveway up to the house but carefully capped so that no extraneous light shot upwards to spoil anyone else's view of the night. Another of Elayne's simple solutions.

Katriona slid the car up to the house and walked round to the back door to let herself in. She was greeted by the muffled barks of Molly and Alice, as they smothered her in doggy kisses. Then Elayne's sleepy face appeared round the kitchen door.

'Hello, love. It's good to have you home.'

There was something unusually poignant in Elayne's voice this evening. Almost as if she'd wondered whether Katriona would come home tonight.

'It's good to be home,' she responded, giving her partner a deep kiss and holding her tight. 'It's been quite a journey.'

They both knew Katriona wasn't just referring to the

drive home. Such was their closeness that Elayne had been aware for a while now how much Katriona struggled to maintain a healthy balance between her love of living where they did and her desire to be actively involved in detecting.

She was wise enough to realise that trying to talk Katriona into being sensible was never going to work, and using emotional blackmail had never been her style. Hanging onto someone you love so that they feel strangled was not the kind of relationship either of them wanted. It had to be a free choice on both sides, and Katriona was always grateful for the space Elayne gave her, and found she loved her more for doing it.

Despite the lateness of the hour, it was a short step from their first warm embrace to a shared surrender into passion and delight.

The day after an Inverness trip was usually scheduled as a day off for them both. They often indulged in a lie-in, sometimes with breakfast in bed. A large window making up most of one side of the bedroom opened out onto a little balcony so that in summer they would take breakfast out there and relish the view. In winter, they would do the same from the bed.

This morning, Elayne had got up before Katriona was awake, so when she opened her eyes, she could hear her partner pottering in the kitchen, talking to the dogs and presumably making a brew. She grabbed her dressing gown and wandered through. Elayne was at the Aga, busy preparing toast, along with scrambled eggs and smoked salmon. There was a fabulous smell of roasted coffee.

'Mm. That looks good.' Katriona put her arms around Elayne's waist. 'Morning.'

'Morning.' Elayne turned to kiss her. 'Do you want breakfast in here or do you want to go back to bed?'

'We might as well eat in here since we're up.'

'Well, one of us is.' Elayne laughed, indicating Katriona's clothing.

Katriona smiled. 'I love pithering about in the morning.'

'I know.'

Elayne busied herself finishing off the cooking, while Katriona pulled knives and forks out of a drawer and placed them on the old pine table which Elayne had rescued from a skip. She let her fingers trace the grain in one of the wooden strips making up the polished surface. So rich and beautiful. So like Elayne herself.

They sat down to eat, the dogs snuffling around their feet and 'hoovering up' stray crumbs that somehow escaped from the table top.

'What do you want to do today?' Elayne asked.

They usually took a venture out somewhere on their day-off which would always include an excellent walk for the dogs. Somewhere a bit further afield than their usual daily walks – as long as Elayne did the driving. That was a stipulation Katriona had put in place early on, when she realised how tiring the drive could be, going to and back from Inverness in one day.

'I dunno. Do you fancy Waternish? We could stop off in Stein for lunch. And maybe visit Deborah's woolshop. We haven't been for a while.'

Making handspun yarn was one of the new skills Elayne had acquired since moving here, along with fulfilling her life-long ambition to keep her own flock of sheep.

Deborah, a delightful lady in her fifties, had got Elayne started with the basics, helping her to choose a suitable spinning wheel and teaching her how to sort and card the fleeces when the sheep were sheared by Dughall – another islander – in the spring. Deborah also had a shop, from which she sold exquisite yarns and wonderful creations knitted up by some of the local women in Waternish. She described herself as a 'woolaholic' and her enthusiasm was catching.

'Yeah, I'd like that.' Elayne smiled. 'I'll do the washing-up while you get dressed, and we can be off in the next – what – hour?'

Katriona laughed. Although in theory it only took a few minutes to have a shower and get ready, she knew the extent of her ability to 'pither' and it was a luxury she liked to indulge on a day off. She left Elayne to it.

It was a while later, as she was brushing her hair in the bedroom, when she heard Elayne call through to her.

'Hey, Kat. Isn't that your mate, Jack?'

'What?' Katriona came back into the kitchen, hairbrush in hand, where Elayne had her laptop on the table, streaming a live news channel. On the screen was an image of Jack Foster holding a press conference. 'Turn the sound up a bit.'

The image cut to a photo of a young girl with long red hair. Foster's voice was speaking over it.

'… Helen Clarke. We believe she was the last person to see Emily Hough alive, but she has not been seen since the night of the murder. It is imperative that we speak with her – obviously.'

The screen cut back to a live picture of Jack Foster, sitting behind a desk, in the midst of the flashing lights of photographers. He coughed, as if a little embarrassed at his over-enthusiasm, and picked up a script in front of him that was clearly a prepared statement. Katriona got the distinct impression he had deviated from it.

'She is an important witness in this case, and needed to help with our enquiries,' Foster continued. Then, lowering his papers again, he looked into the TV camera.

'On no account should she be approached. If a sighting is made, please ring this phone number with your information.' He reeled off a number that was also flashed up on the screen, and the item ended with a return to the studio presenter.

'That's odd,' Katriona reflected.

'What is?' Elayne asked.

'That number. It's not the usual national helpline number. It's the number of the station where Foster's based. That's not standard procedure.'

Katriona put down her hairbrush.

'Elayne, I'm just going to ring Gavin, if you don't mind hanging on for a minute.'

She was already walking out of the kitchen and heading for her study as she spoke.

9

Gavin picked up the phone for the umpteenth time that morning. All hell had broken loose since that disastrous press conference. This was an outside call.

'DI Pearce.'

'Hi Gavin. It's Katriona.'

'Hello again. Twice in three days. People will talk.' Gavin joked, trying to fend off his irritation with the day so far.

'Sorry if you're busy. Just wondered what all that was about on the news just now.'

'You and me both.'

'Sorry?'

'Can I ring you back? I'll be about ten minutes.'

'Sure.'

Gavin put the phone down and made his way out of his office and down to the main desk. He paused briefly to speak to the duty officer.

'I'm just going out to check on something. If anyone wants me, I won't be available for the next half hour. Right?'

He signed the firebook to confirm he was leaving the building, and marched smartly out to the car park to find his car.

He only drove a short distance but it was far enough to park the car in a quiet alleyway where he wouldn't be seen. He opened the glove compartment, and then released a latch at the back, pulling out a mobile phone. He keyed in a code to activate it, then dialled in Katriona's number. Nothing got stored on this handset.

'Hi Katriona. Sorry about that. Needed a secure line.'

'What on earth's going on?' Katriona sounded anxious now.

'I wish I knew. You heard about the murder on Tuesday?'

'Emily Hough? Yeah. Really sad, that. Elayne was a big fan.'

'Oh, I didn't know she was into classical singing.'

'Elayne is a world of surprises, Gavin. But it sounds like you're having your own surprises at the moment. Is this your case or Foster's?'

'It's supposed to be mine,' Gavin sighed. 'There's something mighty weird going on here, Katriona, and I don't have a clue what it is.'

'Wow. How come Foster took the press conference then?'

'That's part of what's weird. You know I'm not keen on these things, so it's not unusual for someone else to sit in for me, but it *is* unusual – '

'– for Jack Foster to want to show his face in public.' Katriona finished for him. 'So what's his interest in this case?'

'I honestly don't know. Yet. But I do know this is a dirty one. This was no straight-forward burglary-gone-wrong. And Foster turned up at the scene.'

'What?'

'I know. Unheard of. Katriona, can I fill you in on the details? I could use another head to help me, and someone outside the immediate team. And, of course, you know the set-up here.'

'Sure. No problem. Let me just get into my comfy chair.' There was a brief pause. Gavin smiled to himself. He could imagine Katriona curled up, phone in hand, relishing the details – and it made him feel better. It was almost like old times.

He took Katriona back two days, and talked her through his visit to the crime scene, emphasising everyone's certainty that this was no ordinary burglary, that whoever had broken into the house had been looking for something very specific.

'So how come Foster turned up?' Katriona asked when he paused.

'He claimed he was just passing.'

There was a sound of choking down the phone, as if someone was trying to laugh and drink tea at the same time.

'You okay?' Gavin asked.

'Yeah, Elayne just brought a cuppa in. Think she knew it wasn't going to be a short call when she saw me sitting in the comfy chair.'

'Oh, are you supposed to be going somewhere? It's your day off, isn't it?'

'Don't worry. I can take a little time before we set off.'

Gavin smiled again. He knew Katriona's version of 'take a little time' when it came to unravelling a case. He could picture Elayne resigning herself to an extra half-hour of gardening, or playing with the sheep, or whatever it was that she was into these days. He had long been an admirer of her patience when it came to Katriona and her detecting.

He picked up the story, sharing Foster's insistence that the only reason the case had not been handed to him was an administrative error.

Katriona was sceptical. 'Yeah, right. Like he's keen to pick up extra work.'

'Well, that was the first clue I had that he might be involved.'

'What – you mean, you think he has something to do with the actual murder?' Katriona sounded incredulous. 'That's not his style, Gavin, surely? I mean, corruption, back-handers, that sort of thing, but he's never been involved in violence.'

'As far as we know.' Gavin responded carefully.

'That's true.' There was a pause. 'So what was your

second clue?'

'When he came into my office the next day – all casual-like – asking me for an update. And I caught him looking through the forensics report.'

'Yeah, I agree. For a man who tries to avoid work, that's highly suspicious. God, what's he up to?'

'That's not the worst of it, Katriona.'

Gavin went on to explain how they'd found out about the young girl – Helen Clarke – and his concern that she had now disappeared.

'That's what confirmed it for me that Foster was involved somehow. He started to get really anxious that the girl be found, started trying to activate our search protocol as soon as we'd identified her. God forgive me, Katriona, but my first thought was thank God she's gone missing – that means he hasn't got her.'

He heard Katriona gasp.

'So all that stuff this morning – it wasn't in the script?'

'Of course not. You know the procedure. If we're just looking for a witness, we don't do the heavy. That's only if they're an actual suspect. And that's what Foster's done by inference now – turned her into a suspect.'

'So the poor girl has probably seen something and what – gone underground?'

'My guess is that she was witness to something at the house. We know she was there.' Gavin explained about the red coat. 'But whatever it was, she hasn't been seen since, so either she was scared stupid, or threatened by someone, or … I'm running out of ideas.'

'Oh, Gavin. I don't envy you on this.' There was a slight pause, then Katriona continued. 'Well, actually I do. It's quite intriguing from this end. But you're right, there's not enough to go on yet. You'll have to keep working the evidence and keep an eye on Foster.'

'And hope the girl shows up somewhere safe,' Gavin sighed.

'Well, yeah. And that's not a given. Suppose she actually

saw Foster at the crime scene – well, even if she didn't, that broadcast is hardly going to encourage her to come forward.'

'No. That's one of the things we were puzzling over. Why – if there had been a witness – they hadn't reported the murder.'

Katriona didn't respond.

'Katriona. You still there?'

'Yeah. Just a thought. Supposing she *did* see him. She couldn't have known that he was a police officer at that stage, could she?'

'I don't see how. What are you getting at?'

'Well, suppose she *did* try to report it. And somehow – I don't know – bumped into him at that point. I mean, that would be enough to make her run, wouldn't it?'

'Katriona, that's genius.' Gavin started up the car. 'Right. Gotta go. I'll ring later.'

He hung up abruptly and began driving back to the station. Some of the pieces were falling into place. A possible scenario was beginning to form in his mind.

As soon as he got back, he called Charlie into his office and explained what he wanted.

'Remember, be circumspect, Charlie.'

'I'm onto it, Sir.'

Gavin didn't relish his next task but knew it had to be done. He marched down the corridor towards Jack Foster's office. As he approached, he heard Foster on the phone.

'What do you mean it's useless?'

Gavin stopped outside the doorway, listening.

'A decoy? That's ridiculous. You mean we went to all that trouble …'

A pause.

'We'll still get our money, right?'

At that point, Tom came round the corner at the end of the corridor.

'Oh, Gavin. Was just looking for you.'

Too late, Gavin put his finger to his lips. He heard

Foster on the phone.

'Bloody hell. I need to go, but this isn't finished.'

Tom looked across at Gavin and mouthed a silent 'Sorry.' Then spoke aloud.

'I was just wondering if you'd be around at lunchtime. There's a group of us buying Angela a drink – it's her birthday.'

Then, lips moving silently again, 'Come down to the lab.'

Gavin picked up the cue.

'Cheers. That would be great.' He turned into the doorway.

'Foster. A word.'

'What the hell do you want?'

'What do you think I want? I want to know what you thought you were doing this morning. That wasn't agreed. What you said. And it went well outside protocol.'

Foster turned towards him with flashing blue eyes.

'You and your fucking protocol. You're so bloody correct, Pearce. I'm surprised you ever get your prick out of your pants.'

Gavin stopped in his tracks and stared at the man, trying not to gape in amazement. Even for Foster, this was extreme. Apparently, Foster realised this too, and looked away, busying himself with the papers on his desk.

'We need results, Pearce, and pussy-footing round things won't do that. If I've got things moving, I'm not going to apologise for breaking a few rules. Now, let me get on with some real policing.'

Gavin had never crossed swords directly with Foster before, but he recognised bullying tactics when he saw them.

'Let's get one thing straight, Foster. This is not your case, and although *outside* …'

He stressed the word just a little to get his point across.

'… assistance is always welcome – if it is useful – when you are assisting me, you *will* work within the confines of protocol and agreed procedure. Do I make myself clear?'

Foster looked up sharply. He was not used to being

spoken to in this way.

'Or else what, Pearce?' he asked, menacingly.

Gavin stood his ground and said nothing. It was Foster who looked away first.

'Good.' Gavin turned to leave. 'I'm glad we've got that clear.'

Gavin next made his way downstairs to the Forensics lab to find Tom. As he entered the room, he could see several of the team busily working at computers, including someone who looked young enough to still be at school. Tom looked up from something he was fiddling with under a big lamp.

'Sorry about that, Gavin.'

'Don't worry about it. Is it really Angela's birthday?'

'Yeah, that was genuine.' Tom put down his forceps and grinned at Gavin.

'So do you have something for me?' Gavin asked.

'Sure do.' Tom's grin widened. 'Several somethings, in fact.'

'Good. I could do with some good news.'

'Why? Things not going well with Jack the Lad?'

Gavin looked at Tom, sharply. He lowered his voice.

'Just be careful there, Tom. Very careful.'

'Right. Understand. Sorry, didn't mean to be flippant.' Tom started to lead the way across the room. 'Let me introduce you to our latest addition.'

He indicated the youngster Gavin had noticed on the way in. 'This is Bryan. He's only been with us a few weeks. I don't think you've met.'

'No, we haven't,' Gavin confirmed, as he viewed the back of Bryan's head. He wondered why the boy hadn't turned round to acknowledge him, then realised he was wearing ear-pieces which connected him to his computer. He was busy working on something. Tom tapped him on the shoulder. Bryan then turned round and stood up, removing the ear-pieces.

'Bryan, this is DI Pearce.'

Bryan towered above Gavin. For all his baby-looks, he was a tall guy, nearly seven foot, Gavin reckoned.

'Hello, Sir. Glad to meet you.' He was remarkably self-assured for an eighteen-year-old who'd just landed his first job in a highly prestigious field. Gavin guessed it came with being an acknowledged genius.

'Likewise,' he replied.

'Bryan, that computer history you completed last night,' Tom continued. 'It was work for DI Pearce. Do you want to give him your report?'

'Right. Of course. Put very simply, the laptop confiscated from Miss Hough's house had been used last at 4.15 pm, when a number of flashdrives had been placed into one of the USB ports, sequentially. The computer had been left on after the last flashdrive had been removed and had run down its battery, thus switching itself off. Prior to that, it had been running for a couple of hours, mostly visiting on-line sites, including a number of opera houses, both in this country and on the continent, and various hotels in the vicinity of these. There was also some e-mail activity which we're looking into just now, an order placed for character shoes size 6, a selection of curtain fabrics – just viewed, no purchases – a download of Michael Ball singing Sweeney Todd and a brief visit to Amazon for a copy of The Greek Music Drama, an English translation of Nietzsche's lecture at the Basel Museum in 1870. I'm sorry I can't tell you what was on any of the flashdrives as the computer doesn't store that information in its history.' Bryan paused.

Gavin was astounded. The boy had delivered the entire speech without notes.

'Thank you, Bryan. Excellent report.'

He started to move away to consult with Tom, but stopped.

'Character shoes?'

'Yes, sir. Basic black, low-heeled shoes with a leather sole, used in operatic productions to enable easy movement around the stage.'

'Thank you,' He turned back to Tom. 'He's quite something, isn't he?' he muttered, as they crossed back to the other side of the room.

'Definitely a good catch, I'd say. Here let me show you something else. We've been looking at that locket Emily was wearing round her neck.'

'Oh yes? Do you know what the code means?'

'Not yet, but we've retrieved two sets of fingerprints from both the locket and the piece of paper. One of them is – not surprisingly – Emily's. The other is a familial match.'

'Probably her sister, then?'

'Probably,' Tom confirmed. 'Have you got any further with tracking her down?'

'Not really. Charlie's team have found several addresses for her. There's a house in Germany, and another in Costa Rica, I think. And an apartment in Los Angeles.'

'Wow. She must earn a bit, then. What does she do?'

'She's a freelance journalist, but the money's from family not work. She and Emily inherited from the father when they were very young. You've heard of Hough-MacAllister?'

'The jewellery group?'

'That's the one. Well, Hough was the father and MacAllister, the mother.'

Tom whistled. 'That's one mighty combination.'

'As far as we can gather, Emily and Heather set up a number of houses round the globe, which they both used – Emily when she was touring and Heather when she was corresponding or documenting – whatever the right verb is for a journalist.'

'So how come you can't find her?' Tom sat himself on a high stool next to his desk. Gavin could see his mind was already onto the next thing, but that wouldn't stop him from listening to Gavin.

'Presumably she's on assignment somewhere. She's certainly not resident at any of her addresses. I gather she sometimes does undercover work, so maybe this is one of those times. Someone in Charlie's team is trying to speak to one of her regular editors – see if he knows where she is.'

'Poor woman.'

'Sorry?' Gavin was confused.

'Well, imagine being tracked down on an undercover assignment to be told your only remaining relative is dead. And murdered, at that.'

Not for the first time, Gavin found himself intrigued by the meanderings of Tom's mind. 'Yeah, I guess. Do you think that would be worse than finding out at any other time?'

'Maybe not, but there's something awful about being out of reach of your usual world when something like this happens.' A shadow passed over Tom's face. 'Kinda makes you wonder if you'd been there …'

Gavin knew now was not the time to pursue this, so he pulled Tom back on task. 'You said you had several things for me, Tom.'

'Oh yeah.' Tom immediately let go of whatever he'd been thinking about and refocused on his findings. 'We found a partial print.'

'A fingerprint?' Gavin's heart gave a little leap.

'No. A partial bootprint.'

'I thought you said there was nothing at the scene.'

'No, well, there wasn't, but it was when I was dusting for fingerprints – on that door, you remember?'

Gavin nodded.

'I came across a spatial anomaly.' Tom's grin was back.

'Drop the sci-fi. Give it to me in English.'

'Okay. I didn't find any fingerprints, as I told you at the time, but I did find a sort of smudge which shouldn't have been there. So we went back yesterday with some more specialised materials. It's a new technique that allows you to get a remote shoeprint off wood – like on doors and floorboards. Almost like getting a ghost of the original.'

'And you found a footprint on the door?' Gavin was surprised.

'Yeah, like someone had kicked the door open – with the

heel of a boot. It's not much but we've identified a few possibilities that might be helpful.'

'Such as?'

'Well, it's a Doc Marten-type boot, we think, but not the standard tread pattern. Mind you, we've only got a small amount and it's a bit squished – as you'd expect from a sliding kick.'

Gavin raised his eyebrows, encouragingly.

'Yeah, where did I put it?' Tom searched amongst the papers on his desk, still muttering away. 'It's a stroke of luck, really. Whoever was there was so careful with everything else. They must've forgotten for a moment not to touch anything that might leave a mark. Ah, here it is.'

He brandished an A4 sheet with a few lines of printing on it.

'And these are … ?' Gavin enquired.

'All possible boot types that could leave such a heel print. My money's on the one at the bottom.'

'Sendra?'

'Yeah, they're a German company – produce high quality handmade boots, including bikers' boots. I think it's the closest match, but that's more of an opinion than a scientific correlation.'

'I'd trust your opinions over correlations any day, Tom,' Gavin affirmed, his mind already whirling with possible lines of enquiry.

'Though there is other evidence to back up a German connection.' Tom was off, marching to a printer on the other side of the lab. He looked particularly proud. 'We also found traces of latex on some of the door handles.'

'Well, you'd expect that, wouldn't you? If the burglar wore gloves?'

'Well, no, actually. Latex doesn't leave a trace as a rule. That's why people use it. But whoever was wearing these gloves must have caught them on a rough surface or something – just enough to snag some microscopic snippets.'

'Oh? Is that going to be useful to us?'

'Hell, yes.' Tom brandished the phrase with glee. 'It turns out this is a very particular kind of latex. All the manufacturers have their own take on the product. We've managed to run a few tests on the bits we've found and they seem to be a mixture of latex and nitrile rubbers. That particular combination is produced by a German company called MediGloves.'

'Really?'

'Yeah. The substance was produced as part of a German research project to reduce latex allergies within the medical profession. I mean, it could all be coincidence, but it – '

'– might not.' finished Gavin. 'Thanks, Tom. That's great work.' He began to move towards the stairs. 'See you lunchtime.'

'Hold on.' Tom called Gavin back. 'I have yet to play my trump card.'

Gavin turned and waited.

'You don't get the significance of this, do you?' Tom asked.

'Significance?'

'Gavin, if we've got traces of latex from someone's glove …' He slowed his speech down, emphasizing every word. '… we *may* be able to get some DNA from it.'

10

Helen and Petey arrived in Bishop's Stortford during the afternoon. They moored the boat briefly at the Star Marina, just long enough for Helen to disembark.

'So you're happy with the plan?' Petey asked.

'Yes, I think so. I can't see any problem with it.'

Helen's worried face looked very different with a black fringe. She and Petey had spent a hilarious morning cutting and colouring in various stages – in between travelling the remaining length of the River Storth – until they agreed that she was sufficiently disguised not to be instantly recognisable. Helen found her new, much shorter hairstyle made her feel light-headed, and a trifle chilly round her neck, but she was surprisingly pleased with the result.

'I like the way it shows off my nose,' she'd joked, after their third attempt with the scissors.

Just like yesterday, Petey had been busy before Helen had woken. Not only had he bought hair colouring, he'd also acquired a holdall for her which, when she opened it, contained all the essentials she would need for the next few days. Toothbrush and paste, soap neatly packed in a watertight container, a couple of small towels, brush and comb, a six-pack of knickers size 12 – 'that's clever of you,' and a bundle of basic second-hand clothing – jumper, T-shirts and so on.

The holdall had several zippered pockets, inside and out, which she found also held 'goodies'. There was a mobile phone with a new SIM card.

'Don't store any numbers,' Petey had advised. 'And take the card out when you're not using it.' He'd provided a little box she could keep it in, and carefully placed that in another of the holdall's pockets.

'It'll connect to the internet so you can keep an eye on the news, but I really wouldn't suggest you go e-mailing anyone.'

Petey had finally told Helen what he'd heard on the radio last night as they were embarking on the last part of the canal journey. He'd suggested she might go inside to watch the TV broadcast replayed on his laptop. Helen had been profoundly shocked and upset.

'That's him. That's Detective Greysuit,' she'd screamed.

'I thought it might be. His name's Foster, apparently. And he's based at one of the South London Police Stations, local to where you saw him.'

Petey had done some research.

'He's made me sound like a criminal.' Helen was appalled.

'Yep. And he's done it very effectively.'

'But how's he got away with it?'

Petey had paused.

'I guess because no-one else knows that it's really him.'

'I suppose. But why would they think it's me?'

But when they got to the part that offered a description of her, including the usual 'last seen wearing …' and a photo Helen recognised as a recent one from Bev's phone, it became obvious why she was being targeted. Helen had wept in despair at this point.

'That wretched coat,' she'd wailed. 'It nearly got me killed once and now it's threatening to again.'

Petey had let her cry for a while, knowing she would feel better once she'd got over the initial shock and could realise that she still had the upper hand. If the police had any idea where she was, they wouldn't be releasing appeals.

Still, there was something about the TV coverage that had disturbed Petey. Since he had inside knowledge of what had really happened, he knew Foster was lying through his teeth, but he also sensed that the man had manipulated the situation. He wasn't at all sure that Foster's statement to the surrounding press had been what was intended – either by the police press department or indeed, by Foster himself. It had the air of something not very cleverly thought through, particularly in the middle when Foster was warning the public not to approach Helen if sighted. Maybe Foster had overplayed his hand.

He'd shared his feelings with Helen, wanting her to trust that when she'd distanced herself from London, it would be safe to contact the police somewhere else.

'You can't seriously think I'm still planning to report this?' Helen had stared at him in disbelief.

Petey had responded quietly. 'I think you'll have to. What's the alternative, love? You going to stay 'wanted' for ever? Live on the run for the rest of your life?'

'No, of course not. I just thought … I thought I might stay hidden until they realise it's him,' she'd blurted out.

'But they might not realise,' Petey had said. 'Not without your evidence.' He'd let the import of that sink in.

'For your own sake – and for Emily's – at some point, you'll have to trust someone enough to tell them,' he'd suggested gently, and had pulled her into a big hug.

They'd agreed that Helen was sufficiently disguised to risk getting off the boat at the marina, despite the inevitable CCTV. Here it would be much easier to unload her and her belongings, but more importantly, the bike. This normally travelled with Petey, padlocked to the back of the boat, on a miniature deck which was packed with other useful items like a waterproof toolbox and pots of growing herbs.

The plan was for Helen to use the bike to ride to the railway station, less than a mile away, and then to embark on a complex rail journey which would take her out to the east of the country and then north towards Scotland. The route they had chosen involved five different trains, with a possible final destination of Glasgow Queen Street.

Petey had bought all the tickets on-line, with a credit card. Helen had decided not to ask how he managed to have a credit card if he couldn't get a bank account. At this stage, she was more grateful than curious, and had thought maybe it might be best not to know.

They'd debated between them whether to buy a single ticket for the entire journey or individual ones for each stage along the way. Or even, whether there was any benefit in Helen buying one or more of the tickets en route. Helen's priority was to put as much distance as possible between her and London, so she'd persuaded Petey to purchase everything she'd need to get her as far as Scotland.

'That way, you don't need to know where I'm *actually* going. I could get off at any of the points along the way. So if the worst happens …'

'It won't,' Petey had smiled reassuringly, but he'd agreed to her part of the plan. His contribution was to suggest they broke the journey into separate shorter, but easily accessible, sections so that tracking her would be more difficult for any potential assailant. Buying lots of different tickets was also less traceable.

'Let's make this nice and complicated,' he'd suggested when they realised that the most direct route to the north – as far as the on-line booking service was concerned – was to go back into London to pick up an express. They'd agreed that was far too dangerous an option.

There was a bit of a dodgy moment when they realised that collecting the tickets might not be as straightforward as they'd thought. Some of the route they'd chosen qualified for self-printed tickets, but these would require a passenger name to be printed on them, and the passenger to be able to produce ID on request, so they couldn't use that option.

There wasn't enough time to have them posted to an

address – even if they had one - and collecting them at the station had complications if Helen were to try asking at a kiosk. By far the safest option was to use a self-service ticket machine. This didn't involve having to have Helen's name on the tickets, though if they bought them with a credit card, she would need the same credit card to operate the machine. Then Petey spotted that they could pay for the tickets using PayPal and that meant Helen could use her own card in the machine.

'But won't that register that I'm using the card?' Helen asked.

'No, I don't think so. The card itself isn't part of the transaction; it just initiates the machine to work. You need to put in the Reference Number to get your tickets but that's only traceable back to PayPal as far as I can see,' Petey explained.

So Helen arrived at Bishop's Stortford station ready to pick up a handful of tickets. She carried several packets of used bank notes, some sewn into the lining of her 'new' coat – a warm and expensive-looking dark woollen affair with deep pockets inside and out, which Petey had spotted in the window of the Oxfam shop on his shopping trip. She also had a small wad of addressed and stamped envelopes, all printed out by Petey with the address of his PO Box in Battersea.

She parked the bike in the bike rack outside the front of the station and padlocked it, then popped the key into one of the envelopes and placed it in the nearby post box. Petey would collect the bike tomorrow, using his spare key, when he'd had his meeting and asked one of his mates to drive him to the station. She then made her way through the foyer, stopping at the ticket machine, and onto the platform to wait for her train.

This was the shortest train ride of the sequence, taking her only as far as Cambridge where she'd be able to pick up the next link out to Norwich, and then on to Peterborough. She could accomplish this by late evening and then get on the mainline train to Edinburgh – a substantial journey of nearly four hours, which would allow her to get some sleep. From here, it would be a short hop over to Glasgow, if that was where she decided to go. She still hadn't made her mind up.

As she sat on the platform, she had time to reflect on whether she was doing the right thing. Saying goodbye to Petey had been much harder than she'd expected. She'd felt the close bond forming between them over the last couple of days, and while he'd been around to support her, an escape plan seemed feasible – even exciting. Now that she was on her own again, her spirits began to sink. She wasn't cut out for this.

The station was very quiet – fairly typical, she thought, for a late Thursday afternoon. Only two other people appeared to be waiting for the train – an elderly gentleman carrying an umbrella and a newspaper, and a young woman who looked like she'd stepped out of a sixties magazine with her hair piled on top of her head and high-heeled shoes. They were both standing at the other end of the platform, looking expectant. Helen guessed they were regular commuters.

Then suddenly a whole rush of people arrived, mostly about her age, wearing a variety of brightly-coloured clothing and wielding enormous rucksacks attached to their backs. Students, probably. There was a lot of jostling and cheery voices. Helen noticed they were all wearing hiking boots so perhaps they were all on a field trip – or returning from one.

'No, that's not right.'

'I think you'll find it is.'

Two of the students stopped close by her seat.

'No, if you get to level three, it changes completely.'

It was a real shock to the system to be back in the world of other people and their concerns. After the quiet, slow boat trip out here, even the bike ride to the station had seemed fast, and the noise of the traffic deafening, but in a strange way, it had felt less intrusive than people talking, sharing things that mattered to them.

Just as before, when she'd been sat in the café – was it only two days ago? – she was struck by the contrast between the normality of the scenes around her and the strange reality of her own world. It was like – well, like being in an opera or a musical, actually. The idea cheered her a little.

Up until now, she realised, she'd been playing the role of secretive criminal – a role which felt very alien to her. Courageous heroine was much more up her street. She could adopt that persona with a reasonable degree of success, she thought, and it would be much more helpful to her psychologically. She breathed deeply, as if breathing in the new character – just as she would prior to a performance.

In the distance, the train appeared, turning a slow corner into the station. It stopped noisily alongside the platform and all the students rushed to the numerous doors presented and piled on board, searching for seats.

'Here we go, then.' Helen stepped into the next part of her unexpected adventure a little more willingly than she had only forty eight hours before.

11

After the exciting progress reported from Forensics, Gavin felt a bit more optimistic about the case opening up. Sometimes it happened like that. You thought you were getting nowhere, nothing was making sense, then suddenly one small detail changed everything – like one of those complex puzzle boxes when you could spend hours fiddling with the bits and pieces to no effect, then just by chance, you might flick a piece out of place and the whole puzzle box would unravel before your eyes.

The possibility of some DNA was particularly encouraging. It felt like a huge step forward, although the likelihood of it giving them an actual name was extremely remote. Unless – he allowed himself a little fantasizing – unless it turned out to belong to Jack Foster. Placing him at the scene of the crime would change everything dramatically. It would be incredible to have some actual evidence against the man, after all this time.

Then the penny dropped. That was why Foster had turned up on the night they'd found the body. So his DNA could be eliminated from the scene. You had to hand it to him – he was damn clever at covering his tracks.

Gavin's despondency returned, along with a wave of fatigue. It had been a long day. Maybe he'd pack it in and go home. There wasn't much more he could do now.

There was a knock on his office door and Charlie appeared.

'Sir, I've someone here to see you.'

'Okay,' Gavin sighed. Maybe going home would have to wait. 'Did you get anywhere with that task I set you?'

'Yes, Sir. That's why I think you should speak to Constable Whitmore before I show you what I've found.'

A dark-haired woman followed Charlie into the office. She looked apprehensive.

'I'm so sorry, Sir. I've been at my aunt's funeral all day. I hadn't seen the news, else I'd've got in touch earlier.'

Gavin motioned for her to take a seat. 'Right, Constable, tell me what this is all about.'

'I saw her, Sir. Helen Clarke.'

'When? Where?' Gavin's excitement began to rise again.

'Here, Sir. At the station. On the day of the murder.'

'What?' He signalled to Charlie, standing behind the constable, to close the door, but Charlie was already doing so.

'Of course, I didn't realise it was her at that stage. It was in the afternoon, before the body had been found. I was coming into the station yard on foot, and there was someone walking in ahead of me – a young woman.

'She stopped very suddenly and turned round – like she was in a panic over something. I asked if I could help. I thought perhaps she might be a bit overwhelmed by the sight of so many people, or something. It was very busy. Lots of cars coming and going. But she wouldn't stop. She looked really scared. She pushed right past me and just ran off.

'I didn't think any more of it, until I saw DI Foster's appeal. It was replaying in the IT room, just now, when I came on duty.'

'And it was definitely her?'

'Oh, yes, Sir. No doubt about it.'

'Thank you, Constable.' Gavin was ready to get investigating again. This was potentially a huge breakthrough.

'Just one thing. When you realised you'd seen her, did you mention this to anyone else?' he asked, as lightly as he dared. The need to keep this information from Foster was paramount.

'No, Sir,' Whitmore replied, looking puzzled. 'The Sarge was in the room working on something and …' Her voice trailed off and she began to look disconcerted.

Charlie stepped in. 'I saw that Constable Whitmore had recognised the girl before she said anything. Brought her straight up here, Sir.'

Gavin and Charlie exchanged looks.

The constable nervously asked: 'Is there something wrong?'

Gavin smiled reassuringly. 'No, not at all. But for the time being, keep this to yourself, will you? I know that seems a strange thing to ask, Constable, but we're having a few security issues at the moment. Nothing to do with this case – at least not directly. But we're trying to cover the chain of information in general, so it's part of a bigger exercise. You know, blocking the links in one place to see if they turn up somewhere else.'

Even to himself, this sounded lame.

'Sorry about your aunt.'

A change of subject might help. Labouring the point definitely wouldn't. He stood up, indicating the conversation was over, and Charlie obligingly opened the door, shuffling Constable Whitmore out. A quick 'Well done,' smoothed the awkwardness a little as she passed him.

Once she'd gone, Charlie closed the door again.

'Do you think she'll keep quiet?' Gavin asked.

'Probably not,' Charlie replied. 'She'll probably share it with her friends, I'm afraid, but I don't think we can do anything about that, Sir.'

'No, I suppose not. Right. Down to business. This is quite exciting. This is the first sighting we've had of Helen after the murder. Looks like she came here almost straightaway.'

'Yes, Sir. And I believe I know why she didn't get any further in reporting it. As you suggested, Sir.'

'So your search paid off?'

'Well, once Constable Whitmore had narrowed down the timeframe so specifically, it was pretty easy to pick up the CCTV.'

As he was speaking, Charlie produced a DVD which Gavin slotted into his desk computer.

'We were lucky it hadn't been deleted yet. There wasn't much going on that day so normally it wouldn't have been kept, but everyone's been so busy since.'

Charlie pulled an image up on the screen. First, there was some footage showing the back of a young girl with long red hair, coming into the station yard. Sure enough, she suddenly stopped in her tracks and turned abruptly, crashing into PC Whitmore.

'So, what did she see?' Gavin asked hesitantly, praying that Charlie had something concrete.

'This.' Charlie indicated to the screen, which now showed the view from the second camera. Gavin watched a police car pulling into the yard and several officers getting out. One of them was Foster.

So, Katriona had been right.

Gavin fretted for a while over what he should do with this information. It certainly wasn't enough to accuse Foster of anything conclusive, but it was more than enough to confirm his suspicions that Helen Clarke had seen Foster at the crime scene. There was no other explanation for her behaviour. She had clearly been on her way to report what she had seen, and then … No wonder she'd disappeared.

He began trying to build a timeline for her, piecing together the scanty bits of evidence that had been collected so far. A lot of the supposed sightings phoned in by the public would turn out to be bogus, he knew. His officers would spend precious hours trailing through the information, trying to verify it. Only that which could be relied on as accurate would make it as far as his desk. Gavin had done his time as a constable, executing this sort of tedious work. He knew the levels of dedication and boredom involved, so he was always appreciative of what eventually reached him.

In front of him now, he had a transcript of an interview with a taxi-driver who claimed to have delivered Helen to Emily Hough's house, early in the afternoon. He'd remembered her because of 'that ridiculous coat she was wearing – it kept creaking, for goodness' sake. I mean, who wears a coat like that. I couldn't work out what it was to start with. Drove me nuts. Oh, and it was seriously red. Hideous colour.'

Amazingly, there was another statement from a neighbour just across the road from Emily's, who happened to be on her way out to go shopping. She remembered seeing the taxi pull up and someone in a red coat get out, but nothing else. That wasn't surprising. It wouldn't have seemed important at the time. It did, however, allow Gavin to confirm the timing of the taxi-driver's statement. Helen must have arrived just about the time Emily had been murdered.

He wondered if she'd seen the actual crime or only the result of it. And had she, herself, been seen by the criminal? Or criminals? Judging by Foster's reactions since – now that Gavin was sure he'd been there – he guessed not. Perhaps Foster had realised someone was in the house when he was busy searching. Perhaps the noise of him scrabbling around and chucking stuff on the floor had scared Helen off before Foster had actually seen who was there. Perhaps he hadn't known there was someone else there until Helen's identity had come to light. So he might not know if he could be identified himself.

Gavin's mind was going round in circles trying to plot out different scenarios, so he was relieved when the phone rang. It was Constable Maxwell.

'Sir, I've got Herr Brandt on the line. He's a newspaper editor for the *Dusseldorfer Chronik*. He knows Heather Hough. She's done pieces for his newspaper on a regular basis over the last few years.'

'Thanks, Maxwell. Put him through.'

Herr Brandt turned out to be an extremely intelligent and coherent man, whose English was exceptionally good. Gavin was relieved as his German was almost non-existent.

'No, I have not seen her for a few months. She was working on a series of documentaries the last time I spoke to her.'

'You mean for TV?'

'Yes, yes. She'd teamed up with a guy – what was his name? – Dieter Bergmann – that was it. He's a highly proficient camera man. Well-respected over here. He specialises in filming war scenes, disaster areas, that sort of thing. He's good at putting people's noses out of joint – you know, films the stuff no-one wants shown. He works freelance, like Heather.'

'What were they working on?'

'Um …' There was a pause. 'Ah, yes, that's it. Quite an ambitious project, really. They were trying to put together a series about epidemics.'

'Epidemics?'

'Yes. You know, what causes them, how they're managed – that sort of thing. They were travelling around a lot. Visiting various countries that had dealt with serious outbreaks. Some of it was historical, as well as contemporary. I think Heather's hoping to sell it to one of the big TV companies here.'

'Thank you, Herr Brandt. That's really helpful. Do you have any idea where Heather is now?'

'No, I'm sorry. Like I said. She usually comes to me when she has something. It seems strange, though, that she's not been in contact with you. She always picks up the news broadcasts, wherever she is.' He paused again.

Gavin thought it was strange, too. He tried another tack.

'Do you have a contact number for this camera-guy, by any chance? Dieter – what did you say his name is?'

'Bergmann. No. Not to hand. But he has a website. You could Google him.'

'Right.' Gavin closed the conversation, thanking Herr Brandt again for his cooperation. He'd got that prickly feeling back again. Was it possible that this case touched on something bigger? Could it have something to do with Heather? Was that why they couldn't find her? A mental shudder ran through him. He wondered if something had happened to her, too.

He decided to do one last task before he went home. He rang Trish to let her know. She wasn't very impressed. She reminded him they were supposed to be visiting friends this evening.

'Oh, Trish, love. I'd completely forgotten.'

'Of course you had.' The caustic reply was sharper than he'd expected.

'Honey, I'm really sorry. You know what it's like in the middle of a case.'

There was silence.

'Trish. You okay?'

More silence, then … 'No. I don't feel so good. I don't really want to go myself.'

'Then ring and cancel. Sally will understand. I'll be home as soon as I can. Can you get your sister over to sit with you – just 'til I get there?'

A sad voice reached him. 'I've already done it.'

'Trish.' He softened. 'Why didn't you ring me?'

'Because you're busy. And I didn't want to bother you. And I felt – oh, I don't know.' He could hear Trish starting to cry. He was getting used to the inevitable emotional twists and turns of pregnancy.

'Please, love. Just put your feet up. Let Charlotte look after you. You know she loves doing it. I have to speak to the Super, then I'm coming home. Okay?'

'Yes, I know you're right. These bloody hormones.' She

sounded brighter now. 'I'll see you in a bit, then.'

'As soon as I can.'

Gavin hung up, feeling torn between wanting to ditch everything here to rush home and be with her, and knowing that he should go and tell Superintendant Fisher what he suspected.

Chief Superintendant Fisher was a cold and efficient man. He ran a 'tight ship', as they say. He was fair, precise and willing to comment on good work as well as criticise sloppy or careless policing. But, reflected Gavin, he was dry, and that made him appear unapproachable.

The previous Super – Frank Hammond – had been a kind, open man and Gavin had worked with him for years. He had been both respected and trusted by his force, and Gavin had really liked him. When the corruption case had blown up, it was clear to everyone that Frank had nothing to do with it, but he was the man at the top and had done the decent thing in offering his resignation. Fortunately, someone in the higher echelons had seen sense and made him a deal. Frank had taken early retirement and left his career with his honour intact. No-one blamed him for what had happened, except perhaps to think he was a little too trusting.

Gavin would rather have that any day than the sterile environment that now emanated from the top office. Losing both Frank and Katriona had changed the dynamic in the station considerably. Work was not quite as much fun, somehow. Still, he knew he had some great members in his current team, and working with Charlie was a dream.

He braced himself to knock on the Super's office door. He was not looking forward to this interview. Ratting on another officer was never something one chose to do lightly but he recognised the potential consequences of not alerting his boss to this suspicious activity soon enough.

Fisher called him in, and finished a phone conversation abruptly.

'Yes, Pearce. What is it?'

There was no invitation to take a seat as there had been with Frank. No indication from Fisher that he was interested to hear an update, or intrigued as to why Gavin was paying him a visit this late in the day. He gave every impression that Gavin was interrupting something far more important. Gavin brushed off the feeling of standing before the headmaster's desk.

'Sir, we've had a sighting of the girl, Helen Clarke.'

'Oh?'

'Yes, it appears that she came to the station on the day of the murder.'

'Oh?' Again.

'The CCTV shows her coming into the station yard, then suddenly turning and leaving. She bumped into one of our officers as she rushed off. Constable Whitmore.' He explained why the constable hadn't reported this sooner.

'So do we know why she ran off?'

As carefully as possible, Gavin said 'The CCTV coverage shows DI Foster arriving in a squad car on the other side of the yard.'

Fisher glared at him. He was obviously not at all happy at hearing this news. He knew, of course, the history of the corruption case, and the unproven suspicions surrounding Jack Foster.

Then, as Gavin watched, he appeared to accommodate this information into a pre-determined mental programme – as if he were some kind of robot, Gavin thought, who only had a limited number of options on how to interpret received data.

'Right. Proceed with caution. Keep all channels of information regarding this case restricted. Make sure all reports go through you, and only you. Then report to me. At every stage.'

Gavin nodded. 'The procedure is already in place, Sir.'

Fisher looked at him sharply. 'You mean you already had suspicions?'

'DI Foster came to the crime scene on the night of the murder, Sir, even though it wasn't his case. I thought it …'

Gavin searched for an appropriate, professional word.

'… unusual, so I put certain protocols in place. And, of course, you'll be aware of the TV debacle.'

The word slipped out before he could censor it.

'Pearce, I won't have senior officers criticising each other. Whatever your suspicions, your judgements stay outside this office – and, I hope, unreported within the ranks.'

'Sir.' *Damn.*

'This may be nothing more than co-incidence. We cannot afford to undermine the levels of co-operation necessary to carry out an effective investigation. I understand your concerns, given what happened here before I came, but disunity within the station serves no-one.'

'I agree, Sir.' *Though,* Gavin thought, *not quite in the way you intended.*

'Monitoring the DI is *my* responsibility. Yours is investigating this murder.'

Gavin opened his mouth, thinking to point out the inconsistencies inherent in this strategy, then changed his mind. He was not going to get any further with this.

'Yes, Sir.' At least he was covered by the directive if Foster became implicated as the investigation proceeded.

He left the office, feeling extremely gloomy, and knowing that the same conversation with Frank would've gone very differently. But he'd done what he should, he'd covered his own back and had slowed any shenanigans Foster might want to employ. That, he supposed, was something.

He went back to his office, packed up his stuff and headed home to Trish.

12

Katriona woke to the sound of oyster catchers, and a bright, but cold day. There was a light frost on the ground and she knew Elayne and the dogs would already be lochside, mulling over frozen seaweed with the local sheep. She meandered into the kitchen where bright red letters, attached to the fridge door, announced 'Mornin'. She loved that Elayne left her messages like this. She felt blessed – and relaxed, too. Yesterday had been a great day off and had done them both good, breaking the intensity that inevitably built up from working at home.

She reached for the coffee pot – yes, it was warm – and poured a cup. She found herself wondering how Gavin had got on with her idea about Helen Clarke seeing Jack Foster at the station. She hoped he'd have time to ring her and let her know. Perhaps she'd ring him if she didn't hear anything. She made her way back to the bedroom, cup in hand, and started running the shower, thinking through the tasks she needed to complete today.

There wasn't actually that much on her list currently, so maybe she could find time to do some reading. She believed it was important to keep up to date with research and new developments within the policing world, even if she had largely removed herself from living such a technological lifestyle. Her job remained important to her, so she needed to be well-informed, and knew the value of being willing to reflect on her work.

She belonged to an informal, on-line peer review group of professional women, who took the time to support each other as much as possible with insights and genuine criticism. Maybe she'd see who was available today.

Then she could settle down to the latest missive from the Chief Super of Police Scotland. She didn't expect there'd be much detail in it – it was sent out to all officers across the country – but it was important to know what had been said. She guessed it would be mostly motivational 'sing-a-long', as the restructuring of the organisation was so recent, but that was no bad thing. It certainly beat some of the detrimental stuff that used to be circulated round the Met.

Stepping out of the shower, she heard Elayne and the dogs in the kitchen.

'Good walk?' she called through the open bedroom door.

'Lovely.' Elayne wandered in. 'It's really beautiful out there.'

'It's pretty beautiful in here, too.' She gave Elayne a light kiss, then hugged her to her wet body.

'Oh, Kat!' Elayne squealed, as Katriona giggled and let her go. 'Do I need to wear my waterproofs in the morning to speak to you?'

Katriona laughed. 'You could just take off your wet clothes.'

'Sorry, love. No time. I've got that meeting with Donald and Fi, this morning.'

'Oh yeah, I forgot. Sorry 'bout the wet clothing, then.'

'No prob. But I will have to get changed.'

Elayne moved towards the wardrobe. 'Can't turn up to see new clients with soap stains all over my bosom.'

'And such a nice bosom.' Katriona touched her gently.

Elayne smiled, allowing the desire to show through her pretty grey eyes. She kissed Katriona with an unexpected warmth, and Katriona felt her body respond.

Then Elayne put her hands on Katriona's shoulders and firmly pushed her back. 'And that's it for now.'

'Oooh, how can you be so cruel?'

Another smile. 'Practice, I guess. Besides, you must have work to do, as well.'

Katriona sighed.

'Yes, but nothing very exciting today.'

Elayne was already replacing her sodden blouse. 'Will you ring Gavin? Find out if you were right about that girl?'

'I was thinking I might.'

Katriona wrapped a large cream bath towel around her slim, well-toned body and hunted for the hair-dryer in the bathroom cupboard. She brought it into the bedroom to sit in front of a large mirror.

'Don't want to seem pushy, though. It's not my case.' A trace of wistfulness was just detectable in her voice.

'I'm sure he'd be glad of someone to talk things through with. After all, who else is he going to use? Don't forget, Frank's gone as well, now. He's lost most of his old team.'

Elayne crossed the room to stand behind Katriona, smiling at their reflection in the mirror. 'I wouldn't be at all surprised if he rings you, actually.'

She gave Katriona a little squeeze on her shoulders, then turned away to get on with her own preparations. Katriona hoped she was right.

After an hour or so of wading through essential – and some non-essential – paperwork, and then another hour or so of various bits of reading, Katriona went on-line, intending to chat with some of her more regular friends in the support group. She was feeling in need of professional contact today. Some days she found she was quite happy working alone, sitting in her room surrounded by the stunning views. Other days, she was restless, desperately wanting to connect with the busy investigative world.

Today, she felt restless, but the technology was not obliging. For some reason, her internet connection wouldn't remain stable enough for her to have an extended conversation. Maybe there was a storm off-shore. Or maybe the mountains were interfering again. She let her fancies wander. She did feel, sometimes, that the landscape deliberately protected her from sliding back into old, destructive habits. Sometimes, she was able to be grateful for that. Sometimes, it made her fractious. She tried very hard to adopt the grateful route this morning.

She glanced at the clock. Gosh, she hadn't realised she'd been sat here working for so long. Definitely the island interfering, then. She stood up and stretched, then went into the kitchen to see what she could find for lunch. The dogs, who'd been sleeping in their baskets, looked up, expectantly.

'Yeah, yeah. Maybe we'll go out in a bit.'

Molly tapped her tail on the floor in response. Katriona opened the fridge and pulled out some rather gorgeous cheese – a rich, strong cheddar. She cut a big chunk off, and then sliced some smaller pieces to share with the dogs, before adding her own portion to a plate of crusty white bread and a slab of locally-churned butter.

She took it out into the garden, where the sunshine was warm enough for her to sit and eat on the patio, the early morning frost now gone. She watched as the dogs meandered around the lawn, sniffing at blades of grass as if they hadn't been inspected only a few hours ago. How did they manage to retain that fresh approach? Every day, it was always new to them – no matter how familiar. But in part, she understood. She could be like that when she was on a case. The difference was she hadn't learned to exercise her curiosity without it becoming an obsession.

A rather fat robin landed on the bird table, pecking intently at the grain Elayne had put out before leaving for her meeting. Katriona sat quietly, enjoying his search for the perfect mouthful, sifting through the collection of ingredients at his disposal until he found just the one he wanted. Then, suddenly, he flew off, something else catching his fancy.

It was no good. She *had* to ring Gavin. She couldn't resist any longer. She finished her meal and got up to head indoors – just as the phone rang.

'So I was right.' Katriona spoke with a touch of relish. There was definitely something very satisfying about making an intuitive guess that turned out to be correct.

'Absolutely. Good call.' Gavin responded warmly. He was never reticent when it came to acknowledging others' successes. 'But I'm not sure where it gets us. We still can't prove anything without the girl.'

'Have you spoken to Fisher?'

'Yes.' Gavin outlined the unsatisfactory conversation he'd had yesterday with the Super. 'And then this morning, I find Foster's been sent off to Surrey somewhere to do some follow-up or other for a case I didn't even know about – and Celia Whitmore's been seconded to another station.'

'Well, I guess that's one way of keeping the investigation clean.'

'I suppose so. I just hope – I mean, I'm glad Foster's out of my hair for a while, but I'm a bit worried about Whitmore. She seemed the insecure type. Hope she doesn't feel she's being punished or something daft like that.'

'Gavin, you're far too soft. How you ever came to be a copper, I'll never know.' Katriona spoke with fondness.

She heard Gavin laugh.

'You're probably right. It's just that everyone who has even a remote connection to this case seems to disappear.'

'What do you mean?'

'Well, we still have no idea where Helen Clarke is. We can't track down Heather Hough. And the best lead we had for contacting her – that camera man, Dieter Bergmann – well, Charlie's just told me he's been killed in a motorcycle accident in Dusseldorf.'

Katriona gasped. She heard possible pennies dropping at Gavin's end of the phoneline.

'Oh my God,' he said, slowly. 'You don't think that's

significant, do you?'

'I certainly think it's worth following up.'

'Fisher will never swallow that. He had a hard enough time when I suggested Foster was involved, but this is even more tenuous.'

An idea began to form in Katriona's head.

'Gavin, would you like me to see what I can find out? You know I've got connections in Germany. I could ring Stephi Wolff. She's based near Dusseldorf. I could get her to look over the file – entirely unofficially, of course.' She was getting excited by the thought.

There was a pause. Then Gavin's voice: 'Yes. Do it. If you're happy with that. It would at least let us know whether there's anything worth investigating.'

Katriona's heart warmed at the mention of 'us' – even if Gavin hadn't intended to include her in the generic. She didn't ask. As soon as he'd hung up, she rang through to Germany.

Her friend was quite happy to find out what she could. Stephi was a super-efficient person and nothing delighted her more than searching for obscure information. Katriona swore she'd have liked to set up home amongst the stacks, which actually suited her personality better than the modern method of computer and mouse.

Not that this information was obscure. It was just very recent and nothing directly to do with Stephi.

'I'll just have to make sure I cover my tracks.'

'Will that be a problem?'

'Shouldn't be. I think the incident went through …' There was a pause, and the sound of fingers tapping keys. 'Yep, Rudi Siedel's station. Fairly local. He'll be okay with me asking. Anything specific you want me to find out?'

Katriona hesitated. She'd never actually met Stephi, though they had a long-time phone and internet friendship, and had worked together on several international cases, each based at their own end. The whisky theft case which

Katriona had told Gavin about, was one such. She trusted Stephi but wasn't sure how fair it was to involve her in retrieving data outside her jurisdiction.

'We're just wondering if there's anything suspicious surrounding the crash, that's all. The guy has – had – a remote connection to a case we're working on.'

'But this is unofficial, right?'

'Yes, at the moment. I'm just casting a net, so to speak. Throwing it out in all directions to see what comes up.'

'So why the need for secrecy?'

Reluctantly, Katriona suggested it was better that Stephi didn't know.

'Okay,' Stephi sounded put out.

'Are you sure this is alright with you?' Katriona was anxious to keep Stephi happy. She was far too valuable a contact to screw up the friendship between them.

'Yes. Oh, absolutely no problem getting hold of the info. Just annoyed you won't let me in on the background.' Stephi laughed. 'Like you – can't resist a good case.'

Katriona was relieved. She had wondered if she'd asked Stephi to cross a line. It was so difficult communicating only by phone with someone you'd never met.

'Tell you what,' Stephi continued. 'If I find something suspicious, I'll trade you for why you wanted it. Is that a deal?'

'It might well be.' Katriona hedged her bets, thinking it might depend on what Stephi found.

The rest of the afternoon passed quite quickly. Katriona's interest in the case was well and truly ignited now, and she found she was reviewing the evidence to date in her mind. She'd always had a remarkable memory – almost photographic for written materials – but it was rather more difficult trying to recall intermittent phone conversations on a case you weren't even supposed to be working on.

After clearing the most immediate papers on her desk, she put on her boots and took the dogs up onto the moorland behind the house, so she could reflect in the fresh air. That always seemed to help.

Gavin was right. This was a strange case. Usually, a murder in the middle of such a busy place had so much evidence, it took the first few days to wade through it all and sift out what was useful. This had all the hallmarks of being only the tail-end of something much bigger and more far-reaching, as if the absence of useful information was well-practised. Part of an organised structure.

And what was Jack Foster's role in all this? She knew he wouldn't normally choose to be that close to a murder. Theft and contraband was much more his style. Even blackmail. He was more interested in getting rich quick than in violence, and very adept at maintaining himself in a 'managerial' role, letting others do the actual dirty work. That's why he'd never had anything pinned on him before. To be actually in the house when Emily Hough was murdered was the kind of risk he rarely took. There must be an awful lot of money involved this time.

Which begged the question as to what kind of case this could be. Like Gavin, she felt drugs or guns was highly unlikely, given Emily's involvement, but it had to be pretty high profile for Foster to take such a big risk. Information of some sort did seem to be the most likely explanation. She wished she had access to the full files. This was very intriguing.

She rounded the top of the next hillock and stopped to take in the view. Late afternoon mist was beginning to gather, obscuring the distant landmarks and closing off the mountain tops. She could see that the mist was more of a travelling fog a few miles away, bringing in some rain over towards Broadford, so she turned to head back down to the house. The dogs raced on ahead of her, thinking it was a great game to guess which direction she'd take next.

Elayne's car was visible on the driveway, so the possibility of afternoon tea was a strong one. Her mind drifted again. Perhaps Stephi's information would give them a clue.

Katriona had guessed right. When she got back to the house, a steaming pot of tea was waiting for her on the little table in the conservatory. She came into the back porch to take off her boots, and called to Elayne in the kitchen.

'That was clever.'

'Saw you coming down the hill.' Elayne smiled, as she came through the door.

'How'd it go?'

'Really well. It's a fascinating spot they've found. It's got a cave!'

'It's what?' Katriona picked up the tray of dainty cups and saucers to carry through. 'Have we got cake?'

'Oh, yes.' Elayne brandished a cakestand, to which she'd been putting the finishing touches. 'Came back through Portree so I picked up these.'

The cakestand held a collection of tiny cupcakes, each iced in a different colour and topped with a sugar star or heart.

'Wow. Those look so pretty.'

'That's what I thought.'

They moved everything through to the conservatory where they could see the sky was already turning leaden, no sign of the day's sunshine left.

'So tell me about this cave.'

'Well, they've bought several acres of land, and some of it is right on the shoreline. Not easily accessible, but there's a tiny footpath that leads down to a private sandy beach.'

Elayne picked up the teapot. 'We scrambled down to take a look, and they showed me the opening just a bit further up, along the coast. We couldn't get to it today because the tide was in, but apparently at low-tide, you can walk right round to it.'

'Wow. How exciting.'

Elayne paused from pouring the tea and beamed at Katriona.

'That's not the most exciting bit.'

'No?' Katriona helped herself to a couple of the tiny cupcakes and waited for the tale to unfold.

'No.' Elayne was really hamming it up. 'We walked back up to the site where they want their house and … you're not going to believe this …'

'What?'

'There's a back entrance to the cave. Hidden behind some rocks and shrubs – and now it's got a silver birch growing over the entrance. We think it might be an old whisky haunt. You know, like in Whisky Galore?'

They both shrieked in delight.

'How fantastic. Did you go into it?'

'No. Sadly, it's not safe. Too much crumbly rock. But they want me to see if we can stabilise it and maybe incorporate it into the design, somehow.'

'Brilliant!'

'I know. Can't wait to get started. They'd like to see if they can use it as a boat-house, so they'd have their own private access to the ocean.'

'I'm very envious.'

Their shared delight was cut short by the sound of the study phone ringing.

'That's work,' Katriona said. 'I'd better take it.'

It was unusual for someone official to be ringing this late in the day, so Katriona assumed it must be important.

'Hello, DI McShannon here.'

'Ma'am, it's Constable McTavish. The Community Officer in Broadford. I'm sorry to disturb you, Ma'am, but I'm not sure what to do. It's so late in the day, and all the Portree lads have gone home, and obviously I can't refer her to Inverness at this time of day, and at the start of the weekend. I know it's not your job as such but I couldn't think who else to ring.'

Katriona interrupted.

'Constable, you're not making sense.'

'No. Sorry, Ma'am. Let me try to explain. I have a young girl here who wants to report a murder.'

Katriona put down the plate of cupcakes she was still holding, feeling cold shivers running down her back.

'A murder?'

'Yes, Ma'am.'

'Then you need to contact your superior officer.'

'Ma'am, I can't. Like I say, Portree's shut up for the night. Besides, the girl is insistent she won't speak to anyone official. Sorry, Ma'am. She's not being very coherent.'

Clearly not. How could you report a murder without speaking to someone official?

'I'm not really sure what I can do, Constable. It's not my jurisdiction.'

'No, Ma'am. That's precisely why I thought of you.'

'I don't understand. Where's the murder?'

'I'm not sure, Ma'am.'

'But somewhere on the island, right?'

'I don't think so.'

Katriona was starting to get impatient. 'But the girl – she's an islander?'

'No, Ma'am. I believe she arrived on the afternoon ferry. She's travelled up from Armadale. She's in a bit of a state, Ma'am. I found her crying outside the old police station, here in Broadford. Seems she didn't know it had closed down some years ago. 'Course I now live in what was the old police house, so I saw her out my front window. Thought I'd just wander over and see if I could help. When I saw what a state she was in, I brought her in and gave her a cuppa. But like I said, she's not being very coherent. Keeps saying she doesn't know who she can trust.'

Katriona froze. It wasn't possible. She'd got her head too full of someone else's case.

'Has she got a name?'

13

Helen was indeed in a bit of a state. Her journey to the north of England and on into Scotland had not gone as planned. It had started out well enough, with the first few connections coinciding quite nicely, so that her newfound confidence on the platform at Bishop's Stortford had initially flourished, allowing her sense of taking on an exciting adventure to increase. But the further she had travelled into unfamiliar territory, towards an unknown destination, the more her courage had diminished. No longer having anyone to talk her out of self-pity and anxiety, she had found herself slipping back into despair, so that by the time she'd got to Peterborough on her third train, she was beginning to feel this might not have been the best idea.

Here, she discovered she had more than an hour to wait for the Edinburgh train, which was disconcerting. She thought they'd planned a pretty smooth run straight through, so that she wouldn't have to make any big decisions until arriving in Scotland, unless she particularly wanted to. Now she had too much time available to question the wisdom of what she was doing. And she was hungry.

She made her way to the station café, hoping for a warm meal, and found it had just closed. So she had to venture out of the station to see if there was something locally that was still open. She managed to find a fish and chip shop not too far from the station. Thank God. The thought of having to explore a strange city in the dark felt extremely daunting and the possibility, then, of not making it back in time for the next train made her very anxious.

Feeling somewhat better for having some food inside her, although reflecting on how one could tire of persistent fish and chips quite quickly, she made her way back into the station to find the platform for the Edinburgh train. It was already there, waiting to depart. But when she checked the departure board, there was no train for Edinburgh listed. This one appeared to go only as far as Newcastle, and there was no-one around to ask.

She retrieved her new phone from her holdall and did a quick internet search. Yes, she'd missed the last direct train to Scotland. If she took this one, she would have a four-hour wait in Newcastle for a second train that would arrive in Edinburgh early tomorrow morning. If she didn't take this train, she was faced with spending the night in Peterborough.

Her spirits sank. She'd been so proud of the plan she and Petey had put together, but they must have misread the timetables at some point. Uncertain as to what was the best choice, she suddenly remembered the TV broadcast Petey had shown her, and realised that for all the hours – days – she had already been travelling, she still wasn't all that far from London.

Her fear of being recognised and reported was sufficient motivation for her to choose to keep moving. She'd just have to trust that the station at Newcastle had an all-night café, or at least a warm waiting room.

On arrival in Newcastle, Helen discovered a magnificently refurbished station, which had cheered her a little, though it was very eerie wandering around closed shops and ticket centres in the middle of the night, with so few people about.

She wasn't sure whether she found the sight of an occasional security guard reassuring or a cause for alarm.

Knowing she was reasonably well-disguised helped her keep calm enough not to panic and she eventually found a café that was open and warm.

She settled in with a mug of hot chocolate to wait. She began to regret not bringing anything with her to read but then she hadn't really had time to think about those sorts of details before setting off. She got her phone out again and clicked onto the internet, searching through various news sites for any updates that might include her name. She found nothing. Again, that sense of 'is this a good thing? or is it sinister?' Maybe she was already old news.

That thought was more comforting. Maybe they'd found out something that meant the search for her was not so important anymore. Maybe there was new evidence … She began to drift, the warmth of the hot chocolate inside and the café surroundings outside made for a rather somnambulant state.

She felt her eyes closing and settled further into the uncomfortable seat, leaning up against the wall. *Mustn't actually go to sleep … might miss the train.* Her last thoughts before unconsciousness.

She was woken abruptly by the clatter of crockery and someone tapping her on the arm. She jumped violently and opened her eyes to view one of the security guards standing next to the table.

Oh my God. They've found me.

But the guy didn't have a serious look on his face. In fact, he appeared rather to be making an attempt at sympathy.

'Sorry, miss. Not allowed to let you sleep here.'

Helen blinked, trying to bring her mind, as well as her eyes, into focus.

'What?'

'Against the rules, I'm afraid. I've left you as long as I can but my supervisor'll be in soon.'

Helen smiled at him, trying to create the illusion of someone who knew what they were doing.

'Yes, of course. What time is it?'

'About 4.30.'

No wonder she felt so awful. She'd only been asleep a couple of hours.

'Thank you. I need to catch my train, anyway.'

Reassured, the man left her to it. Helen gathered up her things and decided she'd better go on 'walkabout'. If she bought another drink and sat down again, she'd probably fall asleep a second time and that might draw too much attention to her.

She left the café and started meandering around the empty shopping mall, listening to the sound of heavy rain pounding on the roof. She had to keep checking around her so that she didn't bump into the security guard and invite suspicion.

She felt terrible. As well as the lack of sleep, the incident itself had shaken her. She realised how very easily she could be discovered and began to feel forlorn and unconfident again. This was horrible. How had she got into this? Her whole life destroyed …

For the first time in a couple of days, she began to replay the awful scene she had witnessed at Emily's house. Inevitably, the desolation of her current situation – alone, in the middle of the night, in a deserted railway station – brought her to tears once more.

By the time the train to Edinburgh was ready to leave, Helen had lost all her positivity and determination. She'd climbed aboard with red-rimmed eyes and no idea of what she would do when it arrived at its destination.

She managed to sleep a little more on the train, as she knew she'd be woken at the other end, and could relax into it more easily, but the journey was only a couple of hours, so it wasn't long before she found she was back into bleary-eyed consciousness, this time with a pounding headache.

As she stepped onto the platform, looking for somewhere that might sell bottles of water, she heard an announcement for the Glasgow train, due to leave in seven minutes. Since her ticket allowed her to take the journey that far, she decided she'd go with it and delay any major decisions until she got there. She rushed to the right platform, grabbing a couple of bottles of water on the way, since there was no queue as she passed.

That was a stroke of luck, in what was quickly turning into a very busy commuter morning. She made it onto the Glasgow train with thirty seconds to spare, but discovered it was packed and there seemed to be no seats left empty. In fact, there were quite a number of people wandering up and down the carriages, presumably also hunting for somewhere to sit. She parked herself next to a luggage space and decided to wait until things had settled.

The train turned out not to be the direct express to Glasgow, but a local train calling at a number of small stations en route, so after a while the crowd of busy passengers thinned and eventually someone vacated a seat near where she was standing. She plonked herself down, thankfully.

Her headache had dissipated somewhat, due to the water she was now taking in, but she still felt unwell and her energy was draining along with her confidence. She only had less than half an hour now before she would reach Glasgow. She needed to make some decisions, but felt almost incapable of doing so.

The shock and strain of the last few days was taking its toll. She felt bewildered, scared and stupid – stupid for putting herself in this situation. She reminded herself sharply of why she'd done it, picturing DI Foster's face vividly – first, at Emily's house, then in the station yard, and finally, on Petey's laptop. She realised there was no doubt in her mind that this man would not hesitate to have her killed if the opportunity arose. She had to keep going. She had to find somewhere to stay until she could work out what to do.

The train pulled into Glasgow as daylight began to appear. It was still early. People were rushing about, on their way to work or arriving to shop. She stood in the midst of the crowd and wondered what would happen next.

She'd never actually been in Glasgow before. She'd passed through a few times, mostly by car on the way to somewhere else. Oh yes, she and some mates had gone to Loch Lomond for a holiday one year. The reminiscence brought Bev to mind. She'd been on that holiday with her. The memory of her friend choked her up. Morbid thoughts entered her head, thoughts like *will I ever see her again?*

Her eye caught sight of a newsagents' with the morning's papers displayed on stands in front of the wide entrance, leading into the kiosk. Someone had obviously dropped one on the floor earlier and sheets of newsprint were floating about, being kicked and trampled on by passers-by.

She couldn't help herself. She moved slowly towards the shop. Just as she reached the circulating stands of postcards, neatly displayed outside on the concourse, one of the loose sheets suddenly flapped against her legs, caught in the breeze. She reached down to pick it off, and saw exactly what she'd dreaded. A photo of herself, placed invidiously next to a photo of Emily Hough.

She didn't bother to read the text. No need. She knew what it would say. She dropped the newspaper as sheer terror ran through her. A sickening echo of what she'd experienced just three days before. She reminded herself she was not instantly recognisable as the girl in the photo, but her shaking hands betrayed what she was really experiencing inside.

There was going to be no getting away from this. Petey was right. At some point, she was going to have to trust someone enough to report what she'd seen. It wasn't simply a question of keeping herself safe. That was only one part of the equation. She also had a duty. A duty to Emily. She owed it to the dead lady to help the police catch her killer.

But which police? How did you report a murder when one of the people who should be investigating had committed the crime? And here she was, hundreds of miles from the scene, and still facing the same questions. A dawning realisation emerged. No amount of distance was going to solve the problem. It didn't matter how far she went, the issues were going to stay the same. And the real issue, ultimately, was finding someone she could trust.

As she stood in the middle of the surging crowd – lost and forlorn – she suddenly sent up a silent prayer. *Help me. Help me, please.*

Praying wasn't a part of her life as a rule. Not since her parents' car crash. As a youngster, she'd enjoyed the family outings to church and had joined the choir as soon as she was allowed. She had found she liked the music, but mostly she enjoyed the technical challenge of singing in harmony. This was where she'd had her early training in reading music. Sat in the choir stalls, she'd had no choice but to listen to the regular sermons – other than falling asleep – so she'd gained a comprehensive picture of what adults thought religion was about. She'd been happy to join in the community practice at that time.

But after her parents had died, she'd realised that whatever it was she thought she'd been doing when she was praying, it was nothing more than an illusion. She didn't think she'd ever tried to pray since, and her visits to church, despite the singing, had quickly ceased.

Now, in the depths of desperation, something inside was urging her to try again. *If there is an ounce of you that exists, please help me now.*

Later, when she reflected back on that moment, she could only believe her prayer had been answered. As she turned to look around the station, hoping she supposed for some kind of miracle, her eyes fell on a poster. 'Take the magical journey of a lifetime. Follow the Road To The Isles.'

Small glints of recognition ignited in her mind. Recollections of a wonderful holiday when she was a little girl. She remembered a pretty cottage on a hill overlooking astonishing blue seas, huge mountains with strange-sounding names, magnificent sunshine and breath-taking rainbows arching across green valleys. She and her parents, happy together. It had been on an island. What was it called?

She walked towards the poster. Skye. That was it. She remembered thinking what a funny name it was. The sky was supposed to be overhead, not under your feet. She'd half-expected, when they got there, to find herself walking on clouds, and it had become a family joke. She'd liked the idea of living on a bit of heaven. Somewhere she could trust.

The thought hit her like a bombshell. Was this crazy? Well, no more crazy than anything else she'd tried up to now. Surely, surely it would be safe to talk to someone there – so far away from London. The most important thing was that it restored her sense of purpose. It gave her a direction and a destination. If she couldn't find some kind of resolution there, it seemed unlikely she'd find it anywhere, she thought. In fact, the idea of returning to such a beautiful place had really cheered her up.

Refocused now, she hurriedly searched for the Departures board, and learned that a train heading for Mallaig was due to leave in just over ten minutes. Now if that wasn't synchronicity, she didn't know what was. She made her way to the Travel Centre to buy a single, one-way ticket, remembering to send a private 'thank you' from her heart to whoever it was that had listened.

The train journey, onto Fort William and out west to Mallaig, was every bit as magical as the poster suggested. The scenery didn't disappoint and turned out to be as beautiful as her faint memories. Better, possibly, since this was real. The further north and west she travelled, the more the skies cleared, until the landscape was bathed in early morning sunshine, turning everything a golden yellow and making even the finishing vegetation look lush.

Forests of changing deciduous trees, their leaves showing a rich variety of reds and oranges, gradually gave way to swathes of conifers which took on a burnished appearance, patchworked with darker and bolder greens.

Moorland browns were set alight as the low-angled sun began to climb higher. The grey storm clouds, which had been hovering over Glasgow, thinned to reveal a pristine blue sky and a warm autumn day.

The waters of the numerous lochs the train passed by shone with even deeper and even brighter blues, or sparkled with a dazzling display of flashing shards of light, depending on the direction the train approached from, and the interplay of the sun's light with the surface. Some of the lochs were so smooth and calm, they were like mirrors, reflecting back the overhead scenery in immaculate detail, creating amazing kaleidoscopic images. As they crossed Rannoch Moor, the peaty bogs looked like liquid gold, with their mysterious green and brown islets punctuating the vast wilderness.

Accompanying every stage of the way were tremendous mountains. These started out as powerful green presences, with tall, rounded tops towering above what now felt like a tiny train, particularly when they crossed a curved viaduct north of Tyndrum, surrounded on all sides with the beautiful, undulating scenery. But as they approached Glencoe, the mountains took on a more rugged appearance, and Helen gasped in wonder as she saw huge areas of snow on the tops, glinting in the sunshine.

Travelling on this train was unlike any other train journey she'd ever taken. No-one was sat reading or listening to their iPod. Everyone was engaged in looking out of the windows, and an excited camaraderie filled the carriages, as people pointed out spectacular view after spectacular view. The journey lasted over five hours but every moment of it was a sheer joy. They arrived in Mallaig in early afternoon, everyone tired, happy and hungry.

There had been a small refreshments trolley available on board, but only supplying basics like sandwiches, so Helen now found she was ravenous. She'd bought a through-ticket all the way to Skye when she'd been in the ticket office at Glasgow; it included the ferry journey along with the train. Since the ferry didn't depart for another couple of hours, this would give her time to find something decent to eat.

As she made her way along the platform and out onto the street, she had her first sighting of the island. It looked warm and welcoming.

'Unusual that,' said a voice in her ear.

'Sorry?'

She turned to see one of the other passengers from the train. A friendly, fair-haired man who had spent the journey organising his family of four children and a wife, making sure they got to see everything he thought they should. He obviously enjoyed supplying information.

'Skye. Not always that easy to see from here. It's often hidden by clouds. That's why they call it the Misty Isle.'

'Oh, I see.' Helen smiled and quickly turned away. She was still reticent to make contact with people. Not until she'd done what she came here to do. She went in search of food.

The crossing only took thirty minutes. In fact, the island seemed so close, Helen wondered why it took that long. She discovered that much of it was taken up with organising the boat in relation to the dock at each end. The rest was down to the unexpected slow pace of the boat. Having spent a couple of days on the canal, she found she was comforted by the familiarity of the sensation. The slowness of it all allowed one to connect with the passing scenery, the utterly clear water, the changing light.

Halfway across, she looked back to the mainland and saw that the storm clouds had caught up with her, hovering in the distance, cutting off sight of the mountain tops. She could no longer see the snow. By the time they'd disembarked at Armadale, the mainland itself was no longer visible, hidden behind a bank of dense fog – almost as if the island had closed in around her, disconnecting her from everything that had happened, keeping her safe.

She made her way past the few brightly-lit buildings that greeted the tourists now leaving the ferry in a stream of cars and people. There was a pottery, an ice-cream kiosk, which was shut, and a busy shop with designer knitwear in the window. It seemed out of place in this quiet, remote setting. She had a vague memory of visiting it with her parents, all those years ago. It hadn't been so flashy then … she thought.

The light was beginning to fade as the clouds drew in, bringing a delicate drizzle with them. Suddenly, she felt very tired. She'd been travelling for twenty-four hours now. Three days, if you counted the canal trip, too. She needed to stop, but she had to decide where.

In the last few hours, she had made her mind up that she was going to report the murder as soon as she could. Racking her memories, she was sure there had been a small police station in Broadford, which was the first proper town the route north would take her through. She was determined to make her way there before looking for somewhere to stay. She felt if she didn't make that her priority, she might lose her courage again by morning. But first, she needed a coffee.

She knew, from the information on the train, there was a major tourist attraction in Armadale. A castle, with its own museum and a restaurant. She walked the relatively short distance along the road to find it, quite taken aback by the splendour of the setting when she reached it. Vague recollections came back to her again. Yes, the family had been here, she was certain.

She made her way to the restaurant and bought a coffee and a delicious-looking piece of cake. The place was almost deserted.

'You're lucky,' the girl behind the till said, as she paid. 'We're just about to close. Another five minutes and you'd've been too late.'

'Oh, I hadn't realised it was that late.' Helen glanced at the clock above the girl's head. It registered four in the afternoon.

'Out of season hours. Winter timetable.' The girl explained.

'I see.' Helen acknowledged inwardly that she had indeed been lucky. 'I guess there'll be a bus up to Broadford, won't there?'

'No, not now. You've just missed the last one. Did you come off the ferry?'

'Yes.'

'You should've got straight on the bus, then.'

Helen didn't think she'd seen a bus, but then remembered a number of the foot-passengers had boarded a coach. She'd assumed it was part of a tour package.

'So there's no more transport north today?'

'You'll have to get a taxi. Number's on the wall in the entrance, but it'll take Donald a while to get here. He's based in Broadford, so he'll have to travel down specially.'

Helen's heart sank. This wasn't going to be so easy.

'And what time does this place close? I mean, the whole building, not just the restaurant.'

'Everything shuts in half an hour.'

Helen thanked the girl and took her coffee and cake to a table on the side wall to sit below a huge piece of red tartan. Outside was now a dismal grey and the drizzle was turning to serious rain. She consumed her snack quickly and went back to the main entrance to find the taxi information.

The actual journey from Armadale to Broadford didn't take a long time, but Donald had been out on another job when Helen rang. His wife told her she'd send him down to Armadale as soon as he got back, but it was another hour before he appeared. At first, Helen had been able to wander around the gift shop, but when everything shut up for the night, she was forced to sit out on a wall in the carpark, anxiously waiting, as twilight drew in and the rain got heavier. By the time Donald had arrived, she was cold, wet and exhausted.

They'd travelled along the road to the main route up the island at quite a startling pace, especially, Helen thought, that it was now so dark and rainy. She was glad she'd decided to sit in the back of the car, even though Donald had offered her the front seat. It meant she didn't have such a full-on view of oncoming traffic. She was relieved that most of the road seemed to have been updated from the original single-track route, which ran alongside them whenever she glanced to the side. They made it to the main road without incident, and Donald set off towards Broadford at an equally terrifying pace.

She hadn't told him she was heading for the police station. She didn't want to attract attention to herself. She'd just said 'Drop me on the main road in Broadford. I'll be fine from there.' But, of course, that had turned out not to be the case.

She had walked along the deserted street, desperately looking for familiar sights, realising what a futile task this was after so many years – and in the dark. The few street lights did little to help recognition, turning everything into shadowy replicas of their daylight reality. She'd ended up walking quite a distance before she came across a carpark that triggered a memory. Yes, the Co-op, with its lighting illuminating the surroundings. Wasn't the police station just opposite that?

The closer she'd got to her final destination, the more she'd had to fight to keep her courage. Voices in her head were screaming how stupid she'd been to come all this way and expect to find help. Frantic fears of what might happen – or might not happen – filled her mind persistently, no matter now hard she tried to block them. She was shaking again, but she was unsure whether that was due to terror, cold or exhaustion.

So when she'd finally reached the building where she expected to find some kind of resolution, and saw the boarded-up windows and barred door, it was all too much. She'd collapsed onto the wall in tears, no longer having any idea what to do. No longer having the energy to care.

When the gentle, dark-haired man had approached her, introducing himself as the local community officer, she had been relieved and terrified all at the same time, but she was so tired that she had no resistance left, and had willingly allowed him to take her into his house, hoping his offer of tea was genuine.

She'd tried to explain but she knew it made no sense because she couldn't bring herself to tell him everything. She didn't know whether to trust him. She didn't know whether he'd believe her. She didn't even know any more whether the murder had really happened or whether she'd dreamt it.

So when an elegant woman, with long blonde hair and a very composed manner, entered the room, she'd been utterly surprised.

'Hello, Helen. I'm DI McShannon, but you can call me Katriona. I'm a consultant detective for the Serious Crime Division here in Scotland. I don't work for any particular police station and I'm off-duty at the moment. I just happen to live on the island. So I hope you will feel you can trust me with your story.'

14

The moment Katriona saw the girl she recognised her from the photos. The disguise was pretty good. The dramatic change in her hair was sufficient to make her unnoticeable to most passers-by, but to a keen observer, Helen Clarke was still visible. How on earth had she ended up here?

Katriona tried to speak reassuringly as she introduced herself. She wanted to make the girl feel she was now safe, but she knew that getting her to trust a police officer was going to be difficult. Still, she had made her way to a police station – even if it no longer existed – so there must be some part of her that still felt that was the best thing to do.

She saw the fear and exhaustion in Helen's eyes. With the efficiency of a trained police mind, she thought: *That's the weakness. That's my way in.* Shutting down her instincts to comfort the girl, encourage her to get a good night's sleep before attempting to talk, she began to open up the necessary questioning.

'Why don't you start at the beginning, Helen?'

That worked. Taking her back to the last point in time where she had felt okay. It was always a good technique to get fearful people talking. Once they'd got started – remembered that life had been normal before the crisis – they would often feel able to narrate what had happened. It was almost as if that reconnection with a more sane reality gave them something secure to hang onto while they revisited events. There was also something in the invitation that indicated the questioner wanted to hear their side of it. Was not making pre-judgements. That always helped, too.

Katriona was good at this. She knew just when to interrupt and make encouraging noises, and when to be quiet and wait. She also knew how to create a conducive setting. If she was going to get Helen to name Foster, she needed to get McTavish out of the room. She guessed the girl was going to be reticent about voicing that part of her story, so a very private, woman-to-woman talk was more likely to produce results than being listened to by two police officers.

She sat down on an armchair opposite Helen, and smiled.

'Tell you what, let's get some more tea going, first. I could definitely do with a cuppa. Constable McTavish – '

She turned to look at the officer hovering in the doorway, obviously uncertain about his role in this difficult situation.

'Why don't you make another pot and see if you can rustle up some sandwiches or something? The co-op's still open, I think. Go and see what you can find.' She nodded at him, meaningfully. Thank God he was astute enough to get the message.

'Sure. No problem.'

And he disappeared, making sure he closed the front door loudly enough to indicate to the distressed girl that she and Katriona were now alone.

'Take me back to the start,' Katriona encouraged, again. 'When would that be?' It was important Helen didn't realise too quickly that Katriona knew who she was.

'Four days ago.' Helen began, hesitantly.

'Yes. And where was this?'

'In London.' Helen took a deep breath. 'Battersea.'

Katriona played it cool. It was clear that Helen considered that piece of information a dead give-away. She picked up on the less crucial offering.

'London?' She allowed surprise to show on her face.

Then, calmly, 'And what were you doing?'

'I was on my way to an audition. I'm a singer, you see. Well, that's not entirely true. I can sing but I want to be a singer. To study singing.' Her story was beginning to flow now.

'And this guy I know encouraged me to start applying to colleges, after he heard me singing in our local pub. He was really good, helping me sort through the paperwork and stuff.'

She stopped.

'But you don't really need to know any of that.'

'What do I need to know?'

'I was going to …' A pause.

'… someone's house for an audition. One of the colleges was interested in my application and had asked me to arrange an audition with one of their assessors. They ask professional singers to act for them. I think it's a great idea. And such a wonderful opportunity. So I'd contacted …' She faltered. '… this person, and she'd agreed to fit me in unexpectedly, before she was off to a concert in Manchester, on Tuesday evening …'

Helen looked up at Katriona.

'But you know all this, don't you?'

'I certainly know some of it, Helen, but I really need to hear it from your perspective.' Katriona spoke as kindly as she could. She didn't want to spook the girl, and it was vital the information came from her and was not superimposed in any way.

'So, just to clarify, the person you went to see was … ?'

Helen almost whispered her response. 'Emily Hough.'

There was a silence, then '… but she was dead when I got there.' It came out in a rush, and the girl began to cry.

Katriona hunted in her pockets for tissues. 'I guessed as much,' she said, though that wasn't actually true. She'd thought Helen had witnessed the murder, and was disappointed to find this was not the case. Damn Foster, she thought. He's going to get away with it, again.

'So how did you manage to find the body?' Katriona knew the police had found it inside the house, but if Emily had been dead when Helen arrived, it was not obvious how she'd discovered it.

'The front door was open.'

'Oh?'

'Yes, I thought it was odd, at the time.' Helen went on to explain how she'd tried to knock on the door and how it had eventually opened itself. 'I saw Miss Hough on the floor straightaway. 'Course, I didn't know it was her immediately. I went in to find out.'

'That was brave of you.'

'Yes? I suppose it was. I didn't think much at the time.'

She began to tell Katriona how she'd checked the body for life-signs, how she'd recognised it was Emily, how she'd discovered she didn't have her phone with her to ring for help. Katriona encouraged her to share every detail, with appropriate nods and smiles, little 'um's' and 'ah's'. The more she could get Helen back to the scene, the better her recall would be.

'So what did you do next?'

'I didn't … I couldn't …'

She saw fear cross Helen's face as she replayed the scene in her mind. This was it. They'd reached the most crucial part of the story. Helen whispered again.

'There was someone else in the house.'

She looked pleadingly at Katriona, as if asking for permission. Katriona wondered whether she wanted permission to be believed or permission for it not to be true.

'It's okay,' she reassured. 'Take your time. Just tell me *exactly* what happened.' She stressed the word, hoping to help Helen focus accurately on her story. Sometimes, when people had witnessed something really terrifying, they skipped details in the retelling, hoping, perhaps, to avoid the overwhelming horror at the heart of the incident. But Helen was turning out to be a good witness.

'I heard a noise first,' she said. 'Like someone was kicking a door. It came from downstairs.' She paused. Katriona could see she was back in Emily's house.

'No, that's not right. I heard a voice before that. That's right. Because I remember thinking maybe someone was just outside, perhaps coming to the house, and then I'd be able to ask them for help. But then there was the noise. And people coming up the stairs from the cellar. And they were talking to each other, like there was nothing wrong. And saying things about searching the house, I think. I couldn't hear everything clearly.'

'So what did you do?'

'I hid. But that was after I'd heard one guy say he'd taken care of Miss Hough.'

'Really? Is that what he said?'

Helen thought really hard. 'He said something like 'I've taken care of her' or 'I've dealt with her'. He was answering the other guy.'

'There were two of them?'

'Yes, but I didn't know that straightaway. I found a door and rushed through it to get out of sight. It turned out to be a cloakroom. I remember I pushed the door closed, but not completely because it had been open a little way and I thought they might notice if it was different.'

'That was clever of you.' Katriona was genuinely impressed. She didn't think that many people in such a situation would've had the presence of mind to think of details like that. Helen barely heard her. She was totally back in the original scene now, working hard to recall what she'd experienced.

'I had to be careful,' she was saying. 'I had this new coat, you see. I'd bought it especially for the audition. I thought it looked impressive. But it turned out to be such a mistake.' The tears started up in her eyes again, and her face began to crumple.

Oh no, don't fall apart on me, now.

'It was so stupidly noisy.'

'What was?' Katriona was confused.

'The damn bloody coat.' Something about the recollection made Helen angry but Katriona was glad because it had the effect of pulling her back on course.

'It was a red plastic coat, you see.' She looked directly at Katriona, even smiling a little. 'It made a noise every time I moved.'

'Oh,' Katriona began to understand.

'So I had to stand absolutely still, otherwise they'd have heard me. Even so, one of the men thought he'd heard something. But then they noticed the front door was open, and this one guy started shouting at the other about being careless or something. I don't remember exactly what they said because that was when I saw the gun.'

'The gun?' Katriona repeated. This was news. There'd been no report of any shooting.

'Yes, the guy in the leather jacket was carrying a gun. The other guy was – oh, my God – ' Helen gasped.

Katriona waited for her to continue. Obviously, the recollection was overpowering but she guessed the 'other guy' was Foster, and Helen was momentarily remembering who – what – he was.

'I'm sorry.' The girl was sobbing, again.

'It's okay, Helen. Like I said, just take your time.'

'But you don't understand. It's not just that he was there, and I can see his face.' There were tears streaming down her cheeks, now.

'I saw him again,' she cried. 'I saw him when I went to report the murder at the police station.' Great shudders shook her body as she released the last sentence with a huge sob, looking up into Katriona's eyes with fear and horror clearly written in her own.

Katriona reached out a hand.

'I know,' she said, calmly. 'I know.'

Constable McTavish arrived back just after Katriona had got Helen to formally identify Foster from a selection of photos.

Perfect timing, she thought. Helen could do with a break. She also didn't want to involve McTavish in any of this. It wasn't fair.

So the three of them had shared a cuppa, and Katriona made sure that Helen had something to eat, while she considered what was the best strategy from here. She let the conversation drift into less emotional topics for a while – just general chit-chat. The constable seemed to be good at that and she was grateful to see him putting Helen at her ease, as well as taking the responsibility for input off her shoulders temporarily. Eventually, when she'd made up her mind, she left the room to make a phonecall.

'Hello, love. Everything okay?' Elayne's reassuring voice somehow confirmed she was doing the right thing.

She and Elayne had had numerous conversations over the years about how they might deal with various situations related to Katriona's work. There was always a danger that police officers' families could be targeted by serious offenders, so they'd put several emergency strategies in place over time. Bringing home a witness, however, was not something Katriona had ever attempted before.

'Yes. But I need to ask something of you. Something big.'

There was a brief pause from the other end of the phone, then Elayne said, 'So it was Helen, then?'

'Yes.'

'And you want her to stay with us for a few days?'

'Yes.'

Another pause.

'Are you sure that's the best thing to do?'

'Pretty much. She's exhausted. She's been on the run since the murder. I don't know the details of how she ended up here yet, but she's identified Foster, and she's scared. I've got her to trust me, love. And that feels like a big thing for her. I don't want to put her back in the system where she doesn't know who she can trust. Besides, I'd have to drive her over to the mainland to do that. That all seems like a lot of unnecessary work if she could just stay here.'

'Yes, I can see that.'

'But only if you're okay with it.'

'Of course, I am. I'll make up the spare bed. Do you want to cancel this evening?'

Friday nights were usually when the local weekly Ceilidh was held in Elgol, the next township along the tiny, twisting road that ran through Torrin. It was a chance for the community to get together and unwind, and to catch up on the latest news. The inhabitants living in Torrin took it in turns to drive Bill's mini-bus to the event and it was Katriona's turn tonight.

'No, I don't think so. I just won't be home in time to drive the bus. Wondered if you'd do it, tonight.'

'No problem.'

'I'll bring Helen along with me later, in the car. That way we can leave early, too. For the time being, she's just my niece turned up unexpectedly.'

'Fine. I'll feed that into the group when I get there.'

Those who knew Katriona and Elayne only a little would accept the information at face value. The friends who knew them well would read the scenario accurately enough to offer their own protection to Helen, if needed.

'Yeah. That'll help. See you later then.'

Katriona returned to the living room where McTavish and Helen were still busy chatting.

'Right, here's what I think we should do.'

The other two looked at her, expectantly.

'Constable, you don't need to know the details. Suffice it to say that Helen has witnessed a serious crime and now needs protection.'

The constable's face registered a flash of surprise but he covered it quickly.

'My suggestion is that she stays at my house for the next few days while I contact some people on the mainland. As far as the rest of the island is concerned, she's my niece – just visiting for a while.'

McTavish nodded.

'Is that okay with you, Helen?'

'Yes. I – I hadn't thought what I would do. That's very kind.'

'Well, that's only a part of it. If you were still back in … where you live, you'd have to be placed in a safe house. Here is as safe as anywhere there.'

'I suppose it is.'

It was clear Helen couldn't believe her luck. *Well*, thought Katriona, *that makes two of us.*

As they drove the seven miles back to Katriona's home, she persuaded Helen to tell her how she'd managed to get to Skye. Katriona was intrigued to know whether it had been a definite choice to make her way here or whether the destination had 'materialised' as she'd travelled. She was fascinated to hear how Helen had got out of London without being seen.

'What a clever idea.'

'Well, I'm not sure I can really take any credit for that. I never would've thought of it, it hadn't been for … for my friend.' Helen had been very careful not to reveal her friend's name. She obviously didn't want to land him in any trouble after he'd been so helpful.

When she went on to explain about the complexities of the train journey, Katriona understood why the girl was so tired.

'Look, you can take a shower when we get in, and perk yourself up a bit, but I'm going to take you out somewhere this evening before I let you sleep.'

Helen was puzzled, as well as reluctant. Katriona tried to explain.

'I want people to see your face. Don't worry – they won't know who you are. Your disguise is pretty effective and no-one here is going to be expecting to see Helen Clarke from London.'

She could see Helen trying hard to be relaxed about this

latest demand on her energy and courage.

'There are people – good friends – on the island who know what I do, and will quickly cotton on you're someone who needs protecting for a few days. I'll introduce you to a few this evening. That will mean you can call on them for help if Elayne and I are not around for any reason.'

'You mean it's not safe even here?'

'I have no reason to suspect it's not, but I'd rather be safe than sorry. Yeah?'

Helen nodded slowly. 'So where is it we're going?'

While Helen was in the shower, Katriona made her second essential phonecall of the evening.

'Hi, Gavin. It's Katriona. Can you ring me back? I've got something I'd like to run past you.'

'Sure.'

He hung up quickly, obviously recognising her coded words. A few minutes later, her phone rang and she heard Gavin's voice.

'Hi. We're on a secure line now. What's up?'

'Gavin, I've got your girl.'

'What?'

'Helen Clarke. She's turned up on the island.'

'Are you sure? It's not just some hoax or other?'

'No. I'm very sure. She's been travelling north since Tuesday. And she's identified Foster.'

Gavin gave a low whistle.

'Did she see him commit the murder, then?'

'No. She thinks it was the other man who was with him. She didn't see that guy's face, but he was carrying a gun. Does that fit with anything your end?'

'Yeah. The Doc thinks Emily might have been hit with the butt of a gun and knocked unconscious before she fell down the stairs.'

'Right. I wasn't sure how to make sense of that bit of her story.'

Katriona was fitting clues together in her head as she

spoke.

'So where is she now?' Gavin asked.

'I've brought her home. Elayne and I will look after her over the weekend – she's exhausted and still very frightened.'

'I'm not surprised.'

'Then I'll drive her to Inverness on Monday to make a formal statement. We can take it from there, but there's no reason why she can't stay up here with us until you've made arrests and so on.'

'Yes, I guess so. It would definitely be nicer for her than being placed in a safe house here.' Gavin paused. 'Probably safer, too.'

'That's what I was thinking.'

'I'll need to tell Fisher, of course, but no-one else needs to have the details. Well, that's a turn-up for the books.'

Katriona could hear the glee in Gavin's voice.

He continued. 'Who would've thought … Do you think we've finally nailed him?'

Katriona had been suppressing her excitement about this possibility for some hours now.

'I'm not holding my breath, but if we can keep Helen safe, there's a pretty good chance.'

Katriona and Helen arrived at the Ceilidh when it was in full swing. The noise of the cheerful music, and the sounds of clapping and dancing feet, could be heard from outside the little village hall. Helen's eyes opened wide as she got out of the car. They'd had to park at the top of the hill and walk down towards the tiny harbour with its single jetty and jumble of nets and lobster pots sitting alongside.

Cars and vans cluttered the grass verges of the single-track road everywhere they looked, and the dark scene was lit by the lights spilling out of the hall.

A bright moon had appeared as the clouds cleared during the evening, revealing a myriad of stars. The soft light was reflected on the calm surface of the water below them, as they walked down the hill. Katriona felt a moment of deep gratitude and awe – as she always did when arriving in Elgol – but tonight it was spiced with an even deeper sense of thankfulness for the support and security this remote place provided.

She noticed Helen was looking out across the sea at the enormous bay that stretched before them.

'What's that?'

Katriona realised that because she knew the scenery so well, she could recognise the vague shapes looming in the dark, and her memory of the landscape in daylight would supply the missing details. Helen wouldn't have that advantage.

She smiled. 'What's what in particular?'

'Over there.' Helen pointed. 'The sky seems to stop.'

She gestured towards a huge black shadow that shot abruptly upwards from the water, obliterating the stars for a substantial area. Adjoined to it were more black shapes, ranging into the distance.

'That is the *Cuillin*.'

Katriona spoke softly, almost with reverence. Helen caught the timbre in her voice and turned sharply.

'The what?'

Katriona thought for a brief moment of putting her DI's hat back on, but heard the keen interest in Helen's voice – a sense of having touched on something special. Hell, she'd let the girl intrude on her privacy thus far; why shouldn't she share something of the beauty and magic of the island, while she was here?

'The *Cuillin* Mountains,' she explained.

'Wow.' Helen turned back to look again. Katriona guessed she was trying to make sense of something she'd never seen before.

'They're … big,' she said slowly.

'Yes, they are.'

There was a shared moment of silence, then Helen asked, 'Do people go up them?'

'Yes. They're quite famous in the climbing world.

They're not necessarily the highest peaks but they can be difficult to maneuver around because the rock is magnetic, so you can't use a compass up there.'

'Really?' Helen was catching the awe of the place, now. 'So you have to trust the mountain.'

The words slipped out unconsciously, and Katriona smiled to herself. *Yes, you're going to fit in well, here.*

15

Helen followed Katriona down the road, towards the village hall. She was overwhelmed by the immensity of the space around her – so, so different from everything she knew. She experienced a strange sense of connection, an unfamiliar feeling of belonging. It had been a long time.

The joyful sounds of an accordion blasted their ears as they opened the door. The place was heaving. Small huddles of islanders sat along the edges of the room, each with their own set of chairs grouped around a small table. The centre of the hall was cleared of any furniture to make space for the dancing which was currently in full flow, pairs of dancers galloping their way around the perimeters of circles whose members stood clapping and cheering. Then everyone paused to perform a setting motif with their own partner and the whole routine started again.

One or two of the dancers were wearing traditional costume, with tartan sashes or sporrans. There were quite a lot of kilts around, but most people were wearing jeans and trainers.

Helen found she was immediately caught up in the energy of it all, her fatigue temporarily forgotten. She saw Katriona wave to someone on the opposite side of the hall. A woman with brown hair and a kind face got up from her table of friends and made her way across the room towards them, weaving between the dancers as she came, and causing much hilarity as one young man tried to grab hold of her and get her to join in.

When she reached them, she gave Katriona a big hug, as if, Helen thought, reassuring her about something. Then she turned and held out her hand towards Helen.

'Hello, Helen. I'm Elayne, Katriona's partner.'

Helen put her hand in Elayne's, expecting a formal handshake, but felt such genuine warmth in the contact that it seemed natural to be drawn into a hug, too. This was a *good* person. She didn't know quite how it'd happened but she'd landed on her feet coming here. She began to feel truly safe for the first time.

She heard Elayne speak quietly in her ear.

'It's lovely that you found your way to us. You're safe now. We'll take good care of you for the next few days.'

Helen felt the tears welling up in her eyes in response to such a welcome. Elayne pulled her head back so she could look Helen in the face. She smiled a beautiful smile.

'You've found a place where crying is allowed,' she said.

Helen blinked in surprise.

'In fact, the ability to cry is almost a prerequisite here.'

Then she grabbed Helen's hand again and started to lead the way back across the hall, the dancers having temporarily dissipated.

Helen caught the look on Katriona's face as they moved away from the door. The elegant, efficient police officer had been replaced for the moment. Katriona held a very private smile, with a look of deep affection in her eyes, as she watched Elayne. *Yes,* Helen thought, *I can see why you love her.*

Once they reached the table where their friends were sitting, Katriona took over the introductions.

'Everyone, this is my niece, Helen. Just freshly arrived on the afternoon ferry. Helen, I'd like you to meet George – ' A man with a thick ginger beard and almost no hair on top of his head stood up. His blue eyes twinkled as he nodded to her.

'– Louise – ' A woman with long black hair and dark eyes.

'Hi, Helen. Nice to meet you.'

'– and Struan.' The man also stood and offered Helen his chair.

'Struan is one of the island's official outdoor guides, so you can ask him anything you'd like to know about the place.'

Helen thought Struan looked just as an outdoor guide should. He was tall, well-muscled and tanned, with fair hair and a keen look in his eyes, like an eagle, watching everything closely.

Katriona was still talking. 'Helen was impressed by the *Cuillin* when we parked up just now. I was telling her a bit about them.'

Struan's eyes underwent a subtle change.

'*Mo chridhe,*' he muttered, almost to himself.

Helen was about to ask him to repeat what he'd said, worried she was supposed to respond, when the band struck up again, and it seemed almost everyone in the room stood up to join in the reconvened dancing.

Struan stuck out his hand with a questioning look on his face.

'Will I know the steps?' Helen had to shout across the noise.

'We'll make it up, if we need to,' and she was swept away in a flurry of swirling movements and fast skipping.

The dance turned out to be some kind of reel where the steps were relatively straightforward. The complication was the continual change of partners and direction. Helen found herself whirled in this direction and that, in constant succession, each new partner identifying themselves briefly before they charged off to the next person and she was picked up by someone new. By the time the dance ended, everyone was out of breath and collapsing in laughter onto nearby chairs.

'Can I get you something to drink?' Struan was back

again.

'Yes, please.' Helen panted. 'I don't suppose …'

'Water? Yes. We have plenty of it.' Struan laughed, and led her back to their table where a large jug of clear fresh water was being passed around the people sitting there. He poured her a glass which she downed quickly. Everyone laughed.

'Your first Ceilidh?' someone asked.

'Yes. It's … amazing.'

Suddenly, a hush fell over the room. The band conferred and fiddled with their instruments, re-tuning where necessary. A man with long dark hair climbed onto the stage. He looked to Helen as if he was not much older than she was. Everyone she'd met so far – aside from during that crazy dance – had been much older.

He wore jeans and a jumper which had intricate patterns knitted into it, in golds and browns. His face had the healthy weathered look so many of the islanders shared, as if he spent his days mostly outside. His eyes, like Louise's, were dark and conveyed to Helen an inner sense of contentment and knowing. He gave the impression of someone with confidence, despite his young age.

And then he opened his mouth and began to sing.

Helen, like everyone else in the room, was captivated. The sounds that emanated from his throat were not just beautiful, they were enchanting. His voice lilted through the song he'd chosen as if caressing every note. There was no loss of focus at any point, no dying away at the ends of lines, or swallowed, unfinished phrases. He sang with his whole being, as if holding something sacred within him which he was gently releasing to the world to be shared and loved.

And he sang in a language Helen had never heard before. A strange, melancholy language, with unfamiliar vowels and far too many consonants. Helen had a sense of him dressing the enticing melody in fine jewels, and even though she didn't understand the words, she found herself being drawn into a magical world of moorlands, cliffs and oceans.

When he finished, there was thunderous applause, and the singer smiled, coming back to the hall from wherever he'd been, thought Helen, who recognised that feeling. She lent across to Elayne.

'What was that?' she whispered, knowing that Elayne would understand what she meant.

'That, my love, was the Gaelic.'

She pronounced the word strangely, with a short 'a' sound, so that at first, Helen didn't recognise what she'd said. She looked at Elayne.

'The what?'

'Scottish Gaelic. It's the island's native language.'

'Oh, how beautiful.' Helen spoke almost in a whisper. *I have to learn this,* she thought. *I have to know this new – this old – way of singing.*

Next to go up on stage was a pair of older men, carrying their beer mugs with them. They began a rowdy song with a repeated chorus which the audience quickly joined in with. It involved clashing their beer mugs together at regular intervals, which some people also participated in, so that Helen feared there would be a serious accident before they got to the end. The song seemed to be about someone called Somerled and his marauding adventures, but Helen couldn't catch all the words.

The men were followed by a group of young girls who performed a recent pop song but after the first verse, they changed up the tempo and added a Scottish jig into the mix. Everyone clapped along with the rhythm, a couple getting up to dance an impromptu routine. It ended with loud cheers and more applause, and then Helen felt her arm being jostled as a plate of hot pies was passed around. Paper plates and napkins quickly followed before there were too many burnt fingers. And the next act got underway.

It was all delightful, Helen thought to herself, feeling as though she'd stepped into some kind of alternate universe. After a few more songs, the general noise and bustle suddenly died down, and a large case was hoisted onto the stage by two men, closely followed by a young girl with long red hair – rather like her own, Helen reflected, sadly.

The girl opened the case and the men pulled out something covered in wrappings which the girl carefully removed. A harp. But not like any kind of harp Helen had ever seen. It was smaller than a classical harp and had no pedals, and the large soundbox was beautifully decorated with painted flowers and celtic knots.

A hush fell over the room as the girl began to play. The music was magical – a delicate haunting melody accompanied by soft chords and intricate musical ornaments. It brought tears to Helen's eyes. She felt as if someone had opened a magic box of fairy music. She longed to get up and sing with the instrument, and when the girl finished playing she was the first to stand and begin the applause.

'Why don't you go up and sing something?' Elayne's voice was suddenly in her ear. It was almost as though she'd read Helen's thoughts.

'Can I do that? I'm not on the bill,' she responded.

'That's not how a Ceilidh works.' Elayne encouraged. 'You just get up and take a turn.'

'Really?' Helen heard the enthusiasm in her own voice, her desperation to get on stage before the harp disappeared.

Elayne grabbed her hand and led her across the floor.

'Fiona,' she called to the girl who was just beginning to cover the harp up again. 'Would you accompany Helen in something?'

The girl turned and smiled with delight. 'I'd love to. What shall we do?'

Helen only knew a few Scottish songs. She picked a ballad that she'd known since childhood. It had been her mother's favourite. She hoped it would be acceptable.

'Oh, I love that,' Fiona responded, and began to tinkle lines of melody out of the harp. 'What key do you want?'

'E minor.' Helen was in her element now.

The girl began an introduction, attuning Helen to how the music would support her voice, checking that the tempo was what Helen wanted. There was an instant rapport between them as the room became expectantly quiet.

As soon as she began to sing, Helen became another person. As she always did. Gone was the timid, unsure teenager – and the terrified, exhausted runaway. She felt the power rising from her belly and stepped into it whole-heartedly, allowing the song to flow on her breath to the waiting audience.

Fiona turned out to be a brilliant accompanist. She kept the harp in check to begin with, providing just enough background to let Helen establish the song and invite the audience in. Then, as Helen's voice filled the hall and she worked her way deep into the song, she let her harp begin to meander – lightly, subtly – weaving patterns around the melody Helen was singing, dancing with the decorations Helen herself was adding in, as if it knew exactly where they were to go. As Helen reached the climax of the song, Fiona let loose a flourishing crescendo of sound, allowing it to die away under the continuing final note from Helen's mouth.

There was a moment of stunned silence. Then the room erupted. Shouting, clapping, cheering. Everyone stood up to applaud the two girls, who had fallen into a tearful embrace, the emotion of the moment overcoming them both. For the first time, in a long time, Helen felt truly happy.

16

Unless there was a really good reason, Gavin tried not to go into work at weekends. He also had a pact with Trish that he never brought work home. Like all senior police officers, he was always falling short of these ideals, but over the last few years he'd found ways to balance home and work better, and learned how to make good compromises.

So when Katriona had rung on Friday evening with the news about Helen, his plans for this weekend needed completely revising.

With no progress in the case, he'd – foolishly – assumed he could have a quiet couple of days and be able to spend plenty of time at home, looking after Trish. But once that phonecall came, everything changed. It was Trish who'd suggested the compromise this time, and given how unwell she was, Gavin really appreciated it.

They'd set up a temporary office for him in the spare bedroom so he could direct operations from there and only go to the station if really necessary. In his heart, Gavin was pretty sure this arrangement would only last for a few hours. He was certain they'd be issuing an arrest warrant and bringing Foster in by the end of the morning, but at least he could show he'd tried.

He'd decided not to ring Fisher until the morning. He knew the Super had been at some big 'do' the previous night and would not be arriving home until the early hours. Gavin felt that nothing was going to change overnight. Helen was safe. Foster was … wherever the Super had sent him, and had no reason to be suspicious, so he chose to make the phonecall once it was daylight and immediate action could be taken.

'Sir, I'm sorry to ring you at home, but we have an important development. Helen Clarke has been found.'

'Yes? Ah, good. So you have her in custody?'

'No, Sir.' The merest flicker of a thought ran through Gavin's brain. *What a strange thing to say.* Then he recollected the Super had probably spoken to Foster about the case before he left. He'd likely got Foster's version at that point.

'No. She's not actually a suspect as yet. Just a witness.'

'Right. So has she provided you with useful information?'

'Yes, Sir.' Gavin took a deep breath. 'She's identified DI Foster as being at the scene.'

'Has she?'

'Yes, Sir. So I'd like to – '

Fisher cut him short. 'So where *do* you have her at present?'

'She's on the Isle of Skye. As I was saying, I think we should – '

'*What* is she doing there?'

Gavin sighed. Conversations with Fisher never seemed to go as planned.

'It seems, once she realised the man she saw was a police officer, she decided to run away. Somehow, she's ended up in Scotland. She's with DI McShannon. You might remember her, Sir. She used to work here, and now lives – '

'Oh, I remember *her*.' Another interruption, and this one with a trace of dislike colouring the comment.

'The DI lives on the island and has arranged for the girl to stay with her over the weekend. Then she'll drive her over to Inverness on Monday morning to make a formal statement. That's the nearest major police station, and the one that Kat – DI McShannon – reports to regularly.'

Damn. He hadn't meant to give away any intimation that he was still friends with her. He continued sharply before the Super could interrupt again.

'I considered that arrangement was at least as safe as bringing the girl back here, and means we don't need to provide a safe house for her – at least for now.' He hoped this last consideration would assuage the Super a little.

'Right. I see. Yes. That's probably a good idea. Well, thank you for keeping me informed, Pearce. We'll pick up the action on Monday, then.'

Gavin was astonished.

'But, Sir – as I said – she's identified Foster. Surely, we should be bringing him in for questioning?'

A stony silence greeted this outburst.

'Must I remind you again, Pearce, that DI Foster is a senior police officer, who is entitled to the proper procedures?'

'And who has been implicated in a murder enquiry.' Gavin was getting angry, now.

'On the unofficial say-so of a young girl, whom none of us has seen.'

From the Super's point of view, Gavin conceded privately, this was true.

Fisher continued. 'No. Once the girl has made a statement, we'll act. We'll get IPCC to come into the station and have DI Foster questioned under caution.'

'Sir, with respect, I need to be in on the interro – ' Gavin quickly corrected himself, '… questioning.'

'That may be possible, Pearce.'

'I'm the investigating officer.' Gavin exploded.

'Yes. And DI Foster is your colleague. This has to be seen to be above board, Pearce.'

'Sir.' Gavin wondered if when he'd calmed down, he would agree.

'Does anyone else know of the girl's whereabouts?'

'No, Sir. We – I thought that was the safest option.

Obviously, I'll need to let the team know she's been found, but none of them has to know exactly where she is at this stage.'

'Good. Let's keep this tidy until Monday. And be very careful what you share with the rest of your team, Pearce. We don't want to compromise the case at all.'

Gavin hung up, miserably. Maybe he'd have the weekend at home after all. He wandered into the kitchen to make coffee, but as soon as he switched the kettle on, his phone rang. Yes, it was work. Tom.

'Hi, Gavin. Can you come in? I think you should see this.'

'Do you ever go home, Tom? Or do you actually sleep at the station?' Gavin joked, trying to lighten his own mood.

'Nah, just don't sleep.'

Gavin laughed.

'Fair enough. Okay. I'll be there in half an hour or so. I'll ring Charlie to come in, too. I have my own news to share.'

The core team – Gavin, Charlie and Tom – sat in a little huddle in Tom's lab, where Tom had brewed up some coffee for them all and Charlie shared out a packet of biscuits he'd picked up on his way to the station. The place was quiet. Most of the forensics team had taken a space for some time off, having worked three days straight, some of them doing nights, too.

Gavin went first. 'Helen Clarke has turned up.'

'Where?' 'When?' The other two were keen for details.

'I can't tell you much at the moment. She's safe, but she's yet to make a formal statement. However, she has told the officer she's with that she saw Foster at the crime scene.'

Charlie's response to this new information was muted, as if he'd expected confirmation of their suspicions to manifest fairly soon. Tom was more outspoken.

'I knew it,' he exploded. 'I knew he was up to something.'

'What makes you say that?' Gavin asked. He'd shared

very little of his own suspicions regarding Foster.

'Oh, just the way he's been fishing around here this week. At least, until he got sent off on that job the other day.'

'You didn't say anything?'

'What could I say? He's perfectly entitled to come down here and see what we're up to. It's just that he doesn't usually bother.'

'Did he ask about anything in particular?'

'No, not really. And yes – ' Tom caught Gavin's eye. 'I was very careful he only conversed with me, and I didn't give away anything significant. Not that we had much of significance then.'

'But you do now by the sound of things.'

'Yes, yes, yes.' Tom's enthusiasm spilled over. He'd been containing himself since they convened. He got up and crossed to a computer screen.

'We got the DNA results this morning.'

'That was fast,' Gavin commented.

'You betcha. I just happen to know someone at the lab who very much wanted to try out that new restaurant on Dene Street and particularly wanted to go with a very charming forensic scientist.'

Despite the seriousness of their meeting, Gavin and Charlie couldn't help chuckling. There was always something very infectious about Tom's manner.

'So, does it give us anything?' Gavin tried to bring everyone back on focus.

'Well, it didn't to begin with. I had the computer running a search for matches first thing. Found nothing in the British database.'

'But … ?' Gavin prompted, sensing something sinister.

'I thought to try in the European database. And got a match in Germany.'

He pulled up an image of a man's face on the screen.

'One, Hans Gravenburg.' The photo showed a man, probably in his thirties, Caucasian, with dark hair and a scruffy, unshaven appearance. His face was rounded, giving the impression of someone slightly overweight but Tom's next information suggested that was unlikely.

'On a hunch, I looked for him on Interpol's 'Wanted list' …' A new set of images appeared. '… where he goes by the name of Max Schroder aka Alexander Schmidt aka Andreas Schneider.'

With each name, Tom clicked on another image, showing the same man in a variety of different scenes and poses, but in all of them wearing what was obviously his trademark leather jacket.

Tom continued. 'He's wanted for smuggling, espionage and murder.' He paused for effect.

'He's believed to be a paid assassin, available for hire, supposedly specialising in working for industrial companies who need a mess clearing up quickly.'

A stunned silence greeted this announcement. Gavin looked from Tom to Charlie, and back to Tom.

'Good God, Tom. Are you sure? You can't have made a mistake?'

He saw the look on Tom's face.

'Forgive me. I know you never make mistakes. But this seems unlikely.'

Tom came back to sit on his stool again.

'I know,' he admitted. 'I thought that, too. So I e-mailed it all to Angela this morning to check through.'

'Good man. I think, in the circumstances, that was the right thing to do.'

'However …' Tom was up again and back to the screen. 'Deborah's come up with something which would indicate it probably is him.'

He clicked into another programme, showing slides of a cast.

'She made this from the wound in the side of Emily's head.'

'Good Lord. That must have taken some patience.'

'Well, she used a new silica-based resin that can be

poured into body tissues and will come away without sticking when it hardens.'

'Doctor Humphrey seemed to think Emily was hit by the butt of a gun,' Gavin said.

'Yes, that's what Deborah found when she lifted the cast.'

The next photo clearly showed the impression made by the end of a pistol handle.

'And not just any gun. It's a Heckler & Koch P2000 SK. See the imprint here …' He pointed to a partial motif which must have been engraved on the gun's grip.

'… and this bit sticking out at the bottom is the backstrap – interchangeable and personalised. That's one of the advantages of this particular pistol. Another is the ambidextrous magazine release and slide lock – essential for a left-handed gunman. The SK is the compact version of the P2000 – Hans Gravenburg's weapon of choice.'

'So what the hell was he doing in Emily Hough's house?'

Gavin was at a loss to make sense of any of this. It just sounded too incredible. He still felt the lovely lady he'd gained an impression of, would not be involved in seriously criminal activities, and if his instincts were right, she must have been an inadvertent victim. But he knew better than to make assumptions. They would continue to follow all possible lines of enquiry until they found something that made sense.

Charlie's phone rang, and he moved away to a corner to answer it, leaving Gavin and Tom to stare at the computer screen.

'I think …' Tom began hesitantly.

'Go on.'

'I think … whatever was on that flashdrive, was really important.'

'We don't even know for sure there was a flashdrive, Tom.'

'No, but it feels right, doesn't it? And you know what? I don't think this was a crime initiated by Foster. I don't think this is his usual 'make a quick buck' stuff. I think he may have got himself caught up in something bigger.'

Gavin frowned. 'Explain a bit.'

'Well, maybe he's just the guy on the ground. Maybe someone – or some organisation, even – needed that flashdrive retrieving.' He caught Gavin's eye. 'Just for the sake of argument.'

'Okay. Go on.'

'Well, they might send their smuggler-cum-hitman to retrieve it. But they'd need someone who knew the lay of the land at this end, wouldn't they? Someone who could cover the details? I don't know…' Tom faded out. 'I haven't thought it through.'

Gavin picked up the thread. 'I can see what you're suggesting, but that implicates Emily in some kind of espionage, and I still don't feel that's right, somehow.'

Charlie interrupted their musings. 'That was Maxwell, Sir. He's got a Derek Hannaford on the phone from Manchester. The man was ringing to speak to DI Foster – to update him.'

'What?'

'He says he spoke to the DI a couple of days ago about his meeting with Emily Hough.'

Gavin nearly exploded with fury. 'Damn being professional. That man gets implicated further in this, every time I draw breath. Can you get Maxwell to put Hannaford through to the landline in here?'

Charlie spoke into his handset again, as Gavin tried to calm himself. As if this enquiry wasn't complicated enough without a corrupt police officer trying to cover his tracks, and with whom he was not allowed to speak.

He crossed to the lab phone and picked it up.

'Mr. Hannaford? This is DI Pearce. I'm the officer in charge of the investigation into Emily Hough's death. I'm afraid there's been a bit of an administrative hiccup at our end.' He spoke through gritted teeth. 'I was unaware you had spoken with DI Foster, so I was hoping you could fill me in on the details. I understand you had a meeting with Miss Hough?'

'Yes. That is, we had a meeting arranged, but Emily never made it. As I told DI Foster, we were due to meet on Wednesday when she was in Manchester. She was supposed to be performing at Bridgewater Hall in the evening, so we'd agreed to meet in the morning before she went on to the theatre.'

'And what was the meeting about?'

'I don't know.'

'I'm sorry?'

'Well, I presumed she had some kind of story for me. It certainly wasn't an interview.'

'I'm afraid I'm not following, sir. Why would she have a story for you?' As the words left his mouth, he realised he must be talking to a reporter.

'Sorry. Of course. You didn't receive the information about me, did you? I'm the editor of the *Manchester Independent.* Emily and her sister had specifically asked me to meet up with Emily. The newspaper has something of a reputation for breaking significant stories that the London papers won't touch, and Heather – that's Emily's sister – '

'Yes, I know. We've been trying to get hold of her.'

'Oh, isn't she in Geneva?'

'I – What makes you think she'd be there?'

'I understood she was visiting the World Health Organisation.'

Gavin gulped. This was more information than they'd uncovered in days.

'So you have quite a bit to do with Heather, then?'

'Well, yes. She often sends me stuff from overseas to look at. I did tell all this to DI Foster.'

Gavin felt his anger rising again.

'But she didn't tell you what this meeting was about?'

'No. And to ask for a meeting was quite unusual, anyway. She mostly sent me copy – either by e-mail or post, depending … Anyway, I was just ringing to tell DI Foster

I've received a package this morning from Emily.'

Gavin nearly choked. Hi didn't know what to ask first.

'What? How is that – ? Have you opened it?'

'You sound surprised, Inspector. And yes, I have opened it, since it was addressed to me. It contains a flashdrive.'

17

Helen was having the best Saturday she'd had in a long time. Now that the stress of trying to get away from London was over, and her anxieties had been resolved about whether, and how, she should report the murder, she had found herself relaxing into this strange, wonderful place where she'd ended up.

She really liked Katriona and Elayne, though she was a bit scared of Katriona when she was in official mode. She thought their home was beautiful and was suitably impressed when Katriona told her that Elayne had designed it. Although the surrounding landscape seemed very alien to her – so much open space – she could see how the house had been built to maximize the views which the two women seemed to value so much, and felt it 'snuggled' into the landscape just as it should.

Here, she began to realise, was another way of life she'd not encountered before. If nothing else, this ghastly adventure had given her an education. She felt that Katriona and Elayne had incorporated the best bits of a working life with the best bits of Petey's non-working life, but without the boat. They obviously both focused hard on what they did but they didn't seem to be frenetic like most of the working people she knew.

And they seemed to be happy with life. Most of the

people she met day-to-day did very little other than complain when they spoke. These two had that air about them that Petey had – a kind of inner gentleness, a peaceful connection with their surroundings. She decided it must have something to do with living so close to nature. She thought, if she could stay a while, she might try to find out more.

Her bedroom was at the back of the house. It was a small room but one wall had a large window which looked out across the moors towards the Red Hills. She'd found it very eerie waking up to see two enormous mountains staring down at her. She hadn't realised the curtains were still open when she went to bed. It had been so dark outside. She was used to streetlights.

She was also used to noise – people, cars, music. Here, she discovered, when a car passed through the village, you noticed it. For one thing, you could hear it crossing the cattlegrid just up the road from the house.

She'd lain in bed for a while, gazing at the shadows of the clouds scuttering across the mountainsides. The sun was shining intermittently, lighting up the reds and greens of the slopes in fascinating shades, creating an ever-changing scene for her to view. Yes, she began to get it – this contentment that emanated from musing on the landscape. She felt she could happily lie for hours just watching it shift from one set of colours to another.

Eventually, when she'd realised that the voices she could hear were coming from the kitchen, she'd got up and wandered down. Her bedroom was raised just above the level of the ground floor and there was a short flight of stairs connecting it to the utilities room behind the kitchen. Elayne had explained it was what was known as 'one and a half storeys', according to island building regulations, where a limited number of small rooms could be incorporated into the roof space of a house. This restricted the height of new builds so that they didn't intrude on the landscape and were in keeping with the traditional croft houses of the island.

She'd found Katriona and Elayne sitting at the kitchen

table, eating breakfast.

'What can I get you?' Elayne had asked when she appeared. 'Tea? Coffee? Orange juice?'

Helen had found their warm hospitality almost overwhelming. They seemed to have no problem with allowing her to share their home for the next few days, and treated her just as if she were a well-known friend.

Over breakfast, they'd shared their plans for the day.

'You can do as much or as little as you want,' Katriona had said. 'I'm guessing you're quite tired, so take the opportunity to rest up as much as you need to. There'll be people dropping in during the day and you're welcome to stay and chat, or just do your own thing.'

In the end, they'd spent a leisurely morning, mostly chatting over food in the kitchen. A number of visitors had called in to share breakfast or 'elevenses'. These included some of the people she'd met last night.

She recognised George, who stopped by briefly to drop off some vegetables. Apparently, he had an organic small-holding and regularly ran a delivery route on a Saturday to local inhabitants. He brought a young boy with him who shared his ginger hair but this time on the top of his head. Helen had to suppress a giggle at the sight of two almost identical faces but in 'reverse', like a pair of children's toys.

A couple called Sean and Alison popped in at one point, accompanied by two collie dogs, who were warmly greeted by Molly and Alice. All four went out to romp in the garden. Helen had seen the couple at the Ceilidh but had not had a chance to speak to them. Katriona introduced her.

'Sean and Alison have the croft just over the road, so if we're not around for any reason, you can pop over for help, if you need it.'

Sean had given her a warm smile. Helen took to him immediately.

'What do you do on your croft?' she'd asked tentatively.

'Oh, this and that,' he'd responded. 'Mostly, we have a couple of caravans to rent out and a hostel for student field trips.'

'Mostly, you play on your tractor, you mean.' Alison had butted in.

Sean glanced at her, affectionately. 'Yeah, that too.'

They both seemed very laid back and relaxed, as if life didn't present too many big problems for them.

'You must come over and take a look while you're here,' Sean invited. 'Come and meet Betty.'

'Betty?'

'Betty the pig.' Sean grinned. Helen hadn't been quite sure whether he was serious or not. A later check-in with Elayne had confirmed that Betty was indeed a pig and was Sean's pride and joy.

Helen had expressed her desire to see something of the island while she was here.

'I'm sure we can sort out a few sight-seeing trips,' Katriona reassured her.

'No, not just sight-seeing,' Helen mused. 'I'd like to see the island properly – to connect with it.' She turned to Elayne. 'Does that make sense?'

'Absolutely.' Elayne's response was predictably warm and positive. 'I understand completely. You'll be needing some walking boots, then.' And she disappeared into the utilities room to rummage through the cupboard.

While she was out of the room, Katriona said, 'I shan't be around tomorrow. I'm speaking at a rookies' conference in Fort William – about the joys of being a detective.'

'Fort William? That's miles from here.'

'Everything's miles from here,' Katriona laughed. 'But Elayne will make sure you're well taken care of while I'm away.'

'Will you be back in time to drive me to Inverness?'

'Oh yes. I'll be back tomorrow evening. Don't worry. I'm used to travelling the long distances. I just make sure I space them out so I'm not doing it all the time.'

'I'm so sorry.'

'What do you mean?'

'I'm sorry that I'm the cause of you having to do an extra journey.'

Katriona smiled. For all Helen's bravery in facing what she'd done during the last few days, Katriona recognised a huge lack of confidence in her which quickly surfaced when she thought she'd inconvenienced or offended someone.

'It's really not a problem. I'm my own boss, so I can cancel my scheduled trip to Inverness later in the week.'

Helen smiled unsurely in response, and then found herself required to try out thick woolly socks in readiness for the variety of boots which Elayne had managed to find.

After lunch, suitably dressed, the three women accompanied by the two dogs set off for an afternoon walk during a pause in the visitors' schedule. Katriona and Elayne were keen to show off the view across the loch and for Helen to get a closer look at *Blà Bheinn.* When they rounded the bend in the lane and the loch came into sight, Helen reacted in surprise.

'I had no idea that was here.'

'Even though we drove past it last night?' Katriona teased.

'I think I was a bit too 'out-of-it' to notice much from the car,' Helen said. 'And it was very dark.'

'I suppose it was for you. I guess I've got used to that, now.'

They stopped by the old village school, now a field studies centre, to gaze across the blue water, past the sheep grazing along the shore line, to where the mountain towered above the scene in majestic grandeur.

'It looks so close. Would it take long to walk round the head of the loch to see more?' Helen asked.

'Yeah. It's way further than it looks. And actually you can't see much of the mountain from that side. Not at ground level, anyway.'

'Oh.' Helen was disappointed.

'Are you interested in going up there?' A voice spoke

over her shoulder. Helen turned and recognised Struan standing behind her. She guessed the truck parked just along the road was his.

'I don't know,' she answered, the hesitation sounding in her voice. 'I'm not sure I could manage it.'

'It's not too difficult if you're fairly fit.' Struan smiled. 'I'd be happy to take you up.'

'Really?' Helen wasn't sure whether this was a fantastic offer or a terrifying prospect. Probably both.

'The weather's supposed to be okay tomorrow. And I'm not busy. Near the end of the season now. We could take the whole day. Go slowly, so we're walking at your pace. We only need go as far as you want.'

Helen turned to Katriona and Elayne, as if asking their permission.

'I think you should do it,' Elayne encouraged. 'Struan is a fantastic guide, and he really won't push you beyond what you can do.'

She still hesitated.

'You might not get another chance like this, and it'd be a shame to go back to London regretting it.'

Something in Elayne's words hit Helen like a punch to the stomach. It wasn't just the reminder of what she'd temporarily left behind. Helen sensed an idea forming at the edge of her consciousness. Yes, she missed her old life before everything had erupted but she was aware that her desperate longing to return to that, had somehow dissipated over the last twenty-four hours – as if there was something here that was more important. Something she needed to find out about. It didn't make a lot of sense to her but that word 'regret' was definitely key.

She turned back to Struan. 'Then I think I should take the plunge.' She exhaled deeply. Everybody laughed.

'Don't worry,' Katriona said. 'You'll be safe. I promise Struan will bring you back in one piece.'

Helen tried to join in the laughter and keep her apprehension to herself, as they turned off the road and headed over the moors to try out her boots some more.

A couple of hours later, as the house came into sight again, Helen found she was pleasantly tired and more than ready to sit down with the cup of tea proposed by Elayne when they turned for home. She was unprepared for the delightful ritual of teapot, cups, saucers and cakestand which appeared a few minutes after she was instructed to wait in the conservatory. She was used to mugs, and biscuits grabbed from a packet.

'Do you do this every day?' she asked in amazement.

'Whenever we can, yes.' Elayne placed the tray on the low table. 'It's a kind of promise to ourselves – a reminder of the important things in life.'

Helen reflected on how different Elayne's values were from those she met in her usual day. Afternoon tea where she worked was about getting something inside you as fast as possible so you could get on with the next thing. Little time to enjoy the food, let alone relish it. She decided she would try out 'relishing' while she had the chance and helped herself to a piece of chocolate sponge filled with fresh cream and raspberry jam. 'Relishing' turned out not to be too difficult.

'Hello.' A voice called through from the kitchen.

'Hi, Jamie,' Elayne responded. 'Come on through. We're in the conservatory.'

A face Helen remembered from last night appeared in the doorway. It was the boy who'd sung that haunting song in Gaelic.

'I was hoping I'd make it in time for tea,' he grinned. 'Hi, Helen. How're you enjoying the island?'

And there it was again. That difference in perspective. No 'how are you?' spoken automatically, without any interest in the answer. This was a real question expecting a response. And there was that proud passion for the land, again, as well. As if the people who lived here had a deep sense not simply of belonging to the place, but of being cared for by it. She wondered if she was being fanciful. Then decided if she was, it must be the island's influence - which meant she wasn't.

She suddenly realised Jamie was still waiting for an answer. She looked up into his fabulous dark eyes.

'I'm absolutely loving it.'

The words came out unexpectedly. She hadn't noticed the depth of emotion the place was evoking, and her words took her by surprise. Not as much surprise, however, as the instant connection she experienced with Jamie. It was as if a lightening bolt had suddenly shot between them.

'Oh!' She almost jumped physically. Jamie held her gaze, his eyes crinkling round the edges, his already large pupils widening further. She wondered if he had felt it, too. She had an urge to look away, embarrassed, but realised that was what the old Helen would have done. Here was an opportunity to do things differently. So she smiled warmly at him, and was rewarded by a generous smile in return.

'It's lovely to see you again,' she ventured. 'I wanted to tell you how very much I enjoyed your song last night.'

'Thank you.' Jamie expressed a genuine pleasure at receiving the compliment but, unlike many of the boys she knew, there was a humility in the acceptance. Here was someone who knew his talent but didn't need to brag about it. Helen felt a strong desire to draw him into conversation, to find out more about him.

'The language you sang in - Elayne said it was Gaelic, I think?'

'That's right. The native language of the island.'

'Does that mean – do people still speak it?' She was trying so hard to be confident but the question sounded stupid as she heard it. She started an attempt to cover her clumsiness. 'I mean … of course, they must speak it, if you were singing it … I meant …'

'I grew up in a Gaelic household, yes.' Jamie's ease of manner, and matter-of-factness about it, smoothed the conversation along. 'There aren't so many Gaelic-speakers here now as there were, say, fifty years ago, but there are plenty more than twenty years ago.'

'Oh,' Helen was surprised. 'Why's that?'

'Well, for one thing, it's taught in school, now.' Jamie reached for a slice of cake to accompany the cup of tea Elayne had poured for him. 'And for another, we have the biggest Gaelic college in Europe based here.'

'What – here on the island?'

'Yep, did you not know that?' He took a bite of the chocolate cake, licking the cream from round his lips. 'Elayne, this is delicious.'

'Can't take any credit, Jamie. It's one of Linda's finest.' She caught Helen's eye. 'From the Blue Shed Café. We walked past it on the way down to the loch.'

'Oh yes.' Helen was beginning to get a real sense of the community spirit that made this remote place work. Everyone seemed to know everyone else. She turned back to Jamie. 'So tell me about this college. Do they just teach the language, like a night school kind-of-thing?'

'No, it's way more than that. People come here from all over the world. They do courses on the culture – poetry, history … I'm studying music, there.'

Something caught in Helen's throat. She felt tingles running through her, as if she'd touched on something very significant.

'Do you mean, full-time?'

'Yeah. I specialise in voice for my instrument, but there are others learning harp and flute.'

'Oh, how very lovely.'

She wasn't sure at what point Elayne and Katriona left the room. She only knew that a magical new world was opening up in front of her, and she wanted to be part of it. She gradually became aware that she and Jamie must have been talking for hours, lost in their own excited huddle of discoveries.

By the time Elayne called them through for supper, a magnificent smell of roast vegetables emanating from the kitchen, Helen had been invited to a concert to be given by the third year students at the college on Monday evening, and Jamie had been invited to join the walk up *Blà Bheinn* the next day.

18

In contrast to Helen's laid-back and lazy Saturday, Gavin's day was getting more and more intense. After Derek Hannaford's astonishing phonecall, he'd arranged to have the flashdrive couriered down to London and was now anxiously awaiting its arrival. He still had no idea what it contained as Derek had explained he'd been unable to open it.

'I think it's got some kind of encrypted password on it, but I'm no expert in these things.'

When Gavin had shared this information, Tom's eyes had lit up.

'I'm guessing this is a job for you, then,' he'd suggested.

'Can't wait.' Tom spoke over his shoulder as he rushed across the room to 'warm up' his computer for de-coding activities.

Charlie, too, had disappeared not long after the phonecall, saying he wanted to 'check on something. Just an idea.'

While he was waiting for everyone to get back to him, Gavin had contacted Maxwell on the switchboard to set him on a new trail tracking Heather Hough. They'd decided the first move was to discover whether there was any kind of event or conference at the WHO headquarters currently, and then, depending on what they found, for Maxwell to attempt to ascertain whether Heather had visited – or was even still there, though that seemed unlikely.

With his team all busy following their own leads, he'd had time to go and sit in his office for a while and ponder over the morning's discoveries. Tom's ideas did make some sense, though it all seemed a bit extreme. He remained convinced that both Emily and Foster were unlikely characters to be executing international mega-crime but the evidence was pointing towards this possibility. In a way, he preferred to think they had unintentionally got caught up in something bigger, rather than being major players.

In another way, he didn't want that to be true either. He'd been ready to handle a straight-forward burglary that had ended badly. He'd even been pleased that he might, finally, have evidence of foul-play that would remove Foster from his job. The man should not still be able to work as a detective when everyone knew how corrupt he was.

But this – this all indicated something much bigger, something that these two had only been on the fringes of. He was sure Foster didn't have either the intelligence or the balls to get involved in organising something as sinister as this was turning into. He decided to go back to Tuesday night and review all the evidence again, see if there was something he'd missed.

It was late afternoon when the courier package arrived and the team met up again in Tom's lab. Maxwell had brought the carefully-sealed parcel down from reception, and Tom had begun the steady procedure of opening and unwrapping all the layers, placing each one in a plastic bag, until he revealed the padded envelope, with a handwritten address on the outside and a single flashdrive inside.

A small note accompanied it. *For our meeting on Wednesday. Emily.* It was beautifully written – as Gavin had expected from what he'd already seen of Emily's diaries and notebooks – and the paper was expensive enough to count as parchment.

Tom put each item into its own evidence bag so that the pieces could be passed around for inspection.

'Well, it's definitely from Emily.' Gavin felt he was stating the obvious, but that also seemed like a secure place to start. 'And it's post-marked Battersea, so it was sent from here, but the date ...' He held it under a lamp. 'The date is yesterday. It was sent first-class. That doesn't make sense.'

'Sir,' Charlie interrupted. 'I think I can offer an explanation.'

'Please do.' Gavin felt explanations were currently in short supply so he would be grateful for anything that put two and two together sensibly.

'On a hunch, I've just been to visit Annie Thomas – Emily Hough's neighbour. She was the lady who found the body, you remember.'

Gavin nodded, wondering where this was leading.

'She was pretty upset to think she might have compromised our investigation, but I was able to reassure her that she may actually have done the right thing.'

'What do you mean?'

'Well, it turns out she posted the envelope yesterday.'

'What? What was she doing with it?'

'She told me she found it in her shopping bag yesterday morning. She doesn't remember clearly but she thinks she might have picked it up by accident on the day of the murder.'

'What do you mean 'picked it up by accident'?'

'It seems she was in the habit of posting items for Miss Hough, particularly when she was touring and very busy. Miss Hough would leave the post on the stand in the hallway and when Annie went in to check on things for her, she would pick up anything that needed posting. It had been a long-standing arrangement.

'With everything that happened on Tuesday, she wonders whether maybe she picked up the envelope automatically, without registering she'd done it, when she found the body. She definitely had her shopping bag with her that day, she says, but hadn't used it since. Until yesterday – when she found the envelope in it.'

'And she didn't think to contact us?' Gavin exploded.

'She says she wasn't sure what to do. I don't think it crossed her mind that it might be evidence, until I called to see her today. She was just worried it might be something important to Miss Hough and decided she should post it.'

'Good God. Does she realise how much she's compromised the investigation?'

'Well, forgive me, sir, but actually, I think she may have saved it.'

Gavin looked at Charlie in astonishment. 'Saved it? What are you talking about?'

Charlie hesitated. 'May I bring Maxwell in on 'Circumspect', Sir?'

'What?' This was not what Gavin had expected him to say.

''Circumspect'. I believe this impacts on that aspect of the investigation.'

'Okay.' Gavin spoke slowly. 'I think I'm beginning to understand. Do you consider Maxwell can be cleared for this?' He turned to look at the young officer, who cleared his throat and spoke for himself.

'Sir. I believe I know what the Sarge is referring to.'

'You do?'

'Yes, Sir. Piecing together the aspects of this investigation that I've been involved with, I understand there may be some suspicion regarding the involvement of DI Foster.'

Gavin let out a breath. 'And what makes you consider DI Foster may be involved?'

'A number of things, Sir, but mostly his particular interest in the progress of this case when … well, it's not his case, sir.'

It seemed either Maxwell was as bright as Gavin had guessed, or they'd not been careful enough as a team in keeping their suspicions to themselves. He hoped the former.

'Right. Okay.' He turned back to Charlie. 'Are you suggesting that if Annie Thomas hadn't picked up the envelope when she did …'

'… that we would have brought it here as evidence,' Charlie continued for him. 'And that would have made it possible for DI Foster to – '

Tom interrupted him. 'So that's what he was fishing around for. In case we'd found what he was looking for.'

Gavin recalled the one-sided phone conversation he'd overheard from outside Foster's office. The one about the decoy. Foster must have picked up the wrong flashdrive.

'When all the time he was searching the house, it had been right under his nose,' Charlie finished, allowing a slight smile to show on his face, as he looked across at Gavin.

Suddenly, Gavin saw the irony in the situation and roared with laughter, letting out all of the frustration of the last few days.

'Well, I'm glad you were able to reassure Annie she had been most helpful with the case.'

For the next hour or so, Tom worked on the flashdrive, trying to figure out the password to open it, while the other three shared further updates on their individual lines of enquiry.

Disappointingly, Maxwell had found out there had been a conference in progress at WHO headquarters all week, that Heather Hough had been due to attend but she had not shown up.

'She was actually supposed to be giving a short talk as part of the programme,' he reported.

'Really? What was the topic?' Gavin asked.

'Well, the conference was about handling epidemics …'

'Oh, she'd been doing some research in that area, hadn't she?' Gavin remembered his conversation with Herr Brandt.

'That's right, Sir. There was no detailed information on what she was going to talk about but she'd given them a title:

The Cuban Experience.'

'So what happened? Why didn't she make it?'

'I couldn't find that out, Sir. No-one I spoke to knew. She doesn't appear to have sent apologies, or cancelled the date. She just didn't appear.'

'When was the last time someone there spoke to her? Do we know?'

'I got hold of the conference secretary – eventually.' Maxwell rummaged through his notebook. 'Madeleine Wright. She told me Heather had approached her about speaking to the conference a few months ago. Which was unusual, sir. The normal routine is for speakers to be invited. But Madeleine and Heather go way back, apparently. They were at school together. So Madeleine was willing to listen to what Heather's interest was.'

'Which was … ?'

'Well, it seems that Heather wasn't very forthcoming. She kept telling Madeleine that the fewer details she shared in advance, the better. Madeleine had pressed her on this, obviously, but Heather had said something about concern for people's safety.'

Gavin was puzzled. 'Did she explain what she meant?'

'Not entirely. The most Heather would tell her was that she had some ground-breaking research to share, and begged Madeleine to give her a platform.'

'Which Madeleine agreed to, presumably?'

'Like I said, Sir, they'd been friends for years, and Madeleine told me she trusted Heather enough to consider this was a worthwhile enterprise. She'd engineered a twenty-minute slot for her but it was too late to advertise it in the main programme. That had already been printed and circulated. She said that Heather was quite happy about that. Something about not wanting the publicity in advance since there would be plenty of it after she'd spoken.'

Gavin got that sensation again – of being just on the edge of something sinister. Was Heather involved in all this, somehow? He shared his thoughts.

'Do we think this could have something to do with the case?'

Charlie spoke first. 'It does seem possible, Sir. I mean, if Heather had stumbled across something during her research, maybe …'

Maxwell joined in. 'Madeleine said she definitely got the impression Heather had something very exciting to share. She thought, at the time, that Heather just didn't want to lose the possibility of a coup. I mean, she'd won awards in the past for her reporting. But when she didn't contact her as arranged a few days before the conference, Madeleine began to have concerns. She alerted the police over there when Heather didn't show up, but there was no reason for them to launch any kind of investigation, particularly.'

'Well, there bloody well is now,' Gavin said. 'As soon as we're done here, Maxwell, I want you to track down who Madeleine reported this to and get them on the phone.'

'Yes, Sir.'

'Right, Charlie, where are we up to on Emily's movements over the last month?' This was an aspect of the investigation which Charlie had been quietly pursuing since Wednesday.

'She's mostly been in Europe, touring. Concerts in France, Germany and Belgium.'

'Do we have the schedule?'

Charlie handed over a printed sheet with a set of performance dates stretching back over the last four weeks.

'So it's perfectly possible that Emily and Heather met up while Emily was in Europe?' Gavin surmised.

'Absolutely, Sir. We know they had a shared house in Dusseldorf. Emily was performing there, at the Tonhalle, on September the twenty-ninth and thirtieth.

'I got hold of the housekeeper and she confirmed she was asked to prepare the house for Emily to stay there from the twenty-eighth through to the third of October. She says she went in on the first to do a bit of tidying round – at Emily's request – but there was no-one in when she called.

Obviously she has her own key.'

'Did she get any sense that both sisters might be staying there?'

'Well, Sir. She says she did see some of Heather's things around but that wasn't unusual. It didn't necessarily mean that Heather was actually there. What are you thinking, Sir?'

'I don't really know. I'm just wondering if Heather gave Emily something to bring back here, to England. Something that needed a bit of surreptitious maneuvering. Like the flashdrive.'

'Perhaps – ' Maxwell jumped into the conversation. 'Perhaps, Heather had stumbled across something, and she knew Derek Hannaford would be happy to print it, but maybe someone else was trying to stop that from happening. Giving it to her sister would be pretty good cover.' His enthusiasm overflowed and he almost bounced off his seat. 'Sir,' he added, trying to backtrack into a suitably inferior role.

'That's okay, Maxwell. Because that's what I was wondering, too. But unless we can find out what's on the flashdrive, this is all speculation.' He glanced behind him to where Tom was still furiously working at his computer.

'I heard that,' Tom muttered.

'Well, how's it going?' Gavin asked.

'It's not.' Tom slapped his hands onto his thighs and stood up. 'Whoever set up this encryption knew what they were doing. All the usual protocols are just not cracking the code. It's going to take some time - or some more clues.'

At that moment, Tom's phone rang and he turned away to answer it. Gavin continued his conversation with the other two.

'Something really isn't right about all this,' he said. 'I mean, if Heather had got something sensational enough for someone else to kill for, I can't imagine she'd deliberately put her sister at risk.'

'Perhaps they didn't realise that whatever they'd got was that important – or dangerous. Not until Emily was killed, anyway,' Charlie offered.

'Yes, that's possible. It would help if we could work out exactly when Heather disappeared. Was it before or after Emily's death? I mean, if she vanished after Emily was killed, maybe she went into hiding because of what happened to her sister. Tom? What is it?'

Gavin turned towards the forensic scientist as he crossed the lab to join them. He'd just hung up his phone.

'That was Angela.' He paused. 'She's confirmed my findings. The DNA has a 90% probability of belonging to Hans Gravenburg.'

Gavin whistled. Then pulled out his own phone. He'd not been mistaken in his feelings about the case. This was definitely sinister.

'I'll just contact … Helen's bodyguard.' He was careful not to give away any clues as to her whereabouts. 'Let them know how serious this is getting.' He started to move towards the door to make sure of privacy.

'You mean you've found her, Sir?' Maxwell asked.

'Yes. Of course, you weren't here this morning. Yes, she's turned up, but her venue is being kept secret for the time being.'

'Can I let Ms Hutchinson know she's been found, then?'

Gavin stopped in his tracks. Why hadn't he thought of that? Maxwell was definitely turning out to be one of the good guys.

'Thanks, Maxwell. Yes, that's a good idea. And yes, you can tell her that Helen's fine.'

Gavin used the secure line as usual to contact Katriona.

'Everything going okay up there?'

'Yes, it's all fine. Now that she's had a good sleep, she seems to be enjoying herself.'

'That's good.' Gavin tried to sound reassuring but Katriona caught the concern in his voice.

'What's up, Gavin?'

'Tom's got the DNA results back.'

'Gosh, that was fast.'

'Yes, well, I think a certain amount of friendly persuasion went into it, including some of the wine and roses variety.'

'Good on Tom.' Gavin remembered Katriona had always had a soft spot for Tom. 'So what have you found?'

He took a deep breath.

'Katriona, there's more than a 90% probability that it belongs to a German assassin called Hans Gravenburg. And yes, Angela's checked the data.'

There was a resounding silence down the phone. Then – 'Bloody hell, Gavin. What's this all about?'

'That's what we're trying to figure out. But in the meantime, I want you to be *very* careful.'

'What d'you mean?'

'Well, this guy has several aliases and it's thought he's available for hire by big concerns like industrial companies and so on. So … I don't know. Just be on the look-out.'

'What? You can't think he's going to turn up here? No-one knows Helen's here, for goodness' sake.'

'No. I suppose. But I just thought I'd warn you.'

'Okay. I mean, I appreciate that.' Katriona sounded as if she were soothing a well-meaning child. 'But really, Gavin, I can't believe we have any reason to worry.'

19

Elayne was enjoying having the house to herself. Katriona had set off very early for Fort William and she didn't expect her home until the evening. Struan had called for Helen just before nine o'clock as the last remnants of pre-morning darkness had drifted off down the valley, and, as predicted, the sun had started to break through, promising a classic 'clear-Skye' day. Jamie was already in the car, and she'd waved the three of them off, complete with rucksacks, sandwiches and flasks, before turning back indoors with the dogs at her heels to a second cup of coffee and a bagel or two.

It was around midday, when she had taken a pause from sketching and planning to make a light lunch in the kitchen, that she caught sight of a movement by the back door. Since no-one knocked or shouted through, she was immediately on the alert. Regular visitors announced their presence, even if they let themselves in.

She moved around the table cautiously, trying to get a glimpse of whoever it might be without being seen herself. The sleeve of a leather jacket was pushed up against the corner of the window. Someone was outside, listening.

Very quietly, she bent over to whisper to the dogs, who had joined her in the kitchen, hoping for crumbs. She opened one of the cupboard doors, revealing a dog-flap out into the garden. It opened onto the side of the house away from the back door. The dogs always thought it was a great game to play, being allowed through their own secret tunnel. Elayne prayed they would understand the urgency of the game today.

She took Molly's face in her hands and looked into her eyes.

'Find Sean,' she whispered. 'Now. Find Sean.' She pointed to the flap and the two dogs disappeared through it, just as the back door was kicked open.

The leather jacket clothed a short, balding man who radiated aggression through every aspect of his physical presence. Elayne experienced a chill of terror as the man's wild eyes quickly scanned the kitchen and came to rest on her. He was holding a gun.

'Where is she?'

For a brief moment, Elayne was that small five-year-old girl all over again. She felt a sob catch in her throat that tried to become a scream and was stifled by some invisible hand. She began to shake violently and a warm trickle of urine ran down her leg.

'Where *is* she?' the man asked again.

Trying desperately to summon something even akin to courage, Elayne opened her mouth, but no coherent words would emerge. Just a strange strangled sound. The fear circulating her body was so ferocious, she realised she was about to pass out and tried to grab hold of the edge of the table.

The man must have mistaken the move for a gesture of resistance. He crossed the room at speed and slapped her hard across the face.

'Bitch.'

She reeled from the impact, only just catching herself from falling. She expected another blow to follow and instinctively kept her head down. She knew how this went.

But the man waited. Elayne found the anticipation of the next strike was more intimidating than the actual impact would have been.

He spoke again. 'For the last time, bitch, where is she?'

Elayne was still unable to speak but the forced stumble she'd just experienced had freed her body from shock just enough for her to remain on her feet. She sensed the man coming towards her again, accompanied by her own terrifying memories.

Then, as she braced herself for a second blow, something utterly incredible happened. From somewhere deep, deep inside, a raging inferno erupted, rushing upwards from her belly, racing through her chest and exploding into her throat. All she had to do was open her mouth to release the anger and fear that she'd always been unable to express when she had been so little and so vulnerable.

She turned to face him, letting rip an extraordinary stream of inarticulate, primal noises, moving just close enough for him to hit her again so that she was pushed backwards towards the sink. As she fell against the draining board, she reached out and grabbed a knife – a large chef's knife with a pristinely sharp edge - then allowed herself to sink to the floor, apparently whimpering in a closed huddle, in order to hide the blade.

She saw the man's black boots walk round the corner of the table and judging her timing to perfection, she plunged the blade deep into the unprotected flesh of his left calf. He howled in pain, as blood began to seep to the surface and stain his trousers.

'Fuck. You bitch. Fuck,' he shouted in her direction, and started to move away – Elayne guessed to pick up his gun which had dropped out of his hand and skittered across the floor when she stabbed him.

She hooked into the stream of anger now towering inside her, and not letting go of the knife's handle, swung her other arm round to place both hands firmly onto it and pulled downwards with all her strength, pushing the blade further in as she did so.

The man howled again, followed by another stream of

swearing. He was now reduced to hobbling on one leg, his second appearing almost completely incapacitated for the moment by the pain of the wound. He attempted to make his way towards the far side of the kitchen where the gun sat gleaming in a shaft of sunlight. But every step he tried to make was seriously hampered by the additional body he was being forced to take with him.

Strangely, Elayne found she was able to reflect on what a bizarre sight they must make, as she refused to let go of the knife, so that every step the man took – as well as every attempt to shake her off – merely caused him more pain and slowed his progress.

It seemed to take forever for him to move them both the few feet he needed but eventually she could see he was nearly close enough to reach down and pick the gun up.

Then she thought she heard voices in the garden. The man jerked violently and her grip loosened for a split second. He was quicker than her. He jumped out of her reach. And suddenly she felt a rich, sharp pain somewhere on her left side – she wasn't sure whether it was in her shoulder … or her neck …

Then there was shouting and screams and lots of feet, as blackness crowded into her vision. The last thing she experienced was a warm dog's tongue on her face.

Helen passed the sandwich box across to Jamie and exclaimed – for about the fifteenth time so far, 'I just can't take it all in.'

'Yeah, the first time up a mountain tends to be like that.'

The view in front of them was truly amazing. From this height, Helen guessed about halfway up their climb, she could see out across the beautiful loch below to the – now fairly tiny – village of Torrin. Occasional cars passed along the winding road in between the houses and to the head of the loch in the distance, looking for all the world like a model toyset.

'Just wait 'til we get higher up,' Struan joined in the

conversation, taking a swig from one of the flasks. Helen couldn't imagine what it could possibly look like any higher up. She already felt like she was at the top of the world.

It had taken much longer to get to this point than she'd thought it would. For the first half hour, the three of them had walked single-file along a tiny winding footpath almost hidden under flowering heather and prickly gorse. Every so often, it had opened out to reveal the staggering sight and raging sound of waterfalls crashing down a gorge on their left-hand side, each stopping-point more spectacular than the last, until the noise was so loud, she'd had to shout to make herself heard.

Then, suddenly, the noise had completely disappeared, as they'd crossed a boggy field and turned left towards the mountain's steep slopes. Struan had explained they needed to walk into the heart of the corrie opening up in front of them – not visible from the road – before swinging right again up the side of the mountain, along a safe route to the summit.

This had completely surprised Helen who realised she'd just expected to walk straight up the side of the hill, imagining grassy slopes and easy footpaths. The huge sandy boulders, vast upward stretches of slipping stones and shale – which Struan described as 'scree' – and unbelievably steep gradients had astonished her still further. The landscape, once you got up here, was so utterly different from how it appeared when you looked up at the mountain from the roadside. She began to understand the immensity of the dimensions involved.

As they'd turned further into the 'coire' – the small valley surrounded on three sides by parts of the mountain – and begun walking towards a greater height, the village and the loch had disappeared from view, and they'd been gradually enclosed in what felt like a very private world.

Struan had suggested Helen didn't look behind her until they stopped for a break, so it had been a delightful surprise to discover another small loch here, just below them, this one set into the body of the mountain itself, and then beyond that the view of the village she was now enjoying, as it had re-appeared from behind the huge green mound on the side of the coire nearest the road.

'Right, then, let's move on.' Struan began collecting up their various bits and pieces and stuffing them back into rucksacks, and the three of them set off on the next section of walking and scrambling – a technical term, Helen discovered, for using all the limbs available to you, in any appropriate order, to work yourself in a vaguely upward direction over ground which claimed to be a footpath but which actually consisted of rubble, more massive stones and patches of bare rock.

When they had first set off, at sea-level – literally – she'd bounded along the tiny footpath with enthusiasm, turning back after a few minutes to see the others walking already some way behind her, at a snail's pace. She'd waited for them to catch up and begun to make some silly quip about the enterprise proving too much for them, when Struan had interrupted.

'We set a pace at the start we can maintain all the way up. That way we get a steady rhythm going and reduce the levels of fatigue.'

Helen hadn't really understood what he meant but had dutifully fallen in with their ridiculously slow speed, thinking that, at this rate, they'd be lucky to reach the summit by tomorrow.

However, now they were encountering the much steeper and less negotiable parts of the mountain – around two thousand feet above sea-level, Struan told her – she understood. They were, indeed, still moving at the same slow pace, albeit mostly with much smaller steps, but the regularity of each step was now integrated into her brain like the metre of a song, so she found herself automatically placing one foot after the other without needing to think about it, and gradually but steadily, they were progressing up the mountain without tiring themselves excessively.

At the next stop, after they'd begun the right-hand swing across the mountain, and had rejoined a more obvious footpath which gave them glimpses of the treacherous *Clach Glas* 'next door', Helen had to agree that the view was even more breath-taking.

Torrin had disappeared from sight again, now a tiny blip in the landscape stretching out before them, which was magnificent. Mountaintops for miles, away to the south, stood proud and powerful, as if they were a different species inhabiting a world that stood above the mere fiddlings and niceties of the feeble humans living so far beneath them. It felt like an alien world – one whose existence she had never guessed at – and she could well understand the attraction that drew people back up here over and over. It was an utterly magical sight.

She looked out across the slopes nearest to her where a few tiny blobs could be seen in the distance. They seemed to be moving at a much faster pace than her group had been managing.

'Probably army boys out training or something,' Struan suggested. 'Yomping, they like to call it.'

Helen giggled. After the last couple of hours, the idea of running up a mountain seemed insane to her but the name was entertaining.

She watched the figures for a while and could just make out two different groups. One, she thought was a party of three or possibly four, who were a long way in the distance at a much lower height, and who suddenly changed direction and followed their leader off along another route heading away from *Blà Bheinn.*

The other party, if she peered for long enough, looked like a solitary walker. He or she was also moving at some speed but had a weird kind of bobbing movement to their progress, as if one leg was shorter than the other.

'Okay?' Struan was ready for the off again. Helen was learning that they took frequent but short breaks. She guessed that was also a way of keeping the rhythm going.

They started on the next part of the long path, this section a little easier with a gentler gradient.

'Look,' Jamie suddenly shouted, and pointed out into the sky where a huge bird with outstretched wings was gently circling, almost at the same level as they were walking.

'A Golden Eagle.'

He turned to Helen. She was speechless. This day just got better and better. The creature was unbelievably huge. She had no idea birds could be so big. The privilege of being in this new world touched her deeply as she watched the bird dip and soar, and then disappear downwards and out of sight.

'Just checking us out, I think,' Struan laughed. 'Maybe there's a nest somewhere.'

'What – up here?' Helen was incredulous.

'Can you think of a safer place?'

'I guess not. I mean, assuming you've got wings, of course. Not sure it would work for me. I mean, it's a bit far to go to the shops, and I can't just swoop down on a local sheep or something.'

They all chuckled and Helen relished the sense of camaraderie.

It was only a few minutes later when Struan stopped and took out his binoculars. 'Storm coming,' he announced.

'What?' 'Where?' The other two were surprised. The sky above them, and as far as they could see, was perfectly clear.

'Coming in from the East. Look.' And he handed over the binoculars to them. Helen couldn't make out anything significant but Jamie was obviously more used to identifying weather. He pointed out a small grey huddle of clouds, just beginning to accumulate on the horizon.

'That?' Helen asked, with just a hint of derision.

'Believe me,' said Struan, 'at this time of year – well, any time of year, actually – you don't ignore something like that at this height.'

'Okay … I'm happy to take your word for it.' Helen was still a bit dubious. 'What do we do?'

'Nothing yet. It may circle round us. It may dissipate again. If it hits us, we just stand still and wait for it to pass, right?'

'Okay,' Helen said again, but feeling even more dubious.

Struan caught the look on her face. 'Storms up here can build up and pass by very quickly, but moving around up here when visibility is low is not a good idea.'

'Visibility?' Helen queried.

'Yes, it may well bring in snow at this height.'

Since Helen was currently standing in a tee-shirt, she snorted in derision – then decided Struan must be winding her up. 'You're joking, right?'

Jamie butted in. 'No, he's not. I've been caught in a snowstorm up here in June, before now. At this time of year, anything's possible. Protocol is to find shelter if you can, and stay put even if you can't. The possibility of wandering off the edge is a real one.'

Helen suppressed a shudder and took a second look through the binoculars. Sure enough, the small huddle of clouds was already nearer and had become considerably larger.

'Wow, I see what you mean.'

As she lowered the binoculars, she caught sight of the solitary walker she'd been viewing earlier and paused to watch. With the aid of lenses, she could make out it was a man wearing heavy black boots and a black leather jacket. The image instantly brought back horrid recollections and she quickly lowered the 'sights', not wanting to be reminded – but not before she took in that the strange bobbing motion she'd noticed earlier seemed to be a rather pronounced limp. She handed the binoculars back to Struan.

'I get it,' she said quietly, and cast a glance back in the direction of the storm. 'Though how you identified a storm from this distance, I can't begin to guess.'

'Practice.'

She allowed her eyes to drop to the level of the walker for just a moment and was shocked by how much closer to them he was than when they'd first seen him. He really was moving at a fast pace. She couldn't stop an ominous thought from passing through her mind.

'You alright?' Jamie queried. He'd obviously noticed something was up.

'Yes – yes, of course. Just being stupid.'

'Are you sure? Sometimes it gets to people – being this high up.'

'No, honestly. I'm fine. Just remembering something I didn't want to.'

Jamie took her hand and gave it a warm squeeze. He didn't say anything else but Helen got the message. She pushed her silly idea to one side.

It was less than ten minutes later when the storm hit. Struan had already organised everyone into warmer clothes and waterproofs. He moved them along the path to a huge boulder which towered above their heads and behind which they could, to a certain extent, be sheltered from the icy blast which now rushed at them with ferocious intensity.

'Lean up against the rock,' he shouted over the increasing noise. 'And don't move.'

Helen did as she was told, grateful for the respite the rock offered as well as the sense of security, as huge hailstones began to fly past her, sideways.

'Ouch! That hurts.'

Struan shoved her a few inches further along the boulder to reduce her exposure to the wind and therefore the likelihood of being pelted by the ice-bullets being fired at them.

As she changed her line of sight, she was able to see the last of the view disappear in front of her. The outstretched, undulating world of mountaintops was rapidly vanishing as huge swirls of fast-flying snowflakes encompassed it, obliterating the scenery any further away than a few hundred yards, and quickly making Helen feel very disoriented. Struan had been bang on about visibility, then. She shouldn't have doubted him. This was actually quite scary.

Just as she thought it couldn't get any worse, the torrent of snow closed in further so that Helen could now only see the footpath immediately in front of her. She could make out the concerned faces of Jamie and Struan but the rest of the world had turned into a rushing white whirlwind.

Struan moved to place his body in front of her, blocking sight of the storm and shielding her from the worst of the gale. He leaned in towards the boulder, putting his hands out above her shoulders to connect with the rock and hold them both safe.

'It won't last long,' he shouted in her ear.

She looked up to mouth a silent thank you, and just as she did, the wind took a sudden detour, temporarily creating a gap in the white onslaught to her left. For a moment, she was able to see further along the footpath towards the neighbouring peaks.

There, not more than two hundred yards away, was the man in the black jacket. He had obviously taken a different route up, crossing over to *Blà Bheinn* at a lower height so that he could reach this point, coming in the opposite direction to them. And he was still moving towards them.

At exactly the same instant she saw him, he also saw her. She screamed as he pulled a gun from inside his jacket and took aim. Struan had turned to see what she was reacting to, and they both caught a fleeting glimpse before the wind gusted again and brought in another round of thick snow, shutting down the scene.

'I … he …' Helen started trying to explain.

'Shut up. Get down. Hands and knees. Now. Both of you.'

Jamie and Helen immediately sank to the ground.

'Crawl round the boulder. Go on.' Struan shoved them both in the direction they'd just come from. They headed back into the blast of the storm.

'Keep touching the boul – ' His voice was ripped away by the wind.

Helen put one shoulder up against the rock now positioned between her and the approaching gunman. Struan pushed her again, forcing her further into a narrow crevice that provided a small amount of shelter from the wind.

'Stay absolutely still,' he mouthed, and disappeared back around the boulder.

'No,' Helen shrieked, reaching out to try and grab hold of him. Jamie held onto her.

'He knows what he doing.'

'But that man has a gun.' It was ridiculously hard to speak in the strength of the wind and hail punching into her face. 'He's after *me*.' She tried to stress the words – to make the situation clear.

'I know.' Jamie looked down at her. 'We both know.'

Struan had no idea what he was going to do, but of one thing he was absolutely certain. He would know this terrain much better than the gunman. This was his territory. He walked these mountains pretty much every day. He knew every little crevice and foothold. He knew when the landscape changed, such as after a storm like this one, and he knew how *Blà Bheinn* and its weather interacted. This was his home. And he trusted the mountain.

He wouldn't stand a chance confronting the man directly. Struan had no doubts that the gunman's intention was to dispose of all three of them. He wouldn't be leaving witnesses. The order in which he executed this would be irrelevant.

He carefully maneuvered himself down the overhanging side of the footpath onto the rocky slope a few feet below. It wasn't sensible trying to negotiate around a mountain in such atrocious weather and he didn't feel happy about breaking his own rules, but it was by far the best option he had to attempt to get all three of them out of this alive.

Fingertip by fingertip, he began to move sideways across the face of the crag. He hadn't climbed this section often but he knew it was possible. He just needed to ask the mountain to open up to him, show him where the footholds were, where he could grip onto with his hands as he progressed slowly along the most treacherous few feet of his life.

The gunman, who clearly thought nothing of the snow blinding his way, would be edging along the path above him, so Struan should be able to gain an advantage by passing him unseen. He knew exactly what the footpath above him looked like and had calculated the one slim chance he might have.

As he reached the point where he intended to scramble back up onto the path, the storm began to thin, and raising his head tentatively to peer over the edge, he could just make out the heavy black boots exactly where he wanted them to be.

As they huddled together in the crevice, Helen realised she was shaking again. She'd done a lot of that over the last few days. She'd thought all that was over. She'd believed she was safe. How… ? How on earth had the man found her? And now, having run away to keep her old friends safe, she was putting her new friends in danger. This was more than she could bear. She felt the tears stinging the back of her eyes, matching the stings on her face from the hail which seemed to have no problem finding her inside the crevice.

But this time she didn't allow herself to cry. She stuffed the tears back down. This had to stop. She couldn't run any further. There was literally nowhere left to run to. She suddenly made up her mind.

Just as suddenly, the storm stopped.

Helen jumped to her feet and stepped round the boulder, completely surprising Jamie who found himself clutching at air. She also surprised the gunman who, having got himself completely disoriented by trying to continue walking in the swirling snow, had veered off the path and crashed into a large vertical slab of rock which stretched high above his head, obliterating his view of the narrow gap between this particular protrusion and the next one along.

Within a split second, Helen took in the man's back to her and the slight movement beyond him – a hand reaching to pull up a body over the edge of the footpath, a hand which then quickly picked up a large piece of rock.

Reaching deep inside, and feeling for all the world as if she was embodying Tosca, Helen screamed, 'Here, you bastard!', and dived for the side of her own boulder as she did so.

She just caught sight of the gunman swinging round in her direction, then heard the crack as a bullet sliced into the boulder and a sickening thud as Struan's rock collided with the man's skull, followed by a strange gurgling noise.

She risked peering round the corner and saw the gunman staggering and holding his head, blood trickling through his fingers, foam bubbling from his mouth. He didn't drop his gun, though, and began letting rip a series of shots that flew uselessly up into the sky, as he struggled to remain upright. The gunshots created an eerie pattern of repeated sounds, the echoes blending into a hideous melody as he furiously and futilely continued to fire them, regardless of direction.

Helen watched in a kind of ghastly horror as he teetered further and further towards the gap in the rocks, blindly grasping with his other hand for a secure hold, and finally grabbing nothing. He stumbled into the space, realising too late what had happened, as his feet slipped away beneath him and he began to fall over the edge.

Unbelievably, as he went, he used the last of his strength to turn towards her so that the final thing she saw was the crazy wildness in his eyes as he fell backwards through the gap, plummeting down the north face of the mountain, the shards of *Clach Glas* creating a strange backdrop for the useless bullets he was still firing into the air as he fell.

20

'Gavin. Elayne's been shot.'

Gavin brought his car to a halt, leaning over to retrieve his phone from the speaker cradle.

'Oh my God. Is she okay?'

There was a stifled sob at the other end.

'I – we don't know. They're operating on her now. I'm at the hospital. I don't know how bad it is. I wasn't here.' Katriona broke into tears, and the next voice Gavin heard belonged to a man.

'Gavin, this is Sean. I'm a friend of Katriona and Elayne. I live just over the road. I found Elayne.'

'What happened?' Gavin felt those cold shudders returning.

'I don't exactly know. The dogs turned up at the house -'

'The dogs?'

'Yeah. Molly and Alice, you know?'

'Yes, I know – but what were they doing? How are they a part of this?' Gavin was getting confused. Had this been some sort of accident?

'I think Elayne sent them. To fetch help. Probably when she first saw the man.'

'What man?' Gavin snapped. 'What the bloody hell's been going on?'

'I'm sorry, Gavin. All I can tell you is I raced round to

Elayne's, because it was clear from the way the dogs were behaving something was wrong. I mean, they often visit us but not usually on their own – and never before, barking like they were. So, like I said, I raced back to their house, and collected a couple of guys on the way who live opposite. They just happened to be out in their front garden.

'Anyway, when we got to the house, we heard a gunshot. We ran round the back to get in through the kitchen door and found Elayne on the floor – and a whole lot of blood.' Sean paused. It sounded like the recollection was a bit much for him.

'But not all the blood was hers. There was a knife on the floor, and some of the blood was smeared across the tiles, like someone had dragged something. Then we heard the front door slam. That's pretty much it. Of course, we rang for an ambulance straight away.'

Gavin hesitated. He didn't know how much Sean was in the picture. He also wasn't happy about sharing too much on this particular phone. But he wanted details.

'Did you see who it was? Did any of you go back into the street?' He was thinking like a copper. Catch the criminal, number one priority. Of course, Sean's priority would be different.

'No. I didn't see anyone. David – one of the other guys – he went back round the house, but said there was no-one to be seen by the time he got there. Mind you, it's easy enough to get straight onto the moors here, and disappear from view.'

'I'm sure.' Gavin tried to be polite though he couldn't imagine how that could be true. 'What about Elayne? What – where was she shot?'

'As far as I could see, the bullet had gone into her chest, high up near the collar bone …' Sean choked. 'I think it was too high to hit her heart. But she lost consciousness as we arrived. She'd lost a lot of blood very quickly. We did what we could …' His voice trailed off.

'So where exactly are you now?' Gavin was still trying to

get a clear picture of the situation. Surely they didn't have the facilities for dealing with this kind of incident up there?

'Just in Broadford. At the local hospital.'

'And can they deal with this? Doesn't Elayne need expert surgery?'

'Oh, yes. No problem. The doc flew up with Katriona, as soon as they heard.'

'What?' Gavin had no way to make sense of this last statement. He found he was very frustrated with being so far from the scene. But then he heard Katriona's voice again.

'Gavin. It's me, again. Please don't worry. Elayne's in the best possible hands.' She had obviously recovered some of her composure. 'Look, someone's coming from the operating theatre now. I've got to go. I'll ring you back. We'll talk properly.'

And the line went dead.

Gavin felt he was left with more questions than useful information after the call. For instance, how did they know it was a man if no-one had seen him? His guess was that Katriona had shared something with her closest friends about the dangers threatening Helen.

And what about Helen? Where had *she* been while all this was going on? Was she okay? Assuming this was the assassin they were talking about, and not some random burglar, had he now got hold of Helen? Or had they managed to keep her hidden? And then, perhaps the most significant question of all, if this had been the work of Gravenberg, how on God's earth had he found where Helen was?

It was, perhaps, another hour before Katriona contacted Gavin again. In the meantime, he had made it back home from an extended run into Essex to leave Trish and her sister at a very select health farm for the next few days. He and Trish had talked it through, as far as he could – or wanted to – share information with her. She needed some support physically at the moment. *He* felt she needed some anonymity as he was getting further into the case. This was proving way more dangerous than he was used to and he wasn't willing to take any chances. Threatening officers' families was a tried and tested method of keeping coppers 'in line'. They'd agreed on this compromise.

He'd been on his way home when he'd received the first phonecall from Katriona. He hoped this second one would be more satisfactory – in all sorts of ways.

When she rang through, he immediately responded on the safe phone, as she'd clearly expected him to.

'How's Elayne?'

'She's going to be okay.' The relief in Katriona's voice was very evident. 'They've removed the bullet. And yes, I have it in an evidence bag.'

Bless her for still managing to think like a detective in the face of what she must have been going through.

She continued. 'It's mostly soft tissue damage, but it had nicked an artery. That's why there was so much blood. And why she lost consciousness so quickly. She was very lucky.' A small sob escaped down the line.

'I'm so glad, Katriona. Poor Elayne. How come she got tangled up in all this? Sorry, are you up to answering a few questions?'

'Yes. Of course. From your point of view, well, you need to know what's going on, because this is all highly significant in terms of your case, I think.'

'You mean, it was Gravenburg that shot her?'

'Yes. It has to be. There's no other explanation. Elayne's not awake enough to speak yet but we just don't have armed criminals wandering around the island, Gavin. It can't have been a random shooting. Anyway, there's no sign of any robbery or anything like that. He was after Helen, for sure.'

'And where is she?' Gavin asked, hesitantly.

'I don't know.'

'You mean he's taken her?' He felt his worst fears surfacing.

'No. At least, not as far as I know.'

Katriona carefully explained about the separate plans the three of them had decided to pursue for the day and how Helen had, she assumed, set off with Struan and Jamie to go up *Blà Bheinn.*

'I was down in Fort William, teaching at a rookies' conference for the day. Set off ridiculously early, so I didn't see anyone else this morning before I left. I presume they got going safely because there was no sign of them at the house, according to Sean.'

'You haven't been back there?'

'No. I came straight to the hospital.'

'Sean said something about you flying there …'

'Yes. That was a real stroke of luck. Dr. Alanis was at the same conference centre, lecturing for the Surgical Clinic at The Belford for the day.'

'Dr. Alanis? Why do I know that name?'

'Because he's a big name in surgery, based in London. He does a lot of work connected with the police, and he's pioneering new surgical techniques all the time.'

'Oh yes. Wasn't he involved with that multiple shooting at Tower Hamlets a few years back?'

'Yep, that's him. Anyway, our local hospital, like the one in Portree, is too small to have many resident specialists, so they have an arrangement with various clinics at some of the closest mainland hospitals. It just so happens that MacKinnon's, here in Broadford, uses the clientele from the surgical clinic at The Belford in Fort William. So when they put the call through, the clinic approached Dr. Alanis to ask if he would assist. At which point, they discovered I was down there, too, so they arranged for a helicopter to fly us both to the island. Elayne couldn't have been in safer hands.'

'That's pretty amazing.' Gavin was in awe of how the situation had been handled, considering the remoteness of the place. 'So presumably the local police have taken overall charge of the situation?'

'Well, not exactly. The local police on a Sunday is one community officer. McTavish. He's a good guy. He's overseeing the crime scene for the moment. The SCD are arriving from Inverness tomorrow. My mate Andy's going to be leading the team. But there's not a lot they can do just now. Gravenberg's gone to ground. And Helen's presumably still on the mountain.'

'Can't you contact her?'

'No signal up there, Gavin. Believe me, she's in one of the safest places she could be at the moment. It's when they come back down we need to start worrying.'

'Actually, I think there's something we need to start worrying about sooner.'

'You mean, how did Gravenburg find her?'

Gavin thought Katriona was amazingly coherent given everything that had happened. 'Yeah, I've been racking my brains over that one.'

'And what have you come up with?'

'Not much. We were very careful at this end to keep the information secret. I didn't even tell Charlie.'

'So who *did* you tell?'

Gavin paused, not wanting to voice the answer out loud. It had been hurting his head for the last hour, but there was no getting round it.

'Only Fisher.'

Silence. Both of them were stunned by the enormity of the statement. It was Katriona who spoke first.

'Really? Are you sure? You didn't write anything down anywhere, or let something slip by accident that might have given a clue?'

Gavin had reached a strange place of calm about this realisation, having followed through every possibility in his thoughts while waiting for Katriona to ring. He wanted to be mistaken – but he knew he wasn't.

'No. I am absolutely certain. Believe me, I really want to find a mistake that would account for this, but there isn't one. It has to be Fisher.'

'So all that stuff about Foster being sent on another case …'

'… was a load of guff. Fisher was covering for Foster. He knew Foster was involved. The two of them were in it together.'

'Gavin, you do realise what this means?'

'I think it means all sorts of things. Which particular one do you want to pick?'

'Well, I suppose the first thing is that your whole investigation is compromised. Quickly followed up with – watch your back, because you're probably not safe if they think you know too much. Nicely rounded off with – if Fisher's involved, God knows who else is.'

21

It took much longer than Helen expected to climb back down the mountain. She'd presumed that going up was the more difficult task, and had imagined descending would be easy. It seemed only logical.

In reality, this proved not to be the case. In fact, gravity – which one would think might be working in one's favour – only served to encourage slipping and tumbling, since the terrain was just as difficult to maneuver around as it had been on the way up but now she was continually facing into a fall instead of into the rock. She discovered she had to pick her way carefully where the route became less obvious, sometimes turning around to come down a short section backwards, as this felt much safer – insofar as anything did now.

Immediately after the shooting, the three of them had simply stood and stared at each other in silence, all of them deeply shocked by what had happened. Jamie was the most coherent as he hadn't seen the whole incident, having been hidden behind the boulder. He had only emerged when he heard Helen screaming.

Helen didn't remember screaming.

After he'd checked the other two were physically okay, Jamie crossed to Struan. Helen heard him speaking as if he were standing at the other end of a long tunnel.

'Come on, mate. We need to treat everyone for shock. Where's your kit?'

The very practical nature of the question seemed to bring Struan round and he snapped back into being the steady and reliable professional guide. Within minutes, he'd produced water, chocolate and then a warm, sweet cuppa for everyone. Helen was very impressed.

'How did you conjure that out of thin air?'

Struan had smiled. Thank God. She felt they needed him back to normal.

After their adrenaline levels had subsided a little, and the increasing sunshine had thoroughly warmed them through again, they began to talk about what they should do.

'We need to report there's been an accident,' Struan said, 'but I doubt the guy is alive.'

For the first time in her life, Helen felt a real surge of hatred. 'I bloody well hope not.' The sound of the venom in her voice shocked her. 'Oh my God. I can't believe I just said that.'

Struan reached out a hand. 'Don't worry. I think you're probably voicing what all of us are thinking. Which is entirely understandable, given the circumstances.' He paused to make eye contact. 'It doesn't make you a bad person.' He smiled, sympathetically.

Helen shrugged in dismay.

Leaving her and Jamie to sip their hot drinks, Struan had wandered up and down the footpath for a while with his mobile phone, trying to get a signal.

'No, it's no good. I didn't expect it would be at this height. We need to go higher, really.'

'Higher?' The thought of continuing their climb filled Helen with horror.

'But I think that's probably not a good idea, for any of us,' Struan continued. 'If I thought there was the least chance of the guy surviving that fall, I might be persuaded to try going further up to get a signal, but …'

The others were quick to dissuade him. All any of them

wanted was to get back down and off the mountain. They'd packed up their rucksacks again and started the long climb down.

At intervals, Struan had tried his phone again, but Helen could tell he had little expectation of getting reception. In fact, the further they descended, the worse the problem became. She had learned early in her visit that most of the inhabitants in Torrin relied much more on the landline phones, since the surrounding hills generally prevented a signal from getting through.

Finally, after what seemed hours longer than the time it had taken to go up, they regained sight of the car park and Struan's truck. Wearily, they loaded their gear in the back and climbed onto the welcome seating. Helen's feet were hurting dreadfully, but once she sat down, she wasn't sure whether they hurt more than any other part of her did.

There had been only sparse conversation between them as they'd descended. No-one seemed to want to talk about what had happened, apart from a very brief exchange during their first rest. Struan had obviously felt, now that they'd left the actual scene behind, he should give everyone the opportunity to say something.

After a few shared mutterings about how frightening and unbelievable the incident had been, Jamie had suddenly turned to Helen.

'That was by far the most stupid – and the most brave – thing I've ever witnessed.'

There was an uncomfortable pause. Then Helen burst out laughing.

'That was by far the most stupid – and the most brave – thing I've ever done.'

The others had joined in with her laughter and the intense atmosphere was somewhat relieved, making the rest of the walk down easier to bear.

Struan started up the truck to drive them back round the loch to Katriona and Elayne's house. 'I can ring Mountain

Rescue from there,' he said. 'The call will automatically go through the police, so we won't need to make a separate call to them.'

'The police?' Helen was easily flipped back into that anxious place where she'd spent the first part of the week. 'Can't we just tell Katriona?'

'No, not really. I mean, obviously we'll tell her what happened, but she's got no authority on the island as such. This was attempted murder, Helen. We have to report it. They'll want to investigate. I mean, I suppose you know who that man was?'

This was the first time either of the other two had asked Helen anything directly about what had taken place before she'd arrived on the island.

'No, I don't know. I just know I saw someone wearing those same clothes when I …' She swallowed hard. 'I never saw his face.'

Jamie opened his mouth before he could stop himself. 'Then how come he was after you?'

'Because there was someone else there – when I found the body – somebody with him, who must have worked out I was a possible witness.'

The words came out slowly. She looked at Jamie and could see the unspoken question in his eyes. She continued.

'The other man was a police officer.'

'Oh.' Both Jamie and Struan showed signs of comprehension on their faces.

'Oh,' repeated Struan. 'Right, and that's why you're reluctant to report this directly to the police – in case the information gets back to him.'

'Yes.'

'But, Helen,' Jamie spoke softly, 'if this guy – the gunman – was after you, then it seems pretty likely that the police guy knows you're here.'

'I suppose.' *Oh God, was there no end to this?*

'Look,' Struan's calm, reassuring voice cut in. 'Let's just get back and talk to Katriona. I'm sure she'll know what to do.'

Helen knew he was just being kind, but for the moment, that was exactly what she needed.

As they pulled onto the driveway of Katriona's house, it was immediately apparent that something was wrong. There was blue and white tape at some of the windows, and across the footpath which led to the back of the house. Struan came to a halt just as Constable McTavish came out of the front door, holding a large roll of the incident tape.

Helen leapt out of the car. 'What's happened? Oh my God, is everyone alright?'

The constable looked up as Helen flew towards him.

'Helen. Thank God you're okay. We've been trying to track you down.'

'Why? What happened?' Helen asked again.

'There's been an incident here.'

Helen could tell from the careful way McTavish was speaking that something awful had taken place. She willed herself to stand still and face whatever news the constable had waiting for her, as the other two got out of the truck and came up behind her.

'It's Ms. Galloway. She's going to be okay …' He made sure he got the reassurance in quickly, '… but she's been shot.'

'No, no.' Helen wailed. That beautiful woman. How could anyone – ? But she knew how. She'd seen it in the man's eyes as he went over the edge. He must have come here first, trying to find her. She wondered, briefly, if the man had tortured Elayne into telling him where she was.

The constable was continuing to speak.

'I got a call from the hospital. It's okay. Your aunt is there with her. They flew her up from Fort William in a helicopter, specially.'

'My aunt?' Helen had forgotten for the moment all about her cover story.

'Yes.' McTavish continued. 'DI McShannon requested I

came down here to process the crime scene and close it off in preparation for her colleagues from the SCD. They'll be arriving tomorrow. So I was just finishing off. I had another call from her not half an hour ago to let me know Ms. Galloway is in Recovery. They've removed the bullet. No serious harm done. So she'll be able to identify her shooter.'

'There's no need,' Struan cut in.

'Sorry?'

'There's no need,' Struan repeated. 'The man's dead. He came after us – well, Helen – while we were up *Blà Bheinn*.'

'Good God. Then how … ?'

'I need to report a serious incident – to the Mountain Rescue Team. We thought we'd be able to use the landline from here. We weren't up high enough to get a signal when it happened.'

'I'm afraid I can't let you into the house.'

'No. I understand. I don't think there's any rush. It's going to be too dark soon to organise a search, anyway.' Struan turned to Helen. 'I think the best thing we can do is get you reconnected with Katriona. So you can share information. I'll drive you up to Broadford. Jamie, do you want to go straight home or … ?'

'I'll come with you. I'd like to hear what happened, as well.'

Helen felt herself slipping into a daze, as everyone around her started making decisions. Her lovely new 'safe place' was disintegrating just as quickly as her home in London had. She tried to pull herself together.

'Yes, please. I'd like to see Elayne, too. Make sure she's okay. I need to hear what happened. And talk with Katriona about what we should do next.'

A sudden thought occurred to her. 'Where are the dogs?'

'Oh, they're okay.' McTavish beamed. 'They're round at Sean's place, having a hero's supper.'

'Hero's supper?' Helen asked.

'I gather they saved the day – to use a dramatic term.'

Helen wanted more details but McTavish had to say he

didn't know anything more than that they had played a crucial role in getting help.

'It's all a bit confused at the moment.'

You don't say, Helen thought, as she piled wearily back into Struan's truck.

22

After he hung up from speaking to Katriona, Gavin spent some time thinking through the implications of what she'd said. She was right – about all of it. Nothing that they'd discovered, or hypothesized about, so far, was necessarily secret anymore. It was perfectly possibly that every step of the investigation had been reported back to whoever was running the show and had orchestrated the break-in at Emily Hough's. Though actually murdering her was probably not planned – just seen as collateral damage.

He hated that phrase. He hated the way it covered the fact that real people had died and others were now grieving, and the way it was used to lessen the guilt of those responsible.

He felt more certain than ever that Foster was only small fry in something much bigger, but he was no longer so certain about Emily. Until they could get into that flashdrive, they couldn't know what it was she'd been up to.

Damn. The flashdrive. He hadn't told Fisher anything about it, thank God, because it had arrived over the weekend and he hadn't thought the Super would be delighted to have his 'down time' interrupted by mere theories. But he did wonder now whether he should warn Tom.

Was he blowing all this out of proportion? There was no reason to suppose Tom and Fisher would have any contact.

Everything went through him if it needed communicating further up the line. And it wasn't right to throw suspicion on a chief of staff without real evidence because it compromised everyone's confidence in what they were doing. No, Tom knew not to let the flashdrive out of his sight. Besides, if he couldn't work out how to open it, then no-one could. Gavin was certain of that.

He found he was a bit rattled by Katriona's suggestion that he might not be safe, but when he thought it through logically, he realised there was nothing he'd said to Fisher so far that would make him vulnerable. Fisher had made sure Foster was well out of the picture for the time being, so *he* wasn't going to be blabbing anything to Gavin that he shouldn't, and as long as Gavin played dumb about their investigation, he thought he could, for the time being, convince Fisher that he didn't know anything significant.

The biggest problem was how to proceed from here. He was in the habit of informing his superior officer what lines of enquiry he was following, so he couldn't modify that without arousing suspicion; but whatever he decided to follow up next was bound to impact on other areas of investigation, or other police personnel, if they were involved. How could he possibly know who to trust? And if he was wrong, and he chose to keep vital evidence secret because of his suspicions, that was his career down the tube, for sure.

After sitting with his mental battles for half an hour or so, he decided he needed a break and got off the sofa to go into the kitchen and make a coffee. Something about the smell reminded him of the 'old days', talking cases over with Frank Hammond, in a much more conducive atmosphere than the current one. There'd been none of this 'shenanigans' in those days. Gavin had always felt he knew exactly who to trust within the force – and who not to! He missed Frank's reassuring certainty.

Then it hit him. That's who he should talk to now. Frank had been around the block a few times in his career. He knew most of the personnel at the local stations, but he also knew plenty of others from different parts of the system – like members of IPCC, for instance. Yes, it was definitely time to meet up with an old mate.

Having contacted Frank and arranged to go for a drink later in the evening, Gavin took a shower, feeling like he needed to wash away the 'grime' of the last few hours. While he was under the refreshing hot water, he heard his phone ring. When he'd dried off, he wandered back into the living room to discover a message from Tom.

'Hi, Gavin. There's good news and bad news. It's really interesting. Can you drop by the lab in the next hour or so?'

The man truly never went home. Gavin rang him back to say he'd be there later. He decided he'd have something to eat first. He didn't think he'd eaten in hours. He could call into the station on his way to meet Frank.

He got dressed, putting on a new shirt Trish had bought him last week. He missed her already. He might not be able to be at home much at the moment but he valued the time he did spend in the flat with her. The place seemed very empty this evening. Usually, on a Sunday, they'd be sitting down to a curry or a roast about now. They'd often cook it together, too, even though Trish didn't think much of his culinary efforts. She was the director in the kitchen but he played a good enough 'bit part' for the enterprise to be enjoyable, he thought.

Tonight, he could only persuade himself to search through the freezer for something to heat up. His heart just wasn't into doing anything more creative. He hoped she'd ring soon, fitting him in between the aromatherapy massage and the seaweed wrap, perhaps. God, he was feeling sorry for himself.

While his food was heating in the oven – Trish disapproved of microwaves, saying that was no way to treat decent food – he tried to ring Katriona again for an update. He was greeted by unexpected exuberance.

'Elayne's awake and Helen's okay. Gravenberg's dead.'

This was an extraordinary amount of information to take in at one go. Gavin felt his adrenaline flowing again.

'Good Lord. Tell me.'

'I can't. Not just now. They've only just got to the hospital. Look, I'll ring you later on tonight. Explain everything then. Okay?'

Gavin had no choice but to agree since he hadn't any idea what was going on. His frustration returned, briefly. Then he decided that was ridiculously unproductive. There was plenty he could do here until he got the full picture. He ate his meal and set out for the station, hoping for more satisfaction from a conversation with Tom.

'Well, like I said on the phone, there's good news and bad news.' Tom was rushing around his lab, clicking onto various computer screens and moving evidence bags about, as he spoke. 'I'll give you the good news first.'

Gavin felt a twinge of anxiety. It never turned out well when someone proffered the good news first. He waited. Best let Tom present things in his own theatrical way.

'I cracked the password.' Tom turned to Gavin and gave a fist-pump.

'Wow! Well done.' Gavin was immensely impressed and desperate to get a read of what the flashdrive contained but restrained himself from butting in, all too aware that the bad news was still to be declared.

'Do you want to know how?' Tom's eyes glittered with excitement.

Privately, Gavin thought *no, not really*. He wanted the contents, not the account of how to get there. Out loud, he said, 'Of course.'

'I've had the programme running since we got the flashdrive yesterday but even with a password of only eight characters – and even if they were all lower case letters – that's over two hundred and eight billion possibilities, and could take up to a week for the computer to uncover, depending on the level of encryption used. Throw in capitals, digits, more characters …'

'It's a mammoth task. I see that.' Gavin had never stopped to think about passwords before. He was surprised by the maths.

'Most people, however, don't use very complex passwords that are hard to crack.' Tom made his way to one of the computer screens. 'And that's because a jumble of different characters is hard to remember – well, for most people.' He grinned. With his extraordinary mind, Gavin guessed he'd probably have no problems remembering even a twenty-character nonsense word.

'So they use things like a pet's name or an anniversary date, or something like that. Something familiar. Which is why so many passwords are very easy to crack once you know a few personal details.'

'So, is that how you cracked this one? Something personal about Emily?'

'Well, yes and no. She didn't have any pets and Heather was her only family. I tried all the obvious things – birthdays, opera houses, singers' names – you know, the usual.'

Gavin thought that selection sounded far from usual but said nothing.

'But I was getting nowhere. Then I suddenly remembered the locket. You know, the one she was wearing around her neck that the Doc pointed out?'

'Oh yeah.' Gavin had temporarily forgotten about that as no-one had turned up anything that it might relate to. Tom handed him the evidence bag containing it, with its tiny piece of paper bearing the code 2450.

'The number itself is too short to be useful as a password but I wondered if it might refer to something else. So I started rifling through the other evidence brought in from the crime scene. Apparently, *this* was sitting on the piano when the team cleared the front room.'

He picked up another evidence bag, this one containing a large soft-cover book which Gavin could see was an operatic score. Specifically, the score to *Il Trovatore*.

'So I checked what she was due to perform at The Bridgewater the day after she was murdered, to see if she might have been rehearsing this.'

Gavin was, as usual, in complete awe of the workings of Tom's mind.

'And sure enough,' Tom pulled up the programme for the concert on his computer screen. 'She was going to sing some excerpts from the soprano's part. Leonora.'

'Leonora?'

'You're not an opera buff, then?'

'Um, no,' Gavin conceded. 'Are you?'

'Enough to know my key characters, yes. One never knows when that might be important.'

'And clearly it was. Let me guess, you put in Leonora and – '

'Oh no, nothing so simple. Remember the numbers? 2450?'

Gavin nodded.

'Well, if you look in the score …' Tom carefully removed the book from its plastic bag, using latex gloves, and opened it about halfway through, then slowly turned the pages until he found a faint pencil mark next to a line of music.

'Act Two. Scene Four. Bar Fifty.' He paused. 'Leonora singing to her friends.' He added for emphasis.

Gavin wasn't following.

'If I enter the notes from this bar as letters, using F for flat and N for natural to take account of the accidentals – '

'Accidentals?' Gavin interrupted.

'Oh, notes that get changed from the key signature of the piece.' As he spoke, Tom pointed to various tiny symbols placed next to individual notes within the bar he was referring to. Gavin nodded again, just about keeping up with Tom's stream of thought.

'So … if we do that …'

Tom turned to another computer into which the

flashdrive was loaded.

'We get …' he began typing, '… FANCBFGGAFBF.'

'That's extraordinary,' Gavin exclaimed, meaning to compliment Tom on his discovery. Tom, however, was focused in a different direction.

'I know. It's really clever, because it genuinely is a password that would have been familiar and easy for Emily to remember, and completely incomprehensible and uncrackable to anyone else.'

'Except you.' Gavin was determined to demonstrate his admiration.

'Except me.' Tom grinned. 'But then I did have the advantage of seeing inside her locket.'

'Even so, that's phenomenal work, Tom. Now, please hit 'Enter' so I can …' Gavin slowed up as an apprehension of the bad news hit him. 'Oh no, what happened?'

Tom tapped the keyboard and the screen went dark.

'It turns out to be the most protected flashdrive ever, because all we get is …' He paused for a few seconds, watching the screen.

'Another password screen,' he announced, as the familiar little box appeared in front of him.

'Another password?'

'Yes, that I'm afraid is the bad news. This flashdrive is doubly coded – and I have no idea how to crack this second one.'

Gavin left the station feeling more despondent than ever. This case made no sense. Every time the team took a step forward, they hit another obstacle. He hated that. He liked being able to follow up on clues and get either a result or a definite indication that the clue was only a red herring. This continual unravelling uncertainty was beginning to get to him. They didn't even seem to know what the real crime was – or even who had committed it. For all he knew, Emily herself could have been a 'closet' criminal.

It was all so frustrating and he was running out of leads,

not to mention any comprehensive support from his boss. His only comfort was a faint intuitive sense that things were 'always darkest before the dawn'. That was something Frank used to say when carefully-worked cases had become difficult. He was often right. Gavin was pleased he'd thought to ring Frank and very much looked forward to seeing him again.

When he reached the pub, he saw his old boss sitting at a table in one corner, drinks already in. A Guinness for Frank and a lager for him. That brought back memories. Frank waved him over, a warm smile welcoming him.

'Gavin. It's been a while. Great to see you, again.'

Gavin took a stool. 'Frank, how've you been?'

'Not so bad. Slowing up a bit, but generally, I'm okay.'

'And what are you doing to keep yourself busy?'

'Oh, fishing, of course.' A wide grin spread across Frank's face.

Gavin had forgotten about Frank's love of fishing. He'd always been keen for his weekends off when he would disappear to some obscure corner of the countryside and don waders and fishing hat, up to his waist in cold water. Gavin shuddered at the thought. He'd never been able to see the fascination of standing for hours in the cold and wet, on the stiff end of a bit of string, waiting for something to happen at the other. But he respected Frank enough to guess there was more to it than he'd ever been able to see, and was glad his old friend had found pleasure in spending even more time in such a seemingly unattractive pastime.

They talked for a while about home and family, updating each other on recent news, and then Frank, direct as ever, asked, 'So, what can I help you with, Gavin?'

Gavin felt an unexpected surge of emotion. This was what it used to be like. You got stuck with a case, you went and knocked on Frank's door, and he sat and listened to your sorry tale, and somehow saw the connection you couldn't make. Which he would then generously share with you, so you could go back to the case with renewed enthusiasm. He wondered whether Frank still had 'the gift'.

'I've run into a problem which I don't know how to solve.'

'Oh?'

'Yes. It's all a bit delicate, really. I wondered if you'd mind if I talked it through with you – confidentially?'

Frank, ever one to adhere to protocol, paused before answering. 'And this isn't something you can take to your Super?'

It was Gavin's turn to pause. He took a long sip of his lager.

'He's the problem.'

'I see.' Another pause. 'It's Fisher, isn't it?'

'Yes. What do you know about him, Frank?'

'Well, not a lot. I never actually worked directly with the guy. I gather he's not the nursemaiding type.'

'Definitely not.' Gavin spoke with feeling.

'So, is that the problem? People finding the new regime difficult?'

'If only,' Gavin responded. 'Look, if you don't feel you can comment, I totally understand but … can he be trusted?'

Gavin felt terrible asking one senior officer such a question about another senior officer but he knew Frank would realise things must be serious if he was doing so. He was surprised by Frank's response.

'No. I would say not.'

'What?'

'I'm guessing you didn't expect me to say that?'

'Well, no. I was kind of hoping for a bit of Frank-style intuition, even a bit of inside information, but I didn't expect you to come out with such an unequivocal answer.'

Frank lowered his voice a little. 'Well, I can give you some inside information, Gavin, which might be useful to you. And which I feel much more at liberty to share now I'm retired. Something on which I was in no position to act at the time.'

Gavin looked across at his friend. 'Something about the

corruption investigation?'

'Yes. I doubt you'll be surprised by that.'

'No. But then, nothing would surprise me at this stage. But that's another matter. Tell me what you know.'

'It's more a question of what happened. That's why I couldn't act at the time. It was when I was being – shall we say 'persuaded' - to retire. The guy who came to speak to me was called Stevens. Elliot Stevens.'

'He was one of the IPCC officers, wasn't he?'

'Well remembered.'

'I remember because he was the guy who interviewed me. And I'm afraid I took rather a dislike to him.'

'You and me both,' Frank grinned. 'There was something rather too 'flash' about him for my liking.'

Gavin chuckled. 'Yeah. I know what you mean.'

Frank continued. 'But I thought, at the time, that was probably just another sign that I was getting too old for the job. I knew things were changing and I couldn't blame the guy for taking a different approach that felt alien to me.'

'You always were too generous with your good opinion, Frank.'

'Maybe. But I'd rather err on that side in the interests of building a good team, than on the other side, where everyone is suspected of being guilty of something, or not good enough at something else – which appeared to be Stevens' approach.'

'You're right. I think I excused his behaviour on the grounds that he was here to investigate us – so he couldn't afford to be seen to be partial.'

'And I did the same at first,' Frank agreed. 'Until about two weeks after IPCC got involved, I just happened to see him talking to Jack Foster.'

'But he would've had to do that – '

'In the pub.'

'Oh. I see.'

'And a few days later, it was all decided, and the guilty officers were named, and Foster wasn't one of them. And

Stevens turned up in my office – '

'– suggesting you would be wise to take early retirement.'

'And the name he put forward to the appointments board as my replacement was Bertram Fisher.'

23

Katriona finished crying and gave a big sigh. She'd held it together all day – from the moment when she'd received the shocking news about Elayne and all through the hours of anxious uncertainty, first on the adrenaline-packed helicopter ride, which in other circumstances she probably would have relished, then in the hospital waiting room.

She'd reassured Sean he'd done the best he possibly could, kept Gavin informed – even talked through case details with him, explained everything she knew to Struan and the others when they arrived at the hospital and comforted Helen when she expressed how guilty she felt about bringing this situation into their lives, not to mention their home.

She'd sat by Elayne's bed, waiting for her to come round from the anaesthetic and then listening to her horrific account of what had happened. She'd sorted the practical details of organising the oversight of the crime scene, informing the SCD and arranging alternative accommodation for Helen and herself – and, of course, the dogs.

Apart from that one brief moment on the phone to Gavin, she'd been rock-solid in the midst of all the emotions flooding the situation – both hers and everyone else's. Now, in the quiet of the hospital gardens, she'd finally given in and wept. Seeing Elayne lying so still and pale on the clinical white hospital sheets, attached to monitors and drips, had been almost the worst moment of her life. The only saving grace had been the knowledge that Elayne had come through the operation and was going to be alright. The actual worst moment had been when she'd first got the news and was over a hundred miles away. Powerless to do anything.

How could anyone harm her precious, lovely woman? Someone so kind and open – after everything she'd been through as a child. But, of course, Katriona knew. She'd met too many criminals over the years not to know what some people were capable of. What she was still trying to get her head round was what Elayne had said to her after she'd told her story.

'You know, in a strange way, I feel grateful to the man.'

'What?!'

Katriona had tried to restrain her angry response as Elayne was so weak, and barely able to speak. She didn't want to upset her further. She briefly considered the possibility that Elayne was delusional due to the effects of all the drugs.

'Please don't get upset.' Elayne had actually tried to reassure her. 'I only meant …' Her throat had dried up and Katriona had helped her take a few sips of water.

'When he hit me … I remembered … what it had been like …'

She'd closed her eyes for a while, trying to summon the energy to explain. Katriona had forced herself to be patient, realising it was important to Elayne to communicate something of what had gone on for her.

'When I was little, I couldn't fight back, Kat. Not ever.' She'd paused to get her breath. Speaking was obviously a great effort.

'It was kind of therapeutic.'

Katriona had squeezed her hand, gently, keeping her rising tears just below the surface.

'My love …' She'd felt a frail response in Elayne's

fingers. 'Elayne, you need to sleep now. Let it go.'

She'd brushed a lock of Elayne's dark hair off her forehead, delighting in the fact that she was still alive, that she could still touch and hold this beautiful woman, that it wasn't all over.

'I will. But I feel so sad for him.'

'Sad?'

'Imagine having so awful a life that all you want to do is kill people for money …' and she'd drifted off into sleep.

Katriona had been astonished – as ever – by Elayne's compassion, and at a complete loss as to how to understand it. The man had tried to kill her, and not even out of any kind of passion. He hadn't really cared whether she lived or died. It was irrelevant to him. He was nothing more than a killing machine. He made no connection, at any level, with his victims, so it didn't matter to him what happened to them. She'd encountered this type of criminal before. They were just completely disconnected – from other people, from themselves, from life.

For a fleeting second, she had the merest comprehension as she heard Elayne's voice in her head. 'I feel so sad for him.' To live a life so divorced from life …

Then one of the nurses interrupted her thoughts, suddenly standing in front of her, trying to get her attention. Katriona jumped up.

'Is everything okay?'

'Yes, fine. Elayne's awake again, and asking where you are, that's all.'

It was nearly midnight when she and Gavin eventually managed to speak to each other again. Katriona had found her way back into the hospital gardens on a surprisingly warm evening, as long as she kept her coat on. Gavin wanted news of Elayne first and it was wonderful to be able to tell him she'd just left her sleeping peacefully.

'So everything's okay? She'll make a full recovery?'

'Yes. Thank God.'

'And what about you? Are you holding up?'

'I am.' Katriona was a bit hesitant, unsure how much to put into words.

'Will you be able to get some sleep yourself? I suppose you can't go back home?'

'No. The house is sealed off now, ready for the team tomorrow. But that's fine. I've got a room at Effie's. She's my friend who runs the B&B just down the road from here. But I think I'll stay with Elayne tonight … snooze in the chair. Just to be sure.'

'Well, make sure you look after yourself as well.'

Katriona was touched by Gavin's concern. 'I will. Elayne has taught me well,' she joked.

'So, tell me the full story – if you're up to it.'

Katriona found, at this stage of the day, she was reluctant to go back through all the details she'd accumulated so far, not wanting to revisit the emotions she'd temporarily put to one side. But she was first and foremost a detective – and Gavin needed to know what had happened. Every little piece of information could be useful somewhere.

So she forced herself to recount what she knew, careful to use other people's words to describe both shooting incidents so that the reports were as accurate as possible, but avoiding much of the emotional content, so what came over was as close to a police report as she could make it.

When she finally finished, there was silence from Gavin's end. She was appreciative of the space and the respect it implied.

'I think that's everything,' she concluded.

'I think – well, just thanks for being willing to go over it all again. It must be hard for you to take all this in.'

'Yes.' *You have no idea.* There was a shared pause. Katriona guessed Gavin was waiting for her to move the conversation forward when she was ready. She opted for a safer way back in.

'So has anything happened at your end since we spoke?'

'Yep, plenty. I've seen Frank.'

'What? How lovely. Is he okay?'

'Certainly is. He sends his regards, of course.'

'So how come … ?'

'I wondered if he could throw any light on Fisher.'

'What a good idea.' Like Gavin, Katriona had nothing but respect for Frank and recognised the value of his immense experience. 'And … ?'

It was Gavin's turn to tell a story, and he related as much of the conversation as he remembered, sharing Frank's suspicions about both Fisher and Stevens. Katriona also recalled disliking the latter.

'He was always so smug.'

'Yeah, that's kinda what Frank said about him.'

'But, I have to say, I never picked up that he might be part of the whole corruption thing.'

'No, well, he was probably well-practised by the time he was appointed to that rank. Though actually he wasn't that old, was he?'

Katriona tried to picture the man's face but couldn't recall many details.

'I don't remember clearly. I don't even remember talking to him much. It feels like he was a bit of a shadowy figure, working in the background.'

'Really? He didn't interview you, then?'

'Well, no. I was part of the investigating team, if you recall. I'd already been vetted before he came on the scene.'

'Of course.'

'So, I suppose I didn't need to have much contact with him. I reported to Hardcastle, the other guy. Wonder what he's doing now? Stevens, I mean.'

She heard Gavin draw breath. 'What's the betting he turns up to do Foster's interview tomorrow?'

'Is that still on?'

'As far as I know. But …'

'But what?'

'I have no idea where to go from here, Kat. I mean, do we take Helen's statement in the morning, as we'd planned, and use it to interrogate Foster? If I'm even allowed near him. I mean, that would immediately put Fisher et al in the picture, and put Helen's life at risk, again – '

'Gavin, hold on.' Katriona interrupted Gavin's anxious train of thought.

'What?'

'Remember what I said earlier today? About watching your back? It won't just be Helen's life you'll be putting at risk, here.'

'No, I suppose not.'

'Besides, we don't want to show our hand at this stage. None of them know what's happened here, yet. It would definitely be to our advantage to keep it like that.'

'So what do you suggest?'

'Well, put it this way ...' Katriona smiled to herself as the beginnings of a plan began to form. '... Foster isn't the only one who can manipulate the press.'

'Explain.'

'Okay. So how often do you hear in the news that there's been a climbing accident on Skye?'

There was a pause. 'Not very,' Gavin responded, sounding a trifle bemused.

'Precisely. Yet someone gets into trouble and calls out Mountain Rescue several times a month. In the summer, they can be up there looking for people two or three times a week.'

'Really?'

'Yes, really. And it doesn't get reported any further south than, perhaps, a short paragraph in *The Highland Times* and a write-up in the reports book at Inverness. Even if we have a fatality, that rarely warrants more than a mention in *The Scotsman*. I mean, last year, the team carried out a thirty-day search for a guy until they eventually found his body, but I don't expect you knew anything about it, did you?'

'No. So where are you going with this, Kat? I mean, this was a shooting, not a climbing accident.'

'But no-one knows that beyond the few who were

directly involved. No-one will have heard the gunfire from that height.'

'What about Elayne getting shot? That'll get reported, won't it? So, even if the incident on the mountain doesn't get much coverage, the shooting in your kitchen will.'

'People will have no reason to connect the two.'

'I'm not following.'

'It's all a question of what is actually released to the press.' Katriona could see now how this could be managed. 'And given that people's lives could be endangered by releasing all the facts at this stage, I think I can persuade some people I know, that limited reported would be very helpful just now.'

'God, yes. I hadn't thought but releasing information about Elayne would put her in danger, wouldn't it?'

'Precisely.'

'So I come back to my original question – what do you suggest?'

Katriona thought she detected just a hint of exasperation in Gavin's voice.

'I suggest we say something along the lines of: "A report of a shooting incident on Skye was received by Inverness Constabulary late last night."' Katriona use the flat tone of a news reporter. '"It is not known at this stage exactly what happened but sources indicate that a woman was attacked in the remote village of Torrin. No further details have been released so far. The crime scene has been sealed off and investigating officers are beginning work today."'

'You've done this before.'

Katriona grinned. That was sounding more like the ever-optimistic Gavin she used to work with.

'You noticed,' she joked. 'And the advantage of doing it this way is that it keeps the story small but releases just enough information for Fisher and his crew to believe 'mission accomplished' and to wait for confirmation.'

'While we have a few days' grace to get on with more investigating.'

'Exactly. We don't need to mention the incident on the mountain. If anyone picks up on it when the team set out in the morning, it'll be just the usual 'person falling over the edge, now missing'. They'll not confirm a fatality until they find the body and that could take days – weeks, even.'

'What a strange place you live in.'

'Well, it may seem strange to you …' Katriona laughed, gently, remembering how strange she'd felt it was when she'd first moved here.

Gavin interrupted her thoughts. 'So tell me how we manage the details? What happens about Helen's interview? I guess you won't be going to Inverness now?'

'No. And there's no need. As I said before, the SCD team will be arriving in the morning. Andy can take her statement while he's here. I'll talk to him about the need for confidentiality. And I'll get him to take statements from all three of them who witnessed what happened to Gravenberg. When I explain about it all being part of a bigger investigation, there'll be no problem in getting him to hold onto the information for a few days. I mean, it's not as if they need to go looking for a criminal. They know where he is.'

'That's true. I guess it's just a question of confirming the statements, as far as they're concerned.'

'Exactly. So I think it might interest Andy to learn about the wider picture.'

'Is that wise?'

'Yes. He's fine. Anyway, I'll have to tell him the details to explain why it needs to be kept low-key. Not to mention the fact that presumably you'd like the bullet. Normally that would be processed back in Inverness.'

'Of course. I hadn't even thought about that. I'd just assumed you'd send it here. No, you're right. I trust your judgement about this Andy. Maybe he'll be able to shed some light on the case. Fresh pair of eyes and all that …'

'Why? Has something new turned up at your end?'

'Yes, but there hasn't been any chance to bring you up to

date – what with everything you've been going through.'

And Gavin shared the other events in his day before Katriona went back inside to sit by Elayne for the night.

24

The next day turned out to be a busy one for Katriona. She'd managed a few hours sleep in the chair next to Elayne's bed but felt the weariness of not having had enough, and now had a stiff neck to boot. So, trying to co-ordinate the numerous connections she wanted to make was proving hard work.

She'd reluctantly left Elayne after breakfast but the patient was much brighter today and reassured Katriona that she understood her need to visit the crime scene and communicate with the investigating team.

'I'll be back in a while, love. I'll come back with Andy, 'cos he'll need your official statement, if you're up to it.'

'Yes, I can do that. But don't rush, Kat. I'll be fine here. You do what you need to do.'

Katriona had kissed her lightly, ever-conscious of how lucky she was, and made her way out to the carpark. She'd borrowed a car from Dougie's garage which he'd driven up the road earlier that morning, leaving the keys at Reception with a note. *It's the red Ford. Hope Elayne's okay.*

It was a bright sunny morning, for which Katriona was glad. It made her feel more optimistic about everything. She was anxious to get back to the house – not to mention the dogs. She felt the need to restore some kind of normality to life, though she knew that was not really going to happen until the team had finished their job and gone home. Nevertheless, she felt being back in Torrin would help somehow.

She wasn't prepared for what she met. Although the team from Inverness was relatively small – Andy and two other officers plus a two-person forensics team – the house looked horribly busy when she arrived. The sanctuary-like peace that normally greeted her had been banished by the yardage of incident tape, the collection of cars and vans on the driveway, and what appeared to be hoards of people coming in and out of both the front and back doors of the house, as well as milling around outside.

She recognised Struan first.

'What's going on?' she asked, just as a helicopter flew overhead to complete the noisy scene.

'Katriona. How are you? And Elayne, more to the point?' Struan seemed surprisingly relaxed after yesterday's events, and was, in fact, kitted up for another climb.

'She's okay, thanks, Struan. She's doing well.' Katriona felt unexpectedly tearful and was grateful that Struan reached over to give her a big hug, hiding her face temporarily from the people invading her home.

He spoke into her ear.

'Sorry about the chaos. Your team from Inverness arrived about an hour ago, and they've been quite discrete, but now the MR Team have arrived, too, so it's all got a bit busy.'

'Why are they here? At the house?' Katriona pulled back so she could see Struan's face, feeling a little more settled and ready to begin supervising where she could.

'They're just picking me up.'

'You're going out with them?' She was very surprised that Struan wanted to go straight back up the mountain after everything that had happened.

'It makes sense. I know the mountains as well as anyone and I also saw where the body fell.'

'Actually, Sir,' another voice interrupted. 'There's been a

bit of a change of plan. Morning, Ma'am.' Constable McTavish approached the two of them.

'Turns out one of the officers from Inverness is a climber, sir. He would very much appreciate you taking him up *Blà Bheinn* to the scene of the incident. Since this was not a straight-forward climbing accident, the scene needs to be properly processed.'

Damn, Katriona thought. *I hadn't considered that.* She hadn't taken McTavish into consideration, either, when she and Gavin had been discussing how to keep this low-key. She smiled at the Constable. 'I wonder if I could have a word.'

'If you're concerned about the need for confidentiality, Ma'am, please don't be. I've informed the local press they'll get a brief statement later, when you and the team have decided – well, whatever you want to say.' He lowered his voice. 'I still don't know what this is all about but I'm guessing it has something to do with our runaway, so I'm presuming you want limited information released and maximum security where possible.'

Katriona stared in astonishment. This was one very astute young man, but she also sensed he was highly delighted to have found himself in the midst of a Hollywood-style scenario. Keeping everything top-secret seemed to appeal to his sense of the dramatic. She could definitely use that to her advantage.

'Thank you, Constable. You are absolutely correct. At this stage, secrecy is paramount. Please keep what you know to yourself for the time being. I'll speak with the team leader. We need to co-ordinate with London and decide what information will be shared. We'll keep you informed as much as possible.'

After the Mountain Rescue Team had climbed back into their Landrover and set off towards the loch, Katriona made her way tentatively into the house, stepping over markers and bits of tape as she went. She hated to see her beautiful home disrupted like this. She pushed her tears down and took a deep breath, a new understanding dawning for her of the various witnesses she'd had to comfort over the years after their homes had been the scene, first of a crime, then this kind of intrusion.

She saw Andy coming down the stairs just as she passed through the open back door.

'Hi, Katriona. How are you?' He quickly checked himself. 'Sorry. Stupid thing to say. Just haven't seen you in a while.'

Katriona smiled. She liked Andy. He reminded her of Gavin. He had a similar 'clean-cut' approach to his policing. That was where the resemblance ended, though. Whereas Gavin had tidy fair hair, Andy's dark tufts always gave the impression of being out of control. In fact, try as he would, Andy generally had the appearance of someone who'd just got out of bed. This morning's crumpled tweed jacket was no exception.

'I've been fine – up until yesterday.'

'How's Elayne? I heard she'd come through the op okay.'

'Yes. She's doing alright, and she's already saying she'll give you a statement as soon as you want.'

Andy ran a hand through his hair – a familiar gesture of his which probably contributed to his 'tousled' look, Katriona thought.

'That's great, Katriona. We can drive up there as soon as we're through here. It won't take long to finish processing and cleaning up. There's really only the kitchen. Nothing disturbed upstairs, or in the other rooms.'

Katriona breathed a sigh of relief. That fitted what Elayne had told her but her partner's recollection might not have been accurate.

'Oh, and I'm afraid there's a blood trail though the hallway. Seems our man left through the front door.'

'Yes, that makes sense. Elayne said Sean and the others arrived just as he shot her. They came round the back so

Gravenburg will have taken the quickest route in the opposite direction.'

'Gravenburg? So we know who this man was, then?'

'I'm afraid so, Andy.' Katriona met Andy's surprised gaze. 'This is no straight-forward shooting – if there ever is such a thing. I want to put you in the picture but there's a lot of it. We need to find somewhere quiet to talk.'

She moved towards the kitchen door. 'I want to see the crime scene first.'

Andy put out a hand to restrain her. 'Are you sure?'

'Why? What do you mean?'

'Well, just that … you've got to come back and live here when we've all gone home. I was thinking you might not want to see Elayne's blood …' He stopped himself. '… what the kitchen looks like just now. You don't want to be remembering it every time you go in there.'

Katriona was touched by his consideration.

He continued. 'I've seen too many victims never able to go back to their homes, just because of what they witnessed. And this is a beautiful house, Katriona. You don't want to spoil that. And,' he changed the gentle tone of his voice to a more jocular one, 'despite the fact that none of us are London-trained, we do actually know how to process a crime-scene. You can leave it to us.'

'Yes, you're right.' Katriona felt torn between her desire as a detective to investigate the evidence thoroughly, and her love of the tranquil home she and Elayne had made together. She realised Andy was right, though. That precious sense of sanctuary would be gone for ever if she saw what was beyond the kitchen door. She sensed the two halves of her life heading for collision and decided to make her best attempt to keep them separate.

'You're absolutely right. Thanks, Andy. Let's step outside, again.'

In the end, they both left the team to it. Andy said he'd seen everything he needed to and was, Katriona sensed, itching to hear the full story. So they strolled down the road to the Blue Shed Café and ordered bacon buns and hot chocolate, and sat outside in the crisp air and autumn sunshine.

Katriona told Andy everything she knew up to date, piecing together a coherent picture as she went. There was something about telling someone else all the details that helped a case to coalesce. She'd found it more difficult than usual to get a handle on this one because she'd only been on the fringes up to now. What had happened yesterday changed that. She now had a personal stake in sorting this one out.

'So you can see why it's important exactly what we release to the press at this stage,' she concluded. 'And, sadly, what we allow to be known within the Force, too.'

'Yes.' Andy agreed. 'Wow. This is difficult. You're right. Both you and Gavin. This is just the tail-end of something, isn't it? I mean, it does sound like this Gravenburg was just tidying up loose ends for somebody. Elayne just got in the way. From his point of view.'

Katriona didn't want to consider the fact that he would probably have tried to kill Elayne anyway, once she'd seen him.

'The thing is, Andy, at this point, it's difficult to know where to go next. In terms of the incidents here, once they find the body, that's the case done and dusted. Just a matter of writing up a report. It's all very apparent what happened, and there's no investigating to do or anyone to take to trial …'

'I agree.' Andy swallowed a mouthful of bun and picked up his mug. 'I think the most helpful thing I can do is – like you said – complete all the essential admin for both incidents, file them separately for now and talk to the Super. I'll tell him what's going on – I don't need to share all the details. If I explain that the incidents are related and part of a bigger case being run from London, he'll be fine with that. We've done our bit, and co-operated with an on-going investigation. I don't see there'll be a problem.'

'Thanks, Andy. I mean, that makes sense, doesn't it? If you were to try taking on the stuff behind the shootings, you'd be covering the same territory as Gavin. No point in you both working the same case. And let's face it, what happened here – in terms of location, it's almost irrelevant. Most of the case is based in London. Gravenburg would've tracked down Helen wherever she'd ended up.'

'Not so easily, though. The fact that her hiding place was reported straight to Gavin's boss seems to have made things a whole lot easier for him to find her.'

Katriona paused before answering. 'It's just not that straight-forward, is it? When I think about it, I can't see how Gavin is going to carry on investigating. He's going to be hampered at every turn.'

'There is one way forward.' Andy looked directly at her, and Katriona felt a surge of adrenalin at what she thought he was suggesting. She forced herself to respond calmly.

'And what's that, then?'

'Well, it's pretty obvious, Katriona. You're the only one of us with freedom to act, because you're not directly employed by either end. This Fisher-guy has no jurisdiction over you, and as long as you report what you're doing to our Super, you're pretty much free to act as you see fit.'

There was silence between them as the idea worked its way into Katriona's thoughts.

'Look,' Andy spoke again. 'I can certainly recommend you act as liaison between me and Gavin. That only makes sense. But when you look at it logically, you have intimate knowledge of the circumstances in both locations, you know all the key personnel, you've even been dragged into the case itself by Helen coming here. You're the perfect person to do what the rest of us can't.'

25

Gavin read the e-mail with a mixture of disgust and relief.

Interview with DI Foster postponed. IPCC to reschedule. Keep me informed re the girl's statement. Fisher.

The memo was hardly surprising, given what Gavin knew, but it was sufficiently curt to be considered rude and uncooperative. No explanations offered. No reasons given. Foster apparently warranted his full title, whereas Helen was not even credited with her name.

He wondered if Fisher would be expecting him to go storming upstairs to the Super's office, demanding more information. It was certainly his first instinct, but he knew that the postponement actually played right into his hands. The less he had to have contact with either Fisher or Foster at this stage, the easier it would be to continue investigating quietly.

He called Charlie into his office.

'Shut the door, Charlie.' He lowered his voice. 'This is for your ears only.'

'Sir.' Charlie stepped calmly through the doorway, closing the door behind him. Gavin reflected on how unruffled he always appeared, and wished he could manage the same. Perhaps he did outwardly. No-one ever actually told him to calm down so maybe he was successful at keeping the turmoil under wraps.

'Have a seat.' He gestured to the chair on the opposite side of his desk. Charlie dutifully did as he was asked.

'It's about … Well, it's just that …' This was difficult. He tried again. 'I want to emphasize the importance of all information coming through me regarding this case.'

He paused, praying that Charlie would take the hint.

'Sir?'

Gavin sighed. There was no reason why the Sergeant should have any idea what he was referring to. He steeled himself for his next words.

'It appears that the leak may be more extensive than we thought.'

'Oh, I see. Well, that makes sense.'

Gavin was surprised. 'Why do you say that?'

'Well, Sir. It has often occurred to me that in order for our primary … suspect … to continue operating, he would need some organisational support.'

'You've never mentioned the thought before.'

'No, Sir. I had no evidence. It was, as I said, just a supposition. I'm presuming that is no longer the case?'

Gavin struggled inwardly about how he should respond. 'I don't want to put you in a difficult position, Charlie.'

'It seems like I'm in one anyway, Sir. And I'd rather be in a fully-informed difficult position than in one where I don't know how to act.'

'I take your point.'

There was silence between them as each considered how to proceed. Gavin was relieved that it was Charlie who moved things forward. That made it easier, somehow.

'If I may make a suggestion, Sir?'

'Please do.'

'I hope this is not out of place, Sir, but if the investigation is to become … even more circumspect than before, well, it seems to me, you're going to need a team – a small team – of people who you can trust. With full disclosure, Sir. That way, we could, if necessary, move from 'circumspect' to 'clandestine', if the circumstances called for it.'

Gavin was now even more surprised. 'How long have you suspected things are not right?'

'Since the re-organisation, Sir. Perhaps it was easier for me to see it, coming in fairly new at the time, but when the DI in question wasn't dismissed from his post, well, it made me feel uncomfortable, if you know what I mean.'

'I know exactly what you mean, Charlie.'

'So, as I say, it occurred to me that the corruption we were supposedly eradicating from the station, might actually run a whole lot deeper. There was nothing I could do about it then, Sir, but it sounds like there is now.'

Gavin was impressed by the determination in Charlie's voice.

'I really hope so,' he responded, 'but first we need to find a way to continue this case without it becoming compromised.' He stood up to stretch his legs. 'And you're right, the only way to do that is to get a select team together and tell you everything. I think, Charlie, I feel a lunch-time drink coming on.'

Feeling somewhat buoyed up by the response from Charlie, Gavin made his way down to Tom's lab. He didn't think Tom would have any problems about acting outside the system for a while - the unconventionality of it would probably appeal to him – but he hated having to ask others to risk their careers in this way.

'Look, Gavin. It's ultimately about integrity, isn't it?' Tom said when Gavin began to explain the situation to him. 'We each have to do what we consider right. For some people, I guess their first priority is keeping their noses clean and staying out of trouble, but you know that's not me. I can't work somewhere where I know the truth about a case isn't going to be investigated thoroughly.

'Besides …' and he stepped across the lab to remove a specimen from his microscope as someone from the forensic team walked in.

'... technically, I'm not even employed by you lot. Don't forget, we're an independent company these days. You just hire our services, now. Isn't that right, Lucy?'

The young woman who'd just entered the lab, smiled in a distracted way. 'Have you seen my notebook, Tom? I'm sure I had it when I left here a minute ago.'

Tom picked up a turquoise-covered file from besides the microscope and handed it to her. 'You left this, too,' he grinned, waving the specimen slide.

'You're a love.' She gave him a warm smile and walked back out again, her mind apparently already on the next thing.

Gavin admired the way Tom had covered his tracks.

'So, you'd be okay with an informal lunch-time drink to put you in the picture?'

Between his visit to Tom's lab and his arrival at the pub, Gavin received two interesting phonecalls. The first was from a DI in Geneva. Maxwell had finally tracked down the officer whom Madeleine Wright had spoken to when she became concerned about Heather Hough's non-appearance at her conference. It appeared that once the officer heard that his routine enquiries might be related to a bigger case, he'd reported this up the line to his boss, DI Sommer. It was the DI who rang through this morning.

'So you can see we had no reason to do more at the time.' Sommer's English was impeccable.

'Can I ask what you *did* do? Did you just take down the details or did you do any investigating?' Gavin asked.

'We didn't do much, as I said, but I did get my officer to check out some of the obvious things like airline passenger lists and so on, since Ms Wright was so insistent. And, of course, the WHO is a highly significant organisation. It might have turned out to be important. But he couldn't find any evidence that she'd even entered the country. So we had to leave it at that. People are entitled to be private.'

'Of course,' Gavin responded, mentally putting the

thought on the back burner to consider later.

'It sounds like this has become important now?'

Gavin decided to play it cool. 'Oh, we're trying to track her down to inform her about her sister. She was found dead in her house a few days ago.'

'Not Emily Hough? The singer?'

'You know her?'

'No, but I'm – was – a big fan. Always went to see her when she performed here. I was really upset to see she'd died. So this Heather is her sister?'

'Yes.'

'And you don't know where she is?'

'No.' Gavin felt the tension rising.

'And Emily didn't die of natural causes, did she?'

'No … so you can see …'

'Quite. Look, I'll get my officer to do a bit more of a detailed check, if that'll help, but, like I said, it really doesn't look like she arrived here at all.'

Gavin expressed his thanks and gave him a phone number that would connect directly with his desk, without having to go through the switchboard. He didn't want any more information trickling out of his reach.

The second phonecall came as he was driving to the pub where he was due to meet Charlie and Tom. They'd agreed to each make their own way there so as not to arouse suspicion. This one was from Katriona.

'Hi, Katriona. How're things?'

'A bit chaotic at this end, if I'm honest. I've never been on the wrong end of an incident-scene before.'

'It's a bit horrendous, isn't it?' Interrupting Katriona's next sentence, he said, 'Let me ring you back in just a minute. I'm on my way to – a meeting. I'll ring you from the carpark.'

A few minutes later, he pulled up outside The Unicorn, a venue which was a reasonably safe distance from the station and which had plenty of quiet corners for secret meetings.

He reached his secure phone out of its hiding place,

tapping in Katriona's number. He asked about Elayne's progress first and was glad the news was so positive.

'So how's the incident-processing going? Is your mate Andy up to scratch?' he joked.

'Andy? Oh, yes, he's a stickler for procedure.'

'I thought you said it was chaotic.'

'No, I didn't mean … it's just a lot busier than I'm used to, that's all. And it's not much fun being in the centre of it all. At least, not in this way. I suppose I'm not used to not running the show.'

Gavin grinned to himself. He knew Katriona well enough to realise how difficult that would be for her.

'Are they processing both incidents at the same time?'

'Pretty much. At least, as far as they can. They can't do much about Gravenburg until they find the body. And that could take a while.'

'And what about Helen's statement?'

'Andy's doing that as we speak. He's taking statements from everyone who's involved with the two incidents here, so he's doing Helen's statement for you at the same time. They're up in Portree, at the station there.'

'And have you put Andy in the picture? The bigger picture, I should say.'

'Yes.'

Katriona's short answer surprised Gavin. 'What are you not telling me?'

'It's just something Andy said. Don't worry. There's nothing to get concerned about. He's perfectly okay with keeping things quiet at this end and just processing everything that needs it. He'll clear it all with the Super, and he's more than happy to liaise with you.'

'So … ?'

'Let me tell you something else first. That's why I rang. I heard back from Stephi, this morning.'

'She's your German contact, isn't she?'

'That's right. She was going to so some fishing for us about Dieter Bergmann's death, if you remember.'

Gavin thought that seemed like a lifetime ago. So much had happened in the last few days.

'Did she find anything useful?'

'Yes. She found Dieter's body. In the river.'

'What? I thought he was killed in a motorcycle accident.'

'Yes, that was what got reported, but Stephi's seen the file. Apparently, witnesses say they heard a loud noise, like an engine backfiring, and then saw the motorbike driving over the edge of the bridge. Everyone assumed it was a freak accident.'

'But now they're not so sure ...' Gavin butted in.

'Actually, now they're certain.'

'Of what, exactly?'

'That Dieter Bergmann was shot.'

Gavin drew in his breath, sharply. 'So how come Stephi found his body?'

'She's a trained diver, so sometimes she goes out as part of the local team. She was chatting with the guy overseeing the investigation when the news came in it might not have been an accident, so she volunteered to take some of the shifts over the weekend. They recovered the body this morning.'

'So she really has been fishing.'

'I was waiting for you to say that. I thought I'd leave the poor jokes to you.' Katriona's sarcastic remarks came over as friendly banter.

'I presume they haven't had time to process the body, yet?'

'No, but Stephi told them about our interest. I mean, it was the only thing she could do.'

'But not the details?' A surge of panic ran through Gavin's mind. This case was becoming more and more difficult to contain.

'She didn't know any. I hadn't told her anything. She was only supposed to be taking an unofficial look at the file – see if there was anything suspicious.'

There was a pause before Katriona continued. 'She's

invited us over to see everything firsthand, if we want to. She doesn't know what our interest is. Obviously, I'm not at liberty to tell her. That's your call. She'll do her best to keep a lid on it at her end until you advise.'

Gavin hesitated. 'I can't go, Katriona. In the normal course of events, it would be exactly the right thing to do, but if I tell Fisher I'm off to Germany to look at a related incident …'

'I know, Gavin. But I could.'

'What? Go to Germany?'

'Yes.' He heard Katriona taking a deep breath. 'It's what Andy said to me this morning. He said I was the only one of the three of us who was free to act without arousing suspicion.'

'I guess so …'

'Because I'm a consultant,' Katriona continued. 'I'm not actually employed by the Force. They just buy in my services.'

'That's funny.'

'What is?'

'That's almost exactly what Tom said – only an hour or so ago.'

Gavin, Tom and Charlie had a constructive lunch-time meeting. When Gavin filled the other two in on the events of the last twenty-four hours on Skye, they were both deeply shocked.

'Wow, Gavin. I can see why you're so concerned.' Tom's response was forceful. 'We should have Fisher arrested immediately.'

'We can't do that, Tom.'

'Why ever not? The man's responsible for two people being shot at – one of them nearly fatal.'

'Because I believe Fisher is still small-fry.'

Tom's eyes widened but Charlie's reaction was more muted. Gavin invited him to expand on his thoughts from earlier in the day.

'It makes sense that the corruption runs through the system, Tom, if what we're dealing with is something like industrial espionage.' There was a new air of authority about Charlie. 'Individuals can't operate successfully on their own, but they are essential to the guys at the top who don't want to get their hands dirty. The top dogs have to have deniability.'

Gavin regarded Charlie with respect. 'You sound like you know what you're talking about.'

'Just years of observation, Sir.'

'So how do we get to the truth of it all?' A typical Tom question. 'If your hands are tied so much …'

'We have an outside accomplice,' Gavin announced, pausing as three plates of chips arrived at their table. 'Can I get anyone another drink?'

'In a minute, Gavin. More important things first. You're talking about Katriona, right?'

And Gavin explained further what had transpired during the morning. Maybe it was the warm food and the excellent beer, but as they talked and ate together, he began to feel much happier about the possibility of resolving the case. This was a good team coalescing around him. They all had unique and invaluable talents and he could see how they might be able to continue investigating, each of them able to operate in their own field without arousing suspicion, and then contributing to the whole picture. It just might be feasible.

He left for the station an hour later, with a much more positive outlook.

'Where the hell have you been?'

'Sir?' Gavin almost collided with Fisher as he stepped through the entrance to the station.

'I've been trying to get hold of you.'

'Sorry, Sir. I must have turned my phone off.' Gavin reached into his pocket and pulled out his mobile. He was trying to remain calm but inside his thoughts were frantic. It was most unlike Fisher to use this kind of language. He normally presented a completely unemotional front. What had he found out?

As coolly as he could, he looked at the small screen in his hand and said, 'Yes, my apologies. It's switched off.'

He looked up at Fisher's flushed face.

'What did you want me for, Sir?'

'I'm calling a meeting – now – of all the staff. In the briefing room.' And Fisher turned his back, marching briskly along the corridor.

What had happened now? As far as he could recall, Fisher had never spoken to the whole staff before – at least, not since his arrival speech. He heard the door open behind him, and saw Tom and Charlie coming in together, swapping cheery remarks, behaving as naturally as they could.

'Fisher's just called a meeting.' He spoke in a low voice. 'Of the entire staff.'

They exchanged looks.

'Does he know something?' Tom asked, as quietly as possible.

Gavin shrugged.

'No.' Charlie sounded definite. 'It can't be that. He wouldn't do that in front of everyone.' He turned to Gavin. 'Too risky, Sir.'

'I hope you're right. Just be careful.' And he led the way to the briefing room where everyone was gathered.

There was a general air of noisy confusion emanating from the collected personnel. No-one seemed to know what this was about. Gavin found an empty chair at the back of the room and sat down. Fisher entered, and Gavin watched him make his way to the front of the gathering where he waited for silence before speaking.

'It is with deep regret that I must inform you all that DI Foster was found dead in his apartment, this morning.'

26

Helen was enchanted by the tiny harbour at Portree. It was such a pretty scene. She was standing in a street, part-way up a hillside, which gave an excellent view across the town and out to the deep waters between Skye and the island of Raasay. The island was close enough to be seen quite clearly from here.

The tide must have been on its way in because she could see a couple of old-fashioned fishing-boats making their way in-between the tall cliffs on either side of the harbour entrance, sailing towards the dock. One boat had already arrived with its load of lobster creels, and two men were busy unloading their catch onto the quayside.

She turned to Jamie, who had brought her up here when they'd finished at the police station, thinking she'd like to see the view.

'It's perfect. Like a picture book.'

'It's pretty special, isn't it?' He smiled, in that proud, wistful way the islanders had when talking about their home. 'Would you like to go down to the harbour and take a look?'

'I'd love to.' And they set off down the hill towards the busy scene.

Helen was glad of this break from the frantic anxiety of the last day and a half. This morning had been particularly difficult. Having to recall all the details both of yesterday's dramatic incident at the top of *Blà Bheinn* – well, nearly the top, as far as she was concerned – and then of the horrid events surrounding her discovery of Emily Hough's body – was it nearly a week ago? – had left her emotionally drained. But it was done now. No more need to worry, she hoped. At least for the time being.

She was also glad of this opportunity to see something more of the island. Andy had taken Struan's statement back at the house before Struan set off with the MRT but he'd explained the importance of doing Helen's in a more official setting since the implications, particularly of her London story, were huge. He'd suggested they do Jamie's statement at the station, too, to draw less attention to Helen. An outside observer would just assume Andy was – as Katriona described him – a stickler for procedure.

Helen was pleased Jamie had been allowed to come, too. She wanted to spend as much time in his company as possible before … She chose not to finish the thought. The idea of returning to London was becoming less attractive by the day. She was beginning to 'get it' – this passionate love of the island that all its inhabitants shared, whether indigenous or incomer.

She'd managed to see a little of Broadford, too, though she hadn't found that as picturesque as Portree. Katriona had arranged for them to stay overnight at her friend Effie's B&B. In fact, Helen hadn't actually seen anything of Katriona and guessed she hadn't come back there to sleep. If she had, she'd been up mighty early, as she'd already left the hospital to go back to Torrin by the time Helen had arrived to visit Elayne.

It had been wonderful to see her new friend sitting up and chatting, although she tired pretty quickly. Helen had kept her visit suitably short, wondering what she should do next, when Katriona and Andy had turned up to explain their plans. She'd discovered Jamie waiting in Andy's car. He would visit Elayne later in the day. Katriona was being very strict on how many people were allowed at any time and Andy had priority this morning – for obvious reasons.

So she'd sat in the car with Jamie and they'd gone through what had happened to them all over again. Each recounting of the event seemed to get a bit easier, somehow, and sharing it with Jamie really helped. When Andy had re-appeared, they'd set off along the main road to Portree.

It wasn't like any main road Helen had ever seen before, or had even imagined. Huge mountains towering above the handful of cars, fantastic views out across a spectacular blue sea towards first the mainland, then various neighbouring islands. At one point, the car had climbed steeply uphill, a sheer drop to the sea-loch on their right, the road twisting round a sharp hairpin to double back on the other side of the magnificent plummeting gorge at the head of the loch, so that she could look down on the road they'd just come along and see the sparkling water hundreds of feet below her.

This was quickly followed by another loch so that the road ran inland again, tracing the coast and culminating in an extraordinary jumble of high peaks which seemed to be generating their own private storm of dark, broiling clouds.

'That's the *Cuillin*, again,' Jamie explained. 'We've come round the far side of them, now.'

Then, as they'd turned towards Portree, the countryside had calmed down into moorland and scrub and Jamie had suggested that Helen turn round to see the view they were leaving behind. Helen had gasped in wonder as a magnificent collection of mountains joined together to make a breathtaking scene. As she twisted back into her seat, an extraordinary pinnacle came into view in the distance ahead.

'The Old Man of Storr,' Jamie announced.

'The what?'

'It's a high rock, up in the *Quiraing* at the north of the island. You're lucky to see it today. Often the weather's too cloudy or rainy at this time of year.'

They'd travelled on, into the pretty township of Portree, which began with isolated houses and cottages, scattered on the moorland, the greens and browns of the peaty earth and heather burnished by the low-lying autumn sun. As they approached, the houses became more frequent until the country road began to look more like the kind of street Helen was used to, with buildings on both sides and even traffic.

They passed a couple of modern buildings as they drove. One, Andy pointed out to her as the Aros Visitor Centre, and suggested she might like to take in the exhibition while she was here. The second, an impressive, modern building on their left as they came into the town, had a line of blue buses parked in front of it.

'That's Portree High School,' Jamie said. 'It's the only secondary school on the island.'

'Is that what all the buses are for? Bringing the kids in?'

'Yes. A lot of them used to stay during the week in that block over there … The Elgin Hostel, but when they rebuilt the school in 2008, that was turned into an art and computing block.'

'It's long way for some of them to travel,' Helen mused. She'd done a bit of map-studying on Saturday, and knew how surprisingly large the island was.

'I suppose it is,' Jamie responded. 'I guess you get used to it. There are still some local hostels for some of them. Just not on the school campus any more.'

Helen thought the idea of boarding sounded romantic, until she considered it also meant living away from one's family for most of the time.

The car had followed the main road into the town centre where she discovered a square of buildings, all facing each other around the four sides, encompassing a small carpark, a bus terminal and a paved pedestrian area in the middle. The police station, a rather nondescript, elongated building stood next to a grim, imposing structure along one side of the square. This, Jamie told her, was the Sherriff Court House.

It was so unlike anywhere Helen had ever been before, she almost felt she'd stepped into an old story-book. But for all its unfamiliarity, she found she liked it. There was a cosy feel to the place, an intimate sense of safety. She had hoped that would help with the interview she must face and had discovered that it did.

Now, strolling down the tiny street that ran alongside the harbour, interviews over, statements taken, she could almost feel that other world – the fast-paced, busy, stressful world she'd left behind – might not even exist. There was something about this island that encouraged her to let go of who she had been, of things in her past she had never expected to leave behind, and to try believing in a different kind of future.

She had held her dream of becoming a singer for as long as she could remember, but she had come to recognise that much of her fantasizing had been hopelessly unrealistic. She'd always imagined she would be 'discovered', when she was younger. Some mythical agent would just happen to stop off at the burger-bar and hear her singing as she threw chips into the fryer or wrapped the chicken bun in a napkin and box. He would declare her voice was far too amazing to be left behind a counter …

As she'd got older, she'd got more of a handle on the idea that one has to create one's dreams, that a lot of hard work and planning had to accompany the wild longings and visualisations. Accordingly, her aspirations had lowered, as she'd come up against more and more obstacles to success, until her confidence, too, had diminished and made it seem less and less likely that having any kind of career which involved her singing would be possible. It had taken an enormous amount of courage – and much friendly encouragement from Bev – to get her to go to that audition. And look what had happened then.

But something had changed since she'd arrived on the island. Something about the idea of success itself. Her childish interpretation of what success meant – fame, fortune, admiration – seemed to have dissolved in the island's rarefied atmosphere, and she now had glimmerings of something much richer and more real, somehow, though it had yet to materialise in any way she could recognise.

As she stood with Jamie, looking out across the harbour, she found herself wondering how this would all work out and realised she no longer felt anxious. A quiet certainty that all would be well was germinating inside her, and she felt it would have something to do with being here, on Skye.

'And up there …' Jamie pointed above her head, bringing her back to the present. '… is Skye Gathering Hall.'

'What a lovely name. What happens there?'

'Lots of things. Ceilidhs, weddings, pop concerts.'

'Pop concerts? What, here?' Helen was sceptical.

'Oh yes. We've had some big names over the years. Don't forget we've even produced some famous bands of our own. Remember Runrig?'

'Who?'

Jamie looked at her sadly. 'No, I suppose that's before your time.'

Helen punched him in the arm, playfully. 'You idiot. You can't be that much older than me.'

'No. A few years. But I'm a bit of a geek when it comes to rock music – and I know my island's musical history. I mean, the Gathering Games used to be super-important on the social calendar back in the early twentieth century. People would come from all over. Anybody who was anybody would expect to come here at one time. And a big part of the Games was the Ball, held on two successive nights at the Hall. Part of the debutante circuit. And the mid-evening cabaret would include opera, ballet …'

Helen couldn't decide whether he was winding her up, but felt the stirrings of something inside her that made her think he might be telling the truth. If he was, she'd really like to know more of the island's heritage. Even become a part of it …

'Are you still on for this evening's concert?' Jamie broke into her thoughts.

'Definitely. I'm looking forward to it.'

'I'm so glad.' He reached out a hand and grasped hers. His lovely dark eyes stared directly into her face.

'I know it's not been a great time for you,' he said, slowly, 'but I'm really glad you came here.'

She met his gaze and felt her breath catch.

'So am I.' She closed her eyes and let him kiss her.

They caught up with Katriona again at the hospital during the afternoon. Elayne was looking tired but the colour had returned to her face. When Helen knocked on the door to her room, she and Katriona were in an earnest discussion.

'Can we come in? Are you okay with that?' she asked.

'Of course,' Elayne responded. 'And what have you been up to? You look different.'

Helen felt herself blushing. Elayne was probably the most astute person she'd ever met. When Jamie followed her in, Elayne said, 'Ah, good.'

How did she know? But Helen was spared from further embarrassment as Elayne discretely changed the subject to ask about the evening's concert, and a happy, light-hearted conversation ensued.

After about ten minutes, it was clear Elayne was tiring so Katriona suggested they all leave her to sleep, and the three of them made their way to the hospital's café to catch up.

'So, did everything go okay at the station?' Katriona asked.

'Yes. Andy was very …' Helen hunted for a suitable word. '… supportive. He made it a lot easier than it might have been. I'm just glad it's done.' She paused, catching Katriona's eye. 'But I guess it's not over.'

'No, I'm afraid not.' She could see Katriona hesitating.

'I suppose I'll have to go to court, eventually, won't I?' she said, summoning the courage to voice what she'd been trying not to think about all day. But as she said it, she realised she felt differently about her precarious situation now. Somehow, that kiss had changed things.

'Well, maybe,' Katriona responded, 'but you won't have to face DI Foster himself.'

'Really?' Helen was confused. 'Why not? I thought …'

'Because he's been found dead, this morning.' Katriona spoke as gently as she could but Helen sensed that nightmare world she thought she'd escaped from, reaching out to hold her in its grasp.

'I don't understand.'

'No, neither do we. I've just spoken with Gavin on the phone. Seems all they have yet is a report that he was found dead in his apartment. A suspected overdose.'

'Is that likely?' Jamie asked.

Helen looked at him. 'What do you mean?'

'Jamie's right, Helen. The whole thing is highly suspicious. I think I need to tell you a few things. I'd hoped to keep most of this from you, but for your own safety, I think you need to know what kind of situation you've got caught up in. It's much bigger than just – '

'Than just what? Murder? Corruption?' Helen felt an unexpected surge of anger. 'What could be bigger than that?'

There was an uncomfortable silence. Then Katriona spoke in low tones.

'It's looking like this is just the tail-end of a possible international conspiracy.'

Helen stared at Katriona, trying desperately to make sense out of her words. She heard herself say, 'Don't be ridiculous. That's … that's impossible.'

Something inside her snapped and she slammed her fists on the table, standing up as she did so.

'No,' she shouted, glaring at Katriona. 'No. I just won't have it.' And she stormed out of the café.

As she sat in the hospital gardens, Helen was grateful the other two hadn't come rushing after her but had allowed her the space to let off steam alone. She needed that. She wasn't used to experiencing such strong emotions – and so many different ones, all in one day.

It wasn't fair. Just as she'd thought her life was taking a turn for something more settled and much happier, it was all threatening to fall apart again. Why was this happening to her?

But even as she thought it, she realised it wasn't that simple. She wasn't any longer that frightened teenager who would retreat into feeling sorry for herself, every time something didn't go according to plan. She was stronger now. The events of the last week had toughened her up, given her 'backbone' as her aunt would have put it. Although she was extremely upset by what Katriona had said, she knew she wasn't collapsing because of it, as she would have done before. She felt angry, yes, but that was actually energising her into facing what was going on, rather than running away from it.

And underlying this newfound stability was the realisation that she was in love. Not with Jamie – although she suspected that might be on the horizon. No, she was in love with this beautiful island, with its strange old-fashioned ways and its magical scenery.

Suddenly, she knew she'd come here for a reason, and that reason was because she belonged here. She was determined to find a way to stay, and if that meant dealing with an international conspiracy – crazy though that sounded – then that's what she would do.

She stared past the hospital building towards the Red Hills, whose tops she could just see towering above the town. She remembered the powerful scene of mountaintops she'd been privileged to view from *Blà Bheinn* yesterday, and she felt the presence of the mountains sustaining her, as if holding her securely in place. A quiet 'thank you' escaped her lips, followed by a gasp of surprise. She was talking to mountains! This island never ceased to amaze her.

She stood up, wiped her angry tears from her eyes and made her way, calmly, back to the hospital café, where Katriona and Jamie were patiently waiting.

'Okay, tell me everything,' she said.

27

'With respect, Sir, I need to go and check for myself.' Gavin was putting on a pretty good show of exasperation and annoyance.

He'd followed Fisher out of the briefing room and pursued him up the stairs to his office, ejaculating short, urgent questions as he tried to keep up with the brisk pace the Super was setting. He knew it was imperative that he behaved as if he didn't have any suspicions of his boss's part in what was going on, and to do that convincingly, he needed to continue showing his frustration at not being allowed access to anything to do with Foster. In light of their previous conversations, he knew it was what Fisher would expect.

'Pearce, I'm quite sure the Surrey police are perfectly capable of doing their job. They'll send us their report when they've finished investigating.'

'But, Sir,' Gavin exploded, 'the man's been implicated in an ongoing murder enquiry.'

'So you keep saying, Inspector, but you have yet to provide any convincing evidence of that. Have you heard any more from that girl – whatever her name was?'

Nice move, thought Gavin. *Turn the focus back on me, question what I'm doing and check for further information on Helen into the bargain.* He squirmed, just sufficiently to allow an element of apparent embarrassment to show through.

'No, Sir. Still waiting on that.' He thought he saw a satisfied smile pass briefly over Fisher's face.

'So you still don't actually have any reason to go interfering in this one. No, I'll put through a request for the report as per normal procedure in such circumstances, and I'll pass on anything I think you should know.'

Yeah, I'll bet, Gavin reflected, facetiously. He opened his mouth to attempt another objection.

'That will be all, Pearce.'

Gavin's irritation with the man was now genuine. He was unbelievably annoying. However, he knew the man's behaviour was to his advantage in the current situation, and turned to go.

'Oh, and Pearce …' The Super's voice floated over his shoulder. 'Don't go stirring things up within the ranks.'

Back down in Tom's lab, his team reconvened.

'I don't suppose you got anywhere with Fisher?' Tom asked, passing out mugs of tea.

'No. Exactly as expected. He's completely closed the door on access to any privileged information. Says he'll let me see the report when it comes through – if he thinks I need to.'

Tom grinned. 'So your acting skills weren't called into question, then?'

Gavin forced a smile in response. 'No, I think I managed to convey my annoyance. It doesn't actually help us, though. We really do need access to what happened to Foster.'

'I presume you're not convinced by the story of an overdose, then, Sir?' Charlie asked.

'No, I'm not. In all the years we suspected Foster was up to no good, there was never a mention of him taking drugs. Hints he might be dealing, every now and then, but even that was unsubstantiated. He was much more a booze and gambling man.'

'Do you know anyone in the Surrey force?' Charlie

enquired.

'Not sufficiently well to go asking, I'm afraid.'

'Well, you might not, but I believe I can help there,' Tom intervened.

'Really? Let me guess. Another one of your entourage.'

Tom put on a look of fabricated innocence.

'Entourage? I have no idea what you might mean. And this one's called Felicity. Haven't spoken in a while. We must be due a tête-à-tête over an Italian …' and he moved away to dig out his phone from the bottom of a rucksack.

Gavin finished his coffee and made his way reluctantly towards the door. 'I'll be in my office.'

He very much wanted to stay in the company of people he could trust but knew if he spent too much time closeted with the other two in Tom's lab, it would raise suspicions elsewhere.

He climbed the stairs and pushed open his office door. Everything looked exactly the same but he was left with that sick feeling of knowing that nothing would ever be the same again. How could he carry on working here when he knew that his boss was – well, frankly, a criminal? And not just his boss.

He looked gloomily out of the window, across the station yard. There was only one way, and that was to get to the bottom of this case. To actually find some evidence that would conclusively prove Fisher's culpability. And Stevens' involvement, if possible. He suddenly realised it had to be possible, because it was imperative not only to solve the elements of this immediate crime but also to expose the multitudinous layers of corruption he was discovering within the Force. And God knows how big this went.

The thought sent shivers through him. He had to accept that this was no longer just about Emily Hough's murder. This probably wasn't even only about the reasons behind her murder and whatever deals she'd been involved in or information she'd stumbled across – with all the ramifications that might entail.

No, this was both closer to home and more far-reaching than he could ever have imagined. A veritable core of corruption and conspiracy running through the heart of the Metropolitan Police Force itself. The cold impact of what lay before him threatened to reduce him almost to tears. He pushed his emotional response away and turned his mind towards a grim determination to get to the truth – whatever it might cost him personally.

He picked up his internal phone and rang down to Patterson in the archives.

'Jim, can you get me some transcripts from the corruption case a few years back?'

Just before Gavin decided to pack up for the day, Tom rang and asked him to go back down to the lab. When he got there, he found Charlie already waiting. Tom was as enthusiastic as ever.

'I've heard back from Felicity.'

'Any joy?' Gavin asked.

'Yes. She's going to do the post-mortem.'

Gavin looked at Tom in astonishment. 'Even for you, that's quite a coup,' he said. 'How did you pull that off?'

Tom laughed. 'No, I can't take the credit for it. She's the Forensic Pathologist for Reigate Division, so she would've done the post-mortem anyway. But I will take credit for persuading her to share what she discovers – on the QT.'

'Well done. And thanks, Tom.'

'No problem. I'm looking forward to reconnecting with her.' He grinned. 'Anyway, she's already told me that she's suspicious of the overdose theory.'

'Oh?' Gavin pulled up a stool next to Charlie and gestured for Tom to join them.

'Yes, apparently, there was no question that drugs of some sort had been injected into his arm, but she couldn't see any evidence of old puncture wounds, as you would expect from a regular user. At least, on first inspection. Obviously, she's going to follow up on that with a full examination and toxicology report and so on.'

'Well, that fits with what we said earlier, doesn't it?'

'Absolutely. In fact, she hinted she was a little surprised by the readiness of the investigating officer to jump on evidence of an overdose and publicise that as cause of death.'

'I don't suppose she mentioned his name – this officer?'

'She did, as a matter of fact. Because she took an instant dislike to him. Something about his manner. Got right up her nose, apparently.'

'So?' Gavin pushed.

'So – what?' Tom had clearly gone off-track, again.

'What was his name?'

'Oh, sorry. Stevens. Elliot Stevens. He's one of the IPCC guys – '

'I know,' interrupted Gavin. 'Well, that pretty much confirms it, then.'

'Sir?' Charlie queried.

'He's the guy who recommended Fisher for his post. You might remember him, Tom. He was one of the investigating team during the corruption.'

Tom looked hard at Gavin. 'So you think he's in on this?'

'I certainly do.' Gavin hadn't told the other two about his conversation with Frank, yet. There hadn't been time with everything else going on. Now seemed like a good opportunity to let them know of Frank's suspicions. 'And – although I can't be sure – it's a pretty safe bet that he would've overseen the interview with Foster today, if that had actually taken place.'

'So that gave him the perfect excuse to be called into the crime scene this morning, I suppose,' Tom surmised. 'I wondered how come he was there.'

Just then, there was a knock on the door and Maxwell came in, carrying a sheaf of papers. He addressed Charlie.

'Sarge, I've got the first of that information you asked for.'

'Good lad.' Charlie turned to Gavin. 'You'll probably want to hear this, Sir.'

Gavin shifted in his seat. 'What's this, then?'

'I've had Maxwell looking into Miss Hough's finances. Thought we should check on that side of things. See if it throws up anything.' He turned back to Maxwell.

'So what have you found?' He pushed a stool across for Maxwell to sit on and the constable moved it to a convenient work surface where he could lay his papers out.

'Well, Sarge, you were right about Miss Hough's involvement with the jewellery company. She and her sister held controlling shares in the business until ten years ago, from which they both received a substantial income. Then they sold most of their shares to a Judy Whitfield.'

Tom interrupted. 'She's that big diamond expert, isn't she? Discovered the White Magician a few years back, I think.'

'How do you do that, Tom?' Gavin asked.

'Do what?'

'Know all these amazing bits and pieces of information.'

'I just have a healthy interest in the world,' Tom chuckled. 'Am I right?' he asked Maxwell.

'I don't know, Sir. But it seems likely. Apparently, she was another old schoolfriend. Both the Hough sisters had known her since school and kept in touch. She had her own company but when Emily and Heather wanted to reduce their involvement with Hough-McAllister, they approached her to come on board, and sold most of their shares to her.'

'Most?' Gavin asked.

'They both kept a small stake in the business, which seems natural. It was the family business, after all, Sir.'

'And they still had returns from this?'

'Yes, but it looks like neither of them took the profits.'

'Oh?'

Maxwell rifled through his papers. 'Yes, Sir. The company prided itself on its ethical stance. You know, being very upfront about not trading in conflict diamonds, or buying from countries with a poor record of child labour within the industry. They bought most of their diamonds from Canada where there's a Diamond Code of Conduct. And they channelled a significant proportion of their profits into a charitable foundation which the Hough sisters had set up in …'

He paused, leafing through some sheets. '… ah, yes, in Zimbabwe. It's an educational project. They build schools in a number of villages near the Marange diamond fields, which are notorious for the use of children in their mines. The Foundation works with The Anti-Slavery Society in this country to provide funds for teachers and resources. It's called the Sweet Diamond Project.'

He produced a printed leaflet, giving brief details and displaying a number of photos of children holding books and sitting in classrooms. He passed it over to Gavin.

'It seems that both sisters continued to put their profits into this charity but I'm still chasing the paperwork. I've now got access to Miss Emily Hough's bank accounts but not, of course, to Heather's since we have no grounds to investigate her as yet.'

Gavin grunted in response. 'It all looks legit, but I suppose it could be a front for something.'

'Yes, Sir. I'm trying to get in touch with someone from the Foundation itself to find out more. And I've contacted Emily's solicitor to check on her will.'

Gavin looked up.

'Well, I wondered whether her estate would include a donation. And the Sarge had already suggested I try to find out who the main beneficiary is.'

Charlie jumped in. 'I know it's unlikely she was murdered for her money, Sir, given what we've uncovered so far, but I thought it best to cover all possibilities.'

'Quite.'

'And we don't know what routine investigations might throw up.'

There was a long thoughtful pause amongst the group,

as everyone considered this new line of enquiry.

Maxwell interrupted the silence. 'Oh, and I've made contact with Judy Whitfield. She has a house not far from here and she's working from home today. I thought you might want to visit her, Sir. See if she can tell you more.'

Gavin reflected privately on Maxwell's enthusiasm and efficiency. This young man was going to make a good detective one day. He smiled across to where Maxwell was regrouping his pile of papers.

'Good work, Maxwell. That's an excellent idea. Why don't you and Sergeant Parker go and talk to her?'

Maxwell's face lit up. 'Of course, Sir.'

Gavin felt Maxwell deserved a reward for all the routine background work he'd been doing. And he couldn't go too far wrong with Charlie overseeing the interview.

He continued. 'In the meantime, I have some paperwork of my own to review.'

28

Katriona's disclosures had shocked Helen. Yet, at the same time, she found the story Katriona and Gavin were piecing together, strangely reassuring. It made some sense of the crazy scene on the mountain. If there were 'big' criminals, desperate to keep their activities untraceable, then disposing of small-fry like herself was more logical than some random burglar chasing her to Skye to get rid of his only witness.

But the most reassuring thing that had come out of the conversation was Katriona's plans to keep her survival secret. If these criminals – whoever they were – didn't know she was still alive, then she was safe. At least for the time being. And that meant she could relax into exploring the other surprising elements of the last few days – like what was happening between her and Jamie, and her newfound longing to find a way of staying on Skye.

'Have you got everything you need?' Katriona called up from the kitchen.

'Yep. Be down in a minute.'

The forensic team had finished their job and cleared out of the house by teatime, meaning that Katriona and Helen could get back in to pack up their belongings before they went off to their separate destinations.

Helen came down the stairs to find Katriona looking round the room.

'They did a good job cleaning up in here,' she observed.

'They did.' Katriona agreed. 'More than they would usually bother with. Andy's gift to me.' She smiled a little. 'I have some good friends here.'

She turned towards Helen standing in the doorway. 'I gather some of the neighbours came in to help.'

'This is a good place to live.'

Katriona must have caught some of the wistfulness in Helen's voice. She gave her a quizzical look, inviting her to say more. Helen hesitated. Was she being foolish?

'I … I think I'd like to stay.'

'Well, that's good,' Katriona responded, 'since you'll be here for a while, I think.'

'No, I mean … I think I'd like to come and live here,' Helen said, and heard the words out loud for the first time. She liked how they sounded.

'Really?' Katriona smiled at her, then suddenly crossed the room to give her a hug. Helen was surprised. She felt this was more the kind of thing Elayne would do.

'That doesn't seem ridiculous, then?'

Katriona stood back so she could look into Helen's face. 'Not in the slightest. It's what the island does. It calls people here – the people who belong here, anyway.'

Helen hadn't seen much of this side of Katriona yet, and felt encouraged – as if she, too, had undertaken this strange journey of realisation.

'That's what I feel,' she said. 'As if I belong here.'

'I got a glimpse of that on Friday evening,' Katriona shared. 'When we arrived at the Ceilidh.'

'I remember.' Helen breathed a deep sigh. 'So much has happened since then. I can't believe it's only a few days. I really want to do this, Katriona. I don't know how to make it happen but I know I have to find a way.'

'You will.' Katriona hugged her again. 'I know you will. And Elayne and I will help in any way we can. You'll just have to …' She paused.

Helen picked up her thought. 'I know,' she laughed. 'I

just have to ask the island.'

'You've got how this works,' said Katriona, laughing as well. 'In the meantime, are you okay about staying with Jamie and Louise?'

'I'm delighted.'

When Katriona had explained about her proposed trip to Germany, back at the hospital café, they'd considered the options open to Helen, to make her immediate time here as conducive as possible. Coming back to the house in Torrin by herself wasn't something she wanted to do, and anyway, Katriona and Jamie had insisted she shouldn't be on her own for the time being. Staying on at the B&B was a possibility but nothing like as wonderful as Jamie's offer to have her come and stay at his house, with him and his mum.

'You can have some proper looking-after,' Jamie had declared, and Helen thought that sounded just like what she needed. Not to mention the delightful idea of spending more time in Jamie's company.

Once they'd both packed a bag, and checked everything was turned off that should be, Katriona and Helen sat at the kitchen table with a pot of tea, making last-minute arrangements and watching the sky darken outside while they waited for Jamie to arrive in his car to pick up Helen.

The gentle quietness of the village felt soothing to Helen after another busy and traumatic day. She had a sudden thought.

'Who will look after the sheep while you're away?'

Katriona laughed. 'Oh, don't worry. They mostly take care of themselves. Sean will pop over with the dogs during the day to check on them. I confess I would be unlikely to do much more if I stayed. I don't generally go walking the moors like Elayne does.'

'It must be nice, though.'

'What – walking the moors?'

'Yes, that. But more than that. Spending your days outside in such lovely scenery, just visiting the sheep and …' She trailed off, seeing the twinkle in Katriona's eyes.

'Yeah, until you get the rain. You know, the kind that goes on for days, and then gets joined by the wind, and the biting cold once the snow's settled on the mountains. And the weeks of relentless grey daylight, which only lasts for a few hours anyway in the winter.'

Helen sipped her tea, looking over the top of the mug to see if Katriona was joking.

'Really? Does it get that bad?'

'Well, they say the average time an incomer lasts is about three years. They get through their first winter believing it can't always be like that. Then in their second, they realise it is. So most of them leave before their third.'

'But not you. You stay. You must find a way to cope.'

'My dear – I wouldn't have it any other way. I love the wildness of it. Watching the rain here is very different from, say, watching rain in the centre of London. I might not go out in it much, but I'm happy to sit in our beautiful conservatory and listen to it falling outside – along with the sound of Elayne's knitting needles, of course.'

This was a whole new picture of life on Skye. Helen wondered how she would take to it. Could she learn to love the rain? It wasn't an idea anyone she'd met before had ever suggested. She thought back to the misery she'd felt in the rain when she'd first arrived on the island. But then she'd been alone and frightened – and with nowhere safe to go. The idea of living in this community threw quite a different light on rain and storms.

The sound of a car crossing the cattle grid interrupted her thoughts.

'Do you think that's Jamie?' she said, feeling excitement rising inside her.

'Probably. Go and have a look.'

And she went outside to greet the headlights coming up the driveway, with an eagerness which took her by surprise.

The route to the Gaelic College – *Sabhal Mòr Ostaig*, Jamie called it – took them back along the roads Helen had travelled in the taxi when she'd first arrived on the island, so she found herself reflecting again on how much things had changed in just a few days.

From having what felt like nothing left, she had suddenly found a whole new life opening out in front of her. She tried not to jump ahead of herself but couldn't help relishing in the fact that she was sitting alongside Jamie – with all the possibilities that offered, that she had made such deep connections with Elayne and now Katriona, and that she had somewhere to stay while she began to make some plans as to how she could remain on the island. It almost felt too good to be true when she remembered how she'd felt the last time she'd been on this road. She wondered what other surprises might be in store for her.

'You okay?' Jamie said, and she realised she'd not spoken for quite a while.

'Mm. I'm fine.'

'Only you've not said much since we set off.'

'Just thinking.'

Jamie braked to allow a sheep to move out of the way. 'Anything interesting?'

Helen hesitated. Should she tell Jamie what she'd decided? She didn't want him to think she was trying to move in with him. But something about the island, and her future on it, couldn't be resisted, so she took the plunge. She looked over towards his silhouette. As they were now driving in the dark, she couldn't see his face clearly. That made it a bit safer, somehow.

'I've decided to stay on the island. To come and live here. If I can find a way.'

Jamie kept his eyes on the road but reached out a hand to squeeze one of hers.

'Wow. That's fantastic.'

'Please don't think …' Helen felt the old patterns of panic and lack of confidence resurfacing.

'I don't.' A simple response but enough to reassure her that things between them were good. He obviously didn't spook easily and, she thought, she should've known that and had more trust. She was learning.

A few minutes later, they turned off the road and onto the college campus.

The college was a beautiful place. Although, in the dark, she couldn't see the sea, she could hear it when Jamie gave her a brief tour of the grounds, circling round the back of the student accommodation block. She breathed in the tangy saltiness of the air. It was exhilarating.

Then suddenly, she was enveloped in people, as they made their way to the main hall. This turned out to be a cleverly-converted stone barn. Students, families, friends, even tutors she thought, were all crowding into the brightly-lit venue with an excited air of expectation. Jamie found her a seat and gave her a gentle kiss on the cheek.

'Gotta go.'

'What?'

'Sorry. Didn't you realise? I'm performing.'

Helen felt very stupid. Of course he was. That was why he'd asked her to come. She'd been so engrossed in her own ideas, she hadn't thought at all about what this evening might mean for him. She was disappointed not to be sharing the music with him but, at the same time, was delighted she'd get to hear him sing again.

'Of course. Sorry. Not concentrating,' she muttered. Then pulled herself together. She reached out to grab his arm and looking into his lovely eyes, she said, 'Break a leg. And enjoy yourself.'

'I intend to,' he beamed, and disappeared, leaving her to contemplate the rising excitement around her.

There were all sorts of people filling up the seats, now. Jamie had led her to believe this was an informal affair but the room had that magical feel one gets at a concert hall before the big event begins.

She felt a bit odd, sitting there on her own, while surrounded by people greeting each other, laughing, sharing news … She realised it was the first time she'd been alone since arriving in Broadford, and the implications of that warmed her. She liked the idea of living in such a friendly, not to say, intimate, community. As if to confirm her thoughts, she felt someone sit down next to her.

'Hello, again.' It was Fiona, the harpist from the Ceilidh.

'Hello.' Helen smiled, delighted to have someone to share the evening with, and particularly pleased to connect with Fiona again after their wonderful experience on Friday.

'What a surprise,' Fiona said. 'What brings you here?'

Helen blushed. 'Jamie invited me.'

'I didn't realise you knew him.' There was just a faint trace of teasing in Fiona's voice.

Helen laughed. 'Well, I didn't on Friday.'

Then suddenly there was a lot of 'shushing' and the inevitable coughs and shuffles as the lights dimmed. The last few people took their seats and a line of students filed into the front of the hall. A cheerful round of applause greeted them as they each moved to a chair in front of the stage, most picking up an instrument already placed there, others bringing one in with them.

Helen quickly realised these weren't the usual instruments one expected to find at a concert. There were a few violins, but surrounding them was an interesting collection of accordions, bagpipes and a surprising number of celtic harps, as well as various wooden flutes, some small hand-held drums, which she recognised as bodhrans, and two keyboards.

'That's the college orchestra,' Fiona whispered, as the students sorted the music sheets on their stands. Then loud cheers greeted a rather charismatic character, with long flowing blond hair and sparkling blue eyes, as he walked to the conductor's lectern. He turned to the audience and gave a bow. Then he invited the orchestra to do the same.

'*Fàilte*,' he announced, in a low, rich voice. Helen wondered if he was a singer as well as a conductor. Then, after a few more words in Gaelic, he turned back to the musicians, picked up his baton and the concert began.

It was every bit as wonderful as Helen had imagined it would be – and then some. The performers, despite mostly being quite young, were extremely accomplished. The music was completely unfamiliar to her, much of it traditional Scottish compositions, including many beautiful songs in Gaelic, with original contemporary pieces included at regular intervals. These latter had been written by the students themselves.

At first, she felt a trifle disgruntled. How was she going to enjoy an entire evening of music which she didn't recognise, with lyrics she couldn't understand? But once she'd reminded herself this was, after all, the Gaelic College, she let go a bit and allowed herself to drift into the magic and feel of the music, instead of trying to be 'clever' about it. She wasn't here to prove anything. Just to enjoy herself.

With this shift of perspective, she began to appreciate what she was hearing. And it *was* magical. In the same way that she'd got caught up in the more folksy flavour of the Ceilidh, she found herself catching glimpses of highland scenery, ancient love stories and musical celebrations.

She decided it was no different from listening to an opera she didn't know, in Italian or French – neither of which she spoke, although she had become fluent at singing certain arias over the years as she practised them. She guessed it would be possible to do that with Gaelic, too. The language still sounded very complicated to her ears but she did love the rhythm of it, the soft slippery consonants that reminded her of the wind, the lilting vowels that evoked mountain streams and waterfalls.

During the interval, the audience gathered at the back of the hall where small glasses of wine and fruit juice were being served. There was a loud buzz of appreciative chatter all around her, and when she listened in, she realised quite a lot of it, too, was in Gaelic.

She found Fiona was standing behind her, holding out a glass.

'I guessed you'd want some,' she said.

'Thank you.' Helen took the offered glass. 'Can I ask – I

mean – there seems to be a lot of Gaelic-speaking going on.'

'Yes. We always try to use the language as much as possible within the college.'

'Oh?'

'Well, that's really the point of the college. To keep the language alive.'

Helen considered this. 'What if you can't speak it? What if you came to study here and didn't know the language?'

'It's a requirement of entry. A basic working knowledge of it, anyway.'

'Oh.' Helen felt a huge wave of disappointment hit her. She suddenly realised she'd been holding out hopes of studying here and being one of the students performing on that stage. This place had been part of the imagined future she'd been trying to bring into focus over the last day or so. She knew there'd be a number of obstacles to overcome to make this happen but learning an entirely new language hadn't been one she'd anticipated.

Fiona must have read the disappointment in her face.

'Helen? Were you thinking of applying here?' she asked, gently.

'Um … I must have been. Only I don't think I realised it until now. How on earth does one go about learning Gaelic?'

'By doing one of the college's on-line courses, possibly?' Fiona spoke with that faint trace of teasing in her voice, again. 'By chatting with your friends, by reading books … all the usual ways of learning a new language. It's not so different from learning any other, I don't think.'

'No, I guess not, but …' Helen spoke slowly. 'I don't know any other college where you have to learn a new language in order to get in.'

'And if you went to Italy to study opera … ?'

'I suppose.' Helen suddenly laughed. 'I see your point. Well, okay, I guess it's yet another challenge I'll have to face if I want to stay.'

'Is that what you're planning to do?'

'Yes. I don't know that I'd realised the details of it until now, but yes, that's what I want to do. Somehow. Stay here and learn to sing – how do you say it? - in the Gaelic.'

'Then I'm sure that's what will happen,' said Fiona, with a friendly smile. 'And I very much hope you will bring that beautiful voice of yours to my house on a regular basis to sing with my harp.'

Helen was about to say how delighted she'd be to accept the invitation when a bell rang and everyone started shuffling back to their seats for the second half of the concert.

29

Getting from Torrin to Dusseldorf was no easy task. The simplest flight – a direct route – was from Glasgow, but that involved a considerable car journey from the island first, and as Katriona's car was currently sitting on the conference centre carpark in Fort William, quite a few details needed to be sorted to make this possible.

Katriona had talked through her plans with both Elayne and Andy earlier in the day. Elayne was, of course, totally supportive of her making the trip.

'I'll be fine.'

'Are you sure? I don't have to do this.'

'What? You're going to miss out on the opportunity to work on a big case? Yes, that sounds like you.' Elayne's sense of humour was solidly back in place. That was a good sign. She'd reached out for Katriona's hand.

'Kat, I'm stuck here for the next few days. I'm being well looked after. It makes perfect sense. It's when I get to go home I'm going to need you.'

The conversation with Andy had been more pragmatic.

'If you're ready to go this evening, I'll drive you down to Fort William on my way back to Inverness. It's not too far out of the way.'

When Katriona had tried to thank him for his generosity, he'd said, 'You can fill me in on all the details while we drive,' and had given her a knowing smile.

He picked her up not long after Helen had left for the concert, and they travelled the two-hour journey in companionable conversation, Katriona sharing with him what she knew and speculating about the rest.

'My God, it all sounds … incredible.' Andy's reaction was predictably one of appalled shock when he learnt about the additional personnel at Gavin's end who were apparently involved. 'You hear about these things, but you never quite believe it until you meet it personally.'

'I know. In fact, I'm still finding it difficult to believe, even though I know it must be true. Anyway, that's my news. What's yours? Did you manage to speak with Struan when he came back down?'

'Yes. He and Finlay did a good job. Took plenty of photos, did an annotated sketch for me. Even found another bullet. Struan reckoned most of them had been fired over the edge, or ricocheted there, but they did a thorough search and turned one up. No casings, though.'

'Does it match the one they took from Elayne?' Katriona suppressed the sob this recollection evoked.

'Looks like it. I've been thinking about that. I gather you and Gavin changed your minds about sending the bullet to him?'

'Yes. We decided it was too risky. It's the only piece of evidence we have that links Fisher to what's going on. And even that's circumstantial, and rather tenuous. If Fisher got wind of it arriving in the lab, there's a more than small chance it might go missing.' She paused. 'I thought I'd take it with me – to Dusseldorf.'

'Oh?'

'See if it matches the one that killed Dieter Bergmann, if that's retrievable.'

'So you think the same guy might be responsible?' Andy sounded surprised.

'Well, put it this way – if there *is* a match, that would make some pretty strong connections for us, and give a bit more direction to the investigation. At the moment, we're still floundering around.'

'I see.'

'I mean, if Emily Hough's murder can be linked to Dieter Bergmann … then throw in the flashdrive, and Heather Hough's disappearance, and we've nearly got some kind of coherence to the case.'

'So, you definitely think there's something on that flashdrive that's creating all this chaos?'

'Andy, I don't definitely think anything, but it's got to be worth pursuing. Like Gavin says, we've got to follow all possible lines of enquiry until something makes sense.'

Andy left Katriona at the conference centre where she'd been lecturing only yesterday. It seemed like days had passed since she'd been whisked away on the helicopter, and the strangeness of being back here was difficult. She booked into the hotel, where they were expecting her, and asked for some food to be sent up to her room.

She didn't enjoy being on her own in the sterile environment that the hotel offered but it was pleasant to relax in the bath and try to wash away the tensions of the day, and the food was good when it arrived.

She sat at the small table in her room, feeling sleepy but refreshed. After a quick 'good-night' call to Elayne, she thought she'd round off her evening by doing a bit of research for tomorrow. She knew nothing about Dieter Bergmann so tried a Google search to see what that would throw up.

The website, which Gavin had mentioned to her, gave her a clear picture of a man dedicated to his job. Although he was – had been – still relatively young, he had a string of awards dating back over ten years or so. Some of his work could be viewed on the site. It seemed he had worked with both still photos and videos, at different times. The photos were mostly from his earlier career. He'd then moved over to making short films, working with several eminent, and controversial, directors.

Then, about three years ago, he'd hooked up with Heather Hough and they'd begun making a whole string of documentaries. Katriona picked up the links to a number of newspaper and TV websites to get more information. The pair had been in several recent warzones, mostly concentrating on the atrocities inflicted on innocent civilians. They hadn't been shy about implicating all parties in what they'd found. Not surprising then, if they'd ticked off someone with influence.

She was able to download a segment from one piece about a refugee camp in the Middle East, subjected first to air attacks by an invading faction, then to retaliatory missiles from the home force. It was utterly heart-breaking, and Katriona decided not to dwell there tonight.

She went back to the website and found a link to Bergmann's blog. He turned out to be one of those people who took blogging very seriously. He'd written an entry, religiously, twice a week for several years. Whilst the documentaries had been very much fact-based affairs, the working pair allowing the footage to tell the tale mostly without comment, Bergmann's blog was obviously the place where he let his emotions been known about what he'd filmed.

He wrote passionately about what he saw, often questioning the motives of those who appeared oblivious to the pain and destruction they created in pursuit of goals, all too often, linked to personal profit and greed. But he also balanced this stream of condemnation with plenty of writing about the courage and compassion he'd witnessed at the various places he'd visited.

He and Heather had been to many different parts of the world during the years they'd worked together and she was often mentioned in the blog, and appeared in lots of the photos. There was an obvious affection for her, though it came across rather more as that of siblings than of lovers.

One item in particular caught her eye. During the last

year, in amongst the various countries they'd visited to film for the documentary on epidemics they'd been making, the pair had also made several visits to Zimbabwe to film the progress of a new school being built. Katriona read that this was being funded by a charitable foundation which Heather and her sister had set up to enable children to escape the slavery of working in the diamond mines.

Bergmann was full of praise for Heather and the work she was doing, and reflected on how easily one could make a difference by redirecting both money and will into a situation.

Just before she closed the computer, she decided to look at the most recent blog entry. It described some of the last work the two had been doing and included some cheerful photos.

'And here we both are, about to go into Falkenrath Pharmaceuticals to talk to the CEO.'

The photo was a typical 'selfie', showing both Dieter and Heather, arm in arm and smiling into the camera. They were outside a large, glass and steel-fronted building with lots of people milling around in the background.

As Katriona looked, she had the weirdest sensation that she was missing something important. She clicked on the photo to blow it up to full-screen size and let her eyes roam across the image.

Then she spotted it. With a sharp intake of breath, she picked up her phone to send the link to Gavin.

30

'So what exactly am I looking at?' Tom peered at the screen in front of him, having brought up the blog-site Gavin had instructed.

'Click on that photo.' Gavin pointed a finger at a photo half-way down the page. Tom did so, and the image filled the screen.

'There,' said Gavin, pointing again. 'Just there.'

'Is that … ? It is, isn't it? It's our assassin.'

Gavin nodded, viewing the picture again with a growing sense of satisfaction. At full-size, Gravenburg could be clearly seen, hovering in the background. He seemed to be looking towards the pair engrossed in taking their photo, but his body language indicated he might just have come through the exit from the building on the edge of the scene.

'So how did you find this?' Tom asked.

'Katriona sent it last night. I mean, it might be nothing but it's a tantalising potential piece of evidence.'

'I agree. It definitely gives us a direction to follow.'

'What's all this, then?' An unexpected, and horribly familiar, voice came from the doorway. Fisher.

Gavin turned and stepped smartly in front of the screen.

'Good morning, Sir. What brings you down here?' He tried to keep his cool but his heart was thumping. How much had Fisher heard?

Behind him, there was a sharp snapping sound as all the computer screens in the room went dead.

'Damn,' Tom said. 'Not again. We'll really have to get this looked at.'

'Problem?' Fisher asked.

'Nothing that can't be fixed, I don't think,' Tom replied, smoothly. 'It's probably the overload synchronisation junction – a tad too sensitive.'

Fisher looked at Tom as if he didn't believe a word of it. Gavin hoped it was more a case of 'didn't understand a word of it'.

'It's unusual to see you down here, Sir.'

'Yes, well, I have the autopsy report for you, from Surrey. I told you it would come through. Nothing untoward in it. As expected, DI Foster died of an overdose.' He paused, glaring at Gavin. 'I wanted to hand it over personally. I was told you were in here.'

'Thank you, Sir.' Gavin reached out a hand to take the file. Since he and Tom had already received a copy unofficially, directly from the pathologist, he knew the Super – or maybe someone else in the paper trail – was lying.

As he took the file, he saw Charlie stepping through the doorway behind Fisher, registering a look of alarm on his face.

'Oh, there you are, Charlie,' Gavin tried to cover. 'Tom was just …' He prayed Tom's inventiveness was up to scratch.

'… about to load the files.' Tom picked up his cue, starting to rush around the lab, busily hitting what Gavin guessed were random buttons. 'But the system has temporarily shut itself down, so you'll have to wait a moment.'

'And this relates to … ? Fisher asked.

Tom turned to him, a big grin on his face. 'I was just going to update these two on that course I attended a couple of weeks ago, about the use of constricting algorithms for photographic files in reverse engineering as it relates to the processing of photographic forensic evidence, as outlined in Interpol's latest digest. I've condensed the essential details down to a manageable text, but it'll still take some explaining. You're very welcome to join us, Sir.'

Gavin saw the twinkle in Tom's eyes as he waited for Fisher's reply.

'Not just now. Thank you, er, Tom,' he flustered. 'I have too much important paperwork to attend to. Another time, perhaps.' He turned to go.

'Oh, Pearce. Perhaps you will update me later today on progress? We need to be closing down this case now, you know.'

Gavin let his irritation go. Now was not the time to be detaining Fisher. He allowed a simple acknowledgement of 'Sir' to suffice, and Fisher left the room.

Charlie closed the door behind him. 'What was that all about?'

'Ostensibly, to bring us the post-mortem report on Foster,' Gavin replied, 'but I can't help feeling he was checking up on us. Nicely played, by the way, Tom. How did you kill the computer so effectively?'

'It's a simple device, known as the Tom Mason Omega 13 Override Button. I installed it precisely for emergency situations like this. Can't have all and sundry looking at the evidence.'

Gavin chuckled. 'Well, whatever it's called, thank God it was there. Do you think he heard anything important?'

'No, I don't think so.' Tom pressed something that rebooted all the computers, then moved towards the kettle. 'Coffee?'

As the water came to a boil, Gavin and Charlie dipped into the report, which bore no relation to the one Felicity had given Tom last night.

'I wonder at what point along the line it got 'doctored'?' Gavin took a mug from Tom for himself and passed another to Charlie.

'Well, Felicity says she definitely handed over a complete

report showing her findings and her suspicions to our friend Elliot Stevens. And that was just before she left to meet me for dinner. So there was no question of coercion at her end.'

'Stevens must have worked on it after that,' Gavin surmised. 'No-one would suspect immediately. I mean, it would take a while for your friend to realise she'd not been called to an inquest, wouldn't it?'

Tom nodded, but before he could say anything, there was a knock on the door. He quickly checked what was now visible on the computers before shouting, 'Come in.'

A worried face appeared.

'Bryan. Come in. What can I help with?' Clearly, something was wrong.

'Tom, can I just have a quick word?'

'Sure. Let's find somewhere private.' And Tom scooped the young boy up protectively – even though he towered above him – and led him out of the lab.

Gavin took the opportunity to share the news of the photo Katriona had sent, with Charlie. He didn't dare touch any of Tom's computers, so he could only describe what he and Tom had seen.

'And it was definitely Gravenburg, Sir?'

'Yes.'

'When was the photo taken?'

'The blog was dated the day Bergmann died. So the photo must have been taken only hours before he was shot. That was the day before Emily Hough's murder.'

'Busy man, this Gravenburg.'

'Thankfully, not any more.'

Their conversation was interrupted by Tom's return. He brought Bryan back with him.

'I think you two had better hear this,' he said.

What a crass thing to do, Gavin thought, now back in his office, sat in front of a collection of files. Fancy trying to recruit Bryan to spy on them. Surely Fisher would realise that the boy's loyalty was much more likely to be directed towards a kind and considerate boss who obviously worked with integrity, rather than to a man he hardly knew, who was curt to the point of rudeness and who had no direct authority over him.

The boy had clearly been shaken by the conversation. Not surprisingly. The only good thing about the scenario was that it demonstrated how rattled Fisher must be, if he was willing to stoop to such tactics. However, it also indicated that he might be aware that Gavin and the others were on to him. It was possible, of course, that he was just reacting to pressure put on him from further up the line. After all, no-one yet knew of Gravenburg's failed attempt to kill Helen, so maybe this was an effort to gain information.

It was equally likely that Fisher was suspicious of the cosy group he'd just come across gathered in Tom's lab, and wanted to know what was going on. Particularly since he must now be aware of how disposable those at the lower end of the chain of operatives were, with the news of Foster's death. Yes, that made more sense.

Gavin chuckled to himself. The picture of Fisher getting paranoid about both those 'below' and 'above' him was strangely comforting. Perhaps because it allowed the possibility that Fisher would no longer be able to see the situation clearly, and although this might make him more suspicious, it would also make him fallible. Not to mention that it encouraged Gavin to believe they must be getting somewhere with their investigations, even if they didn't know precisely where.

The knock on his door indicated the arrival of Charlie and Maxwell who had come to report back from their visit to Judy Whitfield last night, and their follow-up trip to the Hough-MacAllister offices this morning to look through the accounts – at Ms Whitfield's invitation.

Once they'd taken him through the basic facts, and Maxwell had familiarised him with how the charity was funded, Charlie sat back in his chair.

'As we expected, Sir, there's no evidence of anything

dodgy,' he concluded. 'Too long a history of ethical trading, backed up by both paperwork and direct action. If there is something untoward there, it's extremely well hidden. We didn't get any sense of non-disclosure during the conversation.'

'So,' Gavin surmised, 'it seems more likely that Heather and Emily would be the targets of a misdeed rather than the perpetrators of one.'

'Well, possibly, Sir, but I don't see how that works, either. The sisters were never a threat to any of the other jewellery businesses. They were totally upfront about who they would trade with and who they wouldn't. And Ms Whitfield seems to have maintained that stance. I can't see any obvious reason for someone wanting them out of the picture.'

'Unless it's something to do with the charity work,' Maxwell offered.

Gavin gestured for him to say more.

'Well, Sir, it's unlikely to be a hate-crime, I think, because Emily's death and Heather's disappearance didn't happen out in Zimbabwe, where you'd expect if they'd annoyed someone with their schools and such like.'

'True.'

'But I suppose it's possible Heather came across something when she was visiting out there. Something that someone might not want made public, Sir.'

'But the use of child slavery in the diamond mines *is* public knowledge,' Gavin said. 'No-one denies it goes on. Sadly,' he added.

'Maybe Heather just got too vocal about it, Sir.'

'Then why kill Emily, too?' Gavin asked. 'No, I feel there's something else going on here. Something we haven't got to the bottom of, yet.'

'I agree,' Charlie joined in. 'I think, however, it's worth doing a bit more investigating around this Sweet Diamond Project. See what it throws up, Sir.'

'It's certainly a lead to follow. Why don't you do some

more digging, Charlie? And Maxwell, I suggest you take a look at this company Falkenrath Pharmaceuticals. Find out what they're all about.'

It still felt like slow-going to Gavin. He hoped Katriona was having more success. As the other two left his office, he turned back to the files he'd been looking at.

He'd already spent some considerable time going over the early interviews from the corruption investigation which Patterson had sent over to his office yesterday. These just involved junior officers – most of whom had now been dismissed from the Force. Some had readily admitted their guilt in taking 'back-handers', or in couriering packages – contents unknown. Others had been more reticent, until the evidence had stacked up against them.

When he saw how many times that evidence had been provided by Foster, Gavin began to understand the picture. It looked like Foster had set up his own organisation of junior officers, willing to run errands for him and to act as liaisons with local gangsters. This was another example of dispensing with those at the bottom of the heap.

Several of those interviewed had tried to implicate Foster but since he was supplying the evidence against them, it looked initially as if no-one was listening seriously.

As he worked his way along the time-line, however, it had become pretty obvious that Foster himself would need to be interviewed. That was the point at which Stevens had entered the scene.

The paperwork Gavin had in his possession stopped there, so he was hoping Patterson had now turned up some more. He hadn't got a sense of Foster working for someone else from what he'd read so far, so was it possible that Stevens had recruited him when he came? Perhaps seeing a ripe opportunity to exploit?

Since he'd not heard anything further from Patterson, Gavin decided to go across to the archives in person.

'Hello, Sir.' The man seemed to be up to his armpits in

boxes of papers. 'I was just going to ring you.'

'Oh good. What have you found?' Gavin picked up a stray piece of paper that had floated to the floor and passed it to Patterson.

'Nothing, I'm afraid.'

'Excuse me?'

'I can't find the transcripts you asked for. Neither paper copies nor digital.'

Gavin was stunned into silence.

'I'm sorry, Sir. I've looked everywhere I can think of, but the box itself is missing. It could've been misplaced but I've a horrid feeling it's been removed.'

'What makes you think that?'

'I've found the Chain of Evidence List. It was signed out by one of the IPCC guys, after they'd finished investigating – and it looks like it's never come back.'

Gavin swore quietly to himself.

'It's easily done, Sir. And we would've had no need to follow it up at this end. IPCC prosecuted, not us. So they would've had copies of all the evidence they needed. Presumably that's why they took the box.'

'Can I see the list?'

'The list, Sir?'

'The Chain of Evidence List.'

'Yes, of course. Now where did I put it … ?' Patterson turned to a desk behind him and rifled through yet more papers.

Gavin knew exactly what he expected to see, and when Patterson presented the sheet with dates and signatures on it, he was grimly satisfied. Stevens' name was at the bottom.

He was just about to hand the board back when someone else's signature caught his eye. 'Who's this?'

Patterson took the list from him and peered at the scrawl Gavin had indicated.

'Hall-Gardiner,' he deciphered, slowly.

'Who?' Gavin didn't recollect having ever come cross anyone in the station with that name.

'Um …' Patterson rubbed his chin as he tried to remember. 'Oh yes. He was that clerk. You remember. From the Home Office.'

'The Home Office?' Gavin was genuinely taken aback.

'You didn't know?'

'No. But then I suppose I didn't have a lot to do with the investigation. But why would the Home Office want the files?'

'I don't know, Sir. It's not my business to ask. If they have the correct authorisation, anyone can take them.'

31

Katriona arrived at Dusseldorf Airport during the afternoon. She scanned the collection of onlookers waiting at the gate. She'd been worried she might not recognise Stephi, having never actually met her, but she was saved any embarrassment by a tall, young woman promptly shouting over people's heads.

'DI McShannon. Over here.'

The authority in her voice – and perhaps the sight of a police badge – caused the crowd to part quickly, creating a gap for Katriona to pass through to where her host was waiting.

'Katriona. It's good to meet you at last.' Stephi greeted her with the traditional European double kiss. She was an elegant woman, smartly-dressed, with blonde hair similar to Katriona's own. She had the clipped, efficient manner so common to German high-fliers, and exuded an air of self-confidence.

This was one very successful woman, Katriona knew, having talked with her a great deal on-line. Highly intelligent, obviously athletic, and now Katriona discovered, extremely good-looking. She could see it might be easy to feel intimidated by her, and understood why her male colleagues were so co-operative.

'I thought we'd go straight to the labs where the body's being held. They've got the forensics on the bullet, as well.'

Katriona had hoped for a cup of tea at least, before they began work. She wasn't used to the fast pace of day-to-day policing, any more. She smiled in response and let herself be led out to the waiting car at the kerbside. She took the passenger seat as offered and willed herself to get up to speed.

'I gather you've brought the bullet from the attempted murder with you.' Stephi's direct manner might take a little getting used to.

'Yes. I thought we could compare it with any you find at this end.'

'Good idea.' Stephi pulled out smartly into the flow of traffic. Once they were moving, she seemed to relax a little. 'Sorry if I seem to be rushing you. Our forensic pathologist has to leave the labs shortly for a prior engagement. It felt important for you to speak with him directly.'

'Of course.'

'After we've done the immediate business, I'll treat you to afternoon tea at The Shennong Tea Lounge, if you like.'

Now that sounded more like it.

Stephi drove Katriona swiftly out of the town centre and headed towards the suburbs, where, she learned, the forensic labs were based. The officer overseeing the case was to meet them there.

'How well do you know this Rudi Seigel?' Katriona asked.

'Oh, only professionally. We've worked together on a few cases in the past. He seems a reliable policeman.'

'Does he know why I'm here?'

'I've told him what I know. That if this really is a murder, it is probably connected to one at your end. After all, you have yet to share any more than that.'

Stephi's harsh German accent added unexpected emphasis to her words, causing Katriona to look across at her to check whether she was really displeased about not being let in on the case so far.

Stephi responded with a dry smile. 'I understand the

need for secrecy, but I'm very much hoping I can persuade you to tell me more later.'

'I will,' Katriona said. 'If we get a match on the bullets, I'll tell you as much as I can.' She knew the phrase was open to interpretation but that was the best she could do at this stage.

They spent the rest of the short journey talking about the landmarks which Stephi pointed out.

When they arrived at the labs, and had signed in, Stephi escorted her along several corridors and down two flights of stairs before they reached the morgue. The building was rather spectacular for a forensic lab. Glass-fronted, very modern and all the walls painted a pale duck-egg blue. It had obviously been purpose-built and, Katriona guessed, fairly recently. The morgue, however, looked like every other morgue she'd ever been to.

'I thought we'd start here. Let you see the body first,' Stephi explained as they entered the room, where a small dark-haired man was waiting.

He spoke to Stephi in German. He sounded annoyed. Stephi responded sharply, then turned to Katriona.

'Let me introduce Dr. Flussen-Hirsch, our forensic pathologist.'

Katriona held out her hand. 'Katriona McShannon.' She attempted a smile, unsure of the reception she would get, but the man was impeccably polite. He shook her hand firmly.

'I'm afraid the doctor doesn't speak English, so I'll have to translate his findings for you.'

Dr. Flussen-Hirsch crossed the room and pulled back a white sheet covering a body on a table. Katriona recognised it as Dieter Bergmann, despite the damage done by several days' immersion in the river. The doctor pointed out the entry wound and began to talk to Stephi. There was nothing complicated here. The bullet had pierced the heart, causing almost instantaneous death. The man had inhaled some water with his last breaths but not much. He had bled out quickly. The doctor confirmed death was by gunshot, not drowning.

What a shocking and miserable end to a fine man, Katriona thought. She felt more determined than ever to find out what this was all about and who was ultimately responsible.

The doctor covered the body up again and, saying something to Stephi, made a quick departure.

'Right. Let's find Rudi. He should be here by now.' Stephi led the way back upstairs to a small office, overlooking the local buildings.

'Have a seat, Katriona. I'll see if I can find him.' She went back into the corridor, leaving Katriona alone in the room.

Katriona glanced at the rather uncomfortable-looking office chair next to the desk and decided to stay standing for the time being. There was a disconnected gloominess about the place that could quickly get depressing, she felt. She was already missing her trees and mountains. She wandered around the small room, casting an eye over the books on the bookcase which stretched up one wall, and glancing at the papers on the table.

On top of the pile was a file labelled 'New products for you to view', written in red pen, in both English and German. A red and blue sticker covered one corner with a name Katriona recognised. Falkenrath Pharmaceuticals.

That was the company Dieter and Heather had been visiting the day he was shot. The one in the photo. She was contemplating peering into the folder when the door opened and a young girl came in. She had long brown hair pulled back into a tidy knot behind her neck and a dainty face with sharp, brown eyes. She said something in German.

'I'm sorry …' Katriona said, then grappled for the one phrase she knew. 'Ich spreche kein Deutsch.'

To her surprise, the girl responded with, 'Oh, you must be the English visitor.'

Katriona registered a note of annoyance. Her visit was supposed to be low-key and private. How many people knew she was here?

'Yes,' she said, giving nothing away. 'How did you know about that?'

'Oh, I was busy being nosy at Reception just now, I'm afraid.' The girl's tone was friendly and her English accent almost perfect. 'I'm Frieda Haase. One of the secretaries, here. Can I get you anything? I presume you're waiting for DI Wolff.'

'I'm fine, thanks. Yes, the Inspector's just gone to find someone.'

'That'll be DI Siegel, I expect. I saw him arrive a few minutes ago. Well, I'll leave you to it then, if you're sure you're okay?'

As she turned to leave, Katriona caught sight of the same red and blue logo on her name badge, pinned to her lapel.

'Oh, there is one thing.'

'Yes?'

'That logo. It belongs to Falkenrath Pharmaceuticals, doesn't it? I wonder if you could tell me what the connection is with the labs? It looks like you'd be the one to know.'

The girl put her hand, almost defensively, up to her badge but covered her gesture with a smile. 'Of course. How clever of you to notice. Yes, they supply quite a lot of the chemicals we use here, as well as various bits and pieces of equipment, through their subsidiary companies.'

'They're a big enterprise, then?'

'Oh yes, worldwide.' There was an element of admiration in the girl's voice.

'So are you a representative for them?' Katriona fished.

'Yes. Well, after a fashion. I'm actually employed by them to act as a liaison. They provide someone for most of the companies they supply to on a large scale. Saves the bother of having travelling salesmen who can, I'm sure you know, get a hard time if they're not particularly well-known. Having someone on the ground, a day-to-day face, makes for much easier channels of communication.'

'And no doubt promotes higher sales,' Katriona offered, trying to keep the cynical edge out of her observation.

'It works very well.' The girl's reply was cold. Katriona felt she'd probably used up all her goodwill. Fortunately, the door opened again and Stephi walked in, followed by a tall, dark-haired man with an easy manner about him.

'Hi, Frieda,' Stephi said. 'Everything okay?'

'Yes, I was just asking our visitor if she wanted anything. I'll get on, now you're here.' And she disappeared down the corridor.

'Katriona, meet Rudi.' Stephi obviously thought nothing about Frieda's presence in the office, so Katriona put her suspicions to one side for the moment, as Rudi greeted her with the assurance of someone who had a natural authority in the world.

'Hi, Katriona. Nice to meet you, though the circumstances are not the best, I think. Stephi tells me that Dieter Bergmann's death may be linked to a case you're working on?'

'Yes. That's right.' Katriona warmed to him straight away. There was no hint of defensiveness or reticence in his question. He sounded as though he would be cooperative. 'We think he may have been shot by the same man we're investigating in England – and Scotland, actually.'

'Oh?' Rudi's eyes widened. 'This is not an isolated murder, then?'

'I don't think so. I'm sorry I can't be more explicit at the moment. I'm afraid much of the case has to be kept confidential. I'll share what I can. But it may be quite easy to identify your murderer.'

'Really? Well, that would save a lot of time and energy. What do you need from us?'

'The forensics on the bullet,' Katriona said. 'I just need to know if it's the same kind of bullet as I have here.' She retrieved the evidence bag out of her briefcase, containing the bullet from Elayne's attack. 'And if it's been fired from the same gun.'

'Well, that's simple enough to do. Let me ring down to Sondra. She can set that up for us.' He picked up the internal phone on the desk and spoke into it.

Katriona pulled Stephi to one side. 'Frieda has an incredibly good English accent,' she commented.

'Oh, yes. I think she was educated at Oxford. She did tell me once but I don't remember the details.'

'She said she's not actually employed by the labs here. That she's a kind of representative for Falkenrath Pharmaceuticals.' Katriona let the question in her statement show.

'Yes. That's right. Why do you ask?'

'Oh, it may be nothing. I'll tell you later.'

Rudi had finished his phonecall and was indicating toward the door. 'We can go down straight away. Sondra has everything available.'

Sondra's lab was remarkably similar to what Katriona remembered of Tom's, but she was entirely different from him. 'Smart, tidy and efficient' were the words that came into Katriona's head. Not that Tom wasn't smart or efficient as far as his thinking went – he could even be tidy when it came to handling evidence – but his brain worked in loops and off-shoots.

Sondra was someone who thought in straight lines, and also didn't appear to have much of a sense of humour. Her long dark hair, hanging straight from top to bottom, summed up her approach to her work. She presented the evidence meticulously, taking the three officers through a series of micro-photographs, after letting them see the actual bullet.

'This is a 9mm bullet. It can be used in any number of pistols.' Her initial observations were what Katriona had expected but as the photos zoomed in on the details, Sondra was able to point out very specific marks on the side of the bullet.

'These were made by the bullet being fired along the

barrel of the gun. In theory, I could compare another bullet and tell you if it was probably fired from the same gun.'

'Like this one?' Rudi asked, holding up Katriona's evidence bag.

Sondra took the bag from him, and using gloves and forceps, very carefully placed it under the photographic microscope on the far side of the room. Clicking onto the computer placed alongside it, she was able to transfer the image she was looking at onto the bigger screen for everyone to see.

Katriona watched as Sondra carefully turned the bullet round under the lens, photographing it from every side and every angle. She then crossed back to where the others were waiting and picked up the remote.

'If we put the two images side by side …'

The screen split into two, both of the bullets now displayed. Sondra pressed the remote repeatedly so it appeared as if the second bullet was rotating. She stopped when the view matched the one of the first bullet she'd loaded.

'Yes,' she said. 'Look, here … and here.' The group peered.

'It looks very much like those marks match the first. Yes, I'd say this second bullet was fired from the same gun.'

32

'Yes. Hall-Gardiner.' Gavin spelt the name out, holding his phone to his ear. With his free hand, he indicated to Charlie who'd just come through the office door, to wait a moment. 'I believe he's a clerk there.'

The voice on the other end responded politely. 'I'm afraid we have no-one here by that name.'

Gavin had a moment's panic, then remembered the box had been returned so the request must have been legitimate. 'This was a year ago. Is it possible he's moved on?'

"Yes. Absolutely. Is there anything I can help with?'

'I'm not sure. I'm trying to follow the history of a box of files from our end. It seems your clerk signed it out at one time.'

'If you can give me the date, I'll see what I can find out.'

Gavin did so, emphasizing the importance of his enquiry and the need for a swift response.

The voice said, 'I'll see what I can do,' and the phone went dead.

'Another lead, Sir?' Charlie asked.

'Well, possibly.' Gavin gestured for him to take a chair. 'I've been going back over the interviews from the corruption investigation, see if there's anything helpful. Only Patterson tells me one of the boxes is missing.'

'Oh.'

'Yes. All the interviews done by Stevens.'

'Well, there's a surprise,' Charlie said.

'I know. I suppose I should've expected something like this.'

'Do you have any leads as to where it's gone?'

'Hell, yes. Stevens was the last guy to sign it out, so we shan't be seeing that again.'

'Then who was that you were just talking to, Sir?'

'The Home Office.'

Charlie gave a start. 'The Home Office?'

'Yes. One of their clerks signed the box out before it disappeared. I was just wondering what their interest was.'

'I suppose they are technically IPCC's employers.'

'Agreed, but they don't usually take a personal interest in a particular case.'

'I suppose not.' Charlie paused.

'Have you got something for me?' Gavin asked.

'Yes, Sir. Some info on that charity. They are involved in a legal battle with the mine-owners at Marange.'

'Really? What about?'

'Well, it's all a bit complicated but it seems that the Foundation were trying to get the mine-owners prosecuted for kidnap, since they were getting nowhere with the child slavery laws. And the mine-owners were responding by suing the Foundation for loss of profits.'

'How on earth did they justify that?'

'They claim the Foundation were stealing their workforce, Sir.'

'Which, I suppose, they were.'

'Except that every child is likely to have left the mines voluntarily – given the opportunity. I gather the Foundation were giving them that opportunity. Providing escape routes, transport, food, shelter … You get the picture, Sir?'

'I do, but I think this mining company will have a hard time proving a case.'

'In any international court they might, but they're bringing a local case – against the government, who license the Foundation to operate.'

'My God, what a mess.' Gavin was appalled by the

duplicity of such people. 'Do we think this might have something to do with our case?'

'As I said before, Sir, it's possible. I don't know how much Heather had got involved in this particular battle but obviously, the more she and Emily funded the schools, the more likely they made themselves targets.'

'Yes, but by using a wanted German assassin? No, I don't think so, Charlie. I agree this might be part of the picture but I think there's something else here.'

At that moment, there was a further knock on the door and Maxwell came in.

'I have some information on Falkenrath Pharmaceuticals, as requested, Sir.'

'Oh, good,' Gavin responded. 'Have a seat and tell us what you've found out.'

Maxwell sat down, as instructed, and opened a large file.

'Well, Sir. They're a huge enterprise. A conglomerate, really. They own any number of other companies and smaller businesses. Their main concern, obviously, is the research, testing and production of new drugs, but they own companies that have all sorts of related interests.'

'Such as?'

'Oh, medicine bottle production, syringes, surgical gloves …' Maxwell read from a printed list. '… intra-venous drips, surgical instruments, monitoring machines … The list is enormous, Sir.'

'So they have a finger in every pie?'

'It would seem so, Sir. But there's more. Obviously, their profits are in the billions but it's impossible to trace any exact figures. They are very clever at covering their turn-over by using some ingenious tax-dodging methods.'

'Such as?'

'Firstly, by making sure each of their companies runs as an independent enterprise, so officially the profits – and therefore the taxes due – are not attributable to them. And I think, but I'm still working on it, that that's a practice they encourage their subsidiaries to use, too. So if I'm right, each individual tax return will be a very small proportion of their overall take.'

'And I guess there's nothing illegal about that,' Gavin offered.

'No, Sir. Just not particularly honest. Their second method is by using charitable giving. Anything they contribute under that heading can be written off as a tax loss.'

'Which is also standard practice.'

'Until you start looking into the actual so-called charities they fund, and the sorts of amounts they're contributing, Sir.'

'Like what?' Gavin asked, his interest piqued.

Maxwell produced a document, several pages long, and passed it over. Gavin gasped.

'There must be several hundreds of charities here.'

"Yes, Sir. That's what I mean. It'll take me a while to go through all of these.'

'Yes. I can see that.' Gavin turned to Charlie. 'Can you put someone else on this, as well?'

'I can, Sir,' Charlie responded.

'And make sure your priority is anything that looks like it's got a connection with what Heather and Dieter were working on.'

'Actually, Sir,' Maxwell said, 'there was one particular charity that caught my eye.'

'What was that?'

'Victoria Orphanage. It's in Zimbabwe, near the Marange diamond mines.'

Both Gavin and Charlie stared at him.

'It seems like such a small concern for an enterprise like this to bother with, and in the same region as Heather's schools ...'

Gavin experienced the inklings of that glow he got when a case started to coalesce. May, just maybe, they were onto something concrete, at last.

'Well spotted, Maxwell. I want you to start with this one. Find out everything you can. Good work.'

'Sir,' Charlie said. 'I'm due to meet with someone from the Anti-Slavery Group, later. They're going to fill me in on the Sweet Diamond Project. I'm thinking I might just ask them what they know about Victoria Orphanage, too.'

'That sounds like a good idea. Now, I'm going to make another trip over to the archives.'

As Gavin made his way through the formally-planted trees, he acknowledged to himself that the reason for this second visit to Patterson's domain had much less to do with the expectation of finding anything new than with the need to stay out of Fisher's way. Despite the Super's insistence that the case should be near to a close, and his request for Gavin to report to his office, Gavin knew that neither event was going to happen today.

He wondered what Fisher hoped to achieve by speaking to him. He knew that Gavin couldn't offer him any solution to Emily's murder other than the one he already had. Perhaps he was contemplating throwing him a bone by now allowing Foster to be accused openly. Since the man was dead, he couldn't deny it. And, as far as Fisher was concerned, Helen was, too, so it couldn't do any harm to let Gavin's story stand and demand that was an end to it.

Except, Gavin thought, *he must know I won't accept all that at face-value.* Even if he didn't know what he did, Gavin would be questioning motives, the circumstances surrounding the deaths of the two 'players', even the change of heart by Fisher. No, it was much better the entire conversation was avoided for the time being. Until Gavin could get more of a handle on what had really happened.

He arrived in Patterson's office to discover the man was nowhere to be seen. After hanging around for a few minutes, he decided to go and search the stacks himself. He had no idea what he thought he was looking for but something was niggling at the back of his head, and he hoped if he gave it enough leeway, it might turn into something tangible.

He found himself walking alongside a shelf with boxes

of records from similar dates to the ones he'd already looked at. These obviously had nothing to do with the corruption case; they would be other cases that had been in the process of investigation coincidentally around that time. He tried to remember what he'd been working on when IPCC had arrived. He thought it had been a break-in, but which one? And why did he suddenly feel it was so important?

Then it came to him. It had been a series of robberies, all with the same M.O., all small-time events with the same suspects being accused in each case – except for one which was different in a few subtle ways. For instance, whereas the others had all been break-ins of small high-street shops and a few post offices, this one had involved a large jewellers'. At the time, Gavin had no evidence to tie the suspects to this robbery but they'd openly confessed to it once they realised they were not going to get away with the others. But unlike the other break-ins, the money taken from the jewellers' had never been recovered.

He remembered thinking it all very odd at the time but, rather foolishly, he'd not followed up on his suspicions – mostly because the station had been thrown into turmoil by the corruption case. He had a confession. He'd also been supplied with a couple of witnesses who'd been able to identify sufficient elements to implicate the men – things like the get-away car, the number of assailants and general physical details. The men had worn masks in all the robberies so no-one was going to be able to give specifics.

Now that he thought back, he recalled all three of the burglars had been given more lenient sentences after confessing to the bigger crime. 'Co-operating with the prosecuting officers', it had been described as. Why was he remembering this now?

Then, suddenly, a clear picture materialised in Gavin's mind. A picture of Stevens walking into the cells where the men were being held. He hadn't known who Stevens was at that stage because he hadn't yet been interviewed by him. In fact, it must have been only just about the time that Stevens had first come to the station. Gavin had assumed he was the burglars' solicitor, so he hadn't queried it. And later, when he encountered Stevens as a member of the IPCC, it had slipped his mind because, by that point, the man was a common sight around the station.

It didn't take too big a leap of imagination to consider the possibility that Stevens had something to do with the men's additional confession and the sudden, very convenient, appearance of witnesses. Not to mention the disappearance of a considerable sum of money. Had Stevens used the burglars to shift some funds around?

Even as he made his way back to Patterson's desk, to ask him to call up the relevant files, he knew it was a useless task. There'd be nothing there. Stevens would've made sure of that. Now if Gavin could just remember who the custody officer had been that day…

And then another thought struck him. Was it possible that someone else was already onto Stevens – or the network to which he presumably belonged? And that someone had informed someone else at the Home Office? Might that account for their interest in the now missing files? And if so, why was Stevens still floating around, apparently a free agent, over a year later, instead of being 'banged up' like he ought to be?

Gavin realised he was now in the world of unsubstantiated mind-wanderings and called himself back to the tasks in hand.

He waited until he was sure Fisher had gone home before he met again with Charlie and Tom. They all reconvened in Tom's lab to share their various thoughts on the case.

Charlie had had an interesting interview with the woman from the Anti-Slavery Group, who was full of praise for Heather's work and the Sweet Diamond charity.

'She couldn't compliment her enough,' said Charlie. 'It seems Heather's contribution has made a substantial difference to the area, Sir. Given the children hope of a different kind of future, she said.'

'And did she know anything about Victoria Orphanage?'

'Yes. Apparently, that was the initial cause of the lawsuit. I got it wrong. It wasn't the mine-owners as such that Heather's Foundation were trying to prosecute, it was the owners of the orphanage – who turned out to be the same people, pretty much. They use the orphanage to home street kids, who they pick up regularly from various cities in the area, and then, of course, insist they work for their board and lodging by going into the mines.

'Heather had cottoned onto this during a visit last year and decided to try to put a stop to it. Hence the counter-claim against her own project. That was an attempt to shut her up, I think.'

'Then they didn't reckon on who they were dealing with,' Gavin said.

'Clearly not, Sir. Though, of course, we don't know whether they've now done something worse, since we can't find her.'

Gavin grunted in agreement.

'So, this orphanage is part-funded by Falkenrath Pharmaceuticals?'

'Yes. It was on Maxwell's list, Sir. He's still following up on that.'

'I feel,' Gavin said, 'almost as if we're dealing with two cases here. On the one hand, there's all this information about Heather's involvement with these children, and the possibility she's ticked off someone who's answerable – possibly – to Falkenrath Pharmaceuticals …' He paused. 'Then there's all this crap going on here around Fisher and Stevens - and God knows who else.' He paused again. 'And somehow they both fit together, don't they? In some way we've not yet understood.'

'I think that just about sums it up,' Tom said. 'Would a chocolate cookie cheer you up a little? You sound so gloomy.' He got up to fetch a packet of biscuits from his rucksack. 'It'll come together, Gavin. It always does.'

Gavin's phone rang. He moved away to a more secluded part of the lab.

'Hi Gavin.'

'Katriona. Good to hear from you. How're things going over there?'

'Fast. Just to fill you in on the basics. The bullets match.'

'They do?'

'Yes. It was definitely Gravenburg who shot Dieter Bergmann.'

Finally. A real bona fide piece of evidence that began to tie things together.

'And this Falkenrath Pharmaceuticals. There's something funny going on there. I can't quite put my finger on it, but …' Katriona told him about her strange conversation with Frieda.

Gavin listened with intrigue. Then filled her in on what his team had turned up relating to the company.

'Now that's interesting.' Katriona's response was spoken with feeling.

'I wonder if – ' Gavin began to say.

' – I could pay them a visit while I'm here?'

Gavin chuckled. 'Yeah.'

'Already on it. I'm planning to go tomorrow. Booked an appointment this aft – Oh my God!'

Gavin heard a squeal of brakes and a scream, then the phone went dead.

33

'What the hell just happened?' Katriona tried to get up off the pavement where Stephi had flung her, crashing them both to the ground, but her head felt woozy. When she put her hand to it, there was blood. She must have hit something on the way down.

'Stay there,' Stephi ordered, getting out her phone to ring for an ambulance. 'You're bleeding quite badly.'

Katriona pulled a wad of tissues out of her bag and held them over where it hurt. Stephi bent over her to inspect the wound.

'Well, either that was a close call by a very drunken driver – or someone just tried to kill you.'

Even through her light-headedness, Katriona knew her confusion wasn't down to the injury.

'That doesn't make any sense, Stephi. Who on earth would consider me a threat? I haven't uncovered anything significant, today. I've only been here a few hours. In fact, hardly anyone knows I'm here.'

Then it dawned on her – Frieda. She must have reported back to someone at Falkenrath Pharmaceuticals. Quite inadvertently, Katriona had stumbled across a connection, a link between the company and what had happened to Bergmann – and therefore Elayne and Helen … and ultimately Emily. Someone must believe she knew more than she actually did. And by trying to dispose of her – or even if the intention had been only to scare her off – they'd just handed her perhaps the biggest clue so far. She became aware Stephi was speaking to her.

'Katriona? Are you alright? You seemed to blank out for a moment there.'

'Stephi, I'm fine. I've just worked something out.' She looked up at the elegant woman standing next to her. 'Thank you. I believe you've just saved my life.'

She removed the sodden tissues from the side of her head, and hunted in her bag for something more effective to stem the bleeding.

'Here,' Stephi said, and handed her the scarf she'd been wearing.

Katriona took it gratefully and pressed it against the wound. 'Is my phone somewhere? I had it in my hand.'

Stephi looked along the pavement, and walked a few yards to investigate something on the ground.

'Yes, it's here,' she said, handing it over. 'I hope now you're going to fill *me* in, as well as Gavin.' Her tone was acerbic.

'I think I better had,' Katriona answered, 'but I'm going to clear that with Gavin, first.' She hit Redial.

It turned out that the wound was not as bad as the quantity of blood had indicated, and although the paramedics wanted Katriona to be taken to the nearest hospital for observation, she declined. She didn't want any delay now on sorting out their next moves. She agreed with Stephi that she should tell her everything because this was now unfolding on her territory and if anything were to happen to Katriona, Gavin would need someone else at this end to keep working the case.

As they'd been on their way to a restaurant for an evening meal, and as Katriona still felt ravenously hungry, once she'd been checked over, she proposed they go ahead and find somewhere to eat where they could talk properly.

Stephi knew just the place and rang for a taxi to take them there.

After a delicious first course of wild mushroom soup with garlic rye bread, which made Katriona feel considerably better, the pair had mulled over the details of the case along with a rather splendid sea-food risotto.

'I'm glad you brought me here,' Katriona said. 'This is fantastic.'

'So is your story, I think. That's the right English word, isn't it – for when something is hard to believe?' Stephi smiled. She had warmed more towards Katriona since being let in on the background story.

'Yes – and yes.' Katriona responded. 'I agree with you, but when you start putting all the bits and pieces together, those are the conclusions you come to.'

They were both silent, briefly, as the waiter brought more wine.

'So how long has Frieda worked at the lab?' Katriona asked.

'Just over a year, or thereabouts.'

'Do you know her well?'

'Not particularly. She's always been very efficient, always there when you need her, always happy to do more than is asked.' Stephi slowed up as she spoke, realisation dawning.

'The perfect spy, then?' Katriona commented.

'But there's never been … I mean, she's never given me any cause to …'

'Nothing ever gone missing, no information got into the wrong hands, or evidence spoiled?'

'Well, only to the extent one might expect in a forensics lab. There are always going to be accidents. I can't think of anything particularly suspicious since she arrived. Except …' Stephi hesitated.

'Yes?' Katriona encouraged, fitting the syllable in between mouthfuls.

'About six months ago, we had a young technician – I don't remember his name – he'd only been with us a short while, when one day he asked if he could speak to me about something. I couldn't stop at that moment but told him I'd be back at the labs the next day.'

'So what happened?'

'I don't know. I never saw him again.'

'What was he working on?'

'Oh, he was training in autopsy. I think we'd had a shooting come in.' Stephi sipped her wine. 'Yes, it could've been the Morgan case. A man, in his fifties, worked for MediGloves – you know, the surgical glove people. I think he was a research director. We never found either his killer or any reason why he should be shot. He's still one of our unsolved cases.'

'And your new technician – he was working on this shooting?'

'I'm fairly sure he was, but like I say, he just disappeared overnight. When I asked where he was the next day, Reception told me his mother had been taken ill and he'd had to leave in a hurry. I never checked up on it. I mean, why would I?'

'Quite,' Katriona agreed. 'But you think now it might be suspicious?'

'Anything's possible, isn't it? After what you've told me tonight, I'll be getting suspicious of myself tomorrow.' She laughed. 'Are you going to try one of those splendid puddings, before we get too serious?'

Katriona opted for a magnificent orange, vanilla and toffee pudding and thought how much Elayne would enjoy coming here.

Stephi suggested Katriona stay at her flat that night, rather than at the hotel where she was booked. They both agreed that was a safer option and Katriona reflected privately she was incredibly relieved for the offer. She really hadn't wanted to be on her own in the circumstances.

She rang Elayne before she settled down for the night, breaking the news of what had taken place earlier as gently as possible, which wasn't easy. But Elayne, as ever, showed she was made of stern stuff.

'Are you okay?'

'Apart from hitting the side of my head on something, I'm fine. I just have a large lump and a small cut – a bit of bruising, too.'

'Take some Arnica,' Elayne suggested. 'You've got some with you?' She was very keen on alternative remedies.

'Already done. You've trained me well, Master,' Katriona joked.

'And aside from that … it hasn't put you off staying to investigate?'

'Not in the slightest.'

'I didn't really think it would, but I thought I'd better check.'

Katriona was suddenly very grateful to have a partner who gave her the freedom to be herself. 'I miss you already,' she said.

'I knew you would.' Elayne was in a playful mood. 'Now leave me alone to get some sleep – and go to bed yourself. You need to get your brain cells in top working order so you can hurry home.'

After Katriona put the phone down, she reflected some more on her event-filled day. She felt very sure that Falkenrath Pharmaceuticals somehow held the key to what was going on. She hoped her visit to their offices tomorrow would provide some leads but she wasn't at all sure how she could make this happen. She could hardly go in accusing anyone. She had no evidence of anything as yet.

There was no point in throwing suspicions around, so her best tactic was to present an innocent front, explain that she was trying to find Heather Hough and the last recorded sighting she had was outside the company's main office, where she was due to meet with the CEO. Just see where that got her.

Next morning found her outside the same glass and steel-fronted building she had seen in Dieter's blog, with Stephi alongside. Her friend was insistent she should not go alone.

'You have no idea what you might encounter,' she'd said, when they talked it through. 'Besides, having me there will give you more authority. A visiting 'cop' can easily be blown off but a resident policewoman cannot. They cannot afford to get on the wrong side of the law in their own city.'

Katriona had to agree with the logic of this, and actually did feel that the two of them acting together might produce better results than her alone. At the very least, it would demonstrate the importance they were placing on the visit – by sending two DI's.

They entered through the impressive glass doors and made their way to Reception, from where they were directed to the top floor via an elevator. Stepping out of the sliding doors, a few minutes later, they saw a large desk with a smart, fair-haired woman dressed in blue - and wearing the now-familiar logo on her name badge - sitting behind it.

'Oh, DI McShannon. I've been expecting you. I'm Margaret Newton. I'm Mr. Anderson's PA. And you must be DI Wolff?' She turned towards Stephi who raised an eyebrow in query. 'Reception sent up a photo and names for you both.'

'My word, that's efficient,' Stephi said.

'Yes, it's rather a neat system,' Margaret replied.

'You're English,' Katriona observed.

'Yes, though I've lived here for some years now. Right. If you're ready, I'll take you through,' and she led the way towards two enormous, floor to ceiling, wooden doors at the end of the landing.

'I've buzzed Mr. Anderson, so you can go on in.' She smiled, knocking on one of the doors and opening it.

Inside was an equally enormous room, equipped at one end with conventional office furniture and at the other with a number of comfy-looking white sofas and a low-slung wooden coffee table. Three sides of the room had glass windows for walls so that from inside one had a spectacular view across the city.

'Good morning.' A large, but not very tall, man stood up from the desk as they entered. He spoke with an American accent. 'DI McShannon, DI Wolff.' He shook each by the hand but kept the desk between himself and his visitors.

'How can I help you?' He indicated for them to sit in two black leather chairs which had obviously been placed specifically for the meeting.

'Sir, thank you for making time to see us,' Katriona began. 'You're probably aware that I'm a visitor from the UK.'

The man nodded assent.

'I'm currently working as part of a team who are trying to find the whereabouts of a reporter named Heather Hough.'

The man didn't bat an eyelid.

'I'm liaising here in Dusseldorf with DI Wolff. This city is Heather's main home.' She paused, waiting to see if Anderson bit.

'So, I repeat,' he said. 'How can I help you?'

'I believe you knew Heather?' Katriona pushed.

'Oh, I see. Well, I'm not sure I'd phrase it that way. Our paths have crossed once or twice, and I know of her work, of course. Is she missing, then?'

Katriona declined to answer directly. 'We're trying to contact her in light of her sister's death.'

Again, the man gave nothing away. 'I'm sorry to hear that,' he said, 'but I'm still at a loss …'

'I think you may have known Dieter Bergmann, too?'

'Yes, in a similar way. Purely through professional events. I was very sorry to hear of his demise. Poor Ms Hough must be having a hard time.'

He stared straight at Katriona, revealing absolutely nothing. She held her ground and stared back.

'I'm sorry,' he said. 'Am I missing something here?'

'Well, sir,' she said, in her sweetest tones. 'We were hoping you could provide a little more information. This office may be the last place the two of them were seen alive together.'

Anderson jerked his head and threw Katriona an incredulous look.

'Here? I think you must be mistaken.'

'No, not at all. They had a meeting with you on the morning of the day Dieter died.'

'No. You've definitely been misinformed. To my knowledge, I have never met with either of them in a formal capacity.'

Katriona was stunned. Either the man was a very practised liar or something serious had happened between the moment of the snapshot taken outside and their non-appearance in this man's office.

Stephi stepped in. 'Are you sure, sir? We have very concrete evidence that they arrived outside the building that day and were planning to speak with you.'

'Did they actually have an appointment?' Anderson asked. Before either Stephi or Katriona could respond, he continued. 'Let me ask my secretary.' He buzzed the intercom on his desk.

'Margaret, can you bring the diary through?' He smiled at the two police officers, for all the world, Katriona thought, as if he were co-operating fully.

Margaret came in, carrying a large desk diary with her, which she handed over to her boss.

'Now, let's see, which day are we talking?'

'The fifth,' Katriona supplied.

Anderson turned the pages, flipping back through the last week or so, until he came to the correct date, then he turned the diary round for them to see. Katriona noticed it was a loose-leaf file but said nothing. She made a good show of tracking down the page with her finger.

'You are absolutely right, Mr Anderson. There's no record of them having an appointment here.' She stood up. 'Thank you for your time. Perhaps if you think of anything that might be helpful, you could contact me?' She handed him a card with her details on it.

'Of course, of course,' he said. 'I'm only sorry I can't be of more help. My secretary will see you out.'

Margaret scooped up the large diary again and led the way across the room to the door. Katriona and Stephi followed.

Katriona was smarting. She knew he was lying but she had no way of proving it. She toyed with the idea of questioning Margaret separately but decided there was little point in this context. The woman was hardly going to call her boss a liar within his hearing.

She made her way back across the landing towards the elevator.

'Oh, DI McShannon,' Margaret called out after her.

She turned and saw the woman walking towards her, a promotional leaflet in her hand.

'I just thought you might like to take one of these. It'll give you some insight into what we do here.'

She passed the leaflet to Katriona with a smile, and turned back to her desk. *What an odd thing to do,* Katriona thought, as she and Stephi stepped into the lift.

They descended to the ground floor in silence, Katriona guessing that Stephi was as frustrated as she was, booked themselves out at Reception and passed through the glass doors back onto the pavement.

'Well, that was a waste of time,' Stephi said.

'I'm not so sure,' Katriona murmured.

'What do you mean?'

'Let's just take a bit of a walk down the street, shall we? Get away from the building.'

Stephi looked at her, puzzled, but did as Katriona suggested. When they'd walked a few blocks away, Katriona turned a corner and went into a nearby department store. She opened the leaflet Margaret had given her and sure enough, tucked neatly inside was a note. It read:

Meet me at Krocus Café. Noon. M.

34

Gavin, like Katriona, had very mixed feelings about the car 'accident'. On the one hand, he was concerned about Katriona's safety and had been extremely relieved to hear she'd not suffered any serious injuries – or worse. On the other hand, he, too, was excited that the incident gave them clues to follow up and seemed to indicate that somewhere along the line, they – like Heather – had ticked someone off.

He was impatient to hear how Katriona's visit to Falkenrath Pharmaceuticals had gone, and in the absence of any new information from anyone on the team, took himself down to Tom's lab to talk some more while he waited for things to move.

Tom's door was closed when he got there, which was unusual. As Gavin tried to turn the handle, he realised it was locked, as well. He was just about to shout through the door in panic, when he noticed the digital board hung on the hook, just above his head.

Top Secret Work. Please identify yourself by keying in your ID number.   Tom. Genius (local).

Gavin laughed. Sometimes it was like working with a teenager. He dutifully tapped in his personal code and heard the click as the door unlocked.

'Mornin', Gavin.' Tom's cheery voice greeted him. 'Do you like my anti-Fisher technology?'

'Oh, is that what it's for?' Gavin closed the door behind him.

'Primarily, yes. I thought I'd keep it jokey enough to piss him off, but it is a serious - and very useful – piece of technology.'

From the look in his eyes, Gavin couldn't tell whether he really meant it.

'And I am actually doing Top Secret stuff, here.'

'What exactly classes as Top Secret in your world, Tom?'

'I'm chasing bullets.'

'Excuse me?'

Tom pointed to a nearby screen which was flashing images of bullets at a furious rate.

'You know I wasn't happy about not being able to inform Interpol about Gravenburg's recent activities – and probable demise?'

'Yes, but you understand why, Tom?'

'Absolutely. But that doesn't make me any happier about it. Apart from the fact that, technically, we're keeping information that we shouldn't be – '

Gavin opened his mouth to object.

'I know, I know.' Tom cut him off. 'Well, aside from that, I've always dreamt of being the hero forensic scientist who tips off Interpol to a key suspect …'

Gavin watched Tom's eyes glaze over as his fantasy world threatened to take over the conversation.

'So chasing bullets is the next best thing?' he prompted.

'Kinda. I thought that when we can release what we know, it might soften up the authorities a little if I could provide an even more complete package of information. Besides, this might be useful to us.'

'So what are you doing?'

'Tracking the bullets from Gravenburg's gun. The lab Katriona visited yesterday sent me the comparison photos of the bullets from Bergman and Elayne.'

He caught the expression on Gavin's face.

'Don't worry. Katriona arranged it before she left the lab

yesterday. She instructed their ballistics expert, Sondra Jollenbeck, to contact me directly, not to go through the usual channels, so the photos were sent on a secure line.'

'Still …' Gavin muttered.

'Still what?'

'Well, it might account for what happened to Katriona last night.'

'I guess so. I hadn't thought of that. She would've made the arrangements earlier in the day, wouldn't she? Before she suspected anything.'

'I gather she was pretty suspicious of this Frieda character straight away, but I'm sure she would have taken that into account when she spoke to your ballistics contact. It just gives us another person to be concerned about.' He shrugged. He couldn't do anything about that for the moment so he pursued what Tom had been investigating. 'So tell me the details.'

'I've been using the identifying marks on those bullets to compare to bullets from other shootings held in Interpol's files. It's no wonder they've got Gravenburg on their 'Wanted List'. He's got a string of potential murders, as long as my arm, attached to his name. This positive identification is going to be immensely valuable to them in closing a lot of cases.'

'Really? Well done, Tom.'

'But there's more.'

Gavin grinned. There always was 'more'.

'I then started running the comparison through other data bases. See if there are other unclosed cases with a match.'

'Anything?'

'A couple in Germany, from a few years back. One was a guy who was suspected of international espionage himself. The other was a policeman, name of Kassmeyer.'

'Do we know what he was investigating at the time?'

'Not yet, but I'm working on it. I was just about to start hunting for details when you came.' He crossed the room to the kettle. 'Thirsty work, this. I presume you'll have one, too?'

Gavin nodded.

Tom continued, 'The ballistics programme is still running, so we may get more names as the day goes on.'

A buzzing sound interrupted him and he looked over to a screen which displayed a list of numbers and Maxwell's name alongside it. He pressed a button and Gavin heard that click again as the door unlocked.

'Oh, Sir. There you are.' Maxwell addressed Gavin. 'You have a visitor.'

The man waiting outside Gavin's office had rather a pompous air to him. Gavin introduced himself and, receiving no reciprocal details, opened his door and gestured for his visitor to enter.

Once inside, the man produced an ID card and said 'Kimberlay. Thomas Kimberlay. Home Office.'

Gavin gasped, then tried to cover it. What had he stumbled over now?

'I gather you were asking after my clerk, Hall-Gardiner.'

'*Your* clerk?' Was he getting closer to actually uncovering something useful?

'Yes, well, he was. He left my sector over a year ago.'

'And that would be … ?'

'Sorry?'

'Your sector. What exactly is your sector?'

The man, who had taken the seat behind Gavin's desk, reached out to pick up a framed photo of Trish and Gavin on holiday together.

'Oh, I see. Well now, I'm sure you understand that a lot of what we do is highly confidential.'

With a very deliberate motion, he moved the photo to the opposite side of the desk from where he'd picked it up and placed it next to a pile of folders.

'I was just wondering what your interest in my man was.'

Gavin's hopes sank. *Here we go again, playing games.* He

replaced the photo next to the lamp.

'If you could just let me get to my notes …' he said, stepping round his desk. Two could play at this game.

'Of course.' Kimberlay was forced to vacate the chair by Gavin's, equally deliberate, movements.

Gavin quickly sat down and made a show of opening a large notebook and turning over the pages.

'Ah, yes.' He made a gesture, indicating the chair on the far side of his desk, but Kimberlay, having lost his first advantage, preferred to remain standing. He looked at Gavin, expectantly.

'I was trying to trace the history of a box of evidence,' Gavin said, as noncommittally as possible.

'Evidence pertaining to … ?'

'An old case of ours.' He was determined to force Kimberlay to show his hand. He was pretty sure the man already knew what he had been looking into.

'I see.' Kimberlay tried a slightly different approach. 'And what had this to do with Hall-Gardiner?'

'He signed the box out at one time.'

'But it was returned?' A hint of anxiety entered Kimberlay's voice.

'Yes,' Gavin answered, levelly. 'But I wanted to ask him what his interest was.' He raised his line of sight to look directly into Kimberlay's face. 'Perhaps you can help with that. As he was *your* clerk at the time.' He knew the words were a direct challenge but it was worth a shot.

'I'm afraid I can't.'

In Charlie's words, Gavin thought, *there's a surprise.*

Kimberlay looked away. 'Perhaps if you could remind me what the case was about … ?'

Gavin considered he had nothing to lose since he was convinced Kimberlay knew this anyway, so he replied 'The corruption case we had here, a year or so back,' and waited to see if that got any response.

'I see,' said Kimberlay, again. He turned back to face Gavin with a rather peculiar smile on his face. 'Well now, DI

Pearce. He signed the box out at my request. We were monitoring the progress of the investigation.' He paused, looking Gavin in the eye. 'But that's all done and dusted now, isn't it?'

Gavin decided to say nothing. He just smiled in response.

'My advice to you, Inspector, is to let it lie. I fail to see what relevance it might have to any current investigations.' He raised one eyebrow to emphasize the question in his statement.

Gavin was determined not to give anything away. 'It might not, but I'd be neglecting my duty if I was less than diligent.'

'With that, I must concur,' Kimberlay answered, rather pompously, and looked down at his hands where he began to make a strange show of inspecting his nails. 'And we can't have that, can we?' Again, that look accompanied by the peculiar smile.

Gavin could not get a read on what the man really wanted. Had he come to warn him off? To find out how much he knew – or suspected? Even to encourage him to delve further?

'Well, I'll be on my way then.' Suddenly, Kimberlay turned to go.

'Oh, by the way, what happened to Hall-Gardiner?' Gavin threw the question nonchalantly over the desk.

Kimberlay gave him a steady stare. 'He moved on. To higher things.' He left the room.

What the bloody hell was that all about? Gavin thought.

It was not long after Kimberlay had left Gavin's office when his phone rang. He'd taken to carrying his secure phone with him now, given the need to keep consistent contact with Katriona. She'd rung to tell him about her visit to Falkenrath Pharmaceuticals.

'I'm very sure he was lying, Gavin.'

'I know the feeling.'

'Why, who's been lying to you?'

Gavin explained about the visit he'd just received. 'The thing is, Katriona, I can't decide whether he was trying to threaten me, caution me or encourage me.'

'Perhaps he wasn't doing any of those. Maybe he was checking you out.'

'Checking *me* out? Oh, hang on a second.'

A knock on his door interrupted the conversation, and Gavin slid the phone under some files, as he said 'Come in.'

It was Maxwell with a package in his hands.

'Parcel for you, Sir. Left at the front desk.' He placed the brown paper bundle on top of the files where Gavin indicated and left again.

Gavin retrieved his phone. 'Sorry. You were saying?'

'Yes. Just that this Kimberlay guy could be aware of some of what's been going on. Maybe he got wind of your interest and genuinely wondered what you knew. Thought he'd come and take a look himself.'

'That still doesn't explain that much, though. I mean, it doesn't tell us whether he's one of the good guys or not.' Gavin began unsealing the sellotape on the parcel, tucking his phone under his chin, so he could use both hands.

'No. You're right.'

'I mean, if the Home Office were already aware of Stevens, or even just suspected him, when he was leading the corruption investigation here, it's just possible they've been monitoring him since and don't want me interfering. But only just possible. It's equally possible that this Kimberlay guy is also 'on the take' and wanted to find out what I knew …' He trailed off.

'Gavin. You okay?'

'Yes.' He paused, looking intently at the contents of the package. 'Katriona. I need to call you back. Something's turned up.'

'No problem. I just wanted to tell you that I have a private meeting in an hour with Anderson's PA.'

Gavin forced his attention back to the conversation.

'Really? How d'you manage that?'

'I didn't. She approached me. Put a note in a leaflet she gave me as I left.'

'Well now, isn't *that* something of a coincidence?'

Gavin rang down to Tom's lab to let him know he was on his way, before resealing the sellotape and picking up the parcel to take with him. He summoned Charlie from his desk to come, too, but said nothing until all three of them were safely locked into Tom's lab.

'So, what have you got for me?' Tom's eyes glittered in anticipation.

'This was just left for me at the front desk. Apparently by a visitor I had earlier.'

'And who was that, Sir?' Charlie asked, handing round the mugs.

'Man called Kimberlay. From the Home Office.'

'Who rattled their cage?' Tom joked.

'It appears that I did.' Gavin shared the details of his conversation, if one could call it that, with Kimberlay. 'Frustratingly inconclusive, I would describe it.'

'Sounds like it,' said Tom. 'So how does this tie in with the parcel?'

'It seems that he handed this in as he was leaving. In fact, he must've gone out to his car to retrieve it and come back in, because he didn't have it with him when he was in my office. Don't know whether that's significant.'

'So what's inside?'

Gavin carefully pulled the sellotape back again to reveal the note on top of a folded newspaper. It read: *Good man, Hannaford. Worth talking to. Kimberlay.*

Tom put on a pair of latex gloves and used some forceps to remove the note. 'I presume you want this kept?'

'Definitely. We don't know where this is going. Hannaford. Why do I know that name?'

'He's the editor of *The Manchester Independent*, Sir,' Charlie said. 'You remember. The guy Emily was going to meet. You spoke with him on the phone.'

And sure enough, a copy of the newspaper in question was revealed as the note was lifted away. It was dated the previous June, and folded in such a way as to highlight a story on page five, in the political section. The headline ran: *Sacked Civil Servant Offered Post In Ministry.*

Gavin read aloud:

Our reporter discovered today that former Home Office clerk, Martin Hall-Gardiner, who was dismissed from his post last year for alleged breaches of security, has now been invited to take up a senior role at the Ministry of Health, working as a liaison between government authorities and various pharmaceutical companies who regularly trade with Britain.

When questioned, a spokesperson from the Ministry said: 'We are delighted to have Mr. Hall-Gardiner on board. His experience, efficiency and expertise as a former Home Office clerk will suit him to his new role admirably.'

Pushed to comment on Hall-Gardiner's dismissal, our source described it as 'an unfortunate misunderstanding which, in no way, should hold back someone so able'.

Mr. Hall-Gardiner himself was unavailable for comment.

35

Katriona had rung Gavin from the car. In the space between leaving Falkenrath Pharmaceuticals and the promised meeting with Margaret Newton, she and Stephi had decided to visit Heather's apartment, so Katriona could get more of a picture on the missing woman. Stephi had contacted the housekeeper to let them in, and she was waiting for them as they pulled up in the carpark.

They followed her round to a back entrance. Katriona was glad their visit was not too obvious. She was aware of the possibility of being observed.

The apartment was both very elegant and soothingly comfortable. Katriona knew both sisters used it from time to time, and it had the feel of somewhere that was actually lived in rather than just visited. The housekeeper, who insisted they call her Hilda, led them through each room, pointing out things she considered important.

'And this is Miss Heather's room,' she said, opening a door into a room with deep russet walls and long golden curtains at the window. The furniture was old-fashioned, beautifully made from wood. Katriona guessed it was mahogany. There was a large bed, several cupboards and sets of drawers, and a writing desk placed under the window.

She crossed the room to look.

'Don't touch anything,' Stephi warned. 'We don't have a warrant to search.'

Katriona moved her hand over a large book with an engraved cover, which was laid on the open desk flap. It appeared to be a diary.

'We might not, but I'm sure Hilda has permission.'

Stephi caught her eye. 'I see what you mean.'

She turned to the woman standing at the door and spoke in German. A short conversation ensued, which resulted in Hilda joining Katriona at the desk and very carefully opening the book where a piece of ribbon acted as a book marker.

It was dated the day before Dieter was shot.

All set for our meeting tomorrow. The information is now safely in England. This will be his last chance to offer an alternative explanation. Then we go public on all the details.

Here, at last, was an indication on how all the events of the last week or so might fit together. She called Stephi over to read the entry.

'Now can we consider a warrant?'

'I would say so, but I'll do it quietly. We still don't know who is involved. No point drawing attention.'

'Agreed.' A further thought struck Katriona. She turned to Hilda.

'Has there been any sign that Heather might have been back here, recently?'

Stephi translated. 'She says there was something in the living room she thought had been moved on her last visit – which would have been on Thursday. And a pair of Heather's shoes has gone missing.'

Stephi spoke again with Hilda. 'She had the feeling Heather had been home but the place was tidy, just as she'd left it, so she couldn't be sure.'

That was hopeful. Maybe Heather was still alive.

They wandered through the rest of the apartment but, not being able to search, turned up nothing else of significance. However, Katriona felt she'd gained a glimpse into Heather's – and possibly Emily's – life. They gave every impression of being two lovely ladies, clearly devoted to each other but also to their work. The word 'passion' rang in her head as she looked around at the haven the two had created. This was not a place for a quick stop-over when travelling; this was truly a home. A place that mattered.

It was a pity they couldn't look in more detail but one thing was now clarified for her. Heather had definitely been onto something, at the very least, dodgy, and potentially illegal. She must have been about to challenge Anderson to his face. The fact that she was prepared to 'go public' meant that she was one of the good guys.

Stephi drove them both back towards the city centre. The café where they were to meet with Margaret was further south along the river, the other side of town from the offices where she worked.

'This is where Bergmann was shot,' Stephi said, as they crossed a bridge. 'I found his body downstream, over there.' She pointed in the direction of a bend in the river.

'Was it far from here?'

'No, but easily hidden from view at that point. The water's very deep and fast just there. That's why it hadn't been spotted sooner.'

Having reached the far side of the river, it was only a few minutes before Stephi pulled up the car and entered a small carpark, off the main street.

'Not many people know this is here,' she said. 'It's very useful.'

They walked along the pavement, a sudden streak of midday sunshine brightening the scene. Katriona noticed several busy shops with colourful displays in their front windows – mostly fashion and shoe shops.

As they approached the café, she could see a collection of umbrella-covered tables with chairs, set out in front of it. Margaret was already sitting at one of them.

'I've ordered for all of us,' she announced, as they joined her. 'I hope that's okay. I'm on my lunch-break, so I haven't much time.'

As she spoke, a waiter came out of the café carrying

three large platters of one of the most splendid salads Katriona had ever seen.

'I didn't think I could go too far wrong with salad,' Margaret continued. 'And there's garlic bread and a selection of pate's to come, as well.'

Katriona spoke for both her and Stephi. 'Thank you, Margaret. Your taste is impeccable.'

'I'm so glad you think so. I hope that will make it easier for you to trust what I'm about to say.'

The garlic bread arrived, and Katriona took a piece, catching Stephi's eye as she did so.

'Do go ahead, Margaret.'

'Well, the first thing to tell you, I think, is that my name's not really Margaret.'

'No?' Katriona couldn't see immediately how that might be relevant.

'No. It's Clarissa Cartwright. I'm British Intelligence.'

Katriona very nearly choked on her mouthful. She stared at the woman.

'It would be helpful if you didn't make too much of a scene, my dear,' she said.

Katriona suddenly realised the authority for this conversation no longer rested with her. She mustered as much dignity as she could and responded, 'I'll do my best.'

'Now,' said Clarissa, 'I don't expect you just to believe me. I have ID here but I'm not going to make a big show of it. 'Walls have' and all that.'

She took her napkin and reached into her bag with the same hand, pulling something out and placing it on the table, neatly covered by the fabric.

Katriona surreptitiously lifted a corner and saw the ID, verifying that this was, indeed, Agent Clarissa Cartwright of MI6. Well, that was unexpected.

'My friends call me Cici. As you might guess. I've been working here in Dusseldorf for quite a few years now, but I'm relatively new to Falkenrath Pharmaceuticals. I started in the secretarial team about a year ago. Working under cover, of course.'

'Oh, I see.' Katriona began to understand. 'So you had doubts about what was happening there?'

'We've been watching various aspects of the company for some time. My job was to ingratiate myself with Anderson. Try to get myself appointed onto his immediate staff, so that I could get a closer look at what was going on. I've been his PA for about six months.'

'What did you suspect him of at that stage?'

'To begin with, mostly corrupt business deals which might be detrimental to the British economy. But it very soon became apparent that the deals were being authorised by a number of British components, including, we thought, some significant figures in government.' She clarified. 'That is, potentially, both in the German government and our own.'

'Good heavens,' Katriona said. 'So how do Heather and Dieter fit into this?'

'Well, that's quite interesting, really. We had plenty of suspicions but not so much in the way of evidence. Our hands are often tied, which rather limits our field of operation.'

Katriona thought that was probably unlikely but let it go.

'We'd also been watching Heather for a while. She has quite a reputation as a reporter for – shall we say – uncovering the dirt. We guessed she was on to something regarding Anderson a few months back. We didn't want to interfere since she could more easily investigate places where we couldn't. But we did want to know what she knew. Sadly, she disappeared before I was able to make contact.'

'So you have no idea where she is, either?'

'No, but she *was* here. She did come to see Anderson on that morning, with Dieter. I don't know what they talked about but I let them into the office, and out again, afterwards.'

'So Anderson was lying?' Katriona wanted confirmation.

'Yes. And that's not unusual for him. He expects me, as

his PA, to cover for him. It's written into my contract. Very carefully, of course. Issues of confidentiality, etc. But it was made very clear to me what was expected when I took on the post.'

Stephi interrupted, producing a photograph.

'And do you recognise him? Was he in the office that day?'

It was now Clarissa's turn to be shocked. 'That's Gravenburg.' She almost whispered. 'I've come across him before. In another context. What's he got to do with all this?'

Katriona and Stephi exchanged looks.

'He killed Dieter Bergmann. Not long after they left Anderson's office,' Stephi said.

'Good God,' Clarissa exclaimed. 'I thought he died in a road traffic accident.'

'It was made to look that way,' Stephi said, 'but now we have proof that he was shot by a bullet from Gravenburg's gun. So I need to ask you again – did you see him that morning? Or any other time, in fact?'

'No. I definitely would have noticed him.' She paused. 'His face is etched in my memory from a previous occasion.'

'We think,' Katriona spoke again, 'that Dieter and Heather had stumbled over something involving the pharmaceutical company, or Anderson, specifically. They came to the office that morning to challenge him to put the record straight, otherwise they would – in Heather's words – 'go public'. Within hours, Dieter was dead and Heather had disappeared.'

She paused to add emphasis to her next words. 'And the following day, Gravenburg turned up in Heather's sister's house in London, looking for something, and killed her, too.'

'That was Gravenburg?'

'We think Heather sent Emily something – '

'The data stick!' A brief look of glee passed over Clarissa's face. 'She'd been cataloguing names and details for a while, I'm sure of it. We were hoping to make contact with her and persuade her to hand it over. Where is it now?'

Katriona suddenly felt she'd shared enough. 'I'm not at liberty to tell you that.'

'But it's vital that you do. That flashdrive could hold the key to all our investigations about the company.'

'It could,' Katriona agreed. 'But it might have other things on there, as well.'

'You mean, you don't know? You haven't seen what's on it?'

There was an urgency in Clarissa's voice that was unsettling Katriona.

'Clarissa,' she said, looking at the woman very directly. 'I can assure you that the flashdrive is safe, and will be handed over to the correct authorities at the appropriate time.'

'Oh, but you don't understand,' Clarissa responded.

'What don't I understand? What are you not telling us?'

Clarissa suddenly became very reserved again. She hesitated before replying.

'I think this is not the place,' she said. She lowered her voice. 'I'll need to get clearance to share anything further with you, I think. Especially in light of what you've told me about Gravenburg. And I thank you for that. It clarifies quite a lot.'

She began rifling through her bag again.

'Look, here are my private contact details. Get in touch with me early this evening. I'll get something sorted and we can meet somewhere more appropriate. I'm afraid I need to go now. If I'm late back, that'll arouse suspicion. I'm always punctual and Anderson will expect that. But promise me, you will be careful. Don't go charging into anything without considering the consequences. And most importantly, keep that flashdrive very, very safe.'

She stood up, turning on a completely different persona. 'Well, it's been lovely to meet you, my dears. I hope we'll see each other soon.'

She gave a big smile and left the café.

Katriona looked at Stephi. 'What did you make of that?'

'I really don't know, Katriona. But I think she might be

right about keeping a low profile for the moment while we figure something out.'

'Maybe. On the other hand ...' She remembered her last conversation with Gavin. 'It's so difficult to know who to trust.'

'Why do you say that?'

Katriona explained about Kimberlay's visit to Gavin. 'And now here's Clarissa, telling us there are, potentially, connections linking government officials with dodgy business deals. And at least some of those deals might be with Falkenrath Pharmaceuticals. It's another department from the Home Office investigating the same stuff we are. But it's actually impossible to tell who, if any of them, is telling the truth.'

They were both silent for a while. Then Stephi said, 'I vote we go to my apartment. Do a storyboard of what we know. See where we've got leads we can work on. Perhaps it'll make more sense if we put it all on paper.'

Katriona smiled, remembering Stephi's love of archiving.

'You're right. Get the muddle out of my head and onto paper. Back to some basic policing. Tell you what. Let's finish with a coffee. My treat. Oh, and I'd better settle the bill.' She laughed. 'Clarissa very conveniently left without paying.'

She called the waiter over and ordered two coffees. The pair sat in the sunshine, drinking and mulling over what had just happened, and allowing themselves some rather more gentle chit-chat before re-engaging their detective brains. It was wonderfully soporific and, for Katriona at least, a much-needed break. She knew her sharp mind worked better these days when she gave herself space, rather than how she used to work, with more of an anxious impatience.

As she sat, sipping from her cup, her eye was caught by a figure in a smart beige suit, on the other side of the street. The woman also wore a large hat set over a dark headscarf and sunglasses. She reminded Katriona of a 1950's filmstar, but there was an unease about the woman's movements that belied her coutured appearance.

As she watched, she realised the woman was crossing the road and moving in their direction. She waited, intrigued, to see where she would go, and was astonished to discover she was walking directly towards their table.

'Stephi.' She alerted her friend, by nodding in the woman's direction.

'Yes, I've spotted her,' Stephi said. 'Got it covered.' She slid her right hand into her jacket.

'Are you armed?' Katriona said, quietly.

Stephi nodded.

The woman came closer. She turned her palms towards them as if to show she was no threat. She smiled hesitantly, then approached their table.

'Please greet me like you know me,' she said. 'I'm probably being watched.' She reached out to Katriona to kiss her on the cheek.

Katriona, very cautiously, responded, as the woman lowered her sunglasses to reveal her eyes and whispered in Katriona's ear.

'I'm Heather Hough.'

36

Gavin's day had suddenly become very busy. All sorts of possible connections were buzzing around in his head, and his attempts to follow up all the leads were threatening to become unmanageable.

Maxwell got Derek Hannaford on the phone for him.

'Ah, Mr. Hannaford,' he began.

'Detective Inspector Pearce. How nice to hear from you again. I'm guessing you've cracked the password, then.'

'Password?'

Things had moved so far since the flashdrive had arrived in Tom's lab, Gavin had temporarily forgotten about their efforts to access its data.

'No, sorry. We're still working on that, I'm afraid. It's turned out to be doubly-secured. Two passwords.'

'My word. That's impressive.' Hannaford responded. 'It must have something mighty important on it.'

'We believe so, Mr. Hannaford. In fact, our surrounding enquiries are suggesting it may be linked to serious corruption in 'high places', as they say.'

'Really.' Hannaford's remark was more of a comment than a statement of surprise.

'You sound as if that's not unexpected.'

'Well, it's not. I knew if Heather was sending something to me, it would be important. And the news of her disappearance really rather confirmed that for me.'

'Yes. I see.' Gavin paused before saying, 'No, it's something else. Do you remember printing a small article about a civil servant called Martin Hall-Gardiner, last June?'

'I do. Very clearly.'

'Would you care to elaborate?' Gavin invited.

'Well, it was one of those stories that had a lot of potential information but not much of it could be verified.'

'Oh?'

'We got an anonymous tip-off that Hall-Gardiner was worth watching, so we began by researching his background, piecing together a career-picture and so on, and tried to get an interview. Of course, at that stage, he'd lost his job as a clerk at the Home Office and was working as a freelance consultant, advising businesses how to approach setting up government contracts, that sort of thing.

'He wasn't keen for us to speak to him, but we persuaded him to let us do one of our portrait features. It was all going nicely until our reporter touched on the reasons for his apparent dismissal from his previous post. He shut up like a clam, refused to continue the project and demanded we close the whole thing down. Said he'd changed his mind.'

'Did he give any specific reasons?' Gavin asked.

'No. My guess was that there was more to the rumours than had become public, and he was worried we might find out something not particularly in his favour.'

'But just refusing to co-operate with you, wouldn't have prevented you from continuing to dig around. In fact, wouldn't it be more likely to have the opposite effect? Didn't it make you suspicious?'

'Yes. Absolutely. I got the distinct impression that someone else was requiring him to remain low-key, because he'd seemed to enjoy the idea of being profiled when we started the story. And then, of course, he was offered this highly-influential post, and suddenly we were being slapped with Official Secrets Act orders and what not. Told to drop the original piece, and to let the new appointment be marked only by a courtesy paragraph – which would be provided for us.'

Gavin whistled. 'I see. So your short article in June – '

'- was the most we felt we could get away with. And I got my knuckles rapped, even for that.'

'I don't suppose … I mean, do you know if he'd cultivated any particular industrial connections?'

'Not officially, but we knew he had shares in a German pharmaceutical company. They'd been gifted to him when he was still working as a clerk. We wondered if they were a reward for services rendered, or even a bribe – but we never found anything conclusive.'

Gavin held his breath as he asked, 'Do you remember the name of the company?'

'Yes. Falkenrath Pharmaceuticals. They're a – '

'I know exactly who they are,' Gavin interrupted.

As he entered Tom's lab to share his latest news, an alarm went off.

'What have I triggered now?' Gavin asked, assuming it must be something to do with his arrival.

'Nothing,' Tom said, cheerily. 'It's another hit on the bullets programme.' He rubbed his hands in glee and crossed over to the computer with the flashing screen to take a look. 'Another hit in Germany, but this time it's an American citizen. Name of Morgan. Let's see …' And he pulled up the details.

'Now that's interesting.'

'What is?' Gavin asked.

'It was his shooting that Kassmeyer was investigating when he was killed.'

'Really? He was the police officer, wasn't he? And they've both come up on your search?'

'Yes.'

'So they were both shot by bullets from Gravenburg's gun?'

'Looks like it.'

'I wonder why no-one made the connection,' Gavin said.

'Maybe they did. Could just be they didn't make the connection to Gravenburg. I mean, knowing two people have been shot by the same bullet, doesn't guarantee you finding the owner of the gun.'

'I suppose,' Gavin admitted, reluctantly. 'Is there any more useful info there?'

'Um …' Tom rolled the cursor down the screen, quickly scanning the text that became available. "No obvious connection between the two guys when they were alive. Morgan's body was processed in the lab Katriona's been visiting. Wait a moment. So was Kassmeyer's. I suppose that makes sense – if he was investigating Morgan's death.'

'What do we know about Morgan?' Gavin asked.

Tom moved the cursor, again. 'He was a research director. Worked for MediGloves, in Germany.'

'Where have I come across that name before?'

'What, MediGloves?'

'Yeah.'

'They were the manufacturers I pinned down for the gloves Gravenburg used when he broke into Emily Hough's house.'

'Oh, yes. I remember now. You said at the time, it might be significant, I think.'

'Well, they were a very specific 'take' on the latex. Very identifiable.'

A sudden idea occurred to Gavin. 'Where's that list that Maxwell printed out - of Falkenrath's subsidiary companies?'

'Over here,' Tom said, walking across to a filing cabinet, piled high with papers. He pulled the sheets down and sifted through them. 'Yep. It's here. They are definitely one of Falkenrath's.'

'It doesn't particularly prove anything,' Gavin said, 'but it is another connection back to them. We still don't have anything conclusive, though. There's nothing to link Gravenburg with Falkenrath, or Anderson.'

'I guess that's why he's been able to operate for so long.

A very careful and efficient assassin. Good at covering his tracks,' Tom observed.

'He's got to have slipped up somewhere,' Gavin said. 'They always do.'

Gavin had asked Hannaford to send him as much of the original research on Hall-Gardiner as he could by e-mail attachment. He booted it off to Charlie as soon as it arrived. Charlie had been doing his own internet searches on the man – and on Kimberlay – since the visit that morning.

'It's beginning to look like Kimberlay was hoping you'd do his dirty work for him, Sir,' Charlie said, when Gavin called him in for an update. 'I think Kimberlay may have had suspicions when Hall-Gardiner worked for him, and was possibly the person responsible for getting him sacked. Since the guy wasn't prosecuted, one has to assume either that the accusations weren't provable, or that someone else's reputation was also at stake.'

'Could that have been Kimberlay himself?'

'Again, it's possible, Sir. And, of course, that would make him nervous now – with Hall-Gardiner in his new position and you digging into the Archives.'

'Except that it was Kimberlay who pointed us in this direction,' Gavin said. 'Have you managed to find out what his 'sector' is?' He made quote marks with his fingers to emphasize his sarcasm.

'No. I just get the 'Information Protected' screen when I try to do a search on his name. He must be involved at a pretty high level. Something to do with Intelligence, I'm guessing, Sir.'

'Like what?'

'MI5? MI6?' Charlie suggested.

'My God, Charlie. What have we fallen over?'

There was a knock on the door and a weary-looking Maxwell came in, with yet more sheets of paper.

'You look dreadful,' Gavin said. 'Did you sleep at all last night?'

'Not much, Sir. I wanted to do as much as I could on that list of charities.'

'Better take a seat before you flake out on us.' Gavin indicated to a chair tucked behind the door. 'So have you found anything interesting?'

'Yes, Sir. I've been working with Harris.'

Maxwell took the seat, gratefully, and moved it closer to the desk, so he could put his papers on it.

'He's relatively new, Sir. You might not know him so well. Turns out he likes tracking information.' He continued, 'We decided to look some more at Victoria Orphanage … you remember, the one in Zimbabwe. Harris managed to find some financial accounts.'

'Good.'

'There's a lot of money going into the place, Sir, but we couldn't see what it was being spent on. The photos of the place show a perfectly sufficient building and facilities but nothing special. Nothing to justify that amount of money being channelled there.'

'So maybe you were right, Maxwell. Maybe Heather did come across something dodgy to do with the Orphanage. Keep digging. See what else you can find out.'

'Yes, Sir.' Maxwell paused.

'Something else?' Gavin asked.

'Yes, Sir. I don't know whether it might be relevant but it certainly struck me as unusual.'

'What's that, then?"

"Well, Falkenrath have a charitable educational programme. They call it Next Generation Scientists – NGS. On the face of it, a kind of club, I suppose … for teenagers studying science. They provide lectures, workshops, that sort of thing.'

'That's not exactly unusual, Maxwell.'

'No, Sir, but they have an entire network of these clubs – in every country they trade with.'

'But that's …'

'Hundreds. Yes, Sir.'

'That must cost a fortune.'

'Yes, Sir.'

Charlie joined in. 'And if they're putting that much into the organisation of these clubs, we can be sure they're getting something back.'

Gavin thought for a moment. 'Just how many of these clubs are we actually talking? I mean, for instance, here in the UK. Is it a big presence?'

Maxwell looked through his sheets of paper and pulled one out.

'In the UK, their biggest base is in London, with a secondary 'hub' in Manchester. They have branches based at all the major universities, and smaller clubs at the big public schools and so on.'

'Good Lord. That really is a network, isn't it? Have you found any information about what they actually do at any of their events?'

'The on-line publicity shows just what I said – lectures, workshops. They invite research scientists, industrial technicians and so on to come and talk to the kids. So it's a way of encouraging the youngsters into following a scientific career, I guess. Except …'

'Except what?' Gavin asked.

'The speakers that Harris and I have had time to follow up on so far, all work for subsidiary companies of Falkenrath. That just feels a bit creepy, Sir.'

'Yes. I see what you mean. Not exactly what one would call an open-minded educational programme. On the other hand, if you have access to a ready-made pool of speakers, already in the industry, why bother to go elsewhere?'

'But that's just the point, isn't it?' Charlie said.

'What is?'

'These speakers are all part of the industry. As opposed to the broader world of science – or even other scientific industries. Yet they're calling this Next Generation Scientists. Sounds more like Next Generation Employees to me, Sir.'

'So you think it's a recruiting ground?'

'Could be, Sir.'

Gavin turned back to Maxwell. 'What do you think? Is that the impression you get?'

'It certainly seems very Falkenrath-focused. And then there's the Action Group, of course.'

'The Action Group?'

'It's like a network of youngsters who want to get involved more at the political level. They organise demonstrations, petitions, lobbying MP's – that sort of thing.'

'Do they now?'

'It's a part of the scientific world, these days, isn't it, Sir? Learning how to acquire funding for research, how government policies affect the kind of products you need to make.'

'It is,' agreed Gavin, 'but presumably that kind of communication goes in both directions. I mean, there's potential there for persuading the policy-makers to accommodate particular products.'

'But that's illegal.'

Gavin smiled at Maxwell's naivety. 'Oh, yes. For any industrial company to do anything more than bid for a contract, or something similar. But, you said it, Maxwell, these are youngsters. Still at school or Uni. So they don't have to declare a vested interest. They can approach an MP about an idea, in the name of science. It's just that the science they're being particularly exposed to is Falkenrath's version.'

'I hadn't thought of that, Sir.'

'I wonder if you could find out who manages this Action Group. There's got to be a central co-ordinator. See what that turns up. Perhaps we could speak to them directly.'

After this latest input of information, Gavin decided he heeded some fresh air, and took himself outside with his phone. He pulled up Trish's number. She was due to come home today but he felt she would still be safer away from

London. *How does one tell one's partner you don't want them to come home?* he thought miserably.

He was desperate for this case to be closed and for life to resume some of its former sanity, but the more they investigated, the murkier the scenario became. It felt impossible to trust anyone they spoke to. There was still so much they didn't know, and so much they were deliberately not being told – and not just by the villains of the piece, who he realised were, at least, beginning to be identifiable. No, they were also being blocked by the supposed 'good guys', the people who presumably had the information they needed to get a clear picture. Hell, they couldn't even be sure who *were* the 'good guys'.

So maybe it wasn't as straight-forward as an old-fashioned game of 'cops and robbers'. Maybe some of the 'good guys' were using decidedly dodgy methods to achieve what they considered were desirable or beneficial ends, and muddying the waters in the process. He knew all sorts of deals were cut to enable industry to flow successfully. The difference between the UK and somewhere like, say, Saudi Arabia, was that the British preferred to keep their deals rather private. Some other countries expected the personal exchanges to be part of the overall transaction and were far less coy about asking for additional persuasion to seal a contract.

He wasn't sure which version he favoured, if either. As a younger copper, he'd always preferred dealing with 'honest thuggery', as he'd called it. You knew where you stood and what you were dealing with. There was something easier about managing someone who knew they were 'bad' and got on with it, anyway. All this underhand stuff was more difficult to negotiate.

He thought, though, that what distressed him most was dishonest people who held positions of responsibility – like government ministers and their civil servants. There was something much sicker about betraying the trust others had put in you to do something good, and then using that situation to your own advantage. And there seemed to be a lot of that going on in this case.

Before he got too depressed, he rang Trish. She sounded much happier.

'Yeah, I'm loving it here. I feel loads better.'

'I'm so pleased, love. You really weren't well before, were you?'

'No. I don't think I'd realised how unwell I was.'

'So, have you got your bags packed?'

'Well, actually, Gavin, I wondered if you'd mind …'

'So she's staying on to the end of the week?' Tom asked.

'Yes. Apparently, she was hesitant about saying anything in case I wanted her to come home, and she didn't want me to feel neglected.'

'How sweet.'

Gavin laughed. 'I do have a soft side, you know, Tom.'

'I'm sure you have,' Tom said, 'but I'd prefer it if you didn't parade it around here. It's totally inappropriate in a forensic lab. You never know what might happen.'

'Well, I might actually make the tea, one day.'

'Is that a hint?' And, inevitably, Tom switched the kettle on.

'So you know of this NGS network, then?' Gavin asked.

'Yes, it was just getting going when I was at Uni. I never got involved. It wasn't my cup of tea.'

'Ha, ha.' Gavin moved over to one of the computers. 'What's this?'

'Oh, just moodling over some photos Charlie has sent down. He's still hunting through all that stuff about Hall-Gardiner. Found some old photos he wanted me to 'tidy up' for him.'

Gavin peered at the screen. 'How old?'

Tom came over to join him. 'These are from his college days, I think.' He clicked on the screen to find the information. 'Yes, it's the Graduation Ball. Him and his mates.'

Then one of those moments occurred that Gavin loved best about policing – when everything suddenly starts to fall into place. He leaned in towards the photo.

'Isn't that Stevens? A much younger version of him?'

'What? Where?'

Tom moved the mouse around to enlarge and clarify the middle portion of the photo, where a group of students were fooling around on the edge of a swimming pool.

'Yes, I think you're right.'

'So, is Hall-Gardiner in this picture?' Gavin asked.

'Yes. He's the one about to be chucked in.'

'So they knew each other from way back?'

Before Gavin could compute all the implications, a buzz on Tom's latest device indicated someone at the door. Maxwell.

'Sir, I've got the name of the NGS Action Group co-ordinator for you.'

'Well done, Maxwell.'

'But I thought you'd like to see a list of the network's patrons, as well.'

Maxwell handed over a printed sheet. Gavin took it and saw a sequence of ten names, in the middle of which was Martin Hall-Gardiner. He passed it to Tom, and was about to make a comment when his secure phone rang.

'Gavin, it's Katriona. I can't believe I'm going to say this again – but I've got your girl. And this time, we're coming in.'

37

Katriona had spent an unexpected afternoon, wandering around the shops. After the surprise of Heather's appearance, it had quickly become apparent how important it was to disguise the situation. Back at the café, Katriona had made a big show of hugging Heather like an old friend and then introducing her to Stephi, who joined in the charade by giving her a double-kiss, as she had done for Katriona when she arrived.

From a distance, this would create the impression that Katriona and Heather knew each other well and that the meeting had been planned. To keep up the cover this provided, the three women had decided it was probably safer to stay in the open for a while, as if they were joining up for a shopping spree or a tourist trip. So they'd – apparently, casually – visited several of the shops and department stores in the area, taking it in turns to act the part and to keep look-out.

Stephi thought she might have spotted a tail at one point but after they'd spent half an hour in a shoe shop, he'd disappeared. 'Typical man – no stomach for shopping.'

Katriona had dutifully laughed and kept her boredom with the enterprise to herself.

When they were sure they'd been left unobserved for a while, Stephi had suggested they go back to her apartment. So they'd made their way to the small carpark where Stephi had left her car, and she had driven them home. Once in the privacy of her flat, they could talk seriously.

'So, where have you been hiding?' Katriona had asked, as she and Heather settled into the smart leather sofa in the living room while Stephi made some tea.

'Here, In Dusseldorf. I believed that would be the last thing they'd expect me to do.'

'How on earth have you managed to stay hidden?' Stephi butted in, sticking her head through a hatchway from the kitchen. 'There have been no end of people trying to track you down.'

'I know, but this isn't the first time it's been necessary for me to disappear.' Heather presented a surprisingly calm demeanour. Katriona felt if she'd had to go through the same experience, she would have been in pieces.

'I've had contingency plans in place for some years now. I've a couple of bank accounts in other names and a nice little bolt-hole on what you might call the 'seedier' side of town. No-one knows the details. Not even – '

She choked, her emotion briefly showing. 'Not even Dieter or Emily. Emily, bless her, didn't even know I had the need for such a place.'

Katriona reached out a hand.

'I'm so sorry about both of them,' she said, gently. 'That must have made it even harder.'

'It's been dreadful,' Heather confirmed. 'The only thing that's kept me going was the desire to expose the people behind it all.'

She took the mug of tea Stephi offered as she rejoined them.

'I've been following what the police were doing locally, as best I could, praying they would turn something up. It was very distressing to begin with – when I thought they were going to write off Dieter's death as an accident.

'So when I saw you,' she nodded to Stephi, 'out with the diving team, my hopes rose. I knew if you found the body, you'd start investigating. And I knew you weren't part of the local team. So that meant someone, somewhere, was raising suspicions.'

'We definitely were, Heather,' Katriona said. 'But unfortunately, 'suspicions' was mostly what we had. Very little in the way of concrete evidence. So how did you know Dieter's death wasn't an accident?'

'Because I saw Gravenburg shoot him.'

Katriona gasped. 'How? How did it happen?'

'We'd just left Anderson's office. You know, at Falkenrath Pharmaceuticals?'

'Yes, we know. We visited this morning.'

'I saw you. That was when I knew you were on my side – and probably looking for me.' She smiled at Katriona, who gripped her hand reassuringly.

'As I said, we'd left his office, having got absolutely nowhere with the man, and Dieter had to leave to go to another photo-shoot he was booked for. So he set off on his bike.

'And suddenly, I saw a man get into a car and start to follow him. And then I realised I recognised him as Gravenburg, because I'd come across him in the files when I was doing a piece on industrial espionage last year.

'I tried to shout Dieter, but he was well out of earshot by then, so all I could do was watch and pray. I saw Gravenburg's car pull up alongside him as they were crossing the bridge, and the next thing I knew, Dieter was flying through the air, with his bike following him into the river.'

'How awful,' Katriona said.

'That was the point at which I decided I'd better disappear. We'd had our suspicions before that. We knew we were being watched, and very likely to get warned off. But I hadn't expected they would actually try to kill us.'

'Why were you such a threat, Heather? What had you been investigating?' Stephi asked.

Heather gave a big sigh. 'Now that's a longer story.'

'But it has something to do with Falkenrath?' Katriona said.

'It certainly does.'

During the next hour, Heather had shared some of the outline details of what she'd been uncovering. As her story began to unravel, Katriona realised this was something Gavin needed to hear firsthand. And when Heather got to the point where she and Emily had been discussing what to do with the flashdrive, a plan began to form in her head.

'I knew Derek Hannaford would be willing to print the story,' Heather said, 'so getting the material to him – and away from Anderson's people – seemed the best strategy. It was Emily who came up with the idea of putting the documentaries – and the research – onto a flashdrive and giving it to her. We neither of us thought she'd be suspected, as long as she stuck to her planned tour schedule.'

'So the flashdrive has all the information on it?' Katriona asked.

'Yes, but God knows where it is now. And all the original footage was in Dieter's flat, so that will be long gone.'

'We have the flashdrive, Heather,' Katriona said, quietly.

'You do?' Heather's look was one of incredulity. 'How? I thought they must've taken it when they killed Emily.'

'I don't think they intended to kill Emily. I think she just happened to be at home when the burglars broke in. Admittedly, one of them was Gravenburg, as it turned out, but Emily wasn't shot.' She hoped that would give Heather some comfort.

'Then how did she die?'

'We're guessing she was using the laptop in her bedroom when they broke in. She probably came out of the room to see what the noise was. Gravenburg hit her with the butt of his gun. Most likely just a reflex action to knock her out so they could search the house unseen. Unfortunately, it knocked her down the stairs and she was killed in the fall.'

'Oh.'

Katriona gave Heather a few moments to assimilate what

she'd said.

'So she probably didn't suffer?'

'No. She was unconscious as she fell.'

'That, I suppose, is something.'

There was a respectful pause from all three women.

'So how do you have the flashdrive? If these two thugs were there to find it?'

And Katriona had told Heather the delightful details of Mrs. Thomas's attempts to be helpful, and how the flashdrive had been posted onto Hannaford, and then couriered back to Tom's lab.

'But Tom, bless him, has only been able to crack one of the passwords. Who came up with the idea of using two?'

'That was Dieter. In amongst his many accomplishments, he could be a bit of a computer geek. He suggested if we each chose a password, then even if the flashdrive got into the wrong hands, it would be useless to them without access to both of us. You see, we didn't even tell each other what password we'd chosen.'

'So how was Hannaford going to open the files?'

'The plan was for Emily to visit him in person while she was in Manchester. Then Hannaford would ring me for my password. It all seemed very clever when we hatched the plan. Emily thought it was great fun. Playing spies and all that. I don't think she realised how dangerous it all was. In fact, I don't think, at that stage, any of us did.'

'So is this now the only copy?' Stephi asked.

'Yes,' Heather answered, sadly. 'All that work, all those lives – and now it's all down to one small data-stick.'

'So,' said Katriona, 'it's vital we get you somewhere safe, and reconnected with the flashdrive.'

'Where is it now?' Heather asked.

'In England, still. And currently, very safe.'

'So, are you thinking I should get out of Germany and go to England?'

'That's precisely what I'm thinking.'

'But I don't see how? That's why I didn't make it to the

WHO conference. I know Anderson's men are going to be watching the airports.'

'Then,' Stephi intervened, 'we'll have to come up with an alternative.'

Katriona and Stephi had started to put their plan into action while Heather was relaxing a little in the bath – a directive from Katriona. Stephi had dug out some clothes that would more or less fit and a holdall for Heather to put her current clothing into. There was no possibility of retrieving anything else of hers at this stage.

Katriona had rung Margaret Newton first.

'If she's really MI5, she'll be able to help,' Stephi argued, as they thought through various ideas for an escape plan.

'Agreed, but she may not be too happy with the idea of me whisking Heather away, without letting her have access first.'

'I think,' Stephi said, 'if you put it to her that it's a case of either getting Heather back to England, or possibly losing her altogether, she might be more co-operative.'

Stephi had been right. After her initial surprise and delight at Heather's re-appearance, Margaret was, at first, insistent that she meet with Heather, but once Katriona had pointed out how quickly a visit to the flat would arouse suspicion, and how precarious Heather's current situation was, she realised the best course of action was, indeed, to enable a quick and secretive escape.

With Margaret's co-operation, Katriona could now ring Gavin to tell him about her extraordinary afternoon. While she was updating him, Stephi interrupted to let her know she'd contacted Rudi successfully, and the first part of the escape plan was underway. A return phonecall from Margaret confirmed she had put the second part in place. All it needed now was for Gavin to make the arrangements at his end.

As twilight descended, a large black, four-wheel drive,

security police car pulled up outside the apartment block where Stephi lived, in full view of the dark blue, nondescript, hatchback that had been parked across the road for the last two hours.

Stephi drew back the curtains a little to check. 'He's here. Everyone ready?'

All three of them were dressed in dark colours, and clothes that allowed for easy movement – such as running for one's life, Katriona thought, grimly.

Stephi buzzed Rudi into the building and they waited anxiously for the knock on the door that indicated his arrival upstairs. She used her spyhole to confirm it was Rudi who had knocked, and opened the door cautiously to let him in.

'Did they see you?' she asked.

'Yes. They're parked directly opposite. The idiots.' Rudi laughed. 'They must know that makes them obvious.'

'Maybe the idea is to intimidate, not to observe,' suggested Heather, as Rudi unpacked a large black bag, sharing out three bulletproof vests.

'So, are you going to tell me what's going on?' Rudi asked.

'Not until we're done,' Stephi answered. 'I'll explain it all, later. Just do what we planned, and I'll meet you at the rendezvous, as agreed.'

Rudi nodded, reluctantly. 'Let me have the keys, then.'

He reached out a hand. Stephi placed her car keys into it, taking the bunch he offered her in return.

He smiled briefly at the group. 'Best of luck, everyone.' He left as quietly as he'd arrived.

Katriona squeezed Heather's hand, encouragingly. 'Here we go.'

Stephi crossed to the window, again, and a few seconds later, they heard the squeal of tyres as Rudi pulled out of the underground garage onto the street and shot off down the road at speed. They heard another engine start up, another squeal of tyres, and Stephi said, 'It worked. They're following him. Let's go.'

Katriona escorted Heather silently down the stairs to the lobby entrance, leaving Stephi to follow, locking the flat as she left. They waited for her briefly inside the front doors of the building, as she caught up, racing past them to the armoured vehicle outside. Then they dashed towards the car doors as they heard the locking system release. Katriona had barely got her feet inside before Stephi set off.

'I'm going by back routes to start off with,' Stephi said. 'Once they realise their mistake, that'll make it more difficult to trace us. Here, Katriona.' She reached inside her jacket. 'You take this. I presume you can shoot?'

Katriona took the gun. 'Yes,' she confirmed, allowing a note of determination into her voice.

Stephi drove them along a number of small backstreets, and then out into country lanes. Katriona could see her checking her mirror every few minutes, but she reported nothing back. Then suddenly, they were alongside a fast-moving motorway.

'Here's where it gets interesting,' she said, maneuvering the car up some banking onto a short sliproad. 'A private police track,' she explained. 'Hold on.' The car lurched sideways as they joined the hard shoulder, crossing into the first available space in the traffic.

'That may have caught their attention. Depends on how efficient their observation systems are.'

She put her foot down, throwing Katriona and Heather back into their seats, and forced her way through the cars around her. A few minutes later, she announced they were now being followed.

'I don't think they'll try anything on the autobahn,' she said. 'It'll be when we turn off that the fun will start.'

Katriona hoped she was right about the motorway. She didn't relish the possibility of a multiple collision, not to mention the idea of putting even more lives at risk. Once it was down to just a 'them and us' car chase, she felt there was a bigger chance of a positive outcome.

Within a few moments, they could see Stephi's guess was

right. The car – a big, black one like their own – was merely keeping a steady distance between the two vehicles. Stephi tried going faster at one point to see what happened, and the second car speeded up but maintained the gap as before.

'No point trying to outrun them here, then,' she said. 'Let's just get to our turn-off and then start something more serious.' It seemed that her priorities were similar to Katriona's.

Five minutes further on, Stephi suddenly said, 'Here we go,' and putting her foot down, shot across the three lanes of traffic to drive down an exit slip road.

The tail car was obviously caught by surprise and very nearly sailed on past the turning, veering off the main road at the last minute and bumping over several raised kerbs, clearly designed to warn sleepy drivers they had drifted out of their lane. It piled down the sliproad after them.

Stephi drove furiously, constantly changing their route from one road to another in an attempt to shake off their followers, but to no avail. They eventually found themselves on a narrow country lane, heading out towards a flat plain.

'Right, Katriona,' Stephi shouted over the noise of the tyres on the bumpy tarmac. 'When I say 'Now', you must shoot at their tyres, okay?'

'Okay,' Katriona shouted back, winding down her window. She motioned to Heather to get low down in her seat.

Stephi pushed the car even faster as they turned a bend and Katriona could see a long straight stretch ahead of them. The hedges that had lined the previous section gave way to ditches on either side of the road, creating a weird pattern of shadows in the headlights.

Stephi waited for the second car to match her speed, then crossed to the other side of the road and slammed her brakes on. 'Now, now,' she shouted at Katriona, as they squealed to a halt and the other car flew past.

Katriona fired a volley of well-aimed bullets at the rear tyres. The car jerked and slid into a skid, veering violently from side to side in front of them as the driver tried to correct the steering, first in one direction, then in the other, desperately trying to slow the car at the same time - which merely served to exaggerate the pendulum motion which the punctured tyres had thrown them into.

'Grab hold,' Stephi shouted again, as she slammed her car into reverse and began driving furiously backward. Katriona wondered how on earth she was keeping the car on the road in the dark, with only reverse lights to guide her. After a hundred yards or so, she slammed the brakes on again, switched to forward gears once more, and set off towards the other car, now at a halt and slewed across the road diagonally, presumably in an attempt to turn and chase them.

Stephi's quick change of direction had taken them by surprise. In the headlights, Katriona could see the driver desperately trying to turn the ignition key. They must have stalled.

'Brace yourselves.' Stephi angled her armoured vehicle slightly to one side so she hit the rear end of the stationary car neatly, sending it skittering away into the ditch on the far side of the road, and creating a gap for them to pass through. She then engaged four-wheel drive and abruptly left the hard carriageway for the softer ground alongside it.

The car bumped and jerked its way across the rough land, and when Katriona turned to look out of the rear window, she saw the other vehicle was stuck in the ditch with three men standing on the road, shouting furiously at each other.

'I don't think they'll be following us, anymore,' she said. 'Nice work, Stephi.'

She could almost hear Stephi beaming in the darkness. 'It was … exciting,' she said.

They continued across rough ground for another five minutes or so, until Katriona saw lights in the distance. The airfield.

It only took another couple of minutes to arrive at the

hangar where a private jet was waiting for them. Katriona quickly bundled Heather out of the car and onboard, greeting the pilot briefly as she made to climb the steps behind her. She turned to Stephi, still rather breathless from the last half hour.

'Thank you.' She reached in to give Stephi a huge hug. 'I'll be in touch.'

Then she climbed through the hatch and took her seat next to Heather, as the plane took off for England.

38

When the plane landed, in the English countryside just south of London, the passengers were met by another large, black car at the airfield. Katriona experienced a moment of anxiety when she looked through the porthole window she was sat next to and saw a big, burly man get out of the driver's door, stepping onto the floodlit concrete.

'Wait here,' she instructed Heather. 'I'll check it out.'

She shouted through to the pilot. 'Be ready to take off again, if we need to.'

She opened the hatchway and cautiously descended the folded-out stairway. There appeared to be only the one person with the car. No-one tried to take a pot-shot at her. Everything was quiet.

She crossed towards the man waiting beside the car.

'Sergeant Charlie Parker, Ma'am. DI Pearce sent me to collect you,' he said.

She relaxed, and shook hands warmly. That was exactly what she and Gavin had agreed.

'So lovely to see you.' She breathed in relief. 'I've heard quite a bit about you.'

'Ma'am?'

'Gavin says you're a good copper.'

'Thank you, Ma'am. He's a good boss to work for. Now, I suggest we get moving as quickly as possible.'

'Yes. Thank you, Sergeant. That's a good idea.'

She motioned for Heather to join her and they got in the car, Charlie pulling out into the darkness as the jet took off again behind them.

There was an hour's drive to get to the station where they'd all agreed to meet up. At this time of night, Gavin had confirmed they'd have the place to themselves, giving them several hours of privacy to hear the details of Heather's story and to decide what they should do next. Katriona was starving and she hoped the reception party would include some food.

Charlie drove them efficiently and smoothly into the city centre, using back streets to find his way into the rear entrance of the station, pulling up right outside the door so that the car would block the view from the security cameras, as Katriona and Heather hurried inside. From there, it was a short trip down to the basement where Tom's lab was located, and Katriona knew the route well.

It was strange being back here. She relished the familiarity of it but was immediately aware of how little she'd missed the place. Yes, she'd definitely made the right decision to leave when she did.

She led Heather along the bottom corridor towards the lights coming from the lab at the end.

'Gavin.' She almost broke into tears when she saw her old friend and had to hide her emotion in a big hug. 'It's so good to see you.'

She felt the warmth in Gavin's response. 'Katriona. You're here at last. We were beginning to wonder if something had happened.'

'Well, it wasn't an entirely uneventful journey.'

She turned towards the other waiting figure, 'Tom,' and she let herself be swept up in his long arms.

'Katriona. We've missed you. You should come back. We've so many new gadgets to show you.'

'I'm sure you have,' she said, delighting in Tom's

optimistic cheeriness. She gestured to the weary-looking woman waiting in the doorway. 'This is Heather,' she said.

It was Tom who took the initiative.

'Heather, have a seat. It's delightful to meet you. Now, tea or coffee? And we have fish and chips in the microwave.'

Once the two women had been 'fed and watered', as Tom put it, the team got down to business.

Gavin started things off. 'Right, Heather. We're hoping you can tell us what on earth this is all about. We seem to have so many leads to follow.'

Heather looked surprised. 'Do you? Well, that should be helpful in completing the picture.'

'Tell us – what *is* the picture?'

'It starts with the documentary series I was making with Dieter.'

'The one about epidemics?'

'That's right. So you know about that?'

'Yes. Herr Brandt told us when we first started trying to contact you about Emily.' Gavin got off his stool to pick up a notepad. 'That's when we began to get suspicious that something might have happened to you, too.' He sat down again. 'So is this all to do with the documentaries?'

'One episode in particular, and then the research we did to follow up.'

'Yes?' Gavin encouraged, but Tom butted in.

'First things first, Gavin. Am I right in thinking these documentaries are on the flashdrive?'

'Yes,' Heather responded. 'And that's the only copy, now.'

'In which case,' Tom said, 'I would suggest you let me start making more copies straight away. To be on the safe side.'

'I agree,' said Gavin. 'You can be doing that while Heather talks.'

Tom produced the precious flashdrive from its evidence bag and inserted it into the computer nearest to where he was sitting. 'If I show you mine, will you show me yours?'

Heather looked blank for a moment, then laughed. 'Oh, passwords, you mean? Of course.'

Tom explained how he'd deciphered Emily's, and tapped it in.

'I guessed it would be something musical,' Heather said, 'but that's really inventive, isn't it?'

'Yes,' Tom agreed. 'Ingenious, I thought.'

'Do you have the locket?' she asked. Tom passed the bag over to her. 'I gave her this. Last year, for her birthday.'

'We found your fingerprints on it.'

'When this is all over …'

Tom spoke gently. 'I'll make sure it gets back to you.' He gave her a minute, then said, 'But first, please put me out of my misery and tell me your password.'

Katriona and Gavin both laughed. They recognised Tom was itching to know what it was he couldn't decipher.

'It's in Hebrew,' Heather said. 'A biblical quotation.'

'Hebrew?' Tom whistled. 'It would've taken me some time to get there.'

'It was designed especially for Hannaford. He's classically trained, specialising in Latin, Greek and Hebrew. He sometimes liked to write his editorials in Hebrew – just for fun. So I knew it would be accessible to him.'

'But not to an outsider.' Tom commented. 'Clever.'

'Can you access it, Tom?' Gavin asked.

'No problem.' Tom began to pull up a series of menus on his screen, loading a Hebrew digital keyboard. 'And presumably right-to-left script?' he asked.

'Yes.'

Tom clicked on something, then went back to the password screen.

'Okay. Tell me.'

'Oh, it's quite obvious, really. "Let there be light".'

Katriona watched the old team huddled round the computer and felt just a twinge of envy. This, she did miss. This working together, with people you knew well and trusted.

She saw Tom give a fist-pump as the flashdrive menu appeared on the screen. She opened her mouth to start taking charge but even as she did so, remembered this wasn't her team anymore. She resigned herself to a back seat and let Gavin take the lead.

'So this is the list of documentaries?' Gavin was pointing at the screen.

'Yes. And this section here,' Heather said, 'is the follow-up research to the one we made in Cuba.'

'Cuba? Not Africa?' Gavin's astonishment was obvious.

'No. This is all about what we found out there, about how they handle their annual epidemic of Leptospirosis.'

There was a stunned silence. Katriona, who had already heard the story, recognised the reaction.

'So, it's nothing to do with the diamond mines at Marange?' Gavin asked.

'Only very indirectly,' Heather said.

'Okay. Time to let go of everything we thought we knew. Take us back to the beginning,' Gavin invited. Everyone except Tom sat down again to let Heather speak. Tom quietly got on with the business of making copies.

'Two things you need to know, to set the scene,' Heather said. 'First is that Cuba has been under this ridiculous trade embargo from America. Set up originally in the 1960's. Second is that huge areas of Cuba suffer every year from Leptospirosis, which is only exacerbated when there are hurricanes, because those result in floods with the inevitable consequences of water pollution, homelessness, evacuation, and so on. It's a massive problem.

'Now, because of the embargo, the Cuban medical research centre – The Finlay Institute – has become self-sufficient. It produces its own medicines, vaccines, health-care programmes, etc. And these health-care programmes include both conventional and alternative medicines.

'The Finlay Institute developed its own vaccine against Leptospirosis in 1998, but it takes nearly an entire year to produce and distribute two million doses of the vaccine. And that's actually only enough vaccine for less than one million at-risk patients, because of the need to repeat the dosage. And, of course, it's expensive to do. In 2007 and 2008, the cost was about three million US dollars. And this is a poor country.'

'Presumably there's something significant about those years?' Gavin asked. 'Since you mention them specifically.'

'Yes. 2007 was a particularly bad year. Atrocious rainfall, widespread flooding, infrastructure damage. So about two million people were considered to be in the 'at-risk' category.'

'With only enough vaccine for half of those?' Tom intervened.

'That's right,' Heather confirmed. 'And the same thing happened again in 2008, when two hurricanes hit Cuba within ten days of each other.'

'So what did they do?' Tom came over to join the group. He'd finished making the first few copies to flashdrives and had locked them securely in one of his cupboards. His computer was now chuntering away quietly to itself, Katriona guessed making back-up copies to hard drives around the lab.

'They used homeopathy,' Heather announced.

Gavin snorted in derision. 'You're joking, right?'

'Not at all. They made a homeopathic version of their own vaccine at a fraction of the cost, manufacturing five million doses in one week. Which, incidentally, didn't need refrigeration, could be administered without the need for a nurse or doctor and could be given safely to children, old people, pregnant women and so on.'

Gavin's face had a look of total disbelief.

'But it didn't work, right?'

'On the contrary. The recorded levels of infection dropped well below the usual thousands predicted in these circumstances – even with the vaccine – to less than a hundred in all. With zero deaths of hospitalised patients.'

'But … that can't be true,' Gavin spluttered.

'Why not?'

'Because everyone *knows* that homeopathy doesn't work,' Gavin said.

Katriona decided now was the time to intervene. 'Elayne uses it all the time.'

'Yes, but she's …' Gavin caught her eye.

'She's what, Gavin?' Katriona felt her hackles rising.

'Err … unusual,' he said, having obviously struggled to find a non-inflammatory word.

'So homeopathy only works on unusual people?' she asked, coolly.

'Yes. No.' Gavin was struggling now. 'Back me up here, Tom.'

'No can do.' Tom grinned cheerily. 'This is fascinating.'

'And it gets more so,' said Heather. 'This medical protocol was, without doubt, an unqualified success. So the Finlay Institute decided to write a paper on what they'd done. The implications for poor third world countries were immense.' She paused before her next statement. 'Only no-one would publish their work.'

'Presumably because there were serious flaws in the data,' Gavin asked, a trifle more hesitantly than his previous outbursts.

'No. They showed me the data when I was there, as well as the paper they wrote. And they gave Dieter copies of the video footage they'd shot during those two years – with pictures of the storms and the devastation caused. And then some interviews with some of the inhabitants who'd been treated, so we could include it in the film we were making.'

'So what was the problem?' Tom asked.

'We couldn't see one. So we decided to investigate.' Heather said. 'That's the research I was talking about earlier. What we uncovered was enough to merit its own documentary.'

'Go on,' Gavin encouraged.

'Well, to put it simply, if it's possible to produce an

alternative medicine for an epidemic that's ten times as effective and five times cheaper, there are going to be people who are not happy with that.'

Katriona could see comprehension dawning in Gavin's eyes, as Heather continued.

'The main world manufacturer of the Leptospirosis vaccine is an American company called Raptor Vaccines. But they're actually owned by – '

' – by Falkenrath Pharmacueticals,' Gavin broke in.

'Yes. And they obviously have a vested interest in keeping research like this, quiet. We began to follow the trail and we came up against instance after instance of the information being blocked. Sometimes, papers went missing. Sometimes the peer reviews that appeared were so damning that it made the data look – as you suggested – seriously flawed. Occasionally, we came across someone who'd been advised that if they proceeded to bring the article to publication, it could cost them their career as a reputable scientist or scientific reporter.'

'Nevertheless,' Gavin said, 'you can see their point. It is a bit … 'out there'.'

'Agreed. We didn't take anything for granted. We followed up every lead we could. Eventually, we made some shocking discoveries. For instance, every time we followed the money-trail, rather than the paper-trail, we found either Raptor or Falkenrath at the end of the line – in some way or other.'

'Like what?'

'Oh, maybe as a sponsor for a magazine that might have published, or for an entirely different project someone was working on. We even started to come across mysterious disappearances or unsolved deaths, that when we looked a bit closer might have had a connection.' Heather paused. 'You have to understand, this research has huge implications. If you can make an effective homeopathic vaccine for one virus, you can make it for any.'

'And that would mean the pharmaceutical companies

losing billions of pounds-worth of business,' Tom said.

'Exactly. Not to mention other interested parties, such as share-holders and contract-brokers. So my guess is that there are other companies involved in the 'conspiracy', if you want to call it that, to discredit research in this area. We just happened to pick up on this one because they're the chief manufacturer for this particular vaccine.'

Gavin spoke again. 'When you say 'conspiracy' …'

'Well, for example, did you know that Falkenrath spends around forty per cent of their profits on publicity?'

'What? Are you sure? That's an enormous amount.'

'Because it's not all obvious. They have an astonishing network of people around the world, proselytising on their behalf, under the auspices of charitable donations.'

Charlie joined in the conversation for the first time since Heather had begun her story. 'Like the NGS Action Group?'

'You've come across them, have you?' Heather said. 'They were the group that propositioned the WHO last year to condemn outright the use of homeopathy in third world countries. That was why I was trying to get a voice at that recent conference. Get the story out first-hand.'

Heather suddenly slumped in her seat. Katriona could see her exhaustion taking over, now that she'd told Gavin the bulk of what she'd discovered. She reached out to take Heather's hand, and turned towards Gavin. 'So you can see what we're up against.'

Gavin had clearly found it difficult to take this all in, but Katriona knew his duty as a policeman would come first. His obligation to investigate.

'All this research you've been doing, that's all detailed on the flashdrive?' he asked.

'Yes.' Heather sighed. 'It's all there.'

Gavin looked around the solemn group in front of him.

'So what do we do now?' he asked.

For the second time, in as many days, an unexpected voice came from the doorway.

'You hand the flashdrive over to me.'

39

The entire group turned to face the speaker. No-one had seen Fisher come in, as the door to the lab was positioned just around a small corner from where they had all gathered to be within reach of the main computer.

Katriona saw a white, serious-looking man, probably in his fifties, with slicked-back grey hair and cold, little eyes. He was dressed in full uniform.

Gavin broke the stunned silence.

'You can't possibly expect to get away with this, Fisher,' he spat, the full venom of the last few days' frustration, very apparent.

'On the contrary,' Fisher spoke coolly. 'It is my subordinate officers who will not 'get away with it', Pearce.' He caught sight of Katriona. 'Huh, DI McShannon. I might have guessed you'd have something to do with this. You always were a thorn in our side.'

Since Katriona had no recollection of ever meeting the man, she was surprised by his statement. She stood up. 'Superintendant Fisher, I presume,' she said.

Fisher made a disgusted, grunting sound. 'Don't try to get clever with me, woman. Just hand over the flashdrive and I'll leave you all to play Andy-Pandy, or whatever it is you think you're doing here.'

Gavin spoke again. 'That's not going to happen, Fisher.

You're outnumbered here. What are you going to do? Take us all on …' He ground to a halt as Fisher pulled a gun.

'If you won't co-operate voluntarily, then yes, that's precisely what I'll do.'

The second he'd seen the weapon, Charlie had stepped in front of Heather. Katriona and Gavin backed away from the armed man.

'You have to be insane,' Gavin said. 'Are you going to shoot us all?'

Fisher appeared to consider this for a moment, then answered coldly, 'Only as many as it takes.'

'For goodness' sake, man. You must see the game is up.'

'You have no idea what you're up against, have you, Pearce? This isn't just a bunch of third-rate burglars you're dealing with here. This is far bigger than you and your little gang could imagine.'

'It's getting easier to imagine by the second,' Gavin said.

Fisher now spoke as if in a conciliatory tone. 'So I'm sure you can see the sense in complying with bigger forces than either of us.'

'Absolutely.' Tom's voice suddenly broke into the conversation, and he pushed his way past Gavin, holding out a small object in his hand. 'Your Super is right, Gavin. No point going up against giants.'

Katriona saw him smile at Fisher as he offered the item he was holding.

'Unless your name is David, of course.'

As Tom had moved closer to Fisher, a young officer Katriona had never seen before had crept silently into the room. She guessed he'd been listening outside for a while as he had his cosh in his hand.

At Tom's cue, he reached down and hit Fisher smartly on the back of his thigh, just as Tom neatly twisted his body to knock Fisher's gun-hand upwards with his right arm, dropping to the floor in a strange crouching position, so that Fisher toppled over him, crashing into the circle of chairs and stools the group had gathered for their meeting.

Gavin jumped over the tangled mess of arms and legs to sit on Fisher's back, holding him down.

Although he was in pain, the man was still resisting. 'What you gonna do, Pearce? Arrest me?' He spoke derisively. 'You don't have the authority to do that.'

'No, but I do,' Charlie said. 'Maxwell, your handcuffs, please.' He reached into his jacket pocket as he spoke, producing an ID card. 'Agent Charlie Parker. MI5.'

It took the collected group a while to understand exactly what had happened during the last five minutes. Gavin and Charlie frog-marched a limping Fisher to the holding cells, as a temporary measure. The custody officer was seriously shocked when he saw them but was quickly reassured by the sight of Charlie's ID. He handed over the medical box for Gavin to administer any necessary first aid, while Charlie made a few urgent phonecalls.

'There's a team on its way,' he said, briefly, and they both sat in silence with Fisher, making sure he didn't do anything stupid, until a group of three people were escorted in. Two were men in dark suits. Charlie shook hands with one of them. The third carried a medical bag, and she checked Fisher over quickly. When she'd finished, one of the men said to Charlie, 'Okay, Parker. We can take over from here.'

Gavin watched as they ushered Fisher along the corridor, then turned to his former sergeant. 'Charlie, I think you may have some explaining to do.'

'Yes, Sir. Sorry about the deception and all, but we decided it was necessary to keep you in the dark. For your own safety, Sir.'

'Charlie. Given the circumstances, I really don't think you need address me as 'Sir', anymore.' Gavin went back into the cell and sat down on one of the benches.

'No. I suppose not,' Charlie said, sitting opposite him. He laughed. 'Old habits and all that.'

'So how long have you – and your crew – suspected

Fisher?' Gavin asked.

'We'd been watching Stevens *and* Fisher for a while before he was appointed here. The corruption case, from our point of view, was the perfect excuse to get someone into the station to work undercover. Our guess was that Stevens would use the situation to his advantage, possibly recruiting someone 'on the ground', so to speak, so it came as no surprise to see the report not implicating Foster.'

This was the most Gavin had ever heard Charlie say in one breath. He let his colleague continue.

'We were, however, somewhat taken aback when he managed to get Fisher appointed as Superintendant. That was quite adventurous.'

'That's one word for it,' Gavin commented.

'We thought Stevens might be Fisher's handler but, like you, we had no proof. So it seemed like observation was the best course of action.'

'I see.' Gavin began to get the picture.

'Sooner or later, we knew we'd come across something that implicated one or both of them, if we were right.'

'So you decided posing as my sergeant was the best way to do that?' he asked.

'It was essential that we work alongside someone we knew was honest. Someone we could trust. We thought you were our best shot – but even then, we couldn't be sure. Hence the need for secrecy.'

Gavin gave Charlie a puzzled look, inviting him to explain further.

'Well, if you were straight, you'd be suspicious of anything that didn't quite fit, and might even start doing some digging of your own. Which, of course, would be independent of anything we did, so would be valuable as additional evidence.' He grinned at Gavin. A rare sight. 'Of course, if you were bent, we certainly didn't want to expose my identity.'

'Okay, okay. I get that. But you couldn't have known anything about this case back then,' Gavin said.

'No, we weren't investigating a case as such. We were investigating the network.'

'Network?'

'A likely network of corruption running through the Force and possibly beyond it. A network which could take on any situation to its advantage, at a moment's notice.'

'I see,' Gavin said, again, and stood up. 'Well, you certainly had me fooled, Charlie. You made a damn good copper. I'll miss working with you.'

'Thank you, Sir.' And Charlie grinned again, holding out his hand for Gavin to shake.

Back in Tom's lab, multiple cups of tea were being handed around. Maxwell had now stopped shaking from the shock of having coshed his own Super and was soaking in the reassurance that Katriona and the others were offering.

'It was very brave of you to take the chance,' Heather said.

'It certainly was,' Katriona backed her up. 'Did you know Fisher was in on it?'

'No, Ma'am. Not for sure. DI Pearce and the Sarge – well, I s'pose he's not my Sarge any more, is he?'

'It appears not.'

'Well, anyway, they've both been very discreet, Ma'am. 'Cos it sounds like they've known for a while.'

'Yes,' Katriona said. 'Since Helen arrived on Skye and Gravenburg came looking for her.' Maxwell looked up in surprise.

'It must have been Fisher who passed on the information,' she continued, 'since Gavin – DI Pearce – hadn't told anyone else. So you can see, you did exactly the right thing.'

Maxwell looked horrified. 'That's … atrocious!' he blurted out.

'I would definitely agree with that,' Katriona said.

'So he and DI Foster were in this together?' Maxwell asked.

'Oh, Son, it goes much further than just those two.' Charlie's deep voice sounded through the doorway as he and Gavin rejoined them.

'Sarge.'

'Not any more, Maxwell. Not any more.' A look of relief crossed Charlie's face. Then he reached out a hand. 'It's been good working with you. You'll make an excellent Sarge yourself one day.'

Maxwell flushed at the compliment.

'Is your name really David?' Gavin asked.

'Yes, Sir. That's how I knew what Tom meant. What he wanted me to do. I have to admit, Sir, when I saw it was the Super …' he trailed off.

'Quite. And where is the culprit?' Gavin looked around to see Tom over by the kettle. 'What the bloody hell was that?' he asked.

'Just a little Tai Chi,' Tom said.

'You could've been killed, you idiot.'

'Nah. He'd still got the safety lock on,' Tom responded, with a wink. 'Want a cuppa?'

Simultaneous arrests were made in several countries during the next day. Fisher very quickly gave Stevens up as his handler, since there was no advantage left to be gained by not doing so. Stevens, however, proved a harder nut to crack. He gave every impression that he expected to get out of the situation cleanly and quickly, but when he heard that several of his colleagues had been arrested, too, he began to have doubts.

Then suddenly, perhaps in the hope of being on the receiving end of a plea bargain instead of his usual position of offering one, he capitulated, naming Hall-Gardiner as the co-ordinator for his particular 'cell'. From there, it was a short step to implicating the Minister who'd appointed Hall-Gardiner recently, and who turned out also to be a college acquaintance.

In Germany, Anderson and a number of employees were

removed from the Falkenrath buildings, Frieda Haase was arrested at the forensic labs and a handful of civil servants and government officials were relieved of their posts.

In America, the CEO of Raptor Vaccines was taken into custody, quickly naming two thugs he'd employed and pointing the way towards the paper trail which Heather had already uncovered.

It was agreed that a copy of the flashdrive should be sent to Hannaford, as originally planned, and that he should get first option on publication. He was told by the Home Office to wait until all the arrests had been made, but once they were happy they'd mopped up the trail, he could go ahead and print as much of the story as he wanted.

Heather asked if she could deliver the flashdrive in person, as a mark of respect, both for Hannaford and for Emily. It was still felt that she might need some protection at this stage so Katriona suggested she travel to Manchester with Heather, on her way back to Skye, and Charlie offered to accompany them both, so he could meet Hannaford in person, as well as providing additional security.

It was at this point that Katriona and Heather hit on the idea of Heather returning to Skye with Katriona for a while. There would be a short space before she was needed again, and the woman could do with some recuperation from the last couple of weeks' ordeal. Skye was the perfect place to do that.

'So what was the connection with the diamond mines?' Gavin had asked her before she and Katriona set off. 'You said it was a very indirect one,' he reminded her.

'Yes. I'd met Anderson out in Zimbabwe last year, when Dieter and I visited the school that Sweet Diamond has been funding.

'We went out to see Victoria Orphanage. See if it was reputable. Anderson was there, doing a publicity call. I didn't know who he was at the time. Nor did I particularly want to. He was cruising round the building, posing with some of the kids for photo-shoots but not actually speaking with any of them. By the time I bumped into him and his entourage, I'd already got a clear picture of what was going on, so I left without introducing myself.

"So when I came across him again, in his office in Germany, I recognised him straight away, and knew my suspicions about the company were well-founded. Of course, as it turned out, he recognised me, too.'

Selected versions of the flashdrive were sent to various magazines and newspapers in the week that followed. One of the British independent TV channels bought the rights to the documentary series and signed a contract committing them to airing it within the next twelve months. A condition Heather insisted on since she didn't want to see the information buried again.

But perhaps the most delighted of all was Tom, as he got to send Interpol an entire file of Gravenburg's assassinations, stretching back over twenty years, and to inform them that Gravenburg could now be officially removed from their Wanted list. He received a commendation for his work and added another sign to his lab door: *Forensic Hero. International.*

Gravenburg's body, as such, was never found. The MRT had officially given up the formal search after about five weeks, having been unsuccessful in their attempts to find him and knowing that, even if the man had survived the fall, after that length of time – exposed and seriously injured – he was unlikely to still be alive.

It was a few weeks later that one of the team took a recreational climb on the north side of *Blà Bheinn*, with his collie Meg, who was trained as a Search and Rescue Dog. Meg had suddenly run off the main track and disappeared from view. Kelvin, her handler, had carefully followed in the dog's direction, eventually finding her sitting obediently beside a pile of human bones. These were shipped off to Tom's lab where he was able to confirm them as belonging to Gravenburg.

Katriona sat in the conservatory, reflecting on how wonderful it was to be back on her beloved island, and more importantly, with her lovely partner, again. Elayne had come home a few days after Katriona and Heather had arrived. They had flown up from Manchester, as far as Glasgow, where they'd picked up Katriona's car from the long-stay car park where she'd left it when she set out for Germany. Katriona had then driven Heather to Skye.

She'd made sure they timed the journey for daylight hours so that Heather could enjoy the scenery en route, since this was one part of the world she didn't actually know. This would also make it possible for them to take the private Glenelg-Kylerhea ferry crossing, and she delighted in sharing the extraordinary views with Heather as the car climbed the mountain pass over *Mam Ratagan* before the road dropped dramatically down into Glenelg.

On the far side of the loch, there was a similar trip up to the tops from Kylerhea, where they were greeted by both snow and rainbows, created by the astonishing sunshine breaking through the clouds just as they reached the peaks.

Heather was swept up in the beauty of it, just as Katriona had hoped she would be. For Katriona, the sense of coming home was only reinforced after the stresses and strains of the previous few days. She'd been glad of the opportunity to take the adventure but she was even more glad to be picking up on her much steadier, quieter life once more, in this beautiful place.

Heather had stayed for the best part of a week, doing a lot of sleeping, before the request came for her to return to London to help compile the various cases of corruption and murder, both attempted and actual, that had touched her life so deeply over the past few months.

During her stay, she'd met Helen, and they had taken a private walk together down to the loch. Katriona guessed Heather was asking her about finding Emily's body, and hoped the ordeal wouldn't be too awful for either of them. A genuine warmth developed between the two as a result of the conversation.

Now things had quietened down a little, and life could get back to normal for a while. Her last phonecall with Gavin was reassuring.

'So, all done and dusted, then.'

'It would seem so,' he said.

She knew he would miss Charlie but she felt sure Maxwell would grow into the role.

'So will you take some time off now? To be with Trish?'

'Once I've got the paperwork done on those latest robberies and – did I mention? – we've turned up a body. In the river. We haven't been able to identify him yet, so Tom's organising DNA tests as we speak.'

Katriona smiled to herself. *You're very welcome to it all, Gavin*, she thought, with only a very small twinge of envy.

40

December was peppered with three very emotional events. The first was Emily's funeral. Now that the case was over, her body had been released for burial and Heather had quickly got on with making arrangements. She was surprised by the volume of people wishing to attend the service and pay their respects, from many places around the globe where Emily had sung. So it came as an immense relief when Emily's local cathedral said they would like to host the ceremony, since Emily had often contributed to their various liturgies and celebrations over the years.

The building was absolutely packed for the occasion with both celebrities from Emily's musical world and 'commoners', as Tom put it, from all other aspects of her life. Performances of glorious and heart-wrenching music were given at various points during the proceedings, mostly by other musicians that Emily had worked with at different times during her career. But perhaps the most moving performance was that given by a young girl with red hair, singing a cappella.

Heather, who gave an extremely poignant eulogy in memory of her sister, had specifically asked Helen to sing for Emily since she'd not been able to do so when Emily was alive. Helen was reticent at first, her old lack of confidence re-emerging when she heard how many famous singers would be present. But when Elayne had quietly reminded her, 'It's not a competition, Helen,' she'd rediscovered her courage and agreed. She decided to sing *Altissima Luce*, the aria she had prepared for her original audition, now feeling like a life-time ago.

Her performance was exquisite, reducing many of her listeners to tears by its sheer beauty and by its honouring of Emily's loss.

It was only just over a week later when the team all met up again for a much happier event. Gavin and Trish's wedding was a splendid weekend of joy, fun and celebration. The hotel they had booked for the occasion was perfect and, amazingly, the weather was, too. An unexpected flush of sunshine warmed the Surrey countryside, so that the guests were able to wander round the lovely gardens during the reception which followed the ceremony.

Trish looked wonderful, now that she was in her second trimester and her body had accommodated itself to her new situation. She wore an 'absolutely gorgeous' dress – as Helen described it – which she'd had specially designed to show off her bump, along with a discreet veil and a delicate bouquet of flowers.

Her sister, Charlotte, who was her only bridesmaid, was dressed in an equally fabulous dress, in a delicate violet, which set off Trish's ivory fabric beautifully.

Katriona thought Gavin looked happier than she'd ever seen him, which was as it should be. She hoped he would be able to relish his new family as much as she did hers, but recognised the struggles he might have to face as a full-time, working police inspector. He was going to need some support in this, and she made a private promise to herself to keep much more frequent contact than she had done previously.

Gavin had asked Tom to be his best man. He had toyed with the idea of asking Charlie, since he knew the man was steady and sensible enough to do the job well, but he'd known Tom for years, and secretly rather looked forward to discovering what Tom's enthusiasm might bring to the occasion. He had, with appropriate foresight, arranged for his bachelor party to happen several days in advance of the main event, which turned out to be an accurate and fortuitous decision, when he woke the next morning on a sailing boat, just off-shore from Monaco.

The wedding itself went without a hitch, everyone laughing and crying in all the right places. The reception was sumptuous, the cake unbelievably tall and the evening meal so good that no-one wanted to move for several hours afterwards.

Katriona and Elayne finished the day by taking a moonlit walk in the grounds beyond the formal garden, Molly and Alice busy scuffling through the woodland that formed the perimeter to the hotel's acreage.

'What a wonderful day,' Katriona said.

'Mm. It's been … lovely,' Elayne responded, hesitantly.

'What's up? Have you not enjoyed it?' Katriona took Elayne's hand and kissed it, gently.

'I've loved every minute of it. But it's made me think.'

'What?' Katriona whispered, almost holding her breath, as she guessed what Elayne was about to say.

'Shall we get married, Kat? I mean, I know we have the civil partnership, but wouldn't it be … ?'

'Absolutely perfect.' And Katriona kissed her deeply, so her tears didn't show too much in the moonlight.

The final, and unexpected, event of the three happened back on Skye, a few days after the women had driven back home. Just as Katriona and Elayne were struggling to bring a 'way-too-enormous' Christmas tree into the house through the back door, an excited Helen appeared.

'I've just received a letter,' she announced. 'From the Gaelic College.'

Katriona knew she had already managed to negotiate a part-time job at the college – acting as a telephone receptionist for the English students who applied to study there. Instead of being paid for her few hours a week, Helen had asked if she could join the basic Gaelic language course – a deal the college were happy to agree to. Little by little, Katriona thought, she was building her new life on the island.

'Is this something to do with your job?' she asked.

'No, it's something much better.' Helen's eyes sparkled with delight. 'Someone has set up a Scholarship – for musical students without funds, to study at the college. It's in memory of Emily. Turns out she had Scottish roots. It's called the Hough-MacAllister Scholarship and they've invited me to audition.'

Gaelic Terms & Place Names

Gaelic spelling *Gaelic pronunciation* (meaning)
English spelling English pronunciation where needed
(Please note that pronunciations are not phonetic but are my own approximations. For an accurate Gaelic rendition, go to **http://www.learngaelic.net/dictionary/index.jsp**)

Mountains on Skye:
A' Chuith-Raing (Round Fold) **Quiraing** kirang
An Cuiltheann *un coolyan* **Cuillin** coolin
Blà Bheinn *blar vain* (Blue Mountain) **Blaven** blarven
Clach Glas *'ch' as in 'loch', at the back of the throat* (Grey Stone)
Gars-Bheinn *gar-vain*
Na Beanntan Dearga *na beeanthun charaku – 'u' as in 'bun'*
Red Hills or Red Cuillin
Sgùrr Alasdair *skoord – a soft 'd', as if blowing* (Alastair's Peak)
Sgùrr nan Gillean *skoord nan gilyan* (Peak of the Young Men)

Mountains on mainland:
Ceann t-Sàile *kown tarlay* **Kintail**
Mam Ratagan *mam rartagan*
Sgùrr Fhuaran *skoord ooran* (Peak of the Spring)
Sgùrr na Càrnach *skoord na karneech – 'ch' as in 'loch'*
(Rocky Peak)

Places on Skye:
Armadale ***Armadal*** *aramadol*
Broadford ***An t-Àth Leathann*** *an tar lihon –breathe through 'h'*
(the broad ford)
Dunvegan ***Dùn Bheagain*** *doon vikan* (Beagan's Fort)
Elgol ***Ealaghol*** *elagol*
Kyleakin kilakin ***Caol Àcainn*** *cool archin – 'ch' as in 'loch'*
(the Narrows of Haakon)
Kylerhea kyle-ray ***Caol Reithe*** *cool rayhu – 'u' as in bun*
(the Narrows of Reatha)

Skye ***An t-Eilean Sgitheanach*** *an chilan skeeahunoch – 'ch as in 'loch'; also* ***Eilean a' Cheò*** *ilan e hyorr* (possibly The Misty Isle)
Stein ***Steinn*** *shcheyn* (Stone)
Torrin ***Na Torran*** *nu torrun – 'u' as in 'bun' (the Little Hills)*
Waternish ***Bhatarnais*** *varturnish (Promontory of the Waterspout)*

Places on mainland:
Inverness ***Inbhir Nis*** *inyud nish* (Mouth of the River Ness)
Fort William ***An Gearasdan*** *un gerastan* (the Garrison)
Mallaig ***Malaig*** *malike – as in 'like'*
Glenelg ***Gleann Eilg*** *gleen eleg* (the Glens of Eilg)

Other terms:
Rum (sometimes **Rhum**) ***Rùm*** *room* (possibly Isle of the Ridge)
cèilidh *kaylee*
Fàilte *falchu – 'u' as in 'bun'* **Welcome**
mo chridhe *mo chreeu – 'ch' as in 'loch', 'u' as in 'bun'* (literally: my heart; often used as a term of affection, as in 'sweetheart')
Sabhal Mòr Ostaig *sowl morr ostike*

The information presented here is necessarily insufficient. I am far from an expert in this area, and do not speak Gaelic, though I keep trying to learn. I have included all the information I know, or have been able to find.

Many variations of pronunciation can be found due to regional and dialectal preferences, and many meanings have become obscure or lost over generations, particularly where the names originate from a Norse word.

Also, the way in which any particular word is pronounced can vary depending on where exactly it appears in a sentence.

This is a language that is very much alive!

Acknowledgments

My thanks to everyone who has read through bits of this book to offer opinion, comments and suggestions.

In particular, thanks are to due to Kayren and Claire, who have stuck with me, every inch of the way, faithfully reading each chapter as it appeared – a mammoth task over the course of two and a half years. I cannot thank you enough for the support you have both shown, and your consistent belief that I would get there.

Thanks, too, to the many boaters I pestered on my local canal in order to get details of Helen's escape just right. Any errors are entirely mine.

A special mention for Richard 'Paddy' McGuire, a mountaineer and climbing guide on Skye, and a member of the Mountain Rescue Team, who happily answered all my questions about *Blà Bheinn* when I rang him out of the blue one day whilst working on chapter 19. Any inaccuracies are all down to my imagination and the odd touch of poetic licence. www.blavenguiding.co.uk

Finally, a huge thank you to the staff at *Sabhal Mòr Ostaig*, who were good enough to entertain the interests and questions of a stray writer who turned up at their door with only one sentence of Gaelic. They listened kindly to my explanation in English and my request to wander around the college grounds, then promptly arranged a guided tour including sitting in on part of a student performance of plays written by the students themselves. What a delightful place! Inconsistencies with the reality of the college are all in my head. www.smo.uhi.ac.uk

About the Author

Rosalin currently lives in the North of England, but her heart will always be on Skye. She shares her home with her family of dogs and cats, some of whom are present in physical form and some in spirit. She has many passions in life, not the least of which is her love of learning. At different times, she has studied education, biology, mathematics, theology, metaphysics, alternative medicine, embroidery, weaving and natural dyeing. She is just now following a personal study course in spinning. She has been selected as a fire marshal for the British Grand Prix, danced for Archbishop Tutu and climbed to the top of *Blà Bheinn* several times. She would be hard-pressed to decide which of those experiences counted as the best.

Blog

https://peaceweaverwrites.wordpress.com

If you have enjoyed this book –

look out for Book 2 later in 2017

Here is a short extract to keep you going.

Chapter One

'Ma'am, we've found a body. Washed up on shore by Uig.'

Constable McTavish's voice, on the other end of the phone, sounded agitated. Katriona asked for details.

'It's definitely male. Looks to be in his forties or fifties. Caucasian. Dressed in warm gear, with heavy boots – looks like he was on a fishing boat or something.'

'I see.' Katriona, a consultant detective for the Serious Crime Squad in Scotland, was reluctant to get involved without going through the appropriate channels.

'Have you called this in?'

'Yes, Ma'am. It's gone through to Inverness, and they're requesting your assistance.'

The small constabulary on the island was overseen from the headquarters at Inverness, a hundred miles away. This could sometimes be inconvenient but, as the crime rate on Skye was so small, and the crimes rarely of a serious nature, it was mostly sufficient.

'Okay, Constable. I'm on my way.' Katriona took the specifics of the exact location and called through to her partner in the kitchen, as she passed by on her way to find suitable clothing from the bedroom.

'Elayne, I'm going to have to go out.'

'Are you? Why?' Elayne's voice drifted across the hallway. It sounded as though her mind was on something else.

'They've found a body. Up at Uig.'

There was a pause, then Elayne appeared at the bedroom

door.

'A body?'

'Yep. Sounds like a fisherman overboard from what McTavish just said. But Inverness have asked for me to go take a look. I don't suppose I'll need to stay long but it'll take me an hour or so to get there.' Skye might be an island but it was a relatively large one, bigger than its Hebridean neighbours.

'I'll come with you, Kat,' Elayne said. 'Keep you company.'

Katriona smiled and gave her a light kiss. 'I'd really like that.' Since the shooting last year when, for a brief period of time, she'd thought she might lose her beautiful partner forever, the two of them had revelled in each other's company even more than they had before.

'If it's straight-forward,' Katriona said, 'maybe we'd have time to go and see Elisabeth at Kilmuir. See how the weaving's going.'

Elayne, although professionally an architect, had fulfilled a life-long ambition since they'd moved into the house she'd designed for them in the tiny village of Torrin, by keeping her own flock of sheep. In the long evenings of last winter, she'd taught herself how to spin the soft fleece, shorn the previous spring by herself and their neighbour Dughall. Some of the yarn she'd produced had been transported up the island to Elisabeth's weaving shed, where it was being incorporated into a mixed fibre blanket.

Katriona pulled on a suitably tough pair of tweed trousers and looked at Elayne, who was leaning against the doorpost, watching her. 'What d'you think?' she asked.

'When is it ever straight-forward when you get involved, Kat?'

The journey up the island and out to the far west was, as ever, dramatic in the views it had to offer. Even before they set out, in their new four-wheel drive – purchased enthusiastically after Katriona's unexpected and exhilarating car-chase in Germany last year – the pair were able to see the fluffy cloud-halos clinging to the tops of their neighbouring mountains, the Red Hills to one side, the edges of the Black Cuillin to the other. Katriona loved living in this spectacular and beautiful valley, where the view was never the same two days in a row, even in winter when it consisted mostly of low-lying grey cloud and rain, so that the mountains were invisible for days, or weeks, at a time. Nothing was static, here. It was always changing. It was so alive.

They headed first along the tiny road into Broadford, their nearest township, where today the sea was sparkling in the spring sunshine; then turned onto the main road towards Portree, with its huge twists and turns, as it travelled inland and out again, round the heads of the lochs along the way, taking them up to dizzy heights, plummeting them down to sea-level, as they went. From Portree, leaving the distant sight of the jagged Quiraing range behind, they followed the quiet road across the heathery peat moors, towards the wildness of the far coast where it encountered the Minches.

This was not a part of the island which Katriona knew so well. Whenever she visited, she felt the bleakness of it, the battered energy along the coastline, as if the landscape itself had set up defences against marauders from the turbulent waters. Yet she knew only a few miles away, and visible on a clear day, sat the enticing islands of the Outer Hebrides with their miles of flat scenery and golden beaches. Quite benign, really, though they shared that element of desolation which could so easily overcome a visitor not used to the emptiness of the geography.

As they tipped over the brow of the hill into Uig, and swung round the steep descent towards the dock, the pretty white cottages of the town became visible, giving the optimistic appearance of a picture postcard. It was always a surprise to Katriona when she came here. The place was so remote, yet this hillside community, huddled together in a relatively confined space, had a comforting and friendly welcome about it. Almost as if it had been air-lifted out of an old-fashioned storybook and dropped into its barren surroundings to lighten the mood. It certainly made a lovely sight if one was returning to the island from Harris or North Uist on the ferry, the tiny houses and the Tyrolean-style church gradually appearing through the inevitable mists that congregated above the water here.

They drove through the town and out towards the dock. Here the atmosphere was more industrial. The buildings were large grey warehouses instead of pretty cottages, and a grimy-looking bar provided brief hospitality for visiting trawlermen. It was a strange contrast to the township only a few hundred metres away.

Katriona saw the police van parked up alongside a queue of cars and lorries, all waiting to board a ferry. Two officers were busy taking statements from the inhabitants of each vehicle before allowing them to board. She caught sight of McTavish and pulled to a halt, parking the car opposite the café.

'Body's over here, Ma'am. You'll need waterproof footwear – the tide's coming in.'

She opened the boot to retrieve her heavy-duty wellingtons. 'We'd better work smartish, then. Is the body anywhere near the water-line?'

'Not yet, Ma'am, but it won't be long. I've taken photos already so we can move it as soon as you've looked.'

Katriona left Elayne in the car, as she and the constable walked round to a small pebbled beach on the far side of the quay. As they approached, she could see the contorted limbs of the corpse, sticking out from under a large black bundle which, on closer inspection, turned out to be a heavy woollen overcoat. The man was lying face-up with open, staring eyes, but his body had become twisted - presumably by the tides - so that he seemed to be wrapped around himself.

She reached down to touch his face. It was hard.

'He's not been dead all that long. He's still got rigor.'

'Yes, Ma'am.'

She walked round the body, viewing it from all angles, asking the usual questions. 'I don't suppose we know who he is.'

'No, Ma'am, but I haven't searched his pockets yet. Thought you should see the body untouched, first.'

Katriona hadn't spoken with McTavish for a while. She now recalled how reliable and thorough he was in carrying out his duties. Always thinking through the implications of his actions, careful to preserve a crime-scene exactly. She shuddered as a recollection of last year's events went through her mind. That was when she'd first met the young constable and been immediately impressed.

Together, they carefully rolled the body into a position where they could access the inside pockets of both the overcoat and the jacket showing underneath. As they did so, the coat fell away from the body. The man's arms which, at first glance, she had assumed were protruding beyond the ends of the coat's sleeves, had not been pushed into the sleeves at all.

'Someone's already been here,' she said.

'Ma'am?'

'This man isn't actually wearing this coat. Someone has wrapped him in it.'

She looked closer at the various patches of exposed skin.

'I'm not even sure he's been in the water, you know. If he has, it's not been for long.'

She pointed out the lack of damage which even a few hours in the turbulent tides of the Minches would cause, and the fact that the skin didn't have the usual sodden stippling that accompanied a drowning followed by extended exposure to water.

'Right, Constable. We'll have to move the body up to dry ground and then call out the Forensics Team. This is looking like a suspicious death.'